HAMMERED

HAMMERED

THE
IRON
DRUID
CHRONICLES

KEVIN HEARNE

DEL
REY

BALLANTINE BOOKS • NEW YORK

Hammered is a work of fiction. Names, places, and incidents either are products of the author's imagination or are used fictitiously.

A Del Rey Mass Market Original

Published in the United States by Del Rey, an imprint of The Random House Publishing Group, a division of Random House, Inc., New York.

DEL REY is a registered trademark and the Del Rey colophon is a trademark of Random House, Inc.

ISBN 978-0-345-52248-1
eBook ISBN 978-0-345-52254-2

Printed in the United States of America

www.delreybooks.com

9 8 7 6 5 4 3 2 1

Del Rey mass market edition: July 2011

Pronunciation Guide

One of the problems you run into when using Norse mythology is that you're messing with the languages of Norway, Sweden, Denmark, and Iceland—plus Old Norse. Old Norse hasn't been spoken aloud by the hoi polloi in seven centuries or so, but scholarly folks like to think they have a decent clue about how things might have sounded. I've used Anglicized spellings for Odin and Thor so that English speakers will have a pretty decent shot at saying them correctly by getting hooked on phonics. And though I use the Icelandic spelling and pronunciation for *most* things, it's not universal. Sometimes I use what the Old Norse pronunciation would be, and here and there I mess with the vowel sounds merely because I want to. You're free to do the same; this guide is not intended to be prescriptive but rather *descriptive* of the way the author would say things, and you are welcome to adopt them or to make fun of me on language bulletin boards.

The Norse Gods

Baldr = BALL dur
Bragi = BRAH gi (I use a hard *g* sound so that the last syllable rhymes with *key*. In Icelandic, the *g* is pronounced like a *y* when it's between a vowel on the left

and the letters *i* or *y* on the right—but I'm doing the Old Norse thing here. God of poetry)

Freyja = FRAY ya (goddess of beauty and war, twin to Freyr)

Freyr = FRAYr (I'm using an Old Norse/Icelandic spelling. There's a rolling of the first *r*, which makes the *f* sound like its own syllable, sort of like a musical grace note. Sometimes the last *r* is dropped in spelling and pronunciation and it's simply FRAY. God of fertility)

Heimdall = HAME dadl (Icelandic looks at a double *l* and pronounces it like a clicking *dl* sound, much like the English word *battle*. Heimdall is kind of like a watchdog god, amazing senses.)

Idunn = ih DOON (goddess of youth, keeper of golden apples)

Odin = OH din (allfather, runecrafter. You'd actually say the *d* like a *th* if you wanted to get old school, but most English speakers say it with the *d* sound.)

Thor = thor (god of thunder)

Týr = teer (god of single combat)

Ullr = OODL er (god of archery)

Vidar = VIH dar (god of vengeance, Odin's son)

Adorable Animals of the Norse

Gullinbursti = GOODL in BUR stih (This is Freyr's golden boar; the name translates to *golden bristles*. Technically it's a construct of the dwarfs, not an animal, but indistinguishable from a boar by sight—except for the size and the shining mane o' gold.)

Hugin = HOO gin (Thought, one of Odin's ravens. Not following the Icelandic rule about the *g* on this one either; this is an Old Norse name with an Anglicized spelling, because I've dropped the second *n* you see in the *Prose Edda* and the *Poetic Edda*, the sources of most Norse mythology.)

Jörmungandr = yor MOON gan dur (the world serpent that will kill us all!)

Munin = MOO nin (Memory, another of Odin's ravens)

Ratatosk = RAT a tosk (squirrel who lives on/in the World Tree)

Sleipnir = SLAPE neer (eight-legged steed of Odin, spawn of Loki and a stallion)

Cool Norse Weapons

Gungnir = GOONG neer (magic spear of Odin)

Mjöllnir = meYOL neer (first syllable rhymes with *roll*; that *me* is almost like a grace note)

Sweet Norse Halls and Furnishings

Bilskirnir = BEEL skeer neer (Thor's hall)

Gladsheim = GLADS hame (hall of the Norse gods)

Hlidskjálf = HLID skyalf (silver throne of Odin)

Valaskjálf = VAL as skyalf (Odin's hall)

Valhalla = Vahl HALL ah (lots of ways to say this one, but I'm going with the easy one for English speakers. Not doing the *dl* sound here for the double *l*, nor for Idavoll)

Place-names in Asgard and Iceland

Alfheim = AHLF hame (translates to *elf home*)

Hnappavellir = NAH pah VEDL er

Húsavík = HOO sah week

Idavoll = IH dah vahl

Jötunheim = YOT un hame (the first syllable rhymes with *boat*. That translates to *giant home*. A single giant is a *Jötunn*, and the plural is *Jötnar*.)

Muspellheim = MUS pel hame (realm of fire)

Mývatn = ME vat n (translates to *Midge Lake*)

Nidavellir = NIH dah VEDL ir (realm of the dwarfs)

Niflheim = NIV uhl hame (translates to *mist home*, often equated with Hel and the land of the dead)

Reykjavík = RAY kya week

Svartálfheim = SVART ahlf hame (translates to *dark elf home*)

Vanaheim = VAHN ah hame (I'd like to say this translates to *home of the vans*, but no, it's *home of the Vanir.*)

Vigrid = VIH grid

Yggdrasil = ig DRAH sil (try to roll or trill the *r*, it's more fun. Name of the World Tree)

Icelandic Town Name with Which You Can Win a Bar Bet

Kirkjubæjarklaustur = Kir kyu BYE yar KLOW stur (Watch all the English speakers try to pronounce the *j* the way they're used to; it's a good time. If they get that right, they'll still screw up the æ sound and pronounce it like a long *a* or long *e* instead of a long *i*. You can win a beer or two with this, guaranteed, and drink all night for free if the bar is full of suckers.)

HAMMERED

Chapter 1

According to popular imagination, squirrels are supposed to be adorable. As they scurry about on this tree branch or that trunk, people point at them and say, "Awww, how *cuuuuute*!" with their voices turning sugary and spiraling up into falsetto ecstasy. But I'm here to tell you that they're cute only so long as they're small enough to step on. Once you're facing a giant bloody squirrel the size of a cement truck, they lose the majority of their charm.

I wasn't especially surprised to be staring up at a set of choppers as tall as my fridge, twitching whiskers like bullwhips, and tractor-tire eyes staring me down like volcanic bubbles of India ink: I was simply horrified at being proven so spectacularly right.

My apprentice, Granuaile, had argued I was imagining the impossible before I left her back in Arizona. "No, Atticus," she'd said, "all the literature says the only way you can get into Asgard is the Bifrost Bridge. The *Eddas*, the skaldic poems, everything agrees that Bifrost is it."

"Of course that's what the literature *says*," I replied, "but that's just the propaganda of the gods. The *Eddas* also tell you the truth of the matter if you read carefully. Ratatosk is the key to the back door of Asgard."

Granuaile gazed at me, bemused, unsure that she'd

heard me correctly. "The squirrel that lives on the World Tree?" she asked.

"Precisely. He manically scrambles back and forth between the eagle in the canopy and the great wyrm at the roots, ferrying messages of slander and vitriol between them, yadda yadda yadda. Now ask yourself how it is that he manages to do that."

Granuaile took a moment to think it through. "Well, according to what the literature *says*, there are two roots of Yggdrasil that drop below Asgard: One rests in the Well of Mimir in Jötunheim, and one falls to the Spring of Hvergelmir in Niflheim, beneath which the wyrm Nidhogg lies. So I assume he's got himself a little squirrelly hole in there somewhere that he uses." She shook her head, dismissing the point. "But you won't be able to use that."

"I'll bet you dinner I can. A nice homemade dinner, with wine and candles and fancy modern things like Caesar salad."

"Salad isn't modern."

"It is on my personal time scale. Caesar salad was invented in 1924."

Granuaile's eyes bugged. "How do you *know* these things?" She waved off the question as soon as she asked it. "No, you're not going to distract me this time. You're on; I bet you dinner. Now prove it or start cooking."

"The proof will have to come when I climb Yggdrasil's root, *but*," I said, raising a finger to forestall her objection, "I'll dazzle you now with what I think so that I'll seem fantastically prescient later. The way I figure it, Ratatosk has to be an utter badass. Consider: Eagles normally eat squirrels, and malevolent wyrms named Nidhogg are generally expected to eat anything—yet neither of them ever tries to take a bite of Ratatosk. They just talk to him, never give him any guff at all, but ask him nicely if he'd be so kind as to tell their enemy far, far away such-and-such. And they say, 'Hey, Ratatosk, you don't have to hurry. Take your time. Please.'"

"Okay, so you're saying he's a burly squirrel."

"No, I'm saying he's turbo-burly. Paul Bunyan proportions, because his size is proportionate to the World Tree. He's bigger than you and I put together, big enough that Nidhogg thinks of him as an equal instead of as a snack. The only reason we've never heard of anyone climbing Yggdrasil's roots to get to Asgard is because you'd have to be nuts to try it."

"Right," she said with a smirk. "And Ratatosk eats nuts."

"That's right." I bobbed my head once with a sardonic grin of my own.

"Well then," Granuaile wondered aloud, "exactly where are the roots of Yggdrasil, anyway? I assume they're somewhere in Scandinavia, but you'd think they would have shown up on satellite by now."

"The roots of Yggdrasil are on an entirely different plane, and that's really why no one has tried to climb them. But they're tethered to the earth, just like Tír na nÓg is, or the Elysian Fields, or Tartarus, or what have you. And, coincidentally, a certain Druid you know is also tethered to the earth, through his tattoos," I said, holding up my inked right arm.

Granuaile's mouth opened in astonishment as the import of my words sank in, quick to follow the implication to its logical conclusion. "So you're saying you can go anywhere."

"Uh-huh," I confirmed. "But it's not something I brag about"—I pointed a finger at her—"nor should you, once you're bound the same way. Plenty of gods are already worried about me because of what happened to Aenghus Óg and Bres. But since I killed them on this plane, and since Aenghus Óg started it, they don't figure I've turned into a deicidal maniac. In their minds, I'm highly skilled in self-defense but not a mortal threat to them, as long as they don't pick a fight. And they still believe that merely because they've never seen a Druid in their territory before, they never will. But if the gods knew I could get to anyone, anywhere, my perceived threat level would go through the roof."

"Can't the gods go anywhere?"

"Uh-uh," I said, shaking my head. "Most gods can go only two places: their own domain and earth. That's why you'll never see Kali in Olympus, or Ishtar in Abhassara. I haven't visited even a quarter of the places I could go. Never been to any of the heavens. Went to Nirvana once, but it was kind of boring—don't get me wrong, it's a beautiful plane, but the complete absence of desire meant nobody wanted to talk to me. Mag Mell is truly gorgeous; you've gotta go there. And you've gotta go to Middle Earth to see the Shire."

"Shut up!" She punched me in the arm. "You haven't been to Middle Earth!"

"Sure, why not? It's bound to our world like all the other planes. Elrond is still in Rivendell, because that's where people think of him being, not the Gray Havens—and I'm telling you right now he looks nothing like Hugo Weaving. I also went to Hades once so I could ask Odysseus what the sirens had to say, and that was a mindblower. Can't tell you what they said, though."

"You're going to tell me I'm too young again, aren't you?"

"No. You simply have to hear it for yourself to properly appreciate it. It involves hasenpfeffer and sea serpents and the end of the world."

Granuaile narrowed her eyes at me and said, "Fine, don't tell me. So what's your plan for Asgard?"

"Well, first I have to choose a root to climb, but that's easy: I'd rather avoid Ratatosk, so I'm going up the one from Jötunheim. Not only does Ratatosk rarely travel it, but it's a far shorter climb from there than from Niflheim. Now, since you seem to have been reading up on this, tell me what direction I must go to find where the Well of Mimir would be bound to this plane."

"East," Granuaile said immediately. "Jötunheim is always to the east."

"That's right. To the east of Scandinavia. The Well of Mimir is tethered to a sub-arctic lake some distance from the small Russian town of Nadym. That's where I'm going."

"I'm not up-to-date on my small Russian towns. Where exactly is Nadym?"

"It's in western Siberia."

"All right, you go to this particular lake, then what?"

"There will be a tree root drinking from the lake. It will not be an ash tree, more of a stunted evergreen, because it's essentially tundra up there. Once I find this root, I touch it, bind myself to it, pull my center along the tether, and then I'm hugging the root of Yggdrasil on the Norse plane, and the lake will be the Well of Mimir."

Granuaile's eyes shone. "I can't wait until I can do this. And from there you just climb it, right? Because the root of the World Tree has to be huge."

"Yes, that's the plan."

"So how far from the trunk of Yggdrasil is it to Idunn's place?"

I shrugged. "Never been there before, so I'm going to have to wing it. I've never found any maps of it; you'd think someone would have made an atlas of the planes by now, but noooo."

Granuaile frowned. "Do you even know where Idunn is?"

"Nope," I said, a rueful smile on my face.

"It's going to be tough to steal an apple for Laksha, then." Yes, the prospect was daunting, but a deal was a deal: I had promised to steal a golden apple from Asgard in return for twelve dead Bacchants in Scottsdale. Laksha Kulasekaran, the Indian witch, had held up her end of the bargain, and now it was my turn. There was a chance I'd be able to pull off the theft without consequences, but there was no chance that I could renege on the deal and not face repercussions from Laksha.

"It'll be an adventure, for sure," I told Granuaile.

An adventure in squirrels, apparently. As I faced the stark reality of being so stunningly correct, gaping slack-jawed at the colossal size of the rodent above me on the trunk of the World Tree, an old candy bar jingle softly escaped my lips: " 'Sometimes you feel like a nut,' " I crooned, " 'sometimes you don't.' "

I'd really hoped Ratatosk would be on the other root, or even hibernating by this time. It was November 25, Thanksgiving back in America, and Ratatosk looked like he'd already eaten Rhode Island's share of turkeys. He was properly stuffed and ready to sleep until spring. But now that he'd seen me, even if he didn't bite off my head with those choppers, he'd go tell somebody there was a man climbing up the root from Midgard, and then all of Asgard would know I was coming. It wouldn't be much of a stealth mission after that.

I had been climbing Yggdrasil without tiring, binding knees, boots, and jacket to the bark all along the way and drawing power from it through my hands, because it was the World Tree, after all, and synonymous with the earth once I'd shifted planes. While I was doing fine and not in any danger of falling off, I could not hope to match Ratatosk's speed or agility. I moved like a glacier in comparison, and Asgard was still miles away up the root.

He chattered angrily at me, and his breath blew my hair back, filling my nostrils with the scent of stale nuts. I've smelled far worse, but it wasn't exactly fragrant either. There's a reason Bath & Body Works doesn't have a line of products called Huge Fucking Squirrel.

I triggered a charm on my necklace that I call faerie specs, which allows me to view what's happening in the magical spectrum and see how things are bound together. It also makes creating my own bindings a bit easier, since I can see in real time the knots I'm tying with my spells.

Ratatosk, I saw, was very firmly bound to Yggdrasil. In many ways he was a branch of the tree, an extension of its identity, which I was dismayed to discover. Hurting the squirrel would hurt the tree, and I didn't want to do that, but I didn't see what choice I had—unless I could get him to pinky-swear he wouldn't tell anyone I was on my way to steal one of Idunn's golden apples.

I focused my attention on the threads that represented his consciousness and gently bound them to mine until communication was possible. I could still speak Old Norse, which was widely understood throughout Europe until the end of the thirteenth century, and I was betting Ratatosk could speak it too, since he was a creation of Old Norse minds.

I greet you, Ratatosk, I sent through the binding I'd made. He flinched at the words in his head and whirled around, the brush of his tail whipping my face as he scrambled up the root a few quick strides before whirling around again, regarding me warily. Maybe I should have moved my mouth along with the words.

<Who in Hel's frosty realm are you?> came the reply, the squirrel's massive whiskers all twitching in agitation. <Why are you on the root of the World Tree?>

Since I was coming up the root from the middle plane, there were only three places I could possibly be coming from. I wasn't a frost giant from Jötunheim, and he'd never believe I was an ordinary mortal climbing the root, so I had to tell a stretcher and hope he bought it. *I am an envoy sent from Nidavellir, realm of the dwarfs,* I explained. *I am not flesh and blood but rather a new construct. Thus my flame-red hair and the putrid stench that surrounds me.* I had no idea what I smelled like to him, but since I was decked out in new leathers, with their concomitant tanning odors, I figured I smelled like a few dead cows, at least, and it was best from a personal safety perspective to frame my scent and person in terms of something inedible. The Norse dwarfs were famous for making magical constructs that walked around looking like normal critters, but often these creatures had special abilities. They'd made a boar once for the god Freyr, one that could walk on water and ride the wind, and it had a golden mane around its head that shone brightly in the night. They called it Gullinbursti, which meant "Golden Bristles." Go figure.

My name is Eldhár, crafted by Eikinskjaldi son of Yngvi son of Fjalar, I told him. The three dwarf names were mined straight from the *Poetic Edda.* Tolkien found the names of all his "dwarves" in the same source, in addition to Gandalf's, so I saw no reason why I couldn't appropriate a few of them for my own use. Eldhár, the name I'd given for myself, meant nothing more than "Fire Hair"; I figured since I was pretending to be a construct, it would be consistent with names like Gullinbursti. *I am on my way to Valhalla at the Dwarf King's request to speak to Odin Allfather, One-Eyed Wanderer, Gray Runecrafter, Sleipnir Rider, and Gungnir Wielder. It is a matter of great importance regarding danger to the Norns.*

<The Norns!> Ratatosk was so alarmed by this that he actually became still for a half second. <The Three who live by the Well of Urd?>

The same. Will you aid me in my journey and thus speed this most vital embassy, so that the World Tree may be spared any neglect? The Norns were responsible for watering the tree from the well, a sort of constant battle against rot and age.

<Gladly will I take you to Asgard!> Ratatosk said. He switched directions again and shimmied backward, courteously extending his back leg to me and carefully holding his bushy tail out of the way. <Can you climb upon my back?>

It took me longer than I might have wished, but eventually I clambered up his back, bound myself tightly to his red fur, and pronounced myself ready to ride.

<We go,> Ratatosk said simply, and we shot up the trunk with a violent gait so awkward that I think I might have bruised my spleen.

Still, I could not complain. Ratatosk was even more than I had imagined: In addition to being extraordinarily large and speedy, he was perfectly gullible and willing to help strangers, so long as they spoke Old Norse. Perhaps I wouldn't have to kill him after all.

Chapter 2

Most visual representations of Norse cosmology are based on the principle of "You can't get there from here." That's because their cosmology isn't magical merely in the sense that it defies all science, it's also internally inconsistent, so that planewalkers like me tie themselves in knots trying to get around. For example, in some sources, Hel is in Niflheim, the elemental realm of ice, and in others Hel is its own domain separate from Niflheim, so you'd literally have to be in two places at once if you wanted to drop by for a visit. Muspellheim, the realm of fire, is just "south," but no one seems to know how to get there. Luckily, I didn't need or want to go to either place; I had to get to Asgard and bring back one of Idunn's golden apples for Laksha so she wouldn't invade my brain and switch it off. (I didn't know if she could invade my brain or not; I hoped my amulet would protect me, but it's not the sort of thing you invite someone to do on a dare.)

Ratatosk was taking me in the right direction, so I was confident that I'd make it to Asgard, bruised spleen or not. What would happen once I got there would probably be a surprise. The worst-case scenario would be that I'd arrive as all the gods were in council by the Well of Urd, right near the Norns, and Ratatosk would dump me in front of them all and say, <Hey, everybody! Eldhár

here has some bad news from Nidavellir!> and then I'd get my ass handed to me in short order.

Perhaps I should try to avoid that.

Ratatosk, how long before we are in Asgard? I asked him as we bounded up the great tree root. It was far, far thicker than a sequoia but gray and smooth-barked instead of red and etched with crenellations.

<Less than an hour,> the squirrel replied.

My, that's fast. Odin will surely commend you for your speed when I tell him how you helped me. Might you know if the gods are in council by the Well of Urd at this time?

<They are early risers. Surely they are finished by now. But the Norns will still be there. Why not simply tell them what the trouble is? Hey.> Ratatosk stopped suddenly, halted by the intrusion of a disconcerting thought, and if I had not bound myself to his fur I would have flown upward for a brief time before gravity pulled me back down. <Shouldn't the Norns be able to see this danger coming? Why do we have to warn anyone?>

Clearly Ratatosk could not think and run at the same time. *This danger comes from outside Asgard,* I explained, then spun him a lie. *The danger comes from the Romans. The Roman Fates, the Parcae, have sent Bacchus and his pards to slay the Norns, knowing that the Norns will not be able to see him coming.*

<Oh.> Ratatosk leapt forward again but then halted abruptly after a few steps, as another thought locked down his motor functions. <Why does the Dwarf King know about this and Odin doesn't?>

Damn inquisitive squirrel. *He found out from the King of the Dark Elves. The entire evil plot was hatched in their, uh, evil minds.* When in doubt, blame the dark elves.

<Ohhhhh,> Ratatosk said knowingly. I got the sense that he thought the dark elves could keep secrets from Odin if anyone could. <When is Bacchus coming?>

The Dwarf King believes he may already be on his way. Time is of the essence. Let your haste commend your duty, Ratatosk.

<I shall.> Reassured and reinvigorated, Ratatosk leapt up the root of Yggdrasil even faster than before. <Is Bacchus a powerful god?>

It is said that heroes have shat kine at the very sight of him. He drives men to madness. But I do not know how he would fare against the Norns. The danger is in the surprise he represents. If the Norns cannot see him coming, then he may be able to catch them unprepared. Their best defense will be my warning, and with your help all the gods of Asgard will have time to prepare a proper welcome for the upstart Roman.

<I hope I will be there to see it,> Ratatosk said with delicious anticipation. <It has been far too long since the gods have taken anyone's nuts.>

His euphemism startled me, until I remembered that I was talking to a squirrel; I confirmed through the images and emotions in our mental bond that he was using the expression to mean the defeat of an enemy, nothing more.

I affirmed his thoughts and then fell silent as I considered the very real possibilities behind my lies. The Norns would be waiting by the trunk of Yggdrasil as we ascended to Asgard. I was certain they'd not know that it was I who was coming—not because I was a god like Bacchus from a different pantheon, but because my amulet protected me from divination—yet they'd probably know Ratatosk would be bringing someone or something with him at this particular time. They'd be curious at the very least, paranoid at the worst, and if the latter was true they might have planned something unpleasant. They might even send someone down the trunk to see who was riding on Ratatosk. As soon as I thought of it, I cast camouflage on myself, my clothes, and my sword as a precautionary measure. The Norse shouldn't be able to penetrate it, if the mythology was to be believed; they were continually fooling one another in the *Eddas* with basic disguises, much less magical ones.

We still had a decently long trek ahead of us, which suggested to me it was an ideal time for a fishing expedition. I told Ratatosk that my creator, Eikinskjaldi, had given me only basic knowledge of Asgard. Would he be so kind as to fill in some gaps in my information? The squirrel was agreeable, so I peppered him with questions from the old myths: Was Loki still bound with his own son's entrails? Yes. Was the Bifrost Bridge still functional, and did the god Heimdall still guard it? Yes. Had the eagle and the wyrm run out of insults for each other yet?

<Not by a long shot!> Ratatosk chuckled. <Want to hear the latest?>

Do tell.

<Nidhogg says the eagle is a cream-shitting feather duster that doesn't even know its own name!>

That's a good one, I acknowledged. *Accurate yet succinct. Did the eagle offer a riposte?*

<Yes, the eagle had a reply. I was on my way down to deliver it, but the Norns told me to come down this root instead to find something unusual. Hey!> He stopped again. <They must have been talking about you, because you're pretty weird.>

It's been remarked upon before, I admitted.

<Well, then, they know you're coming, so that's good,> Ratatosk said, then began sprinting up the root once more. I didn't agree that this was good. Confirmation that the Norns were expecting me sounded extraordinarily bad.

<Anyway,> the squirrel continued, <the eagle said, "Nidhogg can stick the left fork of his tongue into my

cloaca and taste what I think about having a name." But I think he said something very similar three hundred years ago.>

What an odd relationship they have. Speaking of odd relationships, why is Idunn married to Bragi, the god of poets? It wasn't a subtle way to introduce the true object of my foray into Asgard, but I had a feeling Ratatosk didn't require subtlety.

The squirrel slowed noticeably while he thought it over, but he didn't stop this time. <I suppose it is because they enjoy mating together,> he said, then sped up again.

That is undoubtedly part of it, I conceded. *But I think their lives must be very inconvenient. Do not Idunn's apples grow far from the city of Asgard and therefore far from Bragi's audience of the gods?*

Ratatosk chattered shrilly, which startled me at first, until I felt through our bond that he was amused. That sound had been his laughter. <No one knows where they grow. That is a closely guarded secret. But they do live far from Asgard.>

Ah, then my point is made. Where do they live?

<North of the Asgard Mountains. They live on the border between Vanaheim and Alfheim. Their hall is on the Vanaheim side, and on the other side lies the hall of Freyr. You can't miss it.>

I can't? Why?

<Because at night, the mane of the great boar Gullinbursti lights up the sky, even from inside his stable.>

I was told Freyr's hall was in Alfheim, but I did not think it would be right on the border. I would like to visit this Gullinbursti, since he is a construct like myself, but my creators have told me little except how to get to Gladsheim. Perhaps I will visit after I deliver my message. How would I get to Freyr's hall from Gladsheim?

<Run due north,> Ratatosk said. I'd been told nothing

about Asgard from anyone, of course, but by inquiring about the locations of all the famous halls and landmarks from the sagas in relation to Gladsheim, I could gradually gather a sense of the plane's layout and thus make my way around. I think I felt a brief twinge of guilt at taking advantage of the furry fella's gullibility, but I ruthlessly smooshed it and kept asking questions. Information increased my chances of escape without incident, and besides, Ratatosk was full of juicy gossip about the gods. Heimdall was spending a lot of time in Freyja's hall recently. Freyja's cats had just had kittens, but Odin's dogs had eaten three of them. And Odin didn't want anybody to mention Baldr in his presence ever again.

<Speaking of Odin, there's Hugin and Munin circling around!>

Where?

<Look to your left.>

Two distant black shapes chopping the cerulean sky indicated the presence of Odin's ravens. He saw whatever they saw, and I wondered if they could see through my camouflage. I really hoped they couldn't.

I see them now, I said to Ratatosk.

<Your message is for Odin, right? Why don't you just tell them?>

I can't speak to them like I can speak to you. I probably could, but the last thing I wanted to do was bind myself, however indirectly, with the mind of Odin.

<You can't? Well, I can relay a message for you. Just tell me what to say.>

The black specks were growing larger. I couldn't dodge by saying, "I have to give my message to Odin personally," because those ravens were, in a very real sense, Odin himself. They were Thought and Memory. Time to lie some more—and blame the dark elves.

Tell them that Bacchus is coming to slay the Norns, I

said. *The dark elves in Svartálfheim are working with the Romans to get Bacchus into Asgard through a secret tunnel they have been digging for a century. I will give him all the details when I arrive at his throne in Gladsheim.*

<All right, I will tell them.> We stopped abruptly so that Ratatosk could concentrate on talking to the ravens, however he managed such a thing. I didn't hear him make a sound. But after a few seconds, the ravens banked around and returned the way they had come. <Odin is angry,> Ratatosk said, running up the tree again, <but he will await your arrival at Gladsheim.>

Thank you, I said. I wanted Odin in Gladsheim rather than at his other residence, Valaskjálf. He had a silver throne there named Hlidskjálf, and legend had it that he could see everything from there—maybe even camouflaged Druids.

<It will not be very much longer,> Ratatosk added. <Soon we will be in the bones of Yggdrasil and emerge aboveground in Asgard.>

I looked upward and had difficulty focusing on anything much, due to severe squirrel turbulence. All I could make out was that the sky above was gone; we had ascended into the shadow of a huge . . . tract of land. It was the plane of Asgard.

Gritty rocks buttressed clumps of rich brown earth, and wispy roots waved drily in the wind, like the fine hairs that grow wild and unheeded from the edges of old men's ears.

There was no space between the earth above and the trunk of Yggdrasil, no place for the squirrel to go, and I thought he was going to ram us into it—or else keep chugging through one of those neato optical illusions that Bruce Wayne had in front of his cave. But instead he slithered into a large hole in the root of the World Tree, invisible until we were on top of it, and for a brief

time—half a gasp—we were horizontal in a sort of
scoop, a small concavity at the base of a long, wooden
throat that yawned above us. The back wall was
smooth, but the floor we rested on was rugged and littered with the shells of nuts and shed fur. Piles of un-
eaten nuts and a rough nest of leaves could be seen in a
smaller area that winked dimly through a short passage.
I assumed I was looking at the place where Ratatosk
rested during the winters. The inside wall—or, rather,
the opposite side of the root's outer bark—was scarred
and pitted and ideal for climbing, and Ratatosk flipped
himself (and me) around so that he could ascend using
that surface.

We rose through a Stygian shroud of black, its only
sense of depth coming from a hollow whistling of wind
passing through my hair. *How long will we travel in the
dark?* I asked Ratatosk.

<In a moment you will begin to see the light,> the
squirrel replied. <That will be the hole in the root above
the grassy Plain of Idavoll.>

How far above the plain?

<Only a squirrel's length.>

You mean your length?

<Of course. If the hole were at ground level there
would be mud in here.>

*I see the light now. Excellent. You are without a doubt
the finest of squirrels.*

<Thank you,> Ratatosk replied, sounding at once em-
barrassed and proud. He was such an agreeable fellow,
and I smiled briefly at the top of his head before frowning at the light. The unavoidable problem of the Norns
grew closer with every leap upward. I could not coach
Ratatosk out of this; whatever he did, the Norns would
foresee it. But now I feared that they truly shared my
paranoia and that in their eagerness to attack me—the
unseen, uncertain danger on Ratatosk's back—they

would willingly accept collateral damage, wounding both friend and foe. I did not want Ratatosk to come to harm, but neither did I want to have him stop; they would be prepared for such an event. As it stood, he was bringing me directly to them, where they could easily attack me astride the squirrel, flat against the trunk like a target. Bugger it all.

Ratatosk scurried out of the hole in the root and headed down the outside surface, and as soon as I saw the earth perhaps ten feet below, I unbound myself from his fur and leapt off, somersaulting in the air so as to land on my feet. A hoarse shouted curse and a flash of light startled me in midair, then I heard (and felt) Ratatosk scream as I landed, the sting of impact flaring in my ankles and knees. As the squirrel's cries continued, I dropped and rolled to my right, expecting to be crushed underneath him as he fell from the tree. But that didn't happen; his voice cut off abruptly, the bond between our minds snapped, and I glanced up to see naught but a flurry of ashes and bone fragments raining down from the place where he'd clung to the World Tree.

My mouth gaped and I think I might have whimpered. The Norns had obliterated him completely—a creature they'd known for centuries—because of me. It was like watching Rudolph get shot by Santa Claus.

Clearly, the Norns must have thought I represented a dire threat to act so rashly. I tore my eyes away from the horror and watched them warily, keeping still to maximize the effect of my camouflage.

They couldn't see me. Their blazing yellow eyes, smoke curling from the sockets, were still fixed above my head on Ratatosk's swirling remains. They were stooped hags with clawlike fingers, and their faces bore frenzied expressions that mothers warn their children not to make in case they freeze that way. Dressed in dirty gray rags that matched the greasy strings of hair falling from their scalps, they advanced carefully on the tree to make sure the danger they'd foreseen had passed.

It hadn't.

It wasn't long before they vocalized this. One of them tilted her head upon a wattled neck and said, "He is still here. The danger remains."

Danger to whom? I hadn't come to throw down with them. I just wanted some extremely rare produce. They all deserved a swift kick in the hoo-hah for what they had done to Ratatosk, but much as I wanted to deliver it, I didn't see an upside to picking a fight with them when they could vaporize giant rodents. I took a step to my right, an overture to running away, but they must have spied the movement, for their heads all snapped down to lock directly on me with jaundiced, egg-yolk eyes.

"He is there!" the middle one cried, pointing, and then in unison they sang out in a truly ancient language and threw open their hands at me, their dirty fingernails releasing a foul dust into the air.

I didn't know precisely what the dust was supposed to accomplish; most likely, it was my demise. Perhaps, in their old age and infirmity, they thought they were throwing confetti at me—but their behavior did not seem all that warm and welcoming. Rather the opposite, in fact. My cold iron amulet flashed hot for a second, confirming that they had just tried to kill me, and my stomach twisted oddly in my guts, causing me to fart robustly.

Normally I laugh at such things, because there is nothing like a fart to lighten up a tense situation. But this one hadn't been a natural result of my digestion; it was a deadly serious fart, a sign that some small fraction of the Norns' magic was getting past my amulet—perhaps a single speck of that dust—and that worried me.

"He's still alive!" the one on the right cursed, and that dispelled any lingering doubts about their intentions.

I probably should have run for it. But then, if I escaped,

they'd raise the alarm and all of Asgard would be searching for me. That wouldn't end well. Strategically, logically, and even instinctively, in self-defense, I had to take them out. And once a decision like that is made in a moment of crisis, there is no such thing as calm, reasoned execution. There is only action, fueled by the baser parts of our brains.

The rags on the Norns' bony frames were natural woolen fibers, and as such, lent themselves to easy manipulation. As the Norns shoved their claws into pockets for more dust and began to chant something different and more dire in their old tongue, I murmured a binding for the material at their shoulder blades, so that when I finished and willed it done, they were abruptly pulled back-to-back and held in place like a hissing human triangle. That disrupted their spell and caused some wailing and gnashing of teeth. I paused; I almost left them there, bound only by their clothes, seemingly impotent for now. But then abruptly they calmed down and began to rotate in a circle, chanting something low and venomous. Each Norn in turn faced me and pulled a thread from the front of her garment, passing it to her sister on the left. They began to weave the threads, pulling and twisting and chanting all the while as they spun. It was seven kinds of creepy, and I knew I couldn't let them finish whatever they were doing, because it would likely finish me. I drew Moralltach and charged, not caring if they heard me. Their yellow eyes widened as they heard my approach, but they didn't stop chanting their spell, so I couldn't allow myself to stop either. I swept Moralltach through their necks in a single broad sweep, their heads sailed away like ragged balls of gray twine, and thus were the Norse unyoked from the chains of destiny. And thus was I plunged into a galactic vat of doom.

"Damn it!" I shouted, frustrated beyond belief at how badly this had played out. I released my binding and let the bodies slump as they may. I slumped to the ground after them, dragged down by the weight of what I'd just done.

When you steal an apple, you can simply disappear. That had been my plan. But slay a manifestation of fate, and "they *will* find you," as Hans Gruber pointed out in *Die Hard*.

I chewed over the idea of aborting the mission. It had a nice light flavor to it, a piquant savor of surprise. I could try my hand at being unemployed in Greenland. Maybe that would keep me off the radar. Laksha would never find me there, I felt sure.

But the Norse probably would. And Oberon would be miserable. There was the bitter aftertaste.

Still, I had time to think of something better; I had until New Year's to get the golden apple. Laksha wouldn't start looking for me until then, and that would allow me to plan a thorough disappearance.

Except that then I would be running from both Laksha and the Norse. Whether I liked it or not, killing the Norns in self-defense made me an enemy of the whole pantheon. Stealing an apple at this point could hardly make it worse. That being the case, I decided to see the mission through and at least expunge my debt to Laksha.

I wiped Moralltach clean on one of the Norns' gowns and resheathed it before squatting down and sinking my fingers through fallen leaves into the springy turf of Asgard, which was surprisingly akin to a moor—at least in the immediate vicinity of Yggdrasil. The Norns' bodies had turned sickeningly black. I spoke to the earth through my tattoos and it acknowledged me, though it felt strained and far away, as if it had to struggle through a layer of cheesecloth. Obediently it parted to let the bodies of the Norns sink into its peaty depths, and obediently it closed again, leaving no trace of what had happened to them. That chore done, I scoured the earth around the base of the tree to find a few small remnants of Ratatosk, the finest of squirrels. I was glad I had left him feeling good about himself. I carefully placed the fragments of bone in a pouch attached to my belt. Later I would say words for him.

The Norns would be missed when the gods held their council in the morning, so I had until then to steal a golden apple and get out of Dodge. I couldn't afford to linger, but I took a moment to look up at the towering trunk of Yggdrasil and fix in my memory my avenue of escape. Its size beggared the imagination; extending for miles in either direction, it gave the illusion of being an immense wooden wall rather than a cylinder. I assumed that there must be another hole in the trunk somewhere that Ratatosk used to access the root that led to Niflheim. A few minutes' jog counterclockwise found it, and I noted that it looked a bit larger and more well used than the other one. Satisfied that I wouldn't confuse the two holes and take the wrong exit home, I followed the directions Ratatosk had given me—not to Gladsheim but rather directly to Idunn's hall. I ran west and slightly south toward the northernmost range of the Asgard Mountains, and if I got there after nightfall, which seemed likely, I could hope for Gullinbursti's mane to act as a homing beacon. I leeched a wee bit of power from the earth with every step to keep myself fresh and tireless. I'd probably arrive there as Odin was working the gods into a froth over rumors of betrayal in Svartálfheim and invasion from a Roman god. I'd kicked the Norse anthill a good one, and now the gods would come spilling out, seeking something to bite.

Chapter 3

In many ways, I'm disappointed that *Star Trek* never became a religion. The archetypal skeleton was there, but they never strove to make it anything more than a TV show. If they'd capitalized on it, then its adherents would have orders from the nebulous gods of the Federation to explore new worlds and boldly go where no one has gone before; the crew of the *Enterprise* could have been minor gods—angels, perhaps—guiding us through our personal frontiers on a daily basis. Spock could have been the angel of logic on your left shoulder, pointing out fallacious reasoning and suggesting courses of action based on mountains of evidence, while Kirk could have been the angel of emotion on your right shoulder, exhorting you to gird your loins, check your gut, and follow your instincts.

"Kill 'em all, Atticus," imaginary Kirk said in my right ear. "One blow from Moralltach is all it takes. They can't see you; it'll be easy."

"That would be unwise," imaginary Spock said to the fragments of cartilage dangling on my left. A German witch had shot off most of my left ear three weeks ago, and while the healing was going better than the time a demon had chewed off my right one, it still didn't look very good. "A better course of action would be to complete the mission stealthily. The probability of injury or death increases exponentially once your presence is discovered, coupled with time for the alarm to spread."

Kirk kissed his self-control good-bye. "Damn it, Spock, we're on a different plane of existence here, and sometimes you just have to say fuck it and let your balls swing heavy, free, and low. Right, Atticus? Kill 'em all! For Ratatosk!"

"Captain, our mission here is to purloin an apple that confers the vitality of youth to those who consume it, nothing more. Wholesale slaughter is neither advisable nor necessary."

"What is it with you, Spock? Always prudence and caution and tiptoeing through the tulips. Don't you have any stones in your Vulcan panties?"

"My reproductive organs are both present and in perfect working order, Captain, but that is hardly germane to our discussion. One cannot solve every problem through sheer machismo and violence."

"Why not? It works for Chuck Norris."

This is how I entertain myself when I have to run for hours and I can't worry anymore about the ninety-nine ways I could die. I should have brought an iPod.

The moorish demesne of Yggdrasil gave way beneath my churning feet to the Plain of Idavoll, an impressive expanse of untamed grassland that hid plump pheasants, prairie voles, and sleek red foxes. Clouds hung like torn cotton in an achingly blue sky, and a late-autumn breeze blew scents of grass and earth in my face. It was a lovely day, but I could not enjoy it. A novice tracker could follow the trail I was leaving with little difficulty, and even though it was a planned tactic in the coming game of Seek and Destroy the Intruder, I couldn't help but feel nervous about it.

I caught myself wishing that Scotty—the patron saint of all travelers?—could simply beam me across the plain to Idunn's hall. Teleportation was his godlike power—that and getting his engines not only to warp speed, but to warp speed *faster* with nothing more than some auxiliary tubes and mysterious bypasses.

People used to think that Druids were capable of teleportation, but of course that's nonsense. I've never disintegrated my atoms in one place and reassembled them in another. I have, however, run tirelessly for miles, as I was currently doing, faster than any normal man could huff and puff. And I've cheated by taking shortcuts through Tír na nÓg, where any grove can be bound to any Fae woodland on earth—Fae in the sense that it's a healthy forest. Getting to Russia from Arizona took me less than five minutes: I shifted planes to Tír na nÓg, found the knots that led to a forest in Siberia like a railroad in my sight, then pulled myself along them until I was standing on the other side of the globe in the land of borscht and amusing furry hats. In order to make that shift, however, I'd had to get down to the Aravaipa Canyon Wilderness from Tempe, and that had taken me nearly two hours. And once in Russia in a proper forest, it was a healthy three-hour trip overland to the high tundra lake bound to the Well of Mimir.

There were no shortcuts for me now. I'd have to run everywhere. But that, I came to decide, was not necessarily a bad thing. My longing for teleportation waned as I grew accustomed to the feel of the earth and the flow of magic beneath it. As far as ontological projections of human angst about the afterlife go, Asgard is one of the nicer ones. It is somewhat spare in its diversity of life, like the frozen lands the Norse hail from, but it is sharply rendered, redolent of mystery, and a bite of danger wafts about in the air.

Admittedly, the danger part might have been something I was projecting onto the wind. This wasn't a fun run; it was insanely perilous.

Ratatosk had told me I would know immediately

when I'd reached Vanaheim. For one thing, the purple teeth of the Asgard Mountains would loom large in front of me, and for another, the Plain of Idavoll would give way to harvested fields, idyllic farmland dotted with bright points of color on the horizon, where barns and granaries rested like the desultory afterthoughts of an impressionist's brush, all waiting for winter's first snow. I arrived there as the sun was setting in front of me, and I marveled at the imagination of the Norse, who thought that things like the sun and gravity and weather would behave the same way on a floating plane attached to an ash tree as they did on earth.

Still, they'd imagined their paradise well. If I wasn't about to become the Norse's most wanted, I would have liked to linger there awhile.

I kept running past the twilight songs of birds and cast night vision to save myself from injury. I had run for more than eight hours straight at ten miles per hour, and now the Asgard Mountains were close, jutting up into the early evening like towering ziggurats.

Another mile earned me a glimpse of a pale yellow glow shining just north of west over the canopy of a forest I was fast approaching. It was either a very large campfire, which I deemed unlikely, or it was the golden mane of Gullinbursti. Deciding I had run a bit too far south, I altered my course to head straight for it, and before long I stopped for the first time since I'd left the Norns. There was a river to cross here; it definitively marked the traditional border of Vanaheim, according to Ratatosk. I didn't relish a swim, but I didn't appear to have a choice. Flying across as an owl would mean leaving almost everything behind. I shrugged, sighed, and waded in. Everything that needed to be dry was safely tucked into a waterproof pouch anyway.

Fortunately it was a slow stretch of river, its current not particularly strong, and even weighted down with my clothes and sword, I was able to manage without much trouble aside from the chill. I admit it: There was shrinkage.

Figuring the best cure for shivering would be to resume running, I jogged for maybe forty yards toward the pale light before I had to stop again. Just before I entered the trees, the glow flared brightly and something launched itself from the woods. A blinding phosphorous comet streaked into the sky, followed by a rolling rumble of thunder and a dark cloud bank that had not been there moments before. I remained still, dripping onto the earth and getting colder, because those particular flying objects were gods—and they were probably looking for me.

It was the fertility god Freyr, riding on the back of Gullinbursti, and behind him came Thor in his chariot, pulled by two goats. They were headed toward Yggdrasil.

I waited until they were almost out of sight before moving again. I continued straight on my northwesterly path, now sure that I was headed in the right direction and positive that I didn't have far to go.

That was good, because my timetable had just accelerated. I'd been hoping to be gone before anyone discovered the Norns were missing, but that seemed unlikely now. How fast they picked up my trail depended entirely on how fast they set the god Heimdall the task of finding me. He had superlative senses that made him an excellent tracker; if he was nearby, I had no doubt he'd be able to hear my heartbeat and smell my anxiety.

There was nothing for it but to proceed quickly. I suspected that Odin had seen through my ruse by now; he'd had plenty of time to figure out that Bacchus wasn't coming and the dark elves hadn't done anything. Still, he didn't know who or what I was, what my goal was, or where I was. Thus Thor and Freyr were going to Yggdrasil on a fact-finding mission, perhaps along with other gods as well—but not Odin himself. I'd bet Odin was on his way to his silver throne right now, if he wasn't there already. He'd want to search for me and dispatch a proper welcoming party—so that's why I had to act now, before he had a chance to "see all" from his throne. Ratatosk had been a bit hazy on the distance between Gladsheim and Valaskjálf, so there was no telling how much time I had left.

The unmannerly chaos of the woods changed after four miles to measured orchards in stately rows; the branches of pear trees, plums, apples, and more bore silent witness to my passage, and then a slow, deep river curled into view, perhaps the same one I'd crossed earlier. Suspecting this served as the border between Vanaheim and Alfheim, I kept to the south side of it and looked for halls nestled on either shore. Another mile brought me to them.

On the north side of the river, Freyr's hall seemed to grow like a sturdy oak in the middle of a lush garden still blooming late into November; it appeared organically grown rather than constructed, yet I could still discern that here were walls and a watertight roof, as comfortable and secure as any other hall. Spaced randomly about the grounds on carved wooden pedestals were woven baskets overflowing with produce. Wee nocturnal animals were taking advantage of these offerings, and an owl swooped down to take advantage of the wee nocturnal animals. The warm glow of Freyr's hearth fire could be seen through the windows, which were open to the air—as was his door. A path led from his step to the boundary of his garden, which then turned south and widened to kiss the edge of a sturdy, handsome bridge floating above the river. Bold planks would allow three to walk abreast upon it, or it could support large animals and carts.

The path continued on my side of the river once the

bridge touched the shore. It led straight to a stouter, smaller hall, clearly constructed rather than grown, but every inch of it was carved with runes and scenes of brave Viking deeds. I crept closer until I could read the runes. They were skalds of one form or another, proclaiming the hall to be that of Idunn and Bragi, long may they live and love and so on.

My art appreciation was curtailed by the sound of low, intense voices coming from the hall. The door and windows were open, just like Freyr's, and the fire inside was more for its light than its warmth.

"Get closer," imaginary Kirk said. "I want to hear what they're saying."

"I agree," said imaginary Spock. "The additional intelligence might prove to be useful." I told them both I liked it better when they argued, as I picked my way carefully forward until I was crouching underneath the front window of the hall.

The warm, rich voice of a woman fluttered into my ears: ". . . what this means? If the Norns are truly dead, then their prophecies may be null. We could be truly free, Bragi, think of it!"

A sonorous baritone voice rumbled contemplatively. "Ragnarok, null?" A loudy thump and the scrape of chair legs on a wooden floor suggested someone had sat down heavily. "Perhaps then there is hope for us all."

"Yes!" the woman enthused. I assumed her to be Idunn. "And there is hope for us specifically! Do you not understand? Perhaps we could finally have a child! The doom they laid upon us may have died with them!" I heard kissing noises and then a throaty chuckle from the baritone.

"Ah, I see. Only one way to find out, isn't there?" The kissing noises became more frequent, and these were shortly followed by other, less chaste noises and heavy breathing. I sank dejectedly onto my haunches, realizing this might take a while. These were not teenagers who finished such business in a few frenzied minutes. The long-lived knew how to love long.

But the brief snatch of conversation I'd overheard gave me plenty to think about. Idunn had implied that the two of them were cursed with infertility, and their current behavior implied that they couldn't wait to get rid of that curse. Moreover, it implied that they were still in love. Mortals never got a chance to see if their love would last for centuries, but clearly Idunn and Bragi's had. At first I felt a bit envious, and then heartachingly so for the memories it stirred.

There had been a woman in Africa once whom I loved for more than two hundred years. Upon returning to the fringes of eastern Europe with the hordes of Genghis Khan, I'd quickly ascertained that there was little to be gained by staying there. So I crossed Arabia instead, a strange infidel in the Caliphate, then delved deep into the African continent and lost myself in that wondrous land of savanna and jungle and desert. I did not reemerge until the fifteenth century, happily missing the Black Death in the process. Even more happily for me, Aenghus Óg lost track of me for that whole time; were I superstitious, perhaps I'd assign the credit for that to my love. (More likely I had made enough progress on my amulet to shield me from his divination, and until he thought of new ways to track me, I was safe.)

The source of my long attraction to Tahirah had been perfectly matched chemistry, of course, the same frisson that clearly existed between the Norse gods now snogging behind me. Her sharp wit kept up with mine, and her soft dark eyes soothed my restlessness and chained me willingly to her side. Her low musical voice entered my ears like new velvet, and her laugh was so pure that it struck a tuning fork against my bones and gave me shuddering chills down my spine. She was the last person with whom I'd shared Immortali-Tea. Over the two centuries of our marriage she gave me twenty-five children, all of them a joy; I regretted nothing. Perhaps we would still be in love today, still making babies and trying to keep the young ones from inadvertently marrying the descendants of the old ones (I'm sorry, honey, but you can't marry him. He's the great-great-grandson of your brother, you see, who was born back in 1842). I would never know; the Maasai war party we stumbled across ended our chance at eternal love.

The renewed scraping of the chair leg interrupted my reverie and I heard footsteps fading away deeper into the hall, along with some panting and a few wanton giggles.

That was opportunity knocking.

Rising slowly from my crouch, I peeked carefully over the windowsill. The hearth drew my attention first, off to my left. It was heating the contents of an iron pot craned over the flames, which Idunn and Bragi were apparently willing to let stew for some time. Directly in front of me was the kitchen table, a wooden bowl of fruit on it. There were pears, plums, and peaches—but no apples.

Imaginary Kirk spoke up. "Do you dare to eat a peach?"

"Of course I dare," I whispered.

"May I remind you that we are here for a golden apple?" imaginary Spock said. "We should not be distracted by superfluous fruit." I reached my hand through the open window and selected a plum from the bowl, figuring there would be no time to enjoy an entire peach. It was ripe and slightly soft underneath my fingers.

"Attaboy," Kirk said as I took a bite. It was absurdly tasty.

I grinned impishly and hoped it was a sign I could go

with Plan C. I'd planned obsessively for this caper, plotting courses of action based on various contingencies all the way up to Q (but unfortunately hadn't included a duel with the Norns in any of them). Plan C involved leaving a note behind at the scene of the crime. Now the note was taking shape in my mind as I chewed on the plum; all I needed to do was find the apples.

I silently buried the plum pit underneath the window, with a whispered command to the earth. I untied the drawstring to my belt pouch by touch and removed a waterproof package of oilskin, which contained (among other things) some note-sized sheets of paper and a fountain pen for Plan C. I retrieved these after dissolving my camouflage, then quietly entered the hall while its owners took loud delight in each other.

Once past the threshold, I saw to my right a wooden pedestal much like the ones surrounding Freyr's hall. It had been invisible from the window, but it was prominent as one entered the door, ornately carved with figures that were most likely the Norse gods. A basket full of golden apples rested upon it, clearly an offering to anyone visiting. I grinned and continued to the kitchen table with my paper and pen; Plan C was a go. Taking inspiration from the Modernist poet William Carlos Williams, I wrote a brief poem in Old Norse that would no doubt insult Bragi's sense of good taste, since skaldic poets had no patience with free verse:

This is just to say
I have stolen
The plums
That were in
Your fruit bowl

And which
You were probably

Saving
For the Norns
Freyja's tits!
They were delicious
So sweet
And so cold

I signed it, "You're all stupid. You can lick me, Bacchus," and then stuffed every one of the plums into my pockets, leaving only pears and peaches in the bowl. I didn't care if they believed it was written by Bacchus or not. The entire point of the note was to throw them off my trail; they'd be looking for someone with hands capable of writing saucy Modernist poetry, and I was shortly going to be hands-free.

The moment of theft had arrived. Idunn and Bragi were obligingly experimenting with the pleasurable effects of friction in their bedroom, and the golden apples of the gods beckoned invitingly near the open door. Continuing to tread softly, I picked one out of the basket and paused perversely to see if an alarm would sound. Idunn wailed in ecstasy from the back of the hall and demanded that Bragi give her a baby, but I didn't think that counted.

Moving as quickly as I could without making any noise, I went back to the river and tossed in all the plums. My feet left prints leading down to the riverbank, but that was all right. It would be perfect if they thought I'd jumped in; they'd waste their time searching up- and downstream for where I came out on the other side.

I backed slowly away from the bank and had the earth fill in my prints as I walked, leaving the ones leading to the river alone. Eventually I was under the orchard canopy, where the ground was a bit more firm and strewn with fallen leaves that softened my footfalls and disguised them, since there was a bit of moisture remaining in the leaves and they had yet to turn crunchy. Here, I hoped, was where I'd lose anyone trying to track me by smell.

Placing the golden apple carefully in the crook of a tree branch, I stripped off everything and folded it into a neat pile, glad to be out of the damp leather. I wrote another quick note—"You take unusual delight in sheep asses and everyone knows it. Neener-neener, Bacchus"—and set it on top. The sword I placed off to one side. I asked the earth to part for me and it obliged, opening a hole about two feet deep and about as wide. I placed the pile of clothes and my pouch inside with the note on top and then had the earth bury it for me. I paused to say a few soft words for Ratatosk, because his bones were in my pouch. Then I redistributed leaves over the spot and rose, satisfied. If anyone, such as Heimdall, sniffed me out to this point and then dug up the clothes, they'd get nothing but frustrated.

I sure hoped Odin was missing all of this. I took the apple down from the tree and laid it gently on the ground a few paces away. Then I slung Moralltach across my body and adjusted the strap to a custom length so that it sagged ridiculously on my right side. The sword slid down my back and I hitched it up, then got down on all fours so that the strap hung beneath my torso and even brushed the ground. After a few more tugs and shrugs to position the sword properly across my back, I was ready: I triggered the charm on my necklace that let me shape-shift into a stag, and when the transformation was complete, the sword and its strap was fitted snugly around my body.

This procedure had taken much practice and many hours of making custom straps, but it was worth it since it was a part of Plans A through Q. Now I could run much faster and still have the sword available in case I had to fight in close quarters. I gingerly picked up the golden apple between my deer lips and cast camouflage on myself, the apple, and Moralltach. I was exuding a markedly different scent now that I was a deer—my werewolf friends in Arizona confirmed for me that they could not tell, strictly by scent, that I was the same being when I shape-shifted—and unless Odin somehow figured out what was going on, I didn't foresee any trouble getting back to Yggdrasil in maybe five or six hours, compared to the eight it had taken me to get out here. Who was going to see a camouflaged stag running at night across the Plain of Idavoll?

I wasn't naïve enough to seriously believe I'd have no trouble, though. I just didn't foresee it.

Chapter 4

Occasionally I am smitten with an acute case of Smug. It can happen to anyone, but it happens most often to people who think they've been especially clever. I felt a case of it coming on as I got closer and closer to Yggdrasil with no signs of pursuit or even alarm. Through a combination of surprise, speed, and guile, I had thrown an entire pantheon into such confusion that they didn't know their legs from lutefisk. My supreme cock-up with the Norns should have balanced that out, but I was firmly blocking that and choosing to feel the Smug instead.

With about ten miles to go, near the trunk of Yggdrasil but still miles away from the root leading to Jötunheim, my acute case of Smug turned to a gibbering case of Oh, Shit! I believe that's a bona fide psychological term; if it isn't, it should be.

I present my facts to a candid world: When a person steals anything from anyone and runs away, the first thing they say when they realize they're being chased is "Oh, shit!" in whatever language they spoke as a child. It's really not possible to say anything else at that point. Some Britons cling to long-standing tradition and say "Oh, bugger!" first, but once they confirm that they are, in fact, being chased, they invariably correct course and join the rest of humanity in saying "Shit!"

Except for the part where I was a stag and I had an apple between lips that couldn't say it out loud anyway, I went the conventional route. When I saw what was after me, I screamed "Oh, shit!" in my mind and did my best to achieve maximum warp, Scotty and his engines be damned.

A routine paranoid check of my surroundings had revealed two ravens keeping pace above me. They hadn't been there ten minutes earlier, during my last routine paranoid check. It meant Odin knew where I was, and it might also mean he was on his way to intercept me. I'm not sure how well the ravens could see me while I was camouflaged and running in the dark, but clearly it was well enough to locate my relative position. If nothing else, they could follow the sound of my hooves pounding across the plain.

An hour earlier I had seen the golden trail of Gullinbursti and dark clouds of Thor returning to Freyr's hall. They appeared in the sky to the north, since I was returning a few miles to the south to avoid running into just such a party. They knew the Norns were missing, and perhaps they knew about Ratatosk as well; now they were following the trail I'd left them. At least I knew they wouldn't be waiting for me at Yggdrasil.

Yet a whisper of thunder behind me caused me to risk a look. The sound suggested a mass of cavalry, but instead it was only a single horse on the horizon. It was a massive horse, the height of a camel rather than any thoroughbred, and it had eight legs rather than the four I was accustomed to seeing. It was Sleipnir, the steed of Odin, and on its back rode the one-eyed god, spear in hand. Above the horizon, twelve flying horses galloped in the air, each bearing an armored maiden with shield and sword. They were Valkyries, which meant the shit I was in was deeper than the Mariana Trench. They were the

Choosers of the Slain on this plane, the Norse equivalent of the Morrigan except with funny winged helmets, and somehow I didn't think they would choose Odin to die.

I turned tail and ran for it. Cool, a chase scene, I thought manically as I huffed around the apple in my lips. If I'd brought my iPod, I could have loaded in Wagner's "Ride of the Valkyries" for the soundtrack. Though, on reflection, it was dreary stuff and wouldn't lend me any speed. Perhaps it would have been more amusing and inspirational to play something culturally jarring and utterly absurd, like Jerry Reed's banjo anthem for those seventies bootlegging movies; Odin and the Valkyries could play the role of Smokey, and I'd be the legendary Bandit. Odin looked a bit more competent than Sheriff Buford T. Justice, unfortunately, and I wasn't exactly moving like a 1977 Trans Am. The rumble of Sleipnir's hooves was growing steadily louder; he was gaining on me.

Odin's spear, Gungnir, was a neat piece of magic like Moralltach or Fragarach. Thanks to the runes carved on its head, it was always supposed to hit its target, and its target always died. That sort of magic tended to work; I had firsthand experience, using both Fragarach and Moralltach. I wondered, though, what kind of range he had. Did the magic work in such a way that he could simply target me, then give the spear a halfhearted throw in my general direction and let the runes do the rest? Or did he have to be within the range of his natural (albeit godlike) strength to chuck it after me? It was times like this when I wished I had a parietal eye.

The blowing of a war horn forced me to look around. Valkyries don't blow war horns for the fun of it; they do so only with a purpose, as a signal in battle. I was in time to see Odin, still more than a quarter mile away, rise from his saddle and hurl Gungnir up into a high arc, the terminus of which was undoubtedly intended to be

my heart or brain. At the same time, the Valkyries surged
behind it, raising their swords and then pointing them
all at me. My cold iron amulet sprouted frost crystals
and trembled on my chest, and I knew that they had just
chosen me to die. I suppose I could have depended on
my amulet to protect me from their death sentence, but
I'm too paranoid to leave everything up to a hunk of
metal when I have options. What if the amulet didn't affect the targeting until the spear hit my aura? I couldn't
let the spear get within a couple of inches of my skin and
then try to dodge. I wanted to try out something else.

My idea was to shake off both Gungnir's targeting and
the Valkyries' doom by changing the nature of the target.
I bounded for a couple of leaps to the right to avoid the
path of the spear and then did three things in less than a
second: I dissolved my camouflage, changed back into
human form, and stopped running. The apple popped out
of my human lips and I caught it in my left hand. It was
covered in deer slobber but otherwise unmarred.

The stag that Gungnir had been sent to kill wasn't
there anymore, and I heard the spear whistle over my
head before my eyes caught up to see it thud menacingly
into the moor some forty yards along my previous path.
I checked on my pursuit and saw Odin and the Valkyries
pull up to make sure they weren't hallucinating.

They couldn't believe their eyes. The spear that never
missed had just missed. The chosen slain wasn't slain
but prancing around naked in the Plain of Idavoll with
an apple in his hand and a defiant grin on his face. As
they watched, the red-haired demon held up a hand in a
clear signal for them to wait, then strode confidently
toward Gungnir as if it were no more than a common
spear he had thrown himself. Then the creature had the
unmitigated gall to lay his hands on it—Odin's spear!—
and yank it disrespectfully out of the ground. And then
he—he—

Odin bellowed at the Valkyries as he saw what I intended. He was not clad in full armor, but neither was he abroad as an avuncular traveler with a wide droopy hat and a gray cloak. He wore a spectacled helmet and a mail shirt under a tunic made of reindeer hide. He goaded his horse forward, and the Valkyries followed suit.

It had been a long time since I'd thrown a spear or javelin, but it seemed like a good night to pick up the habit again. If Gungnir hit something, then they'd falter and I'd get a chance to put some distance between us; if it missed, then they'd slow down to retrieve the weapon and I'd still get a chance to put some distance between us.

Directing my strength through my back and shoulder and trying to remember my technique, I hurled the spear powerfully at my enemy's strategic weakness—not at Odin, but at Sleipnir. Without pausing to watch its flight, I dropped immediately to all fours and shifted back into a stag, grasping the apple between my lips once more and shrugging against the fit of the scabbard strap. As I raised my head to resume my run, I saw the spear sink home at the base of the mighty stallion's throat, and he reared, neighing in pain and throwing Odin to the ground before he himself toppled.

That almost made me drop the apple. I hadn't expected my aim to be that good; the runecraft must work for whoever threw the spear. The Valkyries immediately whirled around to help Odin, and I shagged it out of there while I had the chance.

Two limp black forms rained out of the sky as I bounded toward the root, and I realized they were the ravens, Hugin and Munin—Thought and Memory. For them to fall meant Odin must be either unconscious or dead. I had to get out of there before I caused any more damage. I recast camouflage on myself, on the theory that the Valkyries wouldn't be able to see me without Odin's help, and worried about what to do next.

Moralltach was a problem. There was no way I could afford to take it with me down Ratatosk's bolt-hole in the root of Yggdrasil. Now that I was being pursued, I wouldn't have the necessary time to climb down that shaft using the excruciatingly slow process of binding my skin to the bark with each step. I had to fly down, but there was no way I could carry the sword as an owl.

I had no choice but to leave it behind. Checking my six as I approached the root, I saw that a few Valkyries had taken to the air again and they were circling aimlessly, looking for me. Hugin and Munin hadn't returned to the sky, so Odin was still out of it. Cursing the necessity, I returned to my human form and unslung the sword from my shoulders after I caught the apple popping from my mouth. I knelt on the ground and asked it to part for me. It did, accepting the sword that I drove straight down to the depth of my elbow, so that it would remain there like a spike in the earth. As satisfied as possible under the circumstances, I carefully closed the earth over it, making sure that the turf on top looked undisturbed, even going so far as to back away ten paces and spending the effort to remove all traces of footprints.

They might find it; if Heimdall knew to look for it, he probably would. But if I simply left while Odin was still zonked, there was no reason they wouldn't assume I'd taken it with me. I already had a reason to come back to Asgard, in any case: I'd promised my attorney and friend, the vampire Leif Helgarson, that I would bring him there to settle an old grudge against Thor the violent way.

I shape-shifted to a great horned owl and picked up

the apple in my talons as gingerly as possible. I couldn't avoid puncturing its thin skin a little bit, but I figured Laksha would just have to deal with it. I flew up to the hole in the root and then, once over the lip, folded my wings against the sides of my body and dove for the bottom.

After swooping out of the hole underneath Asgard, I dove again for the bottom of the root. The Well of Mimir was unattended, as it had been when I arrived. Mimir had long since been beheaded by the Vanir, but I expected that such an important site would be watched. Since it was now Black Friday, perhaps its keeper was off somewhere taking advantage of a DoorBuster sale. I pulled out of my dive, dropped the apple in the snow, and shifted to plain old Atticus. I promptly began to shiver.

Hugging the tree root and clutching the blasted apple, I found the tether to earth and pulled my center along it until I returned to what everyone thinks of as the "real" world. It was just as cold in Siberia as it was in Jötunheim, and I had no clothes. I groaned out loud and took a moment to enjoy the feeling of not being chased. I also needed to give my body a bit of a break. Despite the fact that all the energy I'd used had come from the earth, the rapid shape-shifting was taking its toll; I felt shaky and weak, and my liver wanted to know if it would get to spend some time in its wonted shape.

Unfortunately, the answer was no. I wasn't out of danger yet. The Norse were perfectly capable of following me to this plane, and I had no doubt that they would, sooner or later. Once they followed my clear trail to Idunn and Bragi's hall, they'd start to piece things together. If they found my buried clothes in the orchard, they'd know I came from Midgard; if they found the Norns, they'd know a sword killed them; if they found Moralltach, they'd recognize it as a Fae weapon and chase that lead until they found out the truth—namely, the being responsible for stealing a golden apple and knocking Odin on his ass wasn't a demon or a god but rather a Druid.

I hoped they wouldn't find that out until much later, if at all. My primary advantage right now was my anonymity. Once Odin woke up and couldn't find me in Asgard, he might waste time looking around Jötunheim until someone figured out I'd come from Midgard.

Taking a couple of deep breaths to brace myself and with apologies to my liver, I shifted once more to a stag and picked up the golden apple. The run south to the forest took me only two hours instead of three. I'd never been so relieved to see a friendly bunch of trees; once I shifted planes to Tír na nÓg, I'd be able to recover a cache of clothes I'd left there and make myself presentable. I wanted to shift to North Carolina this afternoon and place the apple in Laksha's hand with cavalier indifference, as if stealing it had been no more taxing than running to the local grocery store.

She had slain twelve Bacchants without breaking a sweat—something I'd never be able to do—so in terms of badass grandstanding, I needed to make this caper appear as if it had cost me nothing, even though it might end up costing me everything. It had already occurred to me that Laksha might be hoping I'd never return from the trip and that the whole arrangement was an elaborate way to marshal me to knavery. Part of her—perhaps a very large part—would be disappointed that I'd succeeded without a scratch to show for it.

Thinking of how surprised she'd be made me smile. I was, in fact, dangerously close to contracting another acute case of Smug. But just before I cozied up to an old oak and shifted to Tír na nÓg, I looked up at the sky and saw two ravens circling above me. To the north, dark thunderclouds were boiling rapidly in my direction.

Odin was awake, those damn ravens really *could* see through my camouflage, and Thor the Thunder Thug was on his way to settle accounts.

Chapter 5

Sometimes people ask me how I got to be so old. It's tough, I tell them. The short answer is to live as best you can while avoiding all the things that will kill you—but that never satisfies anyone. They want specific nuggets of wisdom, like "You probably shouldn't go yachting off the coast of Somalia," or "Never eat sushi in a restaurant where you're the only customer." But even these sound a bit disappointing. "Stay away from the guy who throws lightning bolts," though—that's a classic. Highly recommended.

My amulet wouldn't protect me from a bolt of lightning, so I shifted to Tír na nÓg before Thor could get himself in range. He'd probably set the forest on fire once I left, just for spite.

I remained in Tír na nÓg just long enough to recover my cache of clothes, and then I shifted to another Fae plane, Mag Mell, and luxuriated in a hot mineral spring. It was partially to recuperate and partially to throw off Hugin and Munin; they couldn't follow me to the Irish planes, and that was a blessed pint o' peace.

Another blessed pint was the one served to me by a comely wood nymph in the spring: Goibhniu's Mag Mell Ale. It's a worty and voluptuous brew, quite mouthy, with a smooth yet grainy foundation and a bodacious, provocative finish that couples a whiff of wanton peaches with the innocence of a virgin. If you can get to Mag Mell, it's free.

That's right, there's free beer in Irish paradise. Everyone's jealous.

After a few of those, I had my Smug on for sure, and I shifted to Pisgah National Forest outside Asheville, North Carolina, to visit Laksha. We arranged by cell phone to meet in Pritchard Park downtown, where we sat on the rocks next to a small waterfall. If she was surprised or disappointed by my appearance, she hid it well. After inquiring about the small blemishes on the apple's surface, she took a bite, and I saw true pleasure illuminate the features of the face she inhabited. Her skin, already beautiful, tightened and smoothed and shone with health.

"Satisfied?" I asked.

She nodded. "Very much so. Well done, Mr. O'Sullivan."

"Then I will take my leave," I said, standing up and giving her a short bow. "I'd eat it all up soon, though, because Hugin and Munin are looking for it. Best of luck growing your own tree of immortality."

"That's it?" Laksha frowned. "I get no more civility than that?"

"I have kept my word to you, Laksha. Please judge me by that, and nothing more. As for civility, I leave you in far better circumstances than you left me after you slew the Bacchants. And there is much that demands my attention elsewhere. Please excuse me." With that, I turned on my heel and started jogging back to the Pisgah Forest, for while I appreciated Laksha's adherence to her word and her skills as a witch, I had no desire to cultivate a friendship with her.

I hadn't been lying about the many demands on my attention. The long soak in the hot springs proved to be an

extremely comfortable place in which to confront some
uncomfortable facts. There really wasn't anything for
me to feel smug about beyond the stark fact that I'd
bearded the lion in his den and survived—for now.
There was no way that Odin would let the deaths of
Sleipnir and the Norns slide—nor should he. Though I
could argue that I'd slain them all in self-defense, the un-
yielding, inconvenient truth of it was that I had chosen
to go to Asgard. No one had forced me; I had made
promises and traded one set of problems for another,
much larger set. I did not see any way to trade down to
something more manageable now—except by abandon-
ing everything I cared about.

It used to be so easy for me to run, to care about nothing but myself and the earth underneath my feet. That
had been my modus operandi ever since Tahirah died; I
never stayed anywhere long enough to be bound by
commitments, never entangled myself with the lives of
others, and told myself it was all about avoiding Aenghus
Óg. That was more true than I realized: What I'd truly
been avoiding was love, the strongest binding there is,
and the pain that scrapes at your insides when the bond
is forcefully broken.

It has been more than five centuries. I still miss her.
She smiles in my dreams sometimes and I wake up weeping for the loss.

When we were married, I did not move without
thinking of her first. And now I am in a similar place; I
cannot move without thinking of Oberon, as well as my
duty to Granuaile. I will not, *cannot* abandon them. I
saw that my need to defend and protect them had driven
my choices in recent months—from killing Aenghus Óg
to making an unwise bargain with Leif so that he would
help me dispatch a nasty German coven. Flidais had
told me, back at Tony Cabin, that she knew I would
have run from Aenghus Óg again if Oberon hadn't been

held hostage. And she was right. Likewise, if *die Töchter des dritten Hauses* had not killed Perry and tried to kill both Granuaile and me, I would not have called Leif for help and agreed to take him to Asgard. Those had been rash, desperate decisions, not the sort that would most likely allow me to stay alive. But once bound by the ties of love, there is no other choice one can make and remain human. They'd been simple choices at the time that were now making my life tremendously complicated. My immediate safety was an illusion; the consequences would come home eventually like the prodigal son—a karmic debt, Laksha might have said, but with the usurious rates incurred at a payday loan center.

It was time for me to leave Arizona. There was an annoying Tempe detective named Kyle Geffert who was convinced I'd had something to do with what the media called the "Satyrn Massacre"—and he was right. Thus far my lawyers had kept me from suffering long interrogation sessions in a steel-gray room laced with cigarette smoke, but I didn't see how I could avoid it for much longer.

The lone Bacchant that had escaped that fiasco left knowing positively that the world's last Druid lived in Arizona, and Bacchus would probably be roused by that alone, to say nothing of his reaction if the Norse pantheon had taken my bait and blamed him for my Thanksgiving shenanigans.

A group of fanatic Russian demon hunters who called themselves the Hammers of God thought I was too cozy with the forces of darkness, despite the fact that I'd probably slain more demons than they had. Rabbi Yosef Bialik would probably return to harass me with a few of his friends, now that he knew I kept company with werewolves and witches.

On top of all this, one of my regular customers in the bookshop had asked me last week how I stayed looking so young.

It was time to go.

The idea of moving wouldn't bother me except for what I'd have to leave behind. The fish and chips at Rúla Búla, sipping whiskey with the widow MacDonagh, the simple pleasures of being a practicing herbalist—all would be sorely missed. Too, there was a large waste-land to heal around Tony Cabin, the existence of which was at least partly my responsibility, and I wanted more than anything to spend all my time there righting that particular wrong. But I had chains of obligation to throw off first—proverbial ducks I had to get in a row.

After running for most of the last couple days, I sur-prised myself by asking Oberon as soon as I got home if he'd like to go for a run.

<You're damn skippy I do!> he said. I'd picked him up from the widow MacDonagh's house, where he'd been staying during my absence. The widow wasn't in, which was just as well. If she'd been home, I would have had to sit and chew the fat for a while, and Oberon had been waiting long enough. The widow's cats provided him plenty of entertainment, but she couldn't take him for walks and give him the sort of exercise a very large Irish wolfhound needs.

We jogged through the Mitchell Park neighborhood where I lived, and he brought me up-to-date on what I'd missed.

<The cats are beginning to get used to me,> he com-plained. <They've managed to notice that in all the times I've barked at them and chased them, not once have I killed them. I haven't even bitten them. So now they can't be bothered so much as to raise their hack-les at me. It's depressing. No, you know what it is? Emasculating.>

I chuckled and spoke aloud as we jogged. I often spoke directly to his mind through the bond we shared, but since no one was around to hear me, I enjoyed making use of my breath. "Whoa, five syllables. Very impressive."

<I deserve a treat for that.>

"Indubitably. And we'll go hunting as soon as I can manage. I'm sorry to hear about your emasculation."

<No, you're not. But this will make you sorry. The widow has a long list of medical problems.>

I frowned at him and checked to see if he was joking. "She does?"

<Uh-huh. She explained them to me in detail. Graphically. Sometimes it was even show and tell.>

"Oh. That does make me sorry. She's never said anything about them to me."

<Well, can't you do anything for her?>

I let a few paces go by before I answered. The neighborhood mourning doves were happy and cooing to each other. A stooped old man in Bermuda shorts was trimming down his cloud sage bush for the winter, moving slowly and carefully. He was too preoccupied with his topiary to recognize that I was talking to my dog as we passed. "Yes. I could reverse the aging process with Immortali-Tea, and that would take care of pretty much everything. It repairs cell damage, prevents cancer, increases white blood cells, you name it. But what if I did that for her? What do you think would happen?"

<She'd feel better, Atticus. And that's what matters.>

"True. But you're not thinking it through. The widow's getting close to ninety years old, if she's not there already. Let's say I put her on an intensive regimen of Immortali-Tea and she shed fifty years in five weeks. She would look and feel forty years old, and if I never gave her any tea after that, she could still look forward to living at least another fifty years."

<That would be awesome!>

"No, it wouldn't. People would start asking questions.

Everyone would want to know how she did it. Her friends and relatives especially. She's told you about her kids and grandkids, right?"

\<Right.\>

"Well, her oldest son is sixty-seven. She'd be younger than him. That would be awkward. Her grandkids would freak out because their grandma didn't look like a sweet old lady anymore. So what does she tell them? This nice Druid I know did me a solid?"

\<Well, why not? They couldn't hurt you.\>

"It's not about hurting me. They're going to want to stay young too. And then their friends and relatives will, and before you know it the tabloids will get hold of the story and latch on like seven puppies after six tits."

\<Oh, great big bears, that does sound pretty bad!\>

"And then the government will get involved, because having someone live that long is eventually going to raise flags at the IRS and the Social Security Administration. Her driver's license picture won't match her face. All sorts of questions are going to be asked."

\<But aren't your friends worth that kind of trouble?\>

"The widow by herself would be worth the trouble. But I can't confine it to her. Still, let's say I did. She gets to start life over at forty while her kids all continue to age and die. Would she thank me for her youth when she's standing over the grave of her son? Or the graves of her grandchildren?"

\<Well, probably not. I see your point.\>

"Good. I've been in that position, Oberon, far too many times. I've buried my children and their children and so on. It carves away a piece of you."

\<You've never offered them Immortali-Tea?\>

"Sure I have. It's how I learned all the stuff I just told you—the painful way. And I learned that some people become distanced from humanity, severely troubled, and reclusive when they live too long. Sort of like vampires tend to do, only without the bloodsucking. If their minds aren't trained like a Druid's, they gradually collect neuroses over time, like sunbathers collect wrinkles. Immortali-Tea can't fix batshit insanity."

<You had kids who went batshit insane?>

"Yep. That's why eventually I stopped offering."

<Are you going to have any more?>

"Not soon. Need to be in a place where I can settle down. And this isn't that place. I need to talk to you about that, actually."

<About what?>

I explained to him that we needed to move out of Tempe. "I'll have to go back to Asgard soon, and it'll be a longer trip than the first one. It might be forever, because I might not come back, and if that's what happens, then you need to be good to Mrs. MacDonagh. But if I do return, we'll be leaving right away."

<Where are we going?>

"I don't know yet."

<Anyplace is good so long as there's sausage and bitches.>

"Heh! I never thought of it that way." I smiled. "But now that you've clarified my thinking, I wonder why they don't list those amenities in real estate ads. It seems criminally negligent."

<Human priorities are messed up, Atticus. I've made the observation many times, but nobody cares for the wisdom of hounds.>

"I care, buddy. I believe you to be remarkably wise."

<Then I think it would be wise for you to adopt a French poodle.>

I laughed. "Perhaps when we are safely settled elsewhere."

<Promise?>

"I cannot promise you, Oberon," I said, regret tinge-ing my voice, and I could tell he was disappointed. "But, look, it is good to have a dream so long as you do not let it gnaw at the substance of your present. I have seen men consumed by their dreams, and it is a sour business. If you cling too tightly to a dream—a poodle bitch or a personal sausage chef or whatever—then you miss the felicity of your heart beating and the smell of the grass growing and the sounds lizards make when you run through the neighborhood with your friend. Your dream should be like a favorite old bone that you savor and cherish and chew upon gently. Then, rather than stealing from you a wasted sigh or the life of an idle hour, it nourishes you, and you become strangely contented by nostalgia for a possible future, so juicy with possibility and redolent of sautéed garlic and decadent slabs of ba-con that you feel full when you've eaten nothing. And then, one fine day when the sun smiles upon your snout, when the time is right, you bite down hard. The dream is yours. And then you chew on the next one."

Oberon chuffed, his version of human laughter. <Suf-fering cats, Atticus, you're talking like I'm a twitchy Pomeranian when I'm more emotionally stable than you are. And I'm not missing out on the lizards. I've heard seven of them so far rustling around in the lantana bushes. They like the purple and yellow ones best, not so much the white. What I want to know is, where can I get a bone like that?>

Chapter 6

Here is how you know someone has had a good idea: Other people freely admit to their friends that said idea has changed their lives. Most people today will grant that fire and the wheel are the big two. After that, any attempts to rank the greatest ideas of all time are going to draw lots of argument. You'll have zealots pimping this god or that on the one hand, scientists pimping Darwin on the other, and then practical people pointing at written language and saying, look, fellas, the reason those ideas have gone viral is because someone figured out how to write them down.

On Saturday night, the day after my return from Asgard, I heard about a new life-changing invention (for some): the salad spinner.

"I seriously love my salad spinner," Granuaile confided. "It's changed my life." She said this in her kitchen, where she was busy making me the dinner she owed me for guessing wrong about Ratatosk's size and the ability to enter Asgard via Yggdrasil.

"Excuse me for just a moment," I said, and I exited the kitchen for the living room, where her laptop had access to Wi-Fi in the building. I Googled "salad spinner changed my life" and got more than six thousand hits. There was also a Salad Spinner Appreciation Society on Facebook. It wasn't what I'd call a cultural revolution, but it had potential, and I was willing to find out more. I returned to the kitchen and said, "Sorry about that. Please explain how your salad spinner has changed your life."

"Oh." Granuaile's eyes flicked down, perhaps with a shade of embarrassment. "Well, when you wash lettuce it's tough to get the leaves dry without wasting paper towels and spending all your time patting them dry. If you just leave them wet, then your dressing dilutes and alters the taste you're aiming for. Oil and water don't mix, right? But now," and her voice deepened into a mockery of a Nitro Funny Car drag-race commercial on the radio, "I can use the raw unbridled power of a SALAD SPINNERRR!" Her voice rose at the end of the sentence in maniacal excitement. Her hand plunged down to the handle of her spinner and she worked it furiously, continuing in the same frenzied voice. "SEE the centrifugal force work its MAGIC on the WATERRR! Red leaf, green leaf, spinach, or arugula, it DOESN'T MATTERRR! Just put your wet greens in the spinner and crank that mother 'til ALL the moisture's GONE! SUPER! DRY! SALAD!" Here Granuaile balled her fists at her sides and thrust her hips forward lewdly. "GET SOME!"

That was when I lost it. Up to that point my mouth was hanging open in shock, but when she whipped out the pelvic thrust for nothing more than *a salad*, well, that brought on an epic fit of the giggles. Her performance began looping in my mind's eye, and the absurdity of it kept tickling me so that I couldn't stop. Paroxysms shook me until I fell off my chair, and that made it worse. Tears came to my eyes and I gasped for breath as I slapped the wood laminate of her floor. Granuaile's face turned bright red and she sank down laughing too, laughing both at herself and at my reaction.

Eventually we got around to eating that salad, but not

before our stomachs ached from extended merriment. It was succulence itself: spinach and red leaf lettuce tossed with jicama, white onion, mandarin oranges, and candied walnut pieces. The dressing was a homemade citrus vinaigrette.

This, however, was merely a side. Chef Granuaile MacTiernan set a broiled orange roughy fillet on top of a wild-rice pilaf, then placed on top of that a flash-broiled portobello mushroom that had been marinated in a Beaujolais red wine. Several spears of lightly salted asparagus drizzled with olive oil complemented the fish, and a bottle of pinot noir from the Santa Cruz Mountains did all those snooty and delicious things in our mouths that wine connoisseurs go on about.

"Outstanding," I said, chewing appreciatively. "Truly fantastic."

"I always settle accounts," Granuaile said, and quirked an eyebrow at me.

"That's good to know. I'm the same way. There are a lot of people who would like to settle accounts with me, however, and we should probably speak of it."

"All right," she said. She narrowed her eyes and pointed her fork at me, jabbing it forward to punctuate her words. "But if you're going to try to convince me to give up being a Druid again, you can forget it."

I shook my head with a rueful grin. "You don't have all the information yet." She'd already heard about Ratatosk and Yggdrasil and I'd shared the general look of the plane with her, but I hadn't explained what really happened other than that I'd successfully stolen an apple. Now I recounted everything.

"So Hugin and Munin are looking for you right now?" she asked after I'd finished.

"As we speak, no doubt. The only reason they haven't found me already is that they don't know what to look for. But if Odin ever suspects it was a Druid that slew the

Norns and his favorite horsie, he'll make noise around Tír na nÓg and then they'll find me quickly, because everyone there knows where I am now. I have to move."

"Of course you do, but"—her face clouded—"that means I have to move too."

"Right." I nodded. "And change your name. And cut off all contact with your family and friends to protect them. Unless you *like* having a family and friends. Then you should give up this dream of being a Druid and live happily ever after."

Granuaile slammed her fork down. "Damn it, sensei, I'm not giving that up, I told you!"

"How will your loved ones take this, Granuaile? Look at it from their perspective for a moment. To them it's going to look like I've kidnapped you or that you've joined a cult."

"Well . . . it kind of *is* a cult, isn't it?" she joked.

I chuckled. "I suppose. A very tiny one—here we all are. You can shave your head if you like for verisimilitude."

Granuaile's jaw dropped. "I thought you liked my hair."

Oh, damn. She'd noticed. There's no winning this, change the subject. . . .

"You never answered my question. Aren't your parents going to worry? You won't be able to contact them often, if at all."

She shrugged and puffed a soft dismissal past her lips. "I don't talk to them much as it is. They're divorced. Dad is always on a dig somewhere in the cradle of civilization, and Mom is busy raising her new family in bloody *Kansas*." The way she spat out *Kansas* led me to believe she did not consider it the cradle of civilization. "I let them know I wanted my independence early on and they gave it to me."

"They seem to have set you up well," I remarked, flicking my eyes around.

"Oh, yeah. How does a barmaid afford a condo like this, right? Well, it's paid for by dinosaurs. Mom's new husband is an oily oil man. So greasy he looks like he sleeps in a jar of Vaseline. He has one clump of hair that he's grown really long, and he combs it over pathetically to try to cover up his shiny bald head. I despise him and he loathes me. When I said I wanted to attend ASU, he was only too happy to pay all the bills so long as I agreed to stay out here."

I sighed and closed my eyes. Clearly she wasn't going to miss much of her old life. I'd gone and caught myself an ideal candidate for Druidry. Still, it was best to be thorough, and I still had a couple of disincentives to offer her.

"Granuaile. Did I ever tell you what happened to my last apprentice?"

"No, but I think you're probably going to tell me he died horribly."

"Tragically, yes. Cut down by Moors in the kingdom of Galicia in 997. He was only a couple months away from getting his tattoos and becoming a full Druid. He was utterly vulnerable, you see. Utterly defenseless. And that's what you're going to be for twelve more years. There aren't many shortcuts we can take. This isn't like the movies where you can just feel the Force or learn everything you need to know in a three-minute montage, or those novels where the young hero masters advanced swordplay in a couple of months of lessons on the trail. And all that time you'll be a target in a way I never was, in a way Cíbran never was."

"Cíbran was your apprentice?"

"Yes. I trained him in secret. The locals all thought I was a staunch Christian, the rock of the neighborhood, and never suspected for a moment what I truly was. And back when I was in training, before Christianity, it was perfectly safe to be a Druid. Best possible thing that could happen to a lad, in fact. But you're not in that situation. I'm currently a high-value target, and I'm going to be the gods' most wanted after this next trip to Asgard, no matter how it turns out. If things don't go well, you're almost certainly going down with me. You could be throwing away your whole life."

Granuaile pressed her lips together and smiled tightly. "Nope, you're not scaring me away. Correct me if I'm wrong, but so far the score is Atticus 5, gods 0."

"That's a poor analogy. If they score one, I'm dead and they win."

"Whatever." She held up a hand. "My point is that you kick ass, and it reminds me of something I've been meaning to ask you: How did the Romans ever manage to wipe out the Druids? You can travel to different planes, camouflage yourselves, shape-shift, and fight without ever getting tired—so what happened?"

"Caesar and Minerva," I said. "That's what happened." Granuaile said nothing. She picked up her wineglass and took a sip, raising her eyebrows expectantly, waiting for me to elaborate.

"There was more to it than that," I admitted. "I think there were vampires behind it too. But what I know for certain is that Caesar tromped through Gaul, burning all the sacred groves, and that effectively prevented most Druids from shifting planes and escaping easily. We didn't have the freedom to use any healthy forest we wanted at the time—that became my project afterward. The fires didn't simply burn the wood, you see, they burned away the tethers to Tír na nÓg. It left all the continental Druids stranded here on this plane. Once that was accomplished, Minerva screwed us over by giving Roman scouts the ability to see through our camouflage, and then they could chase us down. The ability to fight without tiring doesn't help when a cohort of legionnaires surrounds you and thrusts their spears from every direction. And that's what they did, make no mistake. It was a systematic slaughter. Some tried to fly away in their bird forms, but they were shot down by archers."

"But surely some of you escaped."

"Oh, aye. Druidry struggled on, especially in Ireland, because it was isolated from the Romans. But then Saint Patrick came along, you know, spreading Catholicism. Lots of lads looked at twelve years of hard study and responsibility, weighed it against the instant acceptance and fellowship of the Christians, and chose the easier faith. And then it was just a matter of attrition. None of the other Druids knew the herblore of Airmid, and they eventually died of old age, if the Romans didn't get them. And one day, the last Druid except for me died without leaving behind a trained Druid to take his place. I couldn't tell you precisely when it happened, but it was most likely the sixth or seventh century."

Granuaile put down her glass and leaned forward. "But you should have destroyed them all! You had the power of the whole earth at your command! You see how things are bound together. Why couldn't you, you know . . ." She faltered, making lame gestures of something breaking apart with her hands.

"Go ahead and ask. Every initiate does at some point."

"Well, can't you break the bonds holding together someone's aorta, for example? Or cause an aneurysm in the brain? Pull out all the iron in the blood?"

"I can't because of this," I said, holding up my tattooed right arm and pointing at it with my left hand. "I know you can't read what these bindings mean yet, but there's a condition woven into these knots. As soon as you attempt to use any of the earth's energy to directly harm or kill a living creature—any creature, mind you, not just a human—you're dead. The only reason the earth grants Druids her power is that we're pledged to protect her life. So if a rhino charges me, I'm not bursting its heart. I'm getting out of the way."

Granuaile stared at me. "That makes no sense."

"Of course it does."

"You just told me how you bound the Norns together and chopped off their heads."

"I bound their *clothes* together—they happened to be wearing them at the time. I performed no magic directly on their bodies. I killed them with my sword."

"That's not protecting life!"

"I was protecting my own."

"But you told me Aenghus Óg used magic to take over Fagles's mind!" She was referring to a binding placed on the Tempe police detective who'd shot me six weeks ago. Since the Tuatha Dé Danann were bound to the earth like me, they had to follow the same rule.

"He did. But that binding didn't directly harm Fagles. Fagles was killed by the Phoenix police."

"But didn't he make Fagles shoot you? Wasn't that harming you?"

"The magic was directed at Fagles, not at me. And Fagles shot me with a completely ordinary, nonmagical gun."

Granuaile tapped her fingernail on the table. "These are really hair-thin distinctions."

"Yes, and they're the sort that Aenghus Óg knew very well."

"Why bother making them? I mean, the earth has to be aware that you're using her power to strengthen your sword arm or make you jump higher and so on."

"Yes. I'm using the power to compete. To prove myself worthy of living another day. Competition, strife, and predation are natural and encouraged by the earth. I still have to be smarter than the other guy, more skilled than the other guy to survive. I can't simply fix everything by melting people's brains."

"Wait. You mess around with skin cells all the time. You give people wedgies by binding the cotton of their underwear with the skin high up on their backs. You started a slap fight between two cops in front of Satyrn."

"No damage was done. The skin never broke. No harm, no foul."

"All right, then, what about the demons? You used Cold Fire on them."

"They're not living creatures of the earth; they're spirits from hell that take on a corporeal form here. But I have to warn you not to try anything standard on them. They are bound together differently than the flora and fauna of earth, so no Druidic magic works except for Cold Fire. It's better just to hack them up. That unbinds them from their corporeal form quite well."

Granuaile puffed an errant lock of hair away from her face and then tucked it behind her ear, thinking through the implications. "Does this *tabu* extend to healing?"

"Not in so many words, but in practice, yes. Messing around with tissues and organs is vastly complicated. It's too easy to make a mistake and do more harm than good, and then you're dead. That's why I never go there with other people; I use magic to heal only myself, because there's no prohibition against screwing yourself up and I know my body extremely well."

"Ah, so that's why you only use herblore for your healing."

I nodded. "That's right. You can perform bindings on harvested plants and the chemicals in them all you want. It's slower than directly healing someone, but it's safer all around. You can't trespass against the prohibition to do no direct magical harm, and it keeps your abilities secret. If people wonder why your teas or poultices are so effective, you can plausibly point to your unique recipes or fresh ingredients or something else, and magic is never an issue."

"Are you positive that you're the last Druid alive today?"

I waggled the flat of my hand in the air in a sorta-kinda motion. "The Tuatha Dé Danann are technically Druids because they're all tattooed like I am. They can do whatever I can do and then some. Best not to call them Druids, though. They like to think of themselves as gods." I grinned sardonically. "Druids are lesser beings, you see. But so far as such lesser beings are concerned, I do believe I'm the last one walking the earth. Unless you want to count all the happy hippie neo-Druids who do seem to love the earth but lack any real magic."

"No, I meant Druids like you."

"Then there are none like me. Until you become one. If you live long enough."

"I'll make it," Granuaile said. "You gave me this completely unsexy amulet to make sure I do." She lifted a teardrop of cold iron strung on a gold chain out from her shirt. The Morrigan had given it to me, and I had passed it on to my apprentice.

"That's not going to save you all the time," I reminded her.

"I know. It seems to me that the thing to do is to simply disappear."

"No, they'll still look for us."

"Who are *they*?"

"The remaining Norse and any other gods who want to make a point that you can't kill gods with impunity."

"What if they think we're dead? Will they still be looking for us then?"

I sighed and smiled contentedly. "You're a constant relief to me, you know. Every time you say something smart it gives me hope that you might become the first new Druid in more than a thousand years."

Chapter 7

Moving sucks.

Most people would nod and agree without question, but saying it that way leaves ample room for interpretation. How much does it suck? Well, it's not as bad as the stink behind a steak house. Nor is it comparable to the slow burn of heartache or the breathtaking agony of a swift kick to the groin. It's more like the secret existential horror I feel whenever I see gummy worms.

I had a girlfriend in San Diego in the early nineties who noticed that I was profoundly unfamiliar with modern junk food. One day as I dozed at the beach, she tested the boundaries of my ignorance by arranging an entire package of gummy worms across my body, assuring me when I opened an eye that these gelatinous cylinders were some sort of new spa treatment called "sun straws" with UV protection built in, and I gullibly accepted her explanation. I woke up with bright death trails of corn syrup crisscrossing my torso, silently and stickily accusing me of wormicide in the hot coastal sun. Even the mighty rinse cycle of the Pacific Ocean couldn't wash them away; they clung to me like soul-sucking leeches. She wasn't my girlfriend after that, and I moved out of San Diego that very night.

It gets worse the longer you wait between moves, because you've had time to accumulate massive piles of crap, even if you try to minimize your consumption like I do.

Looking around at more than a decade's worth of ac-
creted stuff, I was glad this move would force me to leave
it all behind. If I took anything with me, then "they"
would know I'd scarpered off somewhere. Some of my
best twentieth-century goodies were going to be let go—
various bits of detritus saved from previous moves. My
signed copy of the Beatles' *White Album* was going to
stay behind. So were the cherry Chewbacca action figures in the original packaging. I had a baseball signed by
Randy Johnson when he was with the Diamondbacks
and a beer bottle that had once met the lips of Papa
Hemingway. Most of the weapons in the garage would
be left; all I would take was the bow and the quiver of arrows blessed by the Virgin Mary, because those could
come in handy. Other than that, I'd take Fragarach and
Oberon and the clothes on my back, leaving everything
else. The house was easy.

The business was tough. If I was going to make it look
like I planned on coming back, I had to keep it open. But
I had only one remaining employee besides Granuaile—
Rebecca Dane—and I hated to leave her in charge of the
store all by herself, especially since it was the first place
my enemies would look for me. By the same token,
they'd know I'd left town instead of croaked if I packed
it up or sold it; I'd prefer they think me dead.

No matter how I rationalized it, I couldn't help thinking that leaving Rebecca in the lurch would make me
every bit the cocknuckle Thor was reputed to be. Hiring
someone new to help her would only increase my cock-
nucklery.

Added to this was the problem of my rare-book collection. There were seriously dangerous tomes in there,
protected by seriously dangerous wards. I couldn't leave
either the books or the wards in place, but it had to appear as though the rare books were still there.

Problems like that are why I like to have lawyers.

They do all sorts of useful things for me and keep it secret under the attorney-client privilege. After going for a morning jog with Oberon and tuning the TV to Animal Planet for him, I met one of my attorneys, Hal Hauk, at a Tempe bagel joint called Chompie's. Hal ordered a bagel with lox (shudder), and I had a blueberry one with cream cheese.

Hal looked very businesslike, his expression professionally bland and his movements conservative and precise. He seemed to be slightly uncomfortable in his navy pin-striped suit, which was ridiculous because it was perfectly tailored. I knew that meant he was nervous. He hadn't behaved this way since I first moved into Tempe and the Pack hadn't settled my status yet. It made me curious: Had my status changed somehow with the Pack all of a sudden?

"What's got you all twitchy, Hal? Fess up."

Hal's eyes met mine sharply, and I watched with amusement as his shoulders visibly relaxed, but only with a conscious effort. "I am not the least bit twitchy. Your characterization is scurrilous and unfounded. I haven't twitched once in the two minutes we've been here."

"I know, and the effort at locking it down is going to give you indigestion. Why don't you just tell me what's bothering you so you can get it out of your system and relax?"

Hal regarded me in stony silence for a few seconds, then his fingers began drumming in sequence on the tabletop. He was worked up, all right. But when he spoke, I could barely hear him. "I don't want to be alpha."

"You don't want to be alpha?" I said. "Well, then, your dreams have come true. You're not. Gunnar is alpha, and you're doggie number two."

"But Gunnar is going with you to Asgard."

I blinked. "He is?"

Hal dipped his chin in the barest of nods. "It was decided last night. Leif talked him into it. I'm to be alpha until he returns. And if he doesn't . . . well, then I'm doomed."

"Bwa-ha-ha, cue the derisive laughter. You can't be top dog and tell me you're doomed, Hal. Nobody is going to buy that."

"I *like* being Gunnar's second," Hal groused. "I don't want to make those decisions. And there will be plenty to make if he doesn't come back. Scores more if Leif doesn't come back."

"How is Leif, anyway? Is that finger fully grown back?" Leif had lost his finger—and nearly his undead existence—in the fight with *die Töchter des dritten Hauses*, when they managed to torch his combustible flesh.

"Yeah, it's fine, and he's coming to see you tonight, along with Gunnar."

"Good. What's the problem with Leif not coming back?"

"We'll have the bloodiest vamp war in centuries if he's gone more than a month. They're already sniffing around."

"I beg your pardon?"

"The vampires. They want his territory."

"The bloodiest vamp war in history will be fought over Tempe?"

Hal stared at me to gauge whether I was being serious or not. "His territory is a whole lot bigger than Tempe, Atticus. You can't tell me you didn't know."

"Well, yes, I can. Leif and I never talked about his territory, because I'm not interested and he's not a braggart. I know that Leif must be in singular control of Tempe, because I've never seen or smelled another vampire in the city, but I don't know how he could realistically hold any more."

Hal snorted and held his face in his hands. He peered at

me from between his fingers. "Atticus. Leif controls the entire state of Arizona. *All by himself.* He's the baddest of badass vampires. He's the oldest thing walking around this hemisphere, besides you and the native gods." He dropped his hands and tilted his head at me like a curious canine. "You honestly didn't know that?"

"Nope. Why would I care? I'm not a vampire and I don't want his territory. You don't want the whole state for your pack either, am I right?"

"Well, no, but you have to appreciate what's going to happen here."

"No, I don't. I'm moving."

"Wherever you move it's going to be felt. This kind of power vacuum is going to bring every wannabe vamp lord down on this state, all wanting to carve out a piece of it for themselves. And they're going to leave other power vacuums behind them when they go. If Leif doesn't come back, the ripples are going to be felt all over the country, I can guarantee it, and in quite a few other countries besides."

"Well, what do you want me to do about it?"

"Make damn sure both Gunnar and Leif come back. That way I don't have to be alpha and I don't have to worry about fighting off a bunch of bloodsuckers."

"I can't believe Leif is so feared. He's a perfectly reasonable guy."

"To you and me, yes, he is. He works very well with us. But he's absolute hell on other vampires, from what I understand. They're scared of him, and with good reason. You know, he shouldn't have survived getting burned like that."

I crinkled my brows. "No? Why not?"

"That wasn't a normal fire where you could just stop, drop, and roll. That was hellfire, Atticus. It's almost impossible to put out. It would have destroyed any other vampire I've ever heard of."

Silence fell as I considered this. A vampire war would indeed be inconvenient for everyone, but I didn't see how I could prevent it on top of everything else I had to do. I was also able to conclude to my satisfaction that it wasn't really my problem anyway.

Hal said into the silence, "Let's proceed to business, shall we?"

"Yeah, let's." Hal put his briefcase up on the table and took out a legal pad. I told him what I needed: approximately three hundred semi-rare books—nothing remarkable, just old—delivered by FedEx tomorrow morning. I also needed the firm to draw up paperwork to handle the sale of the store to Rebecca Dane after three months for a buck seventy-two.

"Why the seventy-two cents?" Hal wondered aloud.

"Because everyone who looks at the deal will ask the same question. I want Detective Geffert to think it's a significant clue. I hope he builds a conspiracy theory around it. But it's purely there to mess with his mind and waste his time."

Hal shrugged and wrote it down. I also arranged for the firm to provide three months' pay to Rebecca and any additional employees she should choose to hire on her own. "I'll let her know that she is to manage the place and to let anyone who inquires know that I have gone on an extended vacation to the Antipodes." Hal raised his eyebrows but made no comment.

I'd brought a parcel to the restaurant, and it rested next to me on the vinyl material of the booth seat. Now I hefted it onto the table and untied the string around it before removing the top. A truly rare book lay inside in a nest of tissue paper. The green cloth cover with gilt lettering and blind-embossed leaves finally got a reaction from Hal.

"Is that . . . a first edition?" he asked.

"Uh-huh. Extremely rare copy of Whitman's *Leaves*

of Grass. It should fetch at least a hundred fifty grand, probably much more. This goes to Rebecca Dane once she's bought the store—not before." I replaced the box lid, and Hal stared at the book cover until it disappeared from view.

"All right." He shook his head to clear it and get back to business. "What else?"

"I'll need new IDs for myself and my apprentice. Pick some random Irish names."

"All right, email me some pictures. Where's she going to be while you're gone?"

"She'll stick around for a couple days, then move to a secure undisclosed location." Hal looked up at my choice of words. "No, the vice president won't be there."

"All right. Is that all?"

"Almost. Granuaile is to contact you after three months if she doesn't hear from me by then. You're to assume I'm dead if she contacts you in that case." I really hoped this wouldn't be necessary, but it was best to plan for the worst. "I'll need Oberon to be looked after, preferably by Granuaile, and I need to set up a trust for her now."

We worked out the details of that and then Hal said, "I have some news to share with you. You recall that we set an investigator on the trail of this group calling themselves the Hammers of God?"

"Yes."

"The investigator's missing. Presumed dead."

"Hmm. Are we also presuming that the rabbi is returning with reinforcements?" The Rabbi Yosef Bialik had been convinced to leave town without harm, but I'd always assumed he'd be back.

"Yes. Everyone in the Pack will shortly be wearing a thin body armor underneath their clothes. Should be good enough to stop a thrown silver knife."

"They enchant the handles too, so I'd suggest gloves. The idea is to hit you again when you try to pull the knife out."

Hal shrugged. "Magic doesn't scare me. Only silver."

I wondered what it would be like to be scared of only one thing.

After breakfast with Hal, I went to the shop and met Rebecca Dane there. I made her day by telling her she was getting a promotion and a raise, then spent the morning reviewing how to run the shop all by herself. She wouldn't be able to make some of the more complicated teas that required the use of binding, but all the straight herbal stuff was well within her compass, including Mobili-Tea, my best seller for arthritic customers. "You can hire some help if you like. I'm going away for a while, and so is Granuaile. We are going on an archaeological dig in the Antipodes."

"Oh," she said, a faint wrinkle of concern appearing between her eyes. "For how long?"

"It might be months." It would certainly be months. Years. I prepared her for it as best as I could, explaining that the law firm of Magnusson and Hauk would be paying her and keeping in touch. She was excited and flushed with the responsibility. She was fresh and affable, and my regulars liked her. She radiated innocence and served people without a trace of guile or condescension. I hoped that would be enough to save her when people came looking for me and realized that she knew nothing.

My lunch date was Malina Sokolowski, the leader of the Sisters of the Three Auroras. We met in Four Peaks Brewery on 8th Street. She was wearing the same red wool coat she'd worn the first time we met almost two months ago. Her blond hair lay upon her shoulders like a rich nude woman on a divan, sleek and shiny and unapologetically decadent. I felt the eyes of envious men boring into my back as she favored me with a brilliant smile of welcome and a pleased purring of my name.

It was strange to think that I had made peace with a coven of witches, but I had to admit that Malina's crew was different. Though they still took advantage of people and were always, always plotting to exert some sort of control over others, they at least had pretensions of being good citizens otherwise. We had fought side by side and recognized that there was a patch of common ground between us, a sliver of ellipsoid in a Venn diagram of a witch and a Druid where we could meet—meet and pretend that the vast area of the spheres behind us was undiscovered country rather than our comfort zone.

We spoke of small things at first. She inquired after Granuaile and Oberon; I inquired after her coven sisters. Our draughts came: I had a Kilt Lifter and she was drinking the Sunbru Kölsch. We toasted healthy alliances and sighed appreciatively as we set our glasses down.

"Beer like that almost makes me forget the incredible danger we're in," Malina said.

"I beg your pardon? I mean, yeah, the beer's good, but what danger?"

"We've been continuing our divination rituals because we're unconvinced that we've seen the last of the Hammers of God. From what we can tell, the rabbi is definitely coming back with more Kabbalists just like him. But that's not all," Malina said. "Something else is on the horizon. Several somethings. I think one of them is Bacchus. He might be coming here to look for you."

This wasn't a surprise, between what I'd done to his Bacchants in Scottsdale and the blame I'd laid at his door while I was in Asgard. "How soon?"

"Tomorrow at the earliest, if I'm reading things right."

That was a surprise. "Gods Below," I cursed, "I don't have time to deal with that."

"Time?" Malina spluttered. "What about the strength? You can't take on one of the Olympians."

"I seem to remember you doubting I could take on Aenghus Óg," I teased her. "Have I not earned at least a fighting chance against Bacchus? But that's assuming I'd want to fight him, and I don't. What else did you see?"

"Many vampires." If I needed any confirmation that Hal was right about the vampire war, this was it. "How goes the recovery of Mr. Helgarson?"

"Absolutely peachy as far as I know. I'm supposed to see him tonight. But, look, between your coven and me, he's leaving tomorrow."

Malina's lips tightened. "Leaving for good?"

I shrugged. "That's my assumption. This place will be crawling with would-be replacements before long."

Malina grimaced and muttered something in Polish that I guessed was a curse.

"By the way, I'm leaving too."

Her eyes widened and the Polish cursing became more vehement.

"Plus Gunnar Magnusson."

She didn't have words to express her shock at that. Why would an alpha ever leave his pack? "What is going on?" she breathed.

"I can't tell you. But what I respectfully suggest to you, as an ally, is to get yourself out of here. The Hammers of God are coming for you every bit as much as they're coming for me. And you don't want to be around when the vamp war begins. Whoever comes out on top is probably not going to ignore your coven like Leif did."

"No, that's for certain," Malina said, and took a long pull on her beer for courage. "I think your advice is good and we should pursue it, but I don't know where to go. We were counting on this area remaining stable."

"The era of stability is already gone. This city is about

to pass through the Valley of the Shadow of Deep Shit. Best to cut and run while you still can."

"Is that what you're doing? Running?"

"I suppose I'm running from one fight to take part in another. Characterize it however you wish. Look, just pack all your crap into a U-Haul tonight and get out of the state. Stash everything in a storage facility and then take your time finding someplace else to settle down."

"You've done this sort of thing before, I take it."

"Absolutely. Works great. But if you don't like that idea, how about rebuilding your coven? Go back to Poland, pick up some new recruits, take the long view here instead of focusing on short-term losses. That's how you survive."

"That . . . sounds like a very good idea. I don't know if we can get out of here quickly enough, though. We have significant assets tied up here."

"Hand them over to Magnusson and Hauk. Let them liquidate everything and put the proceeds in an offshore account for you. They can also get you new IDs if you need them, and I'd suggest it since the Hammers of God have probably done their homework."

"You advise me well."

"Aw, shucks."

Malina beamed at me for a sunlit time, and then her smile faded as she processed that this leave-taking would probably be our last for a long while. "Will our paths ever cross again?" she asked.

"Perhaps, but not for at least a decade. I'm going to fall off the map if I survive what's coming."

"But you won't share with me what's coming."

"No. Safer if you don't know. Safest to just get out of this place and begin again."

She nodded her understanding and said, "Well, our short acquaintance has been most instructive. On the one hand you're responsible for wiping out half my coven, and on the other you're largely responsible for preserving the lives of those who remain. You were forced into defending yourself in the first case, but you had no obligation to help us in the second. I must conclude that Druids are dangerous but fairly amenable acquaintances, though my sample size is admittedly very small." She smiled. "Whatever you're about to undertake, I hope you'll survive and manage to find us in the future. If we know you're coming, Berta will bake you a cake."

"Thank you. Is there anyplace in particular I should look for you? I'd like to learn how to speak with a proper Polish accent."

She slung a smirk at me and said, "It's safer if you don't know."

Chapter 8

Since this was to be the last night I spent in Arizona, I was hoping that I'd be able to get a full night's rest. It's funny how vampires don't respect that, since they always expect you to let them sleep all day.

After spending the afternoon reviewing tea recipes with Rebecca Dane one last time and hooking her up with herb vendors for resupply, I spent an hour at my kitchen table drawing a map of Asgard based on my observations and Ratatosk's intelligence. Then I went for a run with Oberon in the early twilight of late autumn and returned after sundown to a well-dressed vampire waiting on my front porch. He had an impeccably tailored werewolf sitting next to him.

Normally the two don't mix, but Leif Helgarson and Gunnar Magnusson had several common bonds: They were both lawyers, they were both originally from Iceland, and they both hated Thor. They got along just fine, but I didn't think they were bosom buddies. They'd driven to my house separately—probably because each was too dominant to let anyone else drive. Leif's black Jaguar XK convertible sat in front of Gunnar's silver BMW Z4 convertible. Most of the Tempe Pack drove those, but I'd never asked them why they chose such tiny cars.

<Oh, look, it's a dead guy and a wet dog,> Oberon

said as we stopped jogging in front of my lawn. In the dim glow of the streetlights, Leif and Gunnar rose to meet us, shoving their hands in their pockets to reveal their competing vests—or waistcoats, as they probably thought of them. Leif's was a Victorian burgundy number with matte black satin lining and eight black buttons in two columns of four. He'd gone all the way and had a gold chain wrapped around them leading to a pocket watch; he was even wearing one of those old-fashioned black string ties. Except for the straight pale corn-silk hair and the lack of mustache, he looked like he'd stepped out of the pages of a steampunk novel—and what's more, he didn't look the least bit scorched from his encounter with hellfire.

Gunnar's suit was likewise old-fashioned, but it was gray and silver. His waistcoat was a decadently patterned silver paisley on a cool gray material, lined in gunmetal satin. His tie was the more modern sort, black with a silver paisley design, and he, too, had a gold pocket watch. His hair was a darker blond, much more of a tawny lion's mane, and he'd slicked it back around the sides and let it curl on top. He had thick muttonchops that stopped short of his chin and arced over his upper lip. The choice of colors for his wardrobe seemed odd for a werewolf, until I realized that it was a status thing, like everything else with members of the Pack. As alpha he couldn't show fear of silver, so of course he drove a silver car and wore silver clothes whenever he could. Now that I thought about it, I'd never seen Hal wear silver. He drove a metallic blue car, but that was it. If he wound up being alpha he'd have to get a whole new wardrobe.

<This guy doesn't have that citrus smell that Hal always does,> Oberon observed. <He's letting his inner dog hang out. I approve.>

"Good evening, Atticus," Leif said in his stilted speech.

"Atticus," Gunnar acknowledged me with a gruff

nod. There was some tension between us and always had been, though none of it came from me. I liked Gunnar just fine. His problem was that he didn't know if he could take me in a fight, and neither did his wolves. Since I was also a shape-shifter and centuries older than he was, they might follow me as an alpha if circumstances were right. Gunnar wanted to make sure those circumstances never occurred. He had declared me a Friend of the Pack years ago and then done everything he could to avoid me so that his wolves would have few occasions to compare us side by side. We'd always been cordial to each other, but some of that cordiality had chilled after he lost two pack members in the Superstition Mountains while trying to rescue Hal, who'd been drawn into the fight only because of me.

"Good evening, gentlemen," I said, nodding to each of them in return. "I'm honored by your visit. May I invite you inside for a beer—and some blood?" I gave Leif a goblet full of my blood every so often, and now I wondered if that had something to do with him surviving an attack he shouldn't have survived.

They made noises of graciousness and gave Oberon a friendly scratch or two behind his ears, and then we all went inside.

I got a couple of bottles of Ommegang's Three Philosophers ale out of the fridge for Gunnar and me, then I grabbed a goblet out of the cupboard and a steak knife out of the cutlery drawer and stabbed myself in the arm, allowing the blood to drip freely into the goblet. A small exertion of power shut down the pain.

"I'm told by others that you've recovered fully, Leif," I remarked. "What's your own assessment?"

"Snorri has practically glutted me on bags of donated blood," he replied, referring to the werewolf doctor who worked in a Scottsdale hospital. "And while it has been nourishing, it has also been less than satisfying. There is never the heady aroma of fear or the succulent scent of desire when you feast on a blood bag. Plus, they were refrigerated," he added with a shudder.

"This should be pleasant, then," I said, watching the level of blood rise in the glass. "Though I'm afraid I can't help you with the smells of fear or desire. Would you say that you're as strong as ever, then?"

"Not precisely," Leif said. "Your blood helps tremendously, however. There is something about it, as we have discussed in the past."

"Yes, I'd be curious to know precisely what it is," I said. The goblet was nearly full, so I bound my torn tissue and skin back together to cut off the flow. "You're welcome to as much as I can afford, of course, in the coming days. I owe you at least that much, since you came to such harm on my account."

I wiped a couple of stray drops off my arm with a washcloth and then handed him the goblet. He thanked me and said, "Helping me kill Thor will settle that account quite nicely."

"The same goes for me," Gunnar chimed in. Presumably he was referring to his dead pack members, but they had come to the Superstitions on their own. I'd never asked them to come. If their deaths were on anyone's head, it was Gunnar's, but I let the comment slide. If he'd consider his imaginary account settled by something I was already going to do anyway, there was no need to dispute him.

"A toast, then," I said, raising my bottle. "Perhaps one of you should offer it, since you have stronger feelings on the matter than I do." My feelings were that I'd already done more than enough damage on the Norse plane.

Leif and Gunnar spoke at once as though they'd rehearsed it in stereo: "To killing Thor!" I think one or both of them spit on me in the process, their vehemence was so strong.

"Hear, hear," I said, attempting to sound hearty about it, and we all clinked our drinks and drank deeply. Leif looked visibly healthier almost immediately.

<It's times like these I wish I had opposable thumbs,> Oberon said. <I can't participate in drinking rituals without making loud lapping noises.>

Would you like a treat as a consolation prize?

<That would console me considerably.>

I gave Oberon a treat from the pantry and said to my guests, "So. Have you come to play video games? Maybe kick it old school with a few rounds of Yahtzee?"

"In happier times, perhaps," Leif said drily. "I rather hoped we could discuss details of our trip to Asgard."

"By all means. Please, be seated." I waved at my kitchen table and we all took seats. The map I'd drawn earlier was still there, lying faceup. I turned it over so that it wouldn't distract them. I'd show it to them a bit later. "May I ask who else is coming besides Gunnar?"

Leif steepled his fingers together, elbows on the table, and peered at me from one side of them. "Of course. There are three additional parties joining us. They await only the location of our rendezvous and a meeting time."

"I can give you GPS coordinates. Will that suffice?"

"Admirably."

"Who are these three other parties?" Gunnar demanded. I think Leif had been about to say their names anyway, but he hadn't spoken up quickly enough for the werewolf. If Leif was irritated, he disguised it well.

"Perun, a Slavic thunder god; Väinämöinen, a shamanic culture hero of the ancient Finns; and Zhang Guo Lao, one of China's Eight Immortals."

<I like that last guy's name,> Oberon said. <Who would win in a cage match between him and Pai Mei?> He situated himself on the floor by my feet and I caressed his neck.

Zhang Guo Lao, of course. He's alive and Pai Mei is dead.

<Pai Mei died in like six different movies, so he's obviously capable of coming back to life. He's had plenty of time to recover from those poisoned fish heads Daryl Hannah gave him in *Kill Bill: Two*. He's probably on Facebook right now. Look him up.>

"That's it?" the alpha asked. "Six of us against all of Asgard?" Gunnar was used to having more than six with him on even the most routine hunts.

"I don't care about all of Asgard," Leif explained. "I only care about Thor." Leif had the opposite problem. He'd been fighting alone for so long and shredding everything that he probably thought the six of us would be overkill.

"All of Asgard is going to object," I pointed out. "And they have resources we need to address."

"Such as?" Leif asked. I explained to them what I'd seen while stealing the golden apple—Thor's chariot, Gullinbursti, the ravens Hugin and Munin, and twelve pissed-off Valkyries, plus Odin and all the rest of the gods, not to mention the possibility of calling up the Einherjar, the fallen Vikings who dwell in Valhalla.

"The Einherjar fight every day, preparing for Ragnarok," Gunnar mused. "They are slain and raised again each day on the Field of Vigrid. They have no fear of death, and their numbers must be huge. They're the perfect army. My friends, we are good—but not that good."

"We will not have to face the Einherjar right away," I assured them. "It's just a late-game possibility. The faster we are in attracting attention, the smaller the possibility that the Einherjar will be a problem."

"How do you know this?" Leif said.

I turned over the map I had made earlier and showed it to them. "This is a map of the plane, which I know to be at least partially accurate," I said. "We are going to

emerge from the root of Yggdrasil. But see here? The Field of Vigrid—and Valhalla—are on the opposite side of the plane, according to my source." Ratatosk had told me that and more during our trip up the root from Jötunheim.

"Who's your source?" Gunnar asked.

"Well, he's a . . . he was . . . a squirrel."

"A squirrel!" the alpha spluttered. "You can't trust a squirrel!"

<I'm with the werewolf on this one. Squirrels are dodgy,> Oberon said.

"Look, his information saved me a lot of trouble. He was very accurate about what I could independently verify. There's no reason to believe the rest of it is wildly off-kilter. If we can get Thor to come out and engage us somewhere on the Plain of Idavoll—the closer to Yggdrasil, the better—the Einherjar will not be able to mobilize in time to make any difference. They don't have flying horsies like the Valkyries. They'll have to march the whole way, and it will take them days."

"Yes, I see," Leif said, "but how do we get Thor to come out? Won't he simply sit behind the walls of Gladsheim, or Bilskirnir, and wait for us to come to him?"

"Nah. All we gotta do is ridicule his strength or say something about his mom. He's a bully, right? Bullies don't fight wisely."

"Come now, Atticus," Leif said. "How will he know we are even there, much less respond to a shouted taunt about his dubious parentage?"

"Oh, he'll know all right," I said. "I have a plan, though in its current form it doesn't take into account the abilities of the other members of our party."

"Let's hear it," Gunnar said, and Leif seconded the motion. I told them what I'd been cooking up, and they approved everything but the rubber suits and the climbing gear.

"We will not be needing those, trust me," Leif said. "So when is this going to happen?"

"We leave tomorrow night." Leif looked pleased at this news, but Gunnar seemed less than sanguine.

"Must it be so soon?" the werewolf asked.

"The Hammers of God plus an actual god are coming to slay me, so, yes, it must be. I'd rather be a slayer than the slain."

Gunnar looked at Leif. "That moves up your timetable significantly."

"Yes, but not impossibly," the vampire replied. "Especially if the Druid helps."

"What are you talking about?" This was the part where we were supposed to wish each other good night and meet back here tomorrow at the same bat time. They sounded like they needed me for something else.

Leif turned his ice-blue eyes on me and allowed a small smile to tug at the edges of his mouth. "Territory, naturally."

"Ah, yes, Hal mentioned to me earlier that you control the entire state. Congratulations."

Leif didn't answer, and Gunnar took the opportunity to jump in. "Yes, well, word of his injuries has spread, and some vampires have come to investigate."

"I've heard," I said. "Why don't you serve 'em up a cease-and-desist letter? You guys are good at that."

"That is not how I respond to vampires in my territory," Leif said without humor.

"How do you respond, then?"

"I destroy them."

Oberon spoke up. <Now, see, you can't just drop a line like that without a little something extra. He should get Danny Elfman to compose a chilling soundtrack especially for him, so that when he says macho stuff he can play it back on one of those personal recorders and give the moment its proper melodrama. Or at least he could give us a "Mwah-ha-ha-ha!">

It's difficult not to laugh when Oberon provides commentary like that, but I enjoy the challenge. It keeps me sharp. If I laughed or seemed the least bit amused, Leif would probably not take it well. And if he realized my dog was making fun of him, he'd be sure to take offense. So I carefully kept my expression neutral and said to Leif, "I see. And you'd like my help? As in, tonight?"

"Yes."

That was precisely what I'd been afraid of. I sighed and said, "Leif, I need my sleep tonight, because I have a full day tomorrow and a long night after that getting us to Russia. I can't afford to tax myself tonight if you want to make it to Asgard. Your territorial concerns will have to remain your concerns. I'm sorry."

"There are sixty-three vampires from Memphis at the Arizona Cardinals game right now," Leif said, tapping the table with his index finger. "I could use someone to watch my back."

"How do you know they are there?"

Leif ignored this and answered with another question. "Can I count on you, Atticus?"

"Only to get some sleep. How do you know about the vampires?"

My persistence didn't pay off. He ignored me again and turned to Gunnar to ask him to come. Whenever I asked Leif a question about vampire hoodoo that he wanted to keep secret, he always pretended not to hear. Several months ago I had used this to my advantage. I'd taken him to his first baseball game ever, on a mild June night with the roof open at Chase Field as the Diamondbacks hosted the Padres. I'd known Leif would be curious about the game and the behavior of people in such a crowd, but his questions never ended: If the team mascot was supposed to be a rattlesnake, why was there a bobcat named Baxter running around acting like an idiot? Did this mascot bait-and-switch indicate humanity's primeval fear of fanged creatures? Why do ballplayers seem to have oral fixations on gum, tobacco, or sunflower seeds? And why do some ballplayers feel the need to fondle their groin between every pitch? Is that why they're called ballplayers instead of athletes or competitors or contestants? It finally came to be too much, and I asked him a question I'd always wondered about.

"Hey, Leif, I've been meaning to ask. There's this famous kids' book called *Everyone Poops*. Does that include vampires, since you guys are on a strict liquid diet? I'd imagine the accumulation of hemoglobin could really get you backed up after a while. Is there a special laxative you use or what?" Leif regarded me glacially for a couple of heartbeats, then rose silently from his seat and shuffled past people to the aisle leading to the main concourse. "Hey, get me a beer while you're up," I called. "And a hot dog with mustard and onions." I didn't see him again for three innings, but he came back with a dog and a beer for me.

Gunnar begged off back-watching duty. He had plenty to accomplish himself if he was to have all in order by tomorrow night. "I must arrange things satisfactorily with the Pack," he said. "Can't be helped."

Leif gave up on the werewolf but turned once more to me. "Atticus, you must help. Sleep is an insufficient excuse to stay home when there are so many vampires out there."

<Is he serious? Sleep is the *best* excuse to stay home when there are vampires out there!>

"Don't get me wrong, Leif," I said, "I loves me some vampire huntin'. Nothing like watching a hissing head go flying in one direction while the body falls in another, you know? But trust me when I say that taking the three of us to Tír na nÓg is going to be taxing. You don't want me to be exhausted when I do that."

"You never get tired," Leif pointed out. "You draw strength from the earth."

"You're supposed to say 'Gotcha!' when you catch people in verbal inconsistencies."

"I am aware, but it sounds vulgar."

"Perhaps it does. This isn't a 'gotcha' moment, anyway. I'm speaking of mental exhaustion, not physical. Planewalking isn't a physical strain. It's a mental one. If I'm not fresh, then—"

"Say no more," Leif interrupted. "I understand. I will simply have to kill them all myself."

<There he goes again. I'm telling you, Danny Elfman would love to get hold of those lines.>

Not John Williams?

<If you've got some hopelessly overmatched heroes fighting evil and some Imperial types marching, John Williams is your guy. You need a song to make people reach for a box of Kleenex, talk to Randy Newman. But if

you want creepy atmospherics and spine-shivering chords to back up your casual death threats, you gotta bring in Danny Elfman.>

Gunnar excused himself from the conversation and rose to leave, citing his pack business. We stood and shook hands and bid him good evening. He exited in a flash of silver and I sat back down with Leif.

"So what's going to happen when you show up there, Leif? Do all the southern vampires know what you look like and have little posters of you taped to the inside of their coffins? Are they going to squee and ask for your autograph?"

"I beg your pardon? What was that? Will they screech and ask me . . . ?"

"No, I said *squee*."

"I am not familiar with this verb."

"It's a relatively new exclamation. It's a high-pitched noise of excitement one makes when confronted with a celebrity one worships."

Leif took a moment to digest this and then he arched a blond eyebrow at me. "Tell me, Atticus, have you ever, ah, squeed? Did I conjugate that correctly?"

"Yes, you did. And, yes, as a matter of fact I have squeed."

"Do tell."

"I went to the San Diego Comic-Con a few years back and met one of my favorite authors, and he made me squee involuntarily. I also did a tiny dance and I might have peed a little bit when he shook my hand."

"You did not," Leif stated flatly.

<Liar!> Oberon added.

"Okay, maybe I didn't pee, but I spake truth about the tiny dance or I'm the son of a goat. Authors aren't huge celebrities to most people, but I'm a guy who appreciates a good story well told. Beyond that, though, I think this man might actually possess supernatural powers.

He makes people lose their minds, and I'm sure some of them do lose bladder control as well."

"I see. And who is this author?"

"Neil Fucking Gaiman."

"His second name is Fucking?"

"No, Leif, that's the honorary second name all celebrities are given by their fans. It's not an insult, it's a huge compliment, and he's earned it. You'd like him. He dresses all in black like you. Read a couple of his books, and then when you meet him, you'll squee too."

Leif found the suggestion distasteful. "I would never behave with so little dignity. Nor would I wish to be confronted in such a manner by anyone else. Vampires inspire screams, not squees. Involuntary urination is common, I grant, but it properly flows from a sense of terror, not an ecstatic sense of hero worship."

"It properly flows? Are we having a pee pun party?"

A slight tightening around the eyes was my only visual clue that Leif was amused. Otherwise his face remained impassive and his voice deadpanned, "If I do not aim carefully at my targets tonight, I might cause a big splash at the stadium."

"Oh, very punny. You will show them what yellow cowards they are," I said.

"Right after I flush them out of the crowd."

"You will rain down upon their porcelain skin a deluge of justice."

"Ugh! And I will have to wash my hands afterward."

I chuckled, and Leif's face finally cracked into a grin. It felt good to laugh, but then I wanted to ask Leif if vampires ever peed. Since he'd never answer that, I asked him something else.

"Leif, why is the Memphis nest at the stadium?"

"It's a direct challenge to me. They are symbolically laying claim to all those people."

"If you take them on during the game, there's likely to be collateral damage."

Leif nodded. "They're counting on it."

"That you won't want to hurt innocents?"

"No, that I will not want to cause a scene and leave a bunch of dead vampires lying around with a bunch of dead humans, thus exposing the secret of our existence. But they have miscalculated; I do not care about that anymore. I *do* want to cause a scene. Leaving the stadium littered with undead corpses will doubtlessly make the news. It will let everyone know I am still around and very capable of holding this territory."

"And it will also let everyone know that vampires are real. Isn't that kind of a fatal flaw in your plan?"

Leif dismissed the point with a wave of his hand. "They will never admit the possibility. Science is so very sacred to them now, and scientifically vampires cannot exist, therefore we do not. Vampires are safe by this tautology alone. Any lab results they find outside the norm will be assumed to be contaminated."

"Do you know if these Memphis vampires are very old?"

Leif snorted contemptuously. "I am the oldest vampire on this side of the Atlantic."

"And on the other side?"

The blue ice of his eyes slid coolly from contemplating his empty goblet and regarded me. "The one who created me is still there. And there are . . . others."

"Any of them older than me?" I asked brightly.

"There is one I know of. There may be others. I have never met him, mind; I have heard of him only, but I am told he still hunts." I half-expected him to throw back his head and let rip with a shrill, hoarse cackle worthy of the Crypt Keeper, but he chose instead to remain silent and let the tension build.

I think you're right, I told Oberon. *He needs a sound-track.*

<Hound 1, Druid 0.>

"Do you dare speak his name?" I whispered softly.

Leif rolled his eyes, acknowledging my mockery. "He is called Theophilus."

"Ha!" I barked, amused by the Greek roots of his name. "There's an ancient vampire in Europe whose name means 'loved by God'?"

"I did not say he was in Europe. But, yes, that is the name he professes to the world. I do not know if that is his original name or if he is merely being ironic."

"What's the name of the vampire who created you?"

The vampire narrowed his eyes. "Why do you wish to know?"

I shrugged. "Curiosity."

Keeping his eyes on me to gauge my reaction, he carefully pronounced, "Zdenik."

"That doesn't sound like an Icelandic name," I observed.

"Your sharp ears serve you well. It is a Czech name."

My eyebrows shot up. "You were turned by a Czech vampire in Iceland one thousand years ago?"

"I never said I was turned in Iceland," Leif replied, smirking.

I frowned and reviewed our relationship, realizing that I'd been operating on an assumption all this time. "Touché," I said. "Will I ever get to hear the story of how and where you were turned?"

His smirk disappeared. "Perhaps someday. For now I have some havoc to wreak and territory to defend." He stood up and offered me his hand. I stood as well to shake it, and he shrugged diffidently as he said, "There are only eighty of the young ones scattered about the valley, and most of them are at the football game. See you tomorrow night, Atticus."

<Heh! Only eighty. That was his way of saying he craps bigger than you.>

I don't think vampires poop, I replied.

<Nonsense. Everyone poops.>

We saw Leif to the door and wished him farewell. *Time to hit the hay for the last time in this old house,* I told my hound as I closed the door on the vampire.

<Cool! Can we watch one last movie first?>

All right, buddy. What'll it be?

<I think *The Boondock Saints,* because the Irish guys win. Plus the cat ends badly. It affirms my worldview and I feel validated.>

Chapter 9

I yawned and stretched luxuriously in the morning. I make noises when I stretch, because it feels ten times better than stretching silently. I made my favorite breakfast with a sense of wistful nostalgia, seasoning the kitchen one last time with the smells of cooking. For Oberon, there was a pan full of sausages. I had coffee and orange juice (the kind with pulp in it), toast with orange marmalade, and a fluffy omelet made with cheese and chives, sprinkled with Tabasco. Making a good omelet is like living well: You have to pay attention to the process if you want to enjoy it.

The newspaper was full of headlines shouting about Leif's territorial defense at the football game. STADIUM SLAUGHTERHOUSE, *The Arizona Republic* splashed across its front page. Phrases like "total carnage" and "war zone" were bandied about. I noticed that the body count was sixty-three, precisely the number of vampires he'd mentioned last night, so he'd managed to wipe out the Memphis nest without killing a single human.

And the humans had no idea that one man—or, rather, one vampire—had been responsible for it all. There had been a blackout—Leif's doing, no doubt—and when the lights finally came back on, hours later, there were bodies everywhere. Plus a significant number of sexually harassed fans, some injuries, panic in the restrooms, and a line judge who'd thrown one too many flags and was "accidentally" knocked down by a "disoriented" player. People had exited the stadium using the collective glow of their cell phones, and fantasy football fans shat themselves because Larry Fitzgerald never got a catch, much less a touchdown.

The police suspected it was a gang war. Someone asked Dick Cheney about it and he promptly blamed it on the terrorists. A few of the state's bigoted politicians pointed fingers at illegal immigrants and human trafficking rings, because in their view everything bad was the fault of someone south of the border. Ugh.

<Can I go to work with you today?> Oberon asked.

"Sure, pal. I don't see why not. We won't stay all day though. I'm just packing up my rare books and stocking some random newer ones in there."

<Then where are we going?>

"Well, I have to hide all the rare magic books somewhere safe. And I need to talk to Coyote."

<Really? How's he been? We haven't seen him in months.>

I smiled fondly at my hound's weak grasp of time. "I expect he's fine, Oberon. It's been only three weeks, after all. And he's a survivor."

There was one final chore to attend to before I left my home for good. I slung Fragarach across my back and adjusted the strap because I was wearing a thick leather jacket over my T-shirt. It was too warm for the mild Arizona autumn, but I figured I'd be grateful for it in Siberia and, later, in Asgard. I locked up the house, then plopped down onto the front lawn and methodically removed every single one of the wards protecting my home, every single alarm, and sent my sentry mesquite tree back to quiet sleep. It had saved my skin not long ago against a demon escaped from hell, so I rose and gave it a hug before I left.

<Look at you getting all sentimental,> Oberon chuffed.

"I'm a tree hugger, no doubt about it," I said.

When we got to the shop, Oberon sprawled contentedly behind my tea counter and basked in the sun as I served my regulars their Mobili-Tea. I let them know they probably wouldn't see me around for a while but Rebecca would take care of them in my absence. After they left, there was some dead time in the shop, and I spent it packing my rare books into boxes. Rebecca was to come in later, and I'd prefer her to think that nothing had changed. I doubted she had ever taken a very close look at the books behind glass.

The numerous wards in the shop also had to be dissolved, and I even unmade the binding that prevented people from shoplifting my merchandise and the binding on the trapdoor to my roof.

FedEx dropped off the random rare books Hal had ordered for me, and I called Granuaile to come pick me up. While she loaded the truly rare books into her car, I restocked the shelves with these other works that were all less than two centuries old. There were a few gems in there: a first edition of *Alice's Adventures in Wonderland*, an early edition of *The Origin of Species*, and a signed first edition of *Dune*.

Rebecca showed up at around half past eleven and I tossed her the keys to the rare bookcase, now guarded by nothing more than a pedestrian lock. "If you get time, you might want to catalog the rare books, organize them however you think best."

Rebecca's already large eyes widened further and she nervously fingered the ankh dangling from her neck, one of many religious symbols she wore out of a mixture of indecision and desire for karma points. "Are you sure? I thought that case was off limits."

"Not anymore. I trust you with the whole shop." I

clapped her on the shoulder as I exited. "May harmony find you."

I piled into the car with Granuaile and Oberon and directed Granuaile to drive east to the Bush Highway. It's a winding road favored by training cyclists that follows the Salt River and provides access to Saguaro Lake. We found a place to pull off with a few palo verde trees to serve as landmarks, then carefully hauled the boxes of books one at a time into the desert landscape while Oberon stood sentinel by the car. When we had them all transferred, I sat on the ground lotus style and placed my tattooed right hand on the earth.

"I'm going to make three calls," I explained to Granuaile. "One is to Coyote, and the other two are to elementals. Elementals are a Druid's best friend. We couldn't get much done without them. Gaia takes too long to respond. Even my extremely long life is little more than a half hour of hers, if you see what I mean. The elementals live in the present, though, and they change as the earth does.

"They're going to protect these books while I'm away. And I'm going to tell them to surrender the books to you if I don't come back. One of the books is actually written by me. I wrote it originally in the eleventh century, when it was clear that I was the last of the Druids, and I've recopied it periodically to make sure that none of the knowledge is lost. It is the only written copy of Druid lore in existence."

"But I thought nothing was ever written," Granuaile said. "Because of the oral tradition."

"Right, well, circumstances are a bit different. I'm extraordinarily endangered, aren't I? So this is a long shot sort of fail-safe. It contains all my herblore, all the rituals, and instructions on how to bind yourself to the earth. You'll have to get someone else to bind you—you can't tattoo yourself, trust me. I recommend asking Flidais of the Tuatha Dé Danann to help you. Don't go to Brighid or the Morrigan or you'll get drawn into their power struggle. What?"

Granuaile was shaking her head. "You're coming back, sensei. I don't need to know this."

"Don't be silly. There's a distinct possibility you will need to know. The existence of the universe is living proof that shit happens. Now, pay attention."

"I can't even communicate with these elementals, much less with Flidais," Granuaile protested.

"I'm going to set that up right now. Be patient and I'll show you." I sent my consciousness down into the earth, calling the Sonoran Desert elemental first, asking it to please inform Coyote I wished to speak with him. Then I asked it to help me bury and store the valuable knowledge contained in my books.

Talking to elementals is sort of like writing a mental picture book. They don't use human languages; they speak in images connected with a syntax of emotions. My attempts to render the communication in writing invariably fall short of the true experience, but here is what I sent to Sonora: //Druid spells / Books / Need protection / Aid//

A minute passed by, and then I felt the reply travel up my arm and images formed in my mind: //Sonora comes / Query: Need?//

I formed a picture in my mind of a pit, eight feet deep, with steps leading down into it that would bear our weight. I kept it firmly in my mind's eye, and slowly, to my right, the pit began to form. Granuaile gasped. To her it must have looked like I was pulling a Yoda, but Sonora was doing all the work. A barrel cactus disappeared into the earth and got reabsorbed; grasses and roots tore away as the pit widened and deepened. It took only a couple of minutes.

"Right, now we schlep the boxes down in there." That

took more than a couple of minutes, but once we were finished I had more talking to do with Sonora, as well as with another elemental—an iron one.

"Now, if I just leave these books in the earth, they won't do so well. On top of that, someone who's looking for those books will be able to divine their presence if we don't shield them somehow."

"Who would be looking for them?"

"Bad guys. So I'm going to have an iron elemental encase them all in iron."

"Wicked. Do all the elementals do what you want?"

"Excellent question, and the answer is no. Some are more helpful than others, but in general they've all been more accommodating since I've been the only Druid around to take care of them."

"Wait. *You* take care of *them*?"

"Sure. Why else would they give us access to their power?"

"But I don't understand why they'd need your help. They're beings of super-duper mega-big magical mojo."

"True. And sometimes they get bound against their will by witches and warlocks seeking to steal their mojo for selfish purposes. When that happens, it's a Druid's job to set them free. Happened just a couple months ago, in fact. Three witches bound up the elemental Kaibab, and I was nearby to set it free before they were able to do anything extraordinarily stupid."

<Hey! You mean when we were hunting? That's why you took off?>

Yep.

<You told me a squirrel needed your help. Thought you'd lost your mind.>

"You're talking about the Kaibab Plateau north of the Grand Canyon?" Granuaile asked, and I nodded confirmation. "What happens if an elemental needs your help in China?"

"I hear about it through the elemental grapevine, then I shift planes to Tír na nÓg and back to earth near the spot where the trouble is."

"What if you don't get there in time? I mean, what if an elemental dies?"

"Then you get the Sahara Desert."

I watched her lips. She almost said, "Bullshit," but then she collected herself and said, "The Sahara's been there for millions of years."

"Aye, but it hasn't always been as dry as it is now. Used to be quite a bit wetter, able to support a broader base of life. Then about five thousand years ago, a wizard bound the Sahara elemental and absorbed it into himself."

"How'd he do that?"

"Not well. He went mad trying to contain it and died."

My apprentice frowned. "Wasn't the elemental released at that point?"

"Aye, the power was released, but it no longer had a coherent identity as an elemental. It was wild magic, and it was released around the Nile Delta. Shortly thereafter the Egyptian civilization started building pyramids."

"Are you saying . . . ?"

"No, because I don't appreciate fallacies of causality. Interesting coincidence, though, don't you think?"

She nodded. "Did the elementals tell you all of this?"

"Yes. That was three thousand years before my time. They'll tell you all sorts of secrets if you're nice to them. And they respond more quickly once they get to know you. This iron elemental I'm calling has been fed lots of faeries over the years. He likes me quite a bit. Calls himself Ferris."

Granuaile looked at me sharply. "Stop it, sensei."

"Stop what?"

She huffed and tucked an errant wisp of hair behind

her ear, then squinted her skepticism at me. "Its name is Ferris? As in the word *ferrous*? You can't expect me to believe an iron elemental is as fond of puns as you are."

I smiled. "No, you're right. He allowed me to give him a name, since we've worked so much together over the years." I paused. "I think of him as male, even though elementals have no gender. That's probably sexist of me."

"Probably," Granuaile agreed. "I'll give you a sensitivity point for noticing, though."

<And that brings your grand total up to one. Congratulations!> Oberon said.

"Thanks," I said to them both, and then I returned my attention to the earth, sending my thoughts down through my tattoos.

//Druid needs Ferris / Book protection / Iron cell//

"He's done this sort of thing for me before," I explained. "He knows precisely what to do. Watch."

Granuaile leaned over to see iron seeping up from the ground and solidifying underneath the boxes. It built up like magnetic iron filings along the sides, slowly hardening into a black wall, and then it closed over the top until all we saw was an iron box without a visible weld or seam.

"Wow," Granuaile said. "You could get a job building bank vaults."

"Those books are worth more than anything in a vault. Okay, they're protected from divination now. What's next? Have Sonora fill in the pit?"

She glanced at me, recognizing that I was testing her.

"No, I don't think so," she replied. "The iron will rust if you don't protect it from the next rains. Groundwater will get it."

"Excellent. What should I do?"

"Thank Ferris and call back Sonora to put nonporous rock around the iron, then fill in the pit."

"You're right, we should thank Ferris and Sonora both. Sonora will ask us to do something in return for this favor, and if it's in your power, I think you should do it. You might as well start building goodwill now."

"Ferris won't ask for anything?"

"I've fed him so many faeries over the years that he feels like he owes me." I thanked both elementals and asked Sonora to encase the iron in granite and fill in the pit. We were silent as Sonora worked. After my books were secure under the earth, I introduced Granuaile to both elementals.

//New Druid / Unbound / Wishes speech//

Almost immediately, a black iron marble formed on the surface of the soil.

I pointed at it and said, "That's a little piece of Ferris right there. Pick it up and concentrate on thoughts of welcome and curiosity. Ask if there is anything you can do for him."

Her mouth fell half open and she glanced at me uncertainly. She still had difficulty believing sometimes that this could happen in an age of science. Before she could pick it up, another marble emerged from the ground. This one was solid turquoise.

"Is that one a piece of Sonora?" she asked.

"Yep. This is how you'll communicate with them if I don't come back. Better practice now to get the hang of it. Do Ferris first. He's used to talking."

She gingerly picked up the iron marble between thumb and forefinger, holding it as if it were a repulsive insect.

"Close it in your fist, shut your eyes, and say hello in your mind," I said.

She did as I instructed, and after a couple of seconds she jerked and gave a startled little "Oh!" Wonder chased surprise, which nipped at the heels of shock traveling across her face. Then a smile took over and made itself comfortable.

<Is Ferris telling her she's going to win the lottery or something?> Oberon asked.

Don't know, I told him. *It's not a conversation I can listen in on.*

<Do the elementals even know I'm here?>

Sonora knows you. He calls you Druidfriend, which is the same as giving you a name. He'd just refer to you as a dog otherwise.

<Cool. Why doesn't Ferris know me?>

You're not part of his ecosystem and you never feed him faeries. Ferris thinks about faeries the way you think about pork products.

<Whoa. Are you telling me faeries taste like bacon?>

No, there's only one thing that tastes like bacon

<—and that's bacon!>

Right. I'm merely drawing a comparison. Iron eats magic, and faeries are magical creatures born on a magical plane. So when I serve up some faeries to Ferris, it's the same thing as giving you one of those Bacon Explosion things and chasing it with a nice bacon latte.

<You've never done that for me! Why haven't you done that for me?>

Because I can't. Bacon lattes don't exist.

<Untrue! Logically it must be so. Vampires exist, werewolves exist, and faeries exist. If all those impossible creatures exist, then so do bacon lattes! We could go get one at Starbucks right now.>

Oberon, seriously, I don't believe there's any such thing. I was just making a point.

<You can't fool me! It has to be on their secret menu! That mermaid on the cup is smiling because she knows where the bacon lattes are!>

Come on, Oberon, you're being silly.

<No, I'm not! What's silly is paying five bucks for hot milk and flavored syrup! But now I see what's really been going on all this time! They charge you all that

money because they need it for the R & D! Somewhere on the outskirts of Seattle, there's a secret facility with higher security than Area 51, and inside there are men with poor eyesight and bad haircuts wearing white lab coats, and they're trying to make the Holy Grail of all coffee drinks.>

The bacon latte?

<No, Atticus, I already told you those exist! I'm talking about the prophecy! "Out of the steam and the foam and the froth, a man in white with poor eyesight will craft a liquid paradox, and it shall be called the Triple Nonfat Double Bacon Five-Cheese Mocha!">

Oberon, what the fuck? I was about to ask him if he'd heard that on television when Granuaile's eyes snapped open.

"That was amazing," she breathed. "It was like . . . dreaming, these images in my head, except I could control the dream and say what I wanted without using words."

"That's a cool way of putting it. What did he say?" I asked.

"He hopes that two Druids will mean twice as many faeries for him."

I smiled. "That sounds about right. Time to say hello to Sonora. You'll find him a bit deeper and richer than Ferris. If Ferris is a glass of chocolate milk, Sonora is mousse."

"Wow. Okay," Granuaile said. "But I'm going to think of Sonora as female." She put the iron marble into the pocket of her jeans and picked up the turquoise marble. This time she closed her fist around it confidently and closed her eyes. A small shiver and sharp intake of breath indicated when she'd made contact. She smiled again as she had before.

Right, she'll be busy talking for a bit, I said to Oberon. *Now explain to me how a Double Bacon Five-Cheese Mocha can ever be nonfat.*

<Duh, it can't. That's why the people researching it must have bad haircuts: They've already demonstrated their bad judgment, and only bad judgment could lead one to believe that it might be possible.>

Yeesh. Your logic should come with a warning label. Where'd you hear that prophecy you spouted?

<Well, that's an interesting—hey.> Oberon's ears pricked up and he swung his head to the east. <Someone's coming.>

I followed his gaze and saw flashes of a familiar canine form coming toward us through the desert scrub.

<It's Coyote!> Oberon said, his tail wagging. It was indeed. Or one version of him, anyway: This one claimed to represent the Navajo tribe. He trotted nimbly between the teddy bear cholla with his tongue hanging out to one side and yipped a cheerful greeting at us. Before we could answer, he shape-shifted to a Native American man clothed in blue jeans, boots, and a white sleeveless undershirt. His straight black hair fell down his back from underneath a cowboy hat, and he had a tiny smirk on his face.

"Howdy, Mr. Druid," he said. "You ain't still mad at me, are ya?" His manner suggested that he really didn't care if I was mad or not. He was referring to the way he'd tricked me—even threatened me—to secure my aid in attacking a fallen angel from the Fifth Circle of hell. He spoke in a slow, dry rumble tinged with amusement, and I tailored my voice to suit his manner of speech.

"Naw, I've mellowed out a good deal in the past few weeks."

"Figured you would. How're you, Oberon?" He squatted down on his haunches and beckoned to my hound. Oberon bounded over to him and wagged his tail enthusiastically.

<Can't complain, Coyote, unless you forgot to bring me sausages.>

Coyote laughed, able to hear Oberon's thoughts as clearly as I did. He petted Oberon with both hands, running one hand along his back and massaging his throat with the other. "I'm sorry, Oberon, I didn't have time to stop without makin' Mr. Druid wait. Who's your lady friend?"

<That's Granuaile.>

"My apprentice," I explained. "She's busy talkin' to Sonora right now. We should prob'ly let 'er have a good gab. Wanna take a short walk?"

"Sure, Mr. Druid, that'd be fine with me." He rose from his squat and the two of us walked south, where our conversation wouldn't distract Granuaile. Oberon trailed behind and snuffled happily at the cacti and creosote.

"I'm in need of your special talents," I told Coyote, and explained to him what the immediate future might hold for me in Asgard.

He chuckled. "I was wonderin' when you'd turn to sooee-cide," he said. He turned his head and spat. "Takin' on the Norse. You're crazier than a pink-eyed parrot."

"Well, maybe only crazy like you," I said. "This deal I have in mind might work out pretty well for both of us."

"A deal, huh?"

"Think of it as a trade, if you like."

"A trade?" Coyote's grin became feral, and a light sparkled in his eyes. He wouldn't be able to resist now. He'd bargain until he thought he had the better of me, all the while protesting that I was robbing him. After I proposed the deal, he fell down laughing and clutched at his gut, howling while tears streamed from his eyes. But once I could get him to speak again, we negotiated in earnest until we shook hands on it.

"Meetin' up with you is always interestin', Mr. Druid," he said. "I'll stick around in this area 'til you get back. Unless you don't come back." He looked down at Oberon.

"An' next time we meet, I'll make sure to have a bag o' those chicken apple sausages you like so much."

<Okay, I'll remember that!>

With one final wave, Coyote dissolved back to his canine form and trotted off to the east from whence he came. Oberon and I returned to check on Granuaile, who was rising from the ground and brushing dirt off her knees.

"How'd it go with Sonora?" I asked.

She was glowing with childlike giddiness. "So awesome! She's given me a big job to do, but I can't wait, because it needs to be done."

"What is it?"

"I'm to get rid of all the crayfish in the East Verde River."

My eyebrows shot up. "You weren't kidding. That's a pretty big job." Crayfish were a nonnative invasive species that were slowly killing off the native fish and frogs in the river by eating their eggs and competing for food. "How are you going to be sure you get them all?"

"Sonora's going to guide me—She'll show me where they are and teach me about her ecosystem, how the species and plants are bound together. I can't wait." She hopped up and down and clapped three times in glee. "It's true that the earth is *alive*. I never knew it could be like this, sensei. Is there like a hierarchy of elementals or something?"

"Yes, there is. Thought you'd catch on. Where would you put Ferris in that hierarchy?"

"Lowest level."

"That's right. He's the avatar of a mineral. Tremendously limited in what he can do, but within his limits he's supreme. And since iron is so darn handy, it's good to make friends with iron elementals—but you're never going to need to call up a beryllium elemental, for example, or a molybdenum one. They're out there but they're not hanging by the phone, if you know what I mean. Sonora's at the next level, and his kind are the kind Druids are supposed to protect. They're avatars of a regional ecosystem, and they have massive power but they're also vulnerable to human stupidity. Whenever we draw power from the earth, we're drawing on them, if you see what I mean."

"What's above them?"

"The tectonic plates. They're literally below the ecosystems, but in terms of hierarchy they're the next step up. It's best not to piss them off. You won't have much contact with them. After that you have Gaia herself."

"Wow. What's she like?"

Her smile was infectious, and I found myself smiling back as I said, "Patient. Kind. Much more difficult to talk to. I think it's good that Sonora has entrusted you with that crayfish business and that he's so willing to talk with you."

"*She* is so willing," Granuaile said pointedly.

"Okay, *she*," I agreed, and shrugged my indifference. "It'll be good for you to be out of town for a while. You should take Oberon with you; he'll love hanging out by the river instead of being trapped with Mrs. MacDonagh's fearless cats again."

<Absolutely! Thank you, Atticus, that's very thoughtful!>

I want you to keep an eye out, okay? Patrol while she's busy, warn her when anyone approaches. She hasn't developed a proper sense of paranoia yet.

<Okay, will do.>

"That would be fine, except he'll be kind of squished in my tiny little car," Granuaile said.

"Right. Let's head back into town and stop by the bank. I'll get you some cash; you can use it to rent a truck, and you can go get some camping gear and some giant paint buckets to put the crayfish in."

"Sweet!" Granuaile said, and the three of us piled back into her small Chevy.

<I'm going to miss being able to talk to you,> Oberon said. <But at least Granuaile won't treat me like some ordinary dog.>

Don't go running off and making her worry. We'll go hunting together when I get back, just you and me.

<Where?>

I'm thinking the San Juan Mountains in Colorado.

"After you're finished," I told Granuaile as we cruised back to town on the Bush Highway, "just bring Oberon over to the widow's place. I'll stop by there this afternoon and let her know that you'll be coming."

Granuaile was all bubbles and excitement over her new mission, and it recalled for me my first interaction with an elemental, a bog spirit in Ireland. My sense of wonder had been every bit as profound as Granuaile's. Her temperament, I reflected, was well suited to a Druid's life. She remained giddy until it was time to part ways at a Mill Avenue ATM. I was going to go grab some lunch, and she was going to grab some gear at REI, with Oberon in tow, then rent a truck.

"You come back, sensei," she said, poking me in the chest to make sure I was getting the message. "You can't leave me dangling like this now that you've started. It would be like buying a kid an action figure and then telling him he can't take it out of the package." Her green eyes met mine and I found myself tongue-tied, even though I knew I was supposed to say something reassuring. A few awkward heartbeats passed, and then she gave up on waiting for me to speak. She grabbed my shirt front and pulled me toward her, delivering a quick buss on the cheek. Her scent lingered as she withdrew, a dark-wine-and-floral shampoo with a top note of strawberry lip gloss. She turned her back immediately and strode to her car, shoulders hunched up high as if she expected me to scold her for something. She opened the back door for Oberon to jump in and then circled around to the driver's side, climbing into the car without looking at me.

<That was kind of sweet, but I don't think I could say good-bye like that. I guess I could hump your leg affectionately or something.>

I squatted down and chuckled, hugging Oberon around the neck. *Be good,* I told him. *I'll be back as soon as I can, and then we'll go find a new place to live.*

<I want more room to run,> Oberon said.

I think that can be arranged. I escorted him to the car and he jumped carefully into the backseat. I shut the door behind him and waved as Granuaile drove off.

I sighed happily, replaying her kiss and still enjoying the faint traces of her scent, while simultaneously feeling guilty for even permitting it. I hoped she would do that again someday, and I berated myself for wishing it.

A last meal of the world's finest fish and chips awaited me due north at Rúla Búla, so I shook myself out of my trance and walked that way, determined to savor my last few hours in Tempe.

"Hey, Siodhachan!" a man's voice boomed from behind me, and I ducked instinctively and pivoted on my heels to meet an attack. My right hand flew to the camouflaged hilt of Fragarach over my right shoulder, but I relaxed and left it sheathed when I saw there was no threat. A fit-looking African man was standing in front of Trippie Hippie and laughing at me. "Wow. You're even more paranoid than the last time I saw you."

I felt acutely embarrassed not to recognize someone who knew my true Irish name. He looked friendly, but I had no idea who this guy was.

Chapter 10

"Come to Jesus," the man said, smiling hugely, with his arms open and inviting embrace. He wore a tie-dyed T-shirt in predominantly reds, yellows, and greens, with a white peace sign screen-printed on the front of it. He had on a pair of relaxed-fit blue jeans, and his Chuck Taylors were classically black. He appeared to be an affable sort, and his voice and rugged good looks reminded me of that guy from the Old Spice body-wash commercials.

I still couldn't place him, and it was supremely annoying because I should have been able to. Random strangers don't know my Irish name—most of my current friends don't know it either, including Granuaile. And it's not like he just made a lucky guess: Siodhachan hasn't exactly been in the top one thousand baby names for quite a long time. Whoever he was, he had to truly know me from the old days, or he had a connection with someone who did. I almost took a look at him with my faerie specs, but then I hesitated. What if he really *was* Jesus? If I looked at him in the magical spectrum, my retinas would fry like eggs. I chose to inquire verbally instead.

"Would you like to speak to me in Aramaic?" I asked him in that language. "I can't recall the last time I spoke it. Can you?"

He switched to Aramaic without difficulty. "Of course I can," he replied. His smile remained broad and highly amused. "We spoke it together in England when we were moving around all that treasure of the Templars and planting false clues. You know, I have really enjoyed the results of that little visit to the planet. The theories have been endlessly creative, and it's put food on the table for many a nearsighted scholar."

"Jesus, it really is you!" I rose from my crouch and accepted the offered hug, and we pounded each other's back in a properly masculine fashion. "This is excellent, man; you look good. Who came up with this look for you?"

Jesus gave a small jerk of his head over his shoulder at Trippie Hippie and switched to English. "One of the patrons in this store gave it to me. Wanted to update my image," he explained.

"What's not to like, right?" I asked, returning to English myself. "I imagine this is a far sight more comfortable than the half-naked crown-of-thorns routine."

"That's an understatement. But I especially appreciate that he imagined something closer to my original skin color. It doesn't get much better."

"No doubt. I was just on my way to grab some lunch. Fancy a bite?"

"You buying?" Jesus grinned.

"Sure, I'll pick up the tab. How long have you been here?" The light turned green again and we walked north up Mill Avenue.

"I arrived just before you showed up," he said. "Heard from my mother you wanted to have a beer."

"That's right, I told her that. She was very kind and blessed some arrows for me. And I'm flattered that you decided to accept my invitation."

"Are you kidding?" Jesus snorted. "I'm grateful to you. I tell you truly, nobody ever wants to just hang out

with me. If they're not asking for explanations or inter-
cession, then they're sharing too much information.
'Why, Jesus? Help me, Jesus! Oh, Jesus, that feels good,
don't stop!' That's all I hear all the time. You're the only
guy who asks me to go have a beer anymore."

"There was someone else you used to drink beers
with?"

"Bertrand Russell."

"Oh. He of little faith? Well, I'm glad I could give you
an excuse to come on down."

"I must tell you that I have an ulterior motive," Jesus
said. "I would not wish you to think later that I had told
a half-truth by saying I have simply come down for a beer.
But business can wait."

We passed an extraordinarily sunburned man in wrap-
around sunglasses busking with his guitar. He was
strumming "They're Red Hot"—an old blues tune about
hot tamales—and singing the infectious lyrics in a grav-
elly voice. His open guitar case rested on a planter beside him, and Jesus wagged his head back and forth a
little bit and got his shoulders into it too. "What a de-
lightful riff," he said. "Do you know who wrote this
song?"

"I believe it's by Robert Johnson, a Mississippi Delta
blues man."

"Truly?" The Christian god stopped dancing and
looked at me. "The same one who went down to the
crossroads?"

"The very same."

He laughed and continued walking north, shaking his
head. "My adversary is thumbing his nose at me, I think.
It is enjoyable, though, to be surprised like that. These
brains can't handle omniscience, so I'm a little slow on
the uptake."

Behind us, the guitar player suddenly stopped playing
and said, "What the hell?" I looked back to see him

staring openmouthed at his guitar case, which was inexplicably—miraculously—filled with dollar bills. He whooped and hurriedly closed his case.

"I think you just made his day," I said.

"It was easy enough. Small green pieces of paper."

We arrived at Rúla Búla and I opened the door for my companion, waving him in. We sat at the bar directly opposite the door and ordered our beers. I asked for a Smithwick's; Jesus thought it was a good day for a Guinness. We both ordered the famous fish and chips, and I asked to see the whiskey menu.

"They have a menu specifically for whiskey?" Jesus said.

"Oh, yeah, and it's amazing stuff. They have some liquid courage back there that's over sixty years old. Want to do a shot with me?"

"No, I'd better not," Jesus said, waving his palms crosswise in front of him.

"Aw, come on, I'm buying."

He paused, then said, "Well, all right, I suppose it'll be a new experience."

Awesome! I'd just bullied Jesus into doing a shot with me. Nobody would ever believe it, but I didn't care. We ordered the insanely expensive stuff, seventy-five dollars for a 1.75-ounce pour of premium Irish whiskey, because if you're doing a shot with Jesus, you don't buy him scotch. We raised our glasses to Irish brewers everywhere, and the smoky liquid burned us smoothly as it fell down our throats.

"Wooo!" he said, slamming his shot glass down and coughing a bit. "That's good stuff."

I agreed heartily. "Shall we do another one?" I asked.

"Oh, no," Jesus said quietly, his eyes growing round. "This is one of those situations where I have to stop and ask myself, what would *I* do?"

I laughed and clapped him on the shoulder, and after

adding considerable varnish to the idea of seeking out new experiences, we set aside the idea of shooting more whiskey and settled instead on pounding a couple of Irish Car Bombs, because he had never pounded one before.

We were pleasantly pickled by the time our fish and chips arrived, and we tucked in right away to try to absorb a little bit of the alcohol.

Jesus made yummy noises after a couple of bites and said, "Now, this right here is food for the gods."

"Really? Did you mean to use the plural?"

Jesus winced. "Am I that transparent? I used to whip out these awesome parables on the spot, tied ministers up in knots for centuries trying to explain them to their flocks, but put a couple of drinks in me and I lose all subtlety."

"So you want to talk to me about the gods."

"One in particular, actually, but, yes," he said, dipping a chip into a pool of ketchup. He noshed on it for a moment before continuing. "These are just too good. I think everyone should give them a try, don't you?"

"The world would be a happier place, I cannot deny it."

"Done," Jesus said.

"Beg your pardon? What's done?"

"Hey!" a man sitting two seats down to my left exclaimed. "Where'd these fish and chips come from? I didn't order these."

"Me neither," a young woman said, sitting behind us in the dining room with a male friend. "But it looks like we both got some."

Other patrons were all discovering that they had fish and chips on their tables that they had not ordered and could not remember their waiter delivering. The wait-staff gradually became aware that customers had food on their tables that hadn't been added to the bill. They asked one another who delivered them, then disappeared into the kitchen to ask the cook to explain, and shortly came back out looking for the manager. It was all very odd. I turned back to Jesus and he had a small smile on his face.

"You're looking a bit smug there," I observed with a grin.

"Miracles are so much more fun when people aren't expecting them of you."

"Yes, I've often amused myself with some mischievous bindings for the same reason."

The Prince of Peace chuckled and said, "I know. Now, where was I? Oh, yes! The god I wish to speak to you about is Thor. You and some confederates are planning to kill him, yes?"

"Well, um," I said, caught off guard. "Yeah," I finished lamely. It's not the sort of thing I would normally admit, but you can't lie to Jesus. "Though I'm hoping to confine my participation to serving as a sort of extraplanar taxi service. I'm the get-there-and-getaway car. I'm not really interested in killing him."

"I tell you truly, it is an unwise course of action, and it were best for you to set it aside."

"You are concerned about my personal welfare?"

"Yes, that is part of it. In most of the futures I see, you do not survive."

That statement nearly sobered me up all by itself. I put a brave face on it and said, "Well, I've had a pretty good run at surviving. I think I'll be okay."

"Ah." Jesus nodded, pausing to chew his fish before dabbing at his mouth with a napkin and continuing, "You are thinking of your deal with the Morrigan."

"Heard about that, did you?"

"Aenghus Óg's howling in hell can be heard all the way to heaven. And how do you think the Morrigan's aegis will help you in Asgard? She can travel there, but she cannot usurp the role of the Valkyries. If you fall, they will hardly let you dwell in Valhalla. Nor will Freyja take you to Fólkvangr. They will let Hel take you to her realm, and there you will stay. There will be no journey to Tír na nÓg."

"Well, that gives me something to think about for sure, but more in terms of strategy and tactics than in terms of giving up."

"You are not persuaded by self-preservation. Hmm. All right, then, consider this: Killing Thor will invite retribution from his pantheon not only against you but also against all your friends and family. And the gods of other pantheons will feel compelled to strike against you in solidarity with the Norse."

"They will? But everybody hates Thor—at least, all the people who truly know him. Isn't it just as likely they'll send me brownies or gift baskets of ambrosia?"

Jesus looked thoughtful. "You may have a point there. If you will forgive my coarse language, I believe the politest term I have heard him called by another god is a giant douche."

"I hear ya," I said, nodding. "He is a douche canoe. But he gets great PR with the mortals. They think he's their protector, some kind of hero, but he really should be sent out to sea and set on fire in a proper Viking burial."

Jesus sighed and pressed his fingers to his temples. "The gods will not stand for it, Siodhachan, even though they despise him. You have to consider that this action will make them all aware of how vulnerable they are. They will react poorly."

"Does that include you?"

"I will remain above the fray," he said. He paused, seeming to reconsider, then decided with a small shake of his head that he'd spoken correctly. "There is none who can assail me. But there are friends of mine who might get hurt." He raised his eyebrows significantly and tilted his head in my direction. "You are one of them."

"Really, you're my friend? My buddy Jesus?"

He chuckled. "Certainly a drinking buddy, if nothing else. And you are also a respected elder."

"Ugh, an elder? You're making me feel creaky here."

"Will you not accept my advice? Forgo this business with Thor. It is unsavory and beneath your character."

"I wish I could," I said. "But I cannot forswear my oath to a friend. That would also be beneath me. At great personal risk to his existence, he helped me dispatch a coven of witches who trafficked with hell. I cannot break faith with him now."

Silence fell as Jesus paused to consider. He sipped his Guinness and wiped off the foam mustache with a napkin, then said, "That is indeed a weighty consideration. I cannot advise you to break your word. I was hoping you might exert yourself to be released from your obligation."

"I suppose I could try. But I know already that Leif will insist I follow through. There is nothing he wants more than this."

"You are resolved, then, to seek out this violence and set in motion waves that will ripple across the planes?"

"I wish you wouldn't put it in those terms. It's not like I make a habit out of picking fights. The fights just seem to be picking me recently. There are several looming on the horizon that I'd truly like to avoid. I really don't want to mess with Bacchus or any of the Romans. Or the Greeks, for that matter. They're true immortals, and they scare the pants off me. Oh, and these other guys who seem to have painted a target on my back—maybe you know something about them. Have you ever heard about an organization calling themselves the Hammers of God?"

A thoughtful crease appeared between Jesus's eyes. "Are you speaking of the old Swedish witch hunters?"

"No, they're contemporary witch hunters, based in Russia."

The crease deepened. "Hold on a moment. They sound like assholes."

I blinked, uncertain I'd heard him correctly. "I beg your pardon?"

Jesus grimaced and pointed at his head. "It's this tiny human brain—I have to have a filing system for all this information or I can't keep track of it all. It sounds like these guys would be filed under Assholes Who Do Evil Shit in My Name."

"Jesus. I mean, wow. That's the name of one of your files?"

"One of my largest, unfortunately. But I have it broken down into subfolders. Here we are. Assholes Who Think They're Entitled to Judge and Kill People in My Name." He closed his eyes briefly and then opened them again. "Yes, now I know who you're talking about. The Hammers of God is an organization of mixed faiths who use Kabbalistic sorcerers as their shock troops. What about them?"

"Well, I think you've already answered my question. I wondered if they enjoyed your official sanction."

"No. They definitely do not."

"Interesting. They occasionally slay a demon or two, don't they?"

"Yes, but even a stopped clock is right twice a day. Look, it's difficult to find fault in them when they eliminate beings that don't belong on this plane. But they have defined evil so broadly that they often attack those who do more good than harm. There is no charity or patience within them, and they have made no allowances for the possibility of redemption."

"I see. I don't suppose you'd pay them a visit for me and tell them to lay off, would you?"

He abruptly looked behind him at the door leading out to Mill Avenue, cocking his head as if he'd heard a noise on the street. Then he turned back to me with a grin on his face and said cryptically, "I don't think that will be necessary," before downing the rest of his Guinness in a few long swallows.

Understanding dawned on my face as Rabbi Yosef Bialik entered the restaurant aggressively, followed by nine more Hasidic Jews who all had bushy beards and impressive peyos curling down from their hats. People stopped eating and stared. Hasidic Jews were an unusual sight in Tempe, and these particular fellows had black, grim expressions to match their black, grim clothing. They didn't look like they had come in search of kosher Irish food. In fact, they ignored the host, who asked, "How many today?" and spread themselves out in the entry area to stand in three columns: four in the center column and three on either side.

"Christ, that's a battle formation."

"I know," Jesus said. "It's the Kabbalistic Tree of Life. This will be fun."

Before I could ask him how it possibly could be fun, the man at the very back, nearest the door, drew his breath to speak. His placement in the formation represented Malkhut, the branches of the tree, the sphere of earth, and he shouted, "Yahweh, *higen aleinu mimar'eh ha'aretz*." My Hebrew was a little spotty, but it sounded like he was asking God to shield him from the earth. All ten Kabbalists clapped their hands together with arms held straight out in front of their chests. The sound echoed strangely, as if there had been a pressure change in the air; I *felt* that clap. Apparently many others did too, because suddenly everyone wanted their checks.

I turned on my faerie specs to scout the Kabbalists'

wards and saw . . . nothing. They had no bindings around them whatsoever, no threads for me to see, no auras. They and the space surrounding them were a void in the world.

"They just shut you down before saying hello," Jesus said in low tones.

"Yes, I can see that."

Rabbi Yosef pointed at me and said to his brethren in Russian, "There he is. The pale one."

Jesus didn't miss a beat with the language change. He said in Russian, "Who, me? You're calling me pale?"

"Stay out of this, sir. We have come for him," the rabbi growled, pointing once again at me.

"Howdy, Rabbi." I said this in English, because the rabbi still didn't know I spoke Russian. I smiled and waved, trying to affect an air of unconcern. "You'll never believe who I'm having lunch with. I'd love for you guys to talk." Without giving him a chance to answer, I called to the bartender, an older chap with thinning hair and a properly red nose. "Flanagan, ten draughts of Guinness here for these ambassadors of peace."

"Coming right up!" he said.

"Stop!" Yosef sternly held up a hand, condescending to use English for the first time. "We have not come for drinks," he said, rolling the *r* richly in his Russian accent. "Nor are we here for peace. We are here to serve a judgment; we are here for retribution. For HaShem, and for all people."

At this point, the host spoke up. "Look, if you're not here to eat or drink, you're going to have to leave," he said. The Kabbalists ignored him.

"I don't get to say a few words in my defense?" I asked. "I missed the trial?"

"Nothing you say can deny your actions," the rabbi snarled.

"I don't want to deny them; I want you to appreciate

them properly. I'm not in league with demons—I've been killing them. I even killed a fallen angel. Ask Jesus here; he wouldn't lie to you."

"Enough mockery." He turned his head a bit to one side, addressing his companions behind him. "Begin."

"But you don't understand," I said, gesturing to the handsome man on my left. "I've truly found Jesus."

The host ducked away to call over a bouncer and maybe the police. Customers in the restaurant were dropping money on their tables and exiting out the back, where they could leave through the patio and access the parking lot. The manager emerged through the kitchen door and stood behind the bar, finally aware that something untoward was happening.

"Now what's going on?" he said in exasperation. He was still trying to solve the mystery of the multiplying fish and chips. He looked like the sort who'd start a revolution against the bloody Brits, but he ruined all possible menace (and dignity) he would have otherwise possessed by wearing a loud Hawaiian shirt.

Flanagan bobbed his red nose at the Kabbalists and said, "Those boys in black over there want a piece of Atticus."

"Well, take it outside!" the manager yelled. The Hammers of God weren't listening. They had taken silver amulets out of their pockets and held them in their raised open palms. They chanted in Hebrew, and the amulets flashed in their hands: "Yahweh, *shema koleinu bishe'at hatzorkheinu. Natan lanu koakh l'nakot et oyveikha bishemekha.*" I caught less of that, but it sounded like they were asking God to give them strength—and I think there was something in there about smiting. When the flash faded, the amulets still glowed with a pearlescent sheen. The Kabbalists closed their fists around them and their hands began to pulse redly, like when you put a flashlight behind your palm at night. Then, in concert, they lunged forward on their left legs and threw a punch with their glowing right fists—from all the way across the room—and yelled *"Tzedek!"* (That meant "justice.")

My cold iron amulet sank into my flesh as if a safe had fallen on it, and I was plowed backward into the bar and cracked my spine painfully. "OW!" I cried. Jesus laughed loudly and slapped his thigh.

"Hey, that wasn't funny," I complained, rubbing my back. That blow had clearly been intended to take my head off or punch a hole through my chest—or something equally fatal.

"Are you kidding? I haven't seen combined channeling like that in a long time. Say what you want about their motives, Atticus, but that was *cool*."

I scowled at him. "Did you give them the power for that?"

Christ grinned. "Nah, they're running on Yahweh juice. You heard them."

"But aren't you supposed to be . . . ?"

"Oh, sure, to Christians I am. But not to these guys. Their conception of Yahweh is very different from a Christian's, so they're talking to a different god. Check it out, things are starting to get hairy."

He was speaking quite literally. The Kabbalists didn't look surprised or dismayed that I was still around. If anything, they looked more determined to give me ouchies. The beards of Yosef and the two Kabbalists immediately flanking him were lengthening and threading themselves into tentacular appendages anchored to their jaws, two on either side of their chins. They knotted and hardened into clouts first, then began to glide through the air toward me, about as fast as a man would walk at a leisurely pace. I'd have plenty of time to duck, but it was far, far in excess of the normal growth rate for beards. Once that registered with the remaining customers, they lost all pretense of behaving calmly in a crisis. There was a general exodus for the patio, with more than a few panicked squeals and impolite requests to get out of the way.

The manager objected and gave chase. "Oi! Pay first, *then* run away screaming if you want!"

"That's it," Flanagan said, his thick hands gripping the bar and his eyes wide. "I'm getting back on the wagon and I'm never getting off again. Oh, Jesus, look at that."

"I'm looking," Jesus said. Flanagan flicked an annoyed glance at him but quickly returned his horrified eyes to the facial hair advancing down the length of the bar. I empathized. I'd seen what those beard tentacles could do; they were much stronger than they looked, besides being viscerally dry, itchy, and raspy. Rabbi Yosef had killed an accomplished witch with his beard three weeks ago by strangling her. It had snaked its way past her wards, and now it occurred to me that it might snake past the protection of my amulet as well. Sure, the beard was being controlled magically, but that magic was targeting the hair, not me, and apart from being completely gross, such hair could constrict my windpipe every bit as effectively as a length of rope—and there were twelve such lengths reaching for me now. If even one of them got wrapped around my neck and the iron of my aura didn't counter the magic controlling it, I could be in trouble.

My options were limited. There wasn't much room to swing a sword in the bar, and I wasn't anxious for bloodshed anyway. Besides, after a shot of whiskey and an Irish Car Bomb on top of my Smithwick's, I wasn't exactly sober enough to muster the balance required for sword fighting. Trying to lay a binding on any of the Kabbalists was impossible now that they had warded themselves from the earth; running away would make me seem like the mass of cowardly lunchtime patrons fleeing out the back, and I wanted my buddy Jesus to think I was cool too; that left nothing but hand-to-hand combat, and people did that all the time while drunk.

I've trained in many martial arts to defend myself against myriad weapons but never against beards. There's not a whole lot of precedent. I decided to treat them like whips. Stepping forward to meet the first tentacle on my right, I grabbed it out of the air and yanked hard and down, expecting to pull the Kabbalist's face to the left and perhaps break up their formation.

It didn't go the way I pictured it in my mind.

Chapter 11

There was no tension at all, no sense that the beard was solidly attached to someone's jaw. It felt like I had yanked on a piece of fishing line when the reel button was depressed, allowing yards of ten-pound filament to whiz free every second. It threw me off balance, and the other eleven tentacles abruptly reared back like cobras and struck, punching me eleven times with surprising force. Getting hit with something akin to a giant knotted sailor's rope isn't as bad as getting hit by a bus, but it isn't like getting tickled with butterfly wings either. One of them caught me on the cheek and spun me around to face an amused Christian deity.

"I don't suppose there's any hope of a *deus ex machina* right about now?" I said.

"Nope," he said cheerfully.

I batted away a couple of hairy ropes that were trying to insinuate themselves around my neck and kicked at a few others that were trying to trip me up. "Well, how about some advice, then?"

"Whosoever shall smite thee on thy right cheek, turn to him the other also."

"You're pulling out the King James?" I cried, incredulous. "I don't think that's the verse you ought to be quoting right now. How about 'I come not to bring peace but to bring a sword'? Remember that one? I liked that one. I have a sword here if you'd like to borrow it."

"Nay, that is not my will."

Uh-oh. Code word. What was his will? He'd just told me he didn't want me messing with Thor because it would upset all the pantheons, and I'd responded by saying I was going to do it anyway. That made me a problem. Maybe he could take care of said problem by letting the Hammers of God have their way with me.

"Think I'll turn the other cheek after all," I said, and I bolted to my right and headed for the back patio, where all the other patrons had escaped. As one exits out the back of Rúla Búla, there's a patio bar to the right, an extensive network of misters overhanging the tables, and a large wrought iron gate to the left, which leads to the parking lot of the Tempe Mission Palms Hotel. Said hotel is situated directly behind a concrete block wall on the east side of the patio, separated only by a wide walkway paved in red cobblestones. The gated exit wasn't much of an exit at the moment; another ten Kabbalists were blocking it, letting patrons past but only at a trickle. If I tried to get through there, they'd have me.

The block wall was looking good. It wasn't terribly high, only four feet or so, and I felt sure I could vault it even in my slightly sauced state. My hopes of dashing over there unnoticed were destroyed by the vanguard of the Kabbalists, who must have been told to look out for the redhead with the goatee. I heard one of them shout, "There he goes!" in Russian, and that was the end of my attempt to "flee casually." I sprinted full tilt for the wall, half expecting to feel a hit on my amulet as they hurled one of their "Justice!" strikes at me, or some other magical attack. Nothing of the sort happened. Instead, as I caught some air and I cleared the top, pain exploded in my back. Knives whistled on either side of me, and I understood as I fell that a few of the Kabbalists had thrown their silver daggers at me—daggers they all carried just in case they ran into a werewolf. One of the knives sank into the meat behind my left shoulder blade and another into my kidney on the right side.

Perhaps it would have occurred to someone else—someone from Scottsdale—to bemoan the fate of his leather jacket in such a scenario. But even such slaves to fashion might be distracted from a wardrobe malfunction by a knife in the kidney, because there's no other pain like it. It's the sort of pain that freezes every muscle for fear of increasing the pain, and you don't dare to scream or breathe, because even that much motion will exacerbate it.

I fell heavily to the cobbled walkway on the other side of the wall and nearly blacked out from the pain. I yanked the knife out of my kidney and had a nice cathartic scream of agony, then went to work healing right away, because it could easily be a mortal wound. Poisons seeping into my bloodstream . . .

Treating the Hammers of God with courtesy, I saw, had been a mistake. Their rules of engagement approved deadly force from the start, while mine had been about disengagement. If I had laid into them with all the gusto they'd shown in coming after me, I wouldn't be in these dire straits now. I'd be in different dire straits, to be sure, but perhaps not so personally threatening.

It's bloody difficult to concentrate properly when you're dying of renal failure and all your brain can do is squeal. I turned down the volume on my pain centers from eleven to one and then refocused on knitting up my kidney. It didn't leave me much room to deal with the Hammers of God. My clever, half-formed plan to ditch them somewhere in the maze of shops in Hayden Square would never see fruition. Drawing Fragarach and making a valiant last stand wasn't going to be possible either.

One lucky knife throw in a half-assed ambush had put me down for the immediate future, and I still had another knife in my shoulder I couldn't reach. The cobblestones weren't letting me get through to the earth; there was cement underneath them, no doubt. Every bit of magic in my bear charm would have to be used in keeping myself alive, so I wasn't sure what I'd be able to muster as a defense when they came to finish me off.

Raised voices cut with equal parts fear and anger dimly registered in my head, and the clapping of approaching shoes against pavement signaled more grief to come.

"*Vot on,*" someone said in Russian. *Here he is.* My field of vision quickly filled with black shoes and the severe garb of the Kabbalists.

Then, suddenly, there were a pair of jeans and Converse All Stars inches away from my nose.

"Hello, gentlemen, can we talk for a second?" a voice said in Russian.

A chorus of heated Russian snarls greeted this request, all of them tersely demanding that the first speaker get out of the way, bugger off, and mind his own business. A couple wondered where he had come from.

"I will move, but we will talk first," the voice said firmly yet calmly, and I recognized it as that of Jesus. We were completely surrounded by men in black now. I hoped none of them had picked up the knife with my blood on it. That would be bad. Though I couldn't imagine how it could be worse than sticking it in my other kidney.

The tight whip of Yosef Bialik's voice lashed out at Jesus. "Why do you interfere? This does not concern you."

"I beg to differ," Jesus said, switching to English. "You interrupted my lunch, and my friend has yet to pay the bill."

"You are a friend to this man? This man who consorts with demons?" Bialik replied in the same language.

"Your mom consorts with demons," I said, though it came out as more of a phlegmy cough than a confident assertion. That was about all the fight I had left in me. I didn't have the strength or will to move an inch. The kidney is a complex organ; I'd need a lot more power and leisure than I currently had at my disposal to make it work properly again. I'd knitted it up to keep it from polluting my insides any more, but it wasn't functional. I already had plenty of nastiness to neutralize in my veins, and that was draining me quickly.

"He no more consorts with demons than you do," Jesus said. "You have misinterpreted his actions and have harmed one you should help."

"Who are you?"

"I'm Jesus Christ."

They didn't even blink. "Step aside or we'll kill you too."

"Thou shalt not kill, gentlemen."

One of the Kabbalists—not Yosef—drew his knife from his coat and brandished it threateningly. "We are serious, crazy man. Get out of the way now."

"Let us talk about Atticus O'Sullivan first."

"You asked for it," the Kabbalist growled. He stepped forward and stabbed Jesus in the shoulder joint—not a kill shot, but still a tad excessive if you want someone to move. I heard the fabric of his shirt tear; I heard the *shik* of the knife sinking into flesh; yet Jesus didn't stagger backward or show any sign of the impact beyond the stark fact of the knife protruding from his peace shirt. The Kabbalist might as well have knifed a wooden post for all the recoil he got.

"I tell you truly, that was extraordinarily rude," Jesus said. "I begin to think you do not keep your covenant." He calmly removed the dagger from his shoulder, as you or I might remove a seed stuck between two teeth. He was as immune to the enchantment on the hilt as I was. It came out cleanly, without a trace of blood; I noticed that last bit when he dropped it to the ground.

"What are you?" Rabbi Yosef demanded. "Are you a demon?"

"Hardly," Jesus said. "Rather the opposite. I've already told you once. But no one believes words anymore. I imagine you will need visual proof."

A new source of light blazed above me—not hot, just bright—and I squinted upward to see a white glowing circle hovering above Jesus's head. It began to rise in the air, and then I belatedly realized that Jesus himself was rising. I darted my eyes back to the ground and saw that his shoes had left it. He was levitating.

"I am the Christian god," he patiently explained. "A prophet to your people, Rabbi Yosef. I am a Jew. Will you not pause to listen? I promise you that Mr. O'Sullivan will not be going anywhere."

No one said anything for a few seconds. It's not every day you see a tie-dyed man with a halo floating above the ground. You want to take time to let that shit sink in, store it in your long-term memory.

"We will listen," Rabbi Yosef finally said, working through what he was seeing. Demons can't manifest a halo—it's against the rules. Angels can do it, but they're not the sort to lie and say they're something they're not. Jesus nodded once before descending back to earth. Once his shoes touched the cobblestones, he turned off his heavenly neon.

"You have sensed traces of my friend's magic in places where demons have been, but rather than consider he may have been fighting them, which was the case, you assumed instead that he was summoning them." Jesus continued to explain that it was Aenghus Óg who'd opened a portal to hell in the Superstition Mountains, and I had not only sent most of the demons back to hell personally, I'd also taken care of the fallen angel Basasael.

"But he has befriended a vampire and a pack of were-wolves! Witches too!" the rabbi said. I took that as my cue to speak up, albeit weakly.

"I am removing the vampire and the alpha wolf to-night," I said, which was technically true. The Hammers of God would interpret that to mean I'd be killing them, but that's why I enjoy ambiguity. "Or at least I will if I feel up to it. And the witches have agreed to leave the state."

"There, you see?" Jesus said. "You have been perse-cuting a man who is playing for our team. He offered to buy you beer and you tried to kill him."

"They might still manage it," I said, wincing. I couldn't afford to suppress the pain anymore; I had to use my last dregs of magic to pay attention to blood toxicity. It's just very hard to focus through a haze of torment. "Hey, Son of Man, a little help here?"

"Please be patient, Atticus," he replied. "I need to get an answer from the rabbis before we proceed. Will you, sirs, leave this man alone henceforth? He has done us all great service."

The rabbis all looked at Yosef. He was the one who had called them here. He glared down at me with hatred in his eyes. He didn't want to let me go. Or perhaps he didn't want to admit he'd been wrong. He was having trouble coming up with a reason to pursue me, however. What was he going to do, call Jesus a liar to his face?

"There will be a vampire war for this territory," I said by way of a peace offering. "Pick up today's newspaper and you'll see it's already begun. If you're all about killing the evil minions of the dark lord, there will be plenty coming here in the next couple of weeks."

All the other rabbis looked a bit excited about that. They were nodding their heads, and fires lit in their eyes.

They probably already had wooden stakes hidden in their jackets.

Yosef saw that he could do no more. "Very well," he groused. "I suppose this man is free of hell. We will pursue other prey for now."

"Excellent!" Jesus beamed at him. "Now go and stake some vamps. Especially the sparkly emo ones."

Yosef and the other rabbis just looked at him with dumb incomprehension.

"Never mind," Jesus said, waving them off. "Go in peace." A couple of them bent to get their knives, but Jesus requested that they leave them behind as a gesture of goodwill.

The Hammers of God turned and walked away as sirens began to wail and police drove into the parking lot. They didn't say good-bye and they didn't say they were sorry for ruining everyone's lunch. They didn't even tell Jesus it was nice to meet him.

Jesus watched them go and then clapped his hands together once, keeping them clasped together in front of his chest. "Right. Well, *they're* certainly filed in the right folder, aren't they? Skilled magicians, but sour dispositions. Let's get you out of sight of the police so we can talk." He bent down to pick up all the silver knives, including the one with my blood on it, but left the last knife lodged in my back. I felt this was an egregious oversight at first. Then I realized what he had in mind as he picked up my left wrist and began hauling me prone along the cobblestones toward the Mission Palms Hotel. New pain exploded inside me, and I felt something tear loose in my shoulder where the knife blade had given the muscle a head start on a trial separation. I lost a few minutes there.

I woke up sitting hunched over in the courtyard of the Mission Palms. It can be accessed from the outside without ever crossing the lobby, but still, I wondered why we were unmolested. No one had noticed one man dragging another man across the courtyard? Even supposing I might have been drunk, didn't the knife handle sticking out of my back raise a red flag? Jesus noticed my look of bewilderment.

"I work in mysterious ways. Let's leave it at that."

I grimaced as my ouchies strongly reminded me that they were still there—nerves slapping my brain and saying, "Hey! You paying attention? This shit hurts." I was completely drained now; I couldn't shut anything off or heal myself at all. "Thought we were buddies," I managed to say through clenched teeth.

"We still are. But pain is often instructive, where whiskey and beer are not. Call it tough love."

"Okay, okay. What's the lesson? I'm listening."

"I want you to think about how you got here, Atticus. What was the decision that led you to this moment— a moment where you were almost killed by witch hunters? Follow the causes and effects backward."

It didn't take me long. I had already been thinking of this back in Mag Mell. "It was when I decided to stop running and kill Aenghus Óg if I could."

Jesus nodded. "That's right. When you decided to kill a god, you set in motion a series of events that led you extremely close to your death. Had you remained meek, you would have inherited the earth—"

"What?"

"No, let me finish. And now that you've killed the Norns—yes, I know about that—you have no idea what possible futures lie ahead of you. The aftershocks of that act have yet to be felt, and you're going to be paying for it like you're paying now for Aenghus Óg. Killing Thor would only make it worse, Atticus. Much worse. In all seriousness, there are few ways ahead in which you survive, your deal with the Morrigan notwithstanding. And there are few ways ahead in which the world survives,

Atticus. Do you hear me? The *world* is at stake—this world. Killing Aenghus brought you to the attention of these Hammers of God. Who knows whom else you've attracted by killing the Norns?"

"I'll bet you have a pretty good idea," I said.

"Well, yes, I do, and that's why I'm here to warn you. Things are already looking grim for you, my friend. You've unleashed a significant aspect of Fate, and it rarely chooses a more peaceful and orderly path when given the opportunity to pursue its own course. Please do not make it worse. Killing Thor will set in motion forces you cannot comprehend. The pain you feel now will be a sensual massage compared to what awaits you should you continue."

I signaled that I understood with the barest of nods. It hurt to breathe. It hurt to sit. It hurt to be conscious.

"Lesson learned?" he asked me.

"Yes," I whispered.

"Right. You won't be needing that anymore, then." Jesus stood up from his patio chair and leaned over me, yanking the knife from my back.

"Gaaaaah!"

"Wah, wah, wah, you're such a crybaby," he said. "It's just a flesh wound, as the Black Knight would say. Stand up."

"Wait. Did you just quote the *Holy Grail*?"

"Why not? It was an inspired piece of filmmaking." He winked at me. "Now stand up."

"You don't mean *divinely* inspired, do you?"

Jesus rolled his eyes. "One needs the patience of Job when speaking with you. Come on, I'm trying to help." He hauled me to my feet by my left arm, eliciting another howl of misery. "Remember this the next time you think it would be macho to face down a god."

"Why not let me die if I'm so dangerous?" I asked, leaning heavily against him for support.

"Because you're also the only one with a hope of preventing the worst cataclysms from happening."

"What cataclysms?"

"I can't tell you. That would be cheating. Now be silent."

"You're awful bossy all of a sudden."

"Doesn't do me much good, does it? You're still talking. Hold still."

Jesus put his hand over my mangled left ear, and a pleasant warmth filled my body. The pain melted away and I felt my muscles knitting back together without a fuss. My kidney healed up and the toxins broke down in my blood. He even fixed the holes in my jacket. And, to top it off, my left ear was good as new again.

"Wow, that was so much easier than the way the Morrigan fixed my other one," I said. "Thank you. Seriously."

He beamed and gave me a hug, more sincerely than the man hug we'd traded on our first greeting. "You are welcome. Thank you for the lunch and the drinks," he said pointedly, bobbing his head toward Rúla Búla and my unpaid tab. "And thank you in advance for making wise decisions in the future."

I began to laugh, and Jesus cocked his head sideways at me. "What's so funny?"

"The next time someone asks me if I've been saved by Jesus, I can tell them truthfully I have. I can tell 'em you're my savior. And they will misinterpret that so deliciously."

Jesus sighed and shook his head with one of those boys-will-be-boys expressions. "Druids," he said. Then he pointed over my shoulder. "Hey, here come the cops." I looked behind me and saw no one there. When I turned around, Jesus was gone.

"All right, you got me," I said, looking up. "That was a good one."

But Jesus hadn't been kidding. A moment later, two

officers came through the short outdoor hallway that led to Rúla Búla, and they saw me standing in the middle of the courtyard.

"Sir? We need to talk to you," the first one said.

There are some grassy spots in the Mission Palms courtyard. It's where the palms grow. I stepped onto one and smiled at the police as I drew power from the earth, replenishing my bear charm. Before they could entrap me into what might possibly be hours of questioning, I cast camouflage on myself and scooted out of there, leaving them bewildered and examining their sunglasses for dirt.

Mindful of my obligations, I crept back into Rúla Búla briefly to settle my bill with Flanagan and leave a generous tip. I figured I needed all the good karma I could get.

Chapter 12

There are certain encounters that one knows will never be repeated so long as one lives. The firstborn child can't be born twice; one's virginity, once lost, can never be found again; the sheer awe one feels when laying hands on a giant sequoia cannot be rivaled. Other times escape our notice, slipping by while we are preoccupied, and we do not appreciate their enormity until it's too late to do anything but regret that we had not paid more attention in the present.

For me, the times I always regret are missed opportunities to say farewell to good people, to wish them long life and say to them in all sincerity, "You build and do not destroy; you sow goodwill and reap it; smiles bloom in the wake of your passing, and I will keep your kindness in trust and share it as occasion arises, so that your life will be a quenching draught of calm in a land of drought and stress." Too often I never get to say that when it should be said. Instead, I leave them with the equivalent of a "Later, dude!" only to discover some time afterward that there would never be a later for us. I did not intend to let that happen with the widow MacDonagh.

But as I walked up to her house, I saw that a moment had already passed me by. The widow wasn't on her porch, sipping whiskey and greeting me with a smile. For all that it was painted bright yellow, the house seemed a little forlorn for her absence. A ring of the doorbell and then a knock at the door brought me no welcome. No lights were on in the house—she usually had them on, even at midday—so I told myself that she must be out. Worried that I might have missed my chance to wish her well, I pulled out the lawn mower from the side yard and trimmed her front lawn while I waited for her return. When that was finished and I was still alone, I grabbed a pair of shears and groomed her grapefruit tree, fretting all the while that if she didn't return by nightfall, I'd have to leave and might never see her again. That would mean my last words to her would be "See you soon," which I'd said on Wednesday when I dropped Oberon off at her house. That phrase was such an inadequate farewell that I cringed inside to think I might have to let it stand.

She arrived after four, dropped off by Mrs. Murphy in a ponderous minivan. Mrs. Murphy, a neighbor of the widow's who thought I was nothing more than a punk college kid, seemed relieved to see me waiting on the driveway. She looked a bit harried because her four kids were making plenty of noise in the back, and she might have feared leaving them alone for the brief span it would take to help the widow out of the van.

"Thank you," she gushed as I opened the door and offered my hand to the widow. She backed up and drove off before we could take three steps away; I deduced from this that somebody in the van must have an urgent need to visit the restroom.

"Thank the Lord yer here, Atticus," the widow said weakly. She looked frail and stooped, her cheeks sunken in and her eyes weighted with fatigue. "That Murphy lass is a decent soul, but she's raisin' a right pack o' brats, if ye ask me."

"Well, at least they're Irish brats," I observed. "They could be British."

"Aye, we need to count our blessings, don't we?" She chuckled softly, and the laugh seemed to restore her somewhat. "I see ye mowed me lawn an' trimmed the tree. Yer a dear lad." She patted my shoulder. "Thank ye."

"You're very welcome, Mrs. MacDonagh."

She put her hand on my shoulder for support. "Would ye mind givin' an' old lady a hand up to the porch? I'm not as spry as I used t'be."

"Sure, Mrs. MacDonagh." She favored her left leg as we slowly made our way to her customary chair. "Where have you been? Haven't seen you since I left."

"I've been to the bloody doctor for days on end. He's been stabbin' me with this and scannin' me with that and chargin' me a fortune to tell me I'm not well, which I already bloody knew before I walked through his door."

"What's wrong?"

"I'm older'n Methuselah is what's wrong. Me body's breakin' down, Atticus. It's tellin' me it's tired of bein' so sexy all the time, hee hee."

"Seriously, Mrs. MacDonagh, what's the matter?"

" 'Tis no matter at all." She groaned a little as I eased her into her chair and relieved the weight on her legs. "I'll not trouble ye with it. The list o' me plagues an' agues is a fair mile long, an' the best medicine for me right now is to talk of somethin' else. Will ye be havin' a glass o' the Irish with me?"

"Sure, I have a little bit of time to spend, and there's nowhere else I'd rather spend it."

The widow beamed at me and her eyes glistened with gratitude. "Attaboy. I'll give ye me keys." She fished them out of her purse and handed them to me, and I went inside to pour two glasses of Tullamore Dew on the rocks.

"Ah, that's grand," she said, taking the proffered glass

from my fingers. She took a sip and sighed, her peace of mind restored. "Atticus, I need t'tell ye something. I don't think I'm long for this world. Soon I'll finally be with me Sean, God rest his merry soul. Every third thought is of the grave." She peered at me over her whiskey glass. "That Shakespeare bloke wrote that, didn't he?"

"Yes, he did. You're paraphrasing Prospero from *The Tempest*."

"Hmph. I think he might have been the only Brit to have ever been worth the milk he sucked from his mother's tit. Wise man."

"Can't argue with that," I agreed.

"Right, well, what I'm tryin' to say is that ye've been a blessing to me in my dotage. I thank the Lord for ye and pray for ye, even though ye don't believe in our savior."

"Oh, I believe in him," I corrected her. "I know he works miracles too." I thought of my healed wounds, the multiplying fish and chips, and the guitar case full of dollar bills. "I simply don't worship him."

The widow stared at me, bemused. "Yer an odd duck, lad. I don't know what to think sometimes."

"You know everything you need to know. Jesus was real and still is. Hold on to that and don't let go."

"I've been holdin' on to it for me whole life, Atticus. I'm not going to let it go now."

"Good."

"Me children ought to be comin' to visit soon, figurin' if they can get in one last good suck-up, I'll change me will in their favor. I'm in for a world o' coddlin' and pamperin' if ever I live that long. But if I bugger off before they get here, will ye let 'em know? I'll leave their numbers posted on me fridge."

"Oh." I looked down at my feet. "Mrs. MacDonagh, I don't think I'll be able to do that. I've actually come here to say good-bye."

She set down her glass and looked at me sharply. "Good-bye?"

"I'm buggering off, I guess," I said. "I plan on coming back, but there's a chance I might not, so I wanted to say a couple of things first."

"Where ye goin' to, lad? Didn't ye jest come back from somewhere?"

"Aye, but I have to return for another job, and it's more dangerous than the first one. Granuaile's got Oberon with her right now and they'll be gone for a few days, but when she returns she'll leave Oberon with you, if that's all right."

"Well, how long d'ye think ye'll be gone?"

"At least a week, but up to three months. If I'm not back after that, I'm not coming back."

"Oh, now I'll be worryin' about ye," she fretted. "I'll be watching me *Wheel of Fortune* and some daft man will buy a vowel, and it'll be an *A*, and then I'll wonder where that mad boy Atticus is and what frightful things he's up to now."

"You didn't used to think I was mad," I said.

"Well, that was before ye went around losin' yer ears and growin' 'em back again, growin' so fast it's like one o' those bloody Chia Pet commercials."

"Heh!" I grinned.

"Oh, aye, did ye think that I didn't notice? I might have a gamy leg, but there's nothing wrong with me eyes."

"Nothing wrong with you at all, Mrs. MacDonagh," I said, and my smile was bittersweet. "You're a rare girl."

"Tish, I'm hardly a girl anymore."

"At heart you are. You have a soul as light as a flower petal and a conscience as clear as crystal."

"Oooh, you're spreadin' it on thick, me boy," the widow chuckled.

"Perhaps," I admitted, tilting my head from side to side in an expression of equivocation. We listened to mourning doves cooing in the grapefruit tree for the space of a few heartbeats, and then I turned to her in all seriousness. "But it's been an honor knowing you. That's no lie, not even the white kind. I've known many people, you understand? Untold thousands in my long life. And you . . . well. The world is better for you having lived in it. I wanted you to know."

The widow reached over and patted my hand. "Oh, Atticus, that's awfully sweet of ye t'say."

I covered her hand with mine and squeezed it gently. Then I sighed, relaxed, and enjoyed the cool burn of whiskey on the rocks tumbling down my throat.

Saying good-bye properly afforded me a measure of peace. It was a binding of a different sort, absent of the earth's power, but still hard proof that there is magic yet in the world.

Chapter 13

My hours with the widow passed quickly. I remained with her until sundown, when Leif called me. He and Gunnar picked me up at the widow's house in a rented Ford Mustang GT, since the three of us wouldn't fit into either of their two-seat sports cars. I noticed that it was black instead of silver: Leif must have paid for it.

The tableau made me miss Oberon. He would have had some comment to make about the three-way olfactory deathmatch in the car: Industrial Air Freshener vs. Wet Dog vs. Bouquet of Ancient Corpse. I wished the widow well, gave her a kiss on each cheek, and squeezed myself into the diminutive backseat. Gunnar's hackles were raised already.

"Buckle up, he drives like a maniac," Gunnar advised me. He and Leif were both dressed more practically than they had been the night before, but they still managed to look slightly ridiculous and out of touch. Gunnar had eschewed silver, presumably because he would not be seen by his pack anytime soon. He wore a blue-and-white-striped rugby shirt, which was tight across the chest and shoulders, and a pair of jeans over those clunky tan work shoes one sees on construction laborers. Leif looked fine—black leather jacket, black T-shirt, and black jeans—until you got to his footwear. His jeans were tucked down into lug-soled combat boots that rose to mid-calf and zipped up the side. Without the boots, he could have passed for a hip graphic designer; instead, he looked like an aging wannabe punk rocker who failed to realize his youthful days of rebellion were long past. He also wore the first jewelry I'd ever seen him wear: a necklace with a finely wrought silver pendant dangling in the center of his chest. It was Thor's hammer, the ancient pagan symbol worn throughout Scandinavia at one time the way Christians wore crosses.

"What Mr. Magnusson means is that maniacs drive like vampires," Leif explained. "The esteemed leader of our law firm fails to give me proper credit."

"What are you talking about? I've already given you credit for running four red lights," Gunnar said.

Leif ignored this. "Where to?" he asked me.

"Swing by my house; I need to pick up a quiver of arrows there."

"Very well," Leif said, and he accelerated gently, almost funereally, and I felt a smile coming on. He was making a point to Gunnar, and I had no doubt he would proceed at this snail's pace until Gunnar told him to speed up.

Gunnar was nearly out of patience by the time we made it down to 11th Street, but I was glad we were going as slowly as we were. Once we turned the corner, Leif braked the car and stared down the street. He and Gunnar both sensed something. I flicked on my faerie specs and then I saw it too: Someone with major mojo was messing with my house. The magical spectrum showed me a shining white humanoid standing near my mesquite tree, gesturing with his hands to encourage ivy to shoot out of the ground and engulf my house. Judging by the sheer amount of white noise in his aura, he was probably a god. Waiting in the street, two leopards harnessed to a chariot pricked up their ears at us. They had a bit of white magical interference around their auras too.

"Hey, Leif, you know what? I don't really need those arrows. Back us up and get us out of here."

"Is that—"

"Don't say his name. It's the Roman deity of the vine."

"What's he doing here?" Gunnar snarled. Leif shoved the Mustang into reverse and drove it like a vampire. The tires squealed loudly as he backed onto Roosevelt Street. The leopards growled, and the glowing white figure turned and saw us. So much for the idea of a quiet exit.

"He's after me, obviously. He—"

"Where do we go?" Leif interrupted.

"Hit U.S. 60 and head east." Leif stepped on it and we shot south toward the freeway at criminal speeds through the neighborhood, giving me one last glimpse at 11th Street in the process. I turned off my faerie specs and the white figure resolved into Bacchus, currently leaping toward his singular mode of transportation. He wasn't the effeminate pretty boy of Caravaggio or Titian, and he certainly wasn't the pudgy baby of Guido Reni's imagination; he was more the sturdy, well-muscled figure of Poussin's *Midas and Bacchus*, except his skin was mottled in madness and his eyes burned with rage. Perhaps on a better day he'd look a little more smooth and androgynous, but he was not feeling the languid sot right now; he was visiting us as the primal avatar of apeshit wrath, arms and neck traced in either veins or vines, I couldn't tell which.

"I think we got us a chariot race, boys." I was proud of myself for staying so calm. What I wanted to do was scream, "GO! FUCKING GO, GO, GO!" But the three of us were all supposed to be badasses. Besides our lives, there were serious testosterone points at stake here. None of us could betray a moment's concern or we'd be mocked mercilessly by the others.

"How far is it?" Leif asked me. "This place where we will shift planes?"

"About an hour or two." There were no healthy forests closer than that near the Phoenix metropolitan area. It was one of the reasons I'd chosen it as a place to live, because I was less likely to run across faeries. "Depends on how fast you drive."

The vampire laughed and drove even faster.

"Now you've done it," Gunnar said. "We're doomed." Because he said it deadpan and obviously in criticism of Leif's driving, he wouldn't be docked any testosterone points for that.

Leif wrenched the wheel to the left and we whipped onto 13th Street, headed toward Mill Avenue. He'd be able to take Mill south to U.S. 60, and once there he could really open up.

There was no question of fighting Bacchus. Unlike the Norse or the Tuatha Dé Danann, the Olympians (both Greek and Roman) were truly immortal and could not be killed—only inconvenienced. That tended to give them an advantage in any altercation. Unbidden, an appropriate sentiment bubbled from my lips: " 'Therefore, dear boy, mount on my swiftest horse; and I'll direct thee how thou shalt escape by sudden flight: come, dally not, be gone,' " I said, quoting from *Henry VI, Part I*. Shakespeare's genius was that he had something to say about almost any situation—even fleeing from a Roman god in a Mustang.

Leif flicked an annoyed glance back at me and affected the grumbly voice of old Capulet: " 'Go to, go to; you are a saucy boy.' " He didn't object to the quote itself but to the idea I was starting a Shakespearean quote duel while we were running for our lives.

"Do you think I mean to engage you while you are busy getting us out of trouble?" I asked him. I should have apologized and ended it there, but again I couldn't resist speaking the perfect line from *Hamlet*: " 'My lord, there was no such stuff in my thoughts.' "

Gunnar groaned and planted his face in his hands. He knew what was coming.

Despite Leif's attempts to speed through the neighborhood, Bacchus took a good angle through the air—because his bloody leopards were the flying sort—and caught up with us as we slowed to turn onto Mill. We heard them roar, and Bacchus joined in with a bellow meant to drive us mad with fear. Were any of us vulnerable to such magic, I'm quite sure we would have completely lost our shit. Claws scraped on the roof of the Mustang as we screeched around the corner.

" 'Alack, what noise is this?' " Leif said, grinning, getting into the spirit of the situation—a macabre fatalism that suggested we might as well enjoy ourselves as much as possible. Still, I carefully drew Fragarach from its sheath in case the roof gave way and I had to fend off swipes at our heads. The back of Gunnar's neck was rippling as his wolf fought to get out. He hated being in the passenger seat right now, powerless to do anything but hope we could outrun the god.

We endured a couple more shrieking scrapes against the hardtop, clenching our teeth against the boneshivering sound, and then the Mustang pulled away again under the weight of Leif's booted heel against the accelerator.

"I hope you bought the optional insurance," Gunnar said.

"Of course I did!" Leif said. "What do you think I am, a maniac?"

Horns honked in our wake, and people stomped on their brakes at the sight of a black Mustang being pursued by an airborne chariot. The witnesses would no doubt medicate themselves with an impromptu prescription of booze when they got home.

It was mayhem and Leif loved it. He leaned on the horn and flashed his lights at people to get them to swerve out of the way. " 'Now bid me run, and I will strive with things impossible; yea, get the better of them,' " he boasted, assuming the part of Ligarius from *Julius Caesar*.

The Roman reference reminded me of the perfect line from *Antony and Cleopatra*. " 'Come, thou monarch of the vine, plumpy Bacchus with pink eyne!' " I said, and that made Leif wince, acknowledging that I'd bested him with that one. He was cursing himself for not thinking of it first—if he ever knew it at all. I'd scored a palpable hit—a plumpy one, even—and he'd have a tough time answering it.

We were having a tough time pulling away from Bacchus too. Every time we slowed beneath 50 mph, his leopards tried to claw their way through the roof. He's not a particularly martial god; the thyrsus he carries is topped with a pinecone, and that wasn't going to smash through much besides toilet paper. Still, his raw strength was well known, a trait he shared with his Bacchants, and if he could once grapple with us, we'd be hard pressed to come away with all our limbs still attached. A red light was coming up at the freeway on-ramp. Cars were stacked up four deep in every lane, and Leif wouldn't be able to weave through them.

The vampire gestured to the obstacle ahead of us and said, "That could be trouble. Should we split up," he said to me, "get out of the car and let him go after you, then Gunnar and I will fall on him from behind?"

I twisted in my seat to view our pursuit. The leopards were partially obscuring Bacchus, but that obstruction gave me an idea. "No, I think I might be able to slow him down." Concentrating on the pinecone of the god's thyrsus—which he was brandishing high above his head—I constructed a binding between it and the narrow patch of fur betwixt the eyes of one of his leopards. It would do the beast no harm, but it would be sorely distracted. When I completed the binding, Bacchus became distracted too, for he never expected his thyrsus to fly out of his hand and land precisely between the eyes of his leopard. He cursed as one leopard yowled and started batting at its head while the other continued running, causing the chariot to spin in midair. To deal with it properly he'd have to descend to the ground, and he sank to street level behind us even as we slowed for the stoplight.

Leif and Gunnar craned their heads around once we were stopped and saw Bacchus trying to deal with a very annoyed pair of large cats.

"Oh noes, kitteh haz major angriez!" I said. I turned around to share a laugh with my companions and found them glaring at me. "What?" I asked.

Leif shook a finger and said in a low, menacing tone, "If you tell me I have to talk like an illiterate halfwit to fit into this society, I will punch you."

"And I'll pull out your goatee," Gunnar added.

"Lolcat iz new happeh wai 2 talk," I explained to them. "U doan haz 2 be kitteh 2 speek it."

Leif cocked his fist and I held up my hands. "Okay, okay, I'll stop! Light's green, by the way."

He shook his head and faced forward, stepping on the accelerator. "How you can go from Shakespeare to that meaningless babble is beyond me."

I made no answer, because I was actually worried about the leopard. It was clawing at Bacchus, who had taken firm hold on the pinecone, and he looked mad enough to yank it free forcibly, tearing the fur out in the process. So while they were still in sight, I changed the binding: I loosed the knots to the leopard and instead bound the pinecone between the eyes of Bacchus himself. He could tear off his own skin if he wanted. His barbaric yawp shook our windows as we disappeared from sight, zipping down the on-ramp to U.S. 60.

"Is that it, then?" Gunnar asked. "Did we lose him?"

"Not for good," I said. "He's probably sharp enough to know where we're headed; he's dealt with Druids before. He can fly in a straight line and shave a lot of time off his trip."

"So what I am hearing you say," Leif said, already weaving past human motorists at dangerous speeds, "is that I should go a bit faster."

"Right. But with the proviso that we need to remain alive and uninjured at the end of the journey."

We tried to relax as we drove out to Superior and then took Highway 177 south toward a small town called Winkelman. When one is being pursued by a god, it's extremely difficult to pretend that nothing is amiss, but we tried because machismo demanded it. We spoke of other things, as if we were out cruising instead of fleeing. Leif amused us with what he'd accomplished last night at the stadium, spending a large part of the drive giving us a play-by-play account of how he'd dismantled sixty-three vampires.

"The key to sowing mayhem in the age of electronics is to deprive humans of electricity," he began. "I took out not only the transformer for the city block but the backup generators within the stadium as well. That meant the security cameras were out of it, and only dim flashes of movement would ever be seen by human eyes. Their cell-phone cameras work poorly in low light. I was thus free to travel throughout the stadium and hunt the Memphis nest at my leisure. They had foolishly spread themselves throughout the crowd rather than concentrate their strength in an unassailable position." He grinned wickedly in the rearview mirror. "The young and naïve fell to the hand of experience and guile."

"The papers didn't say anything about irregularities with the bodies, but they probably didn't discover them until today sometime," I said. "I'm sure tomorrow's headlines will be engrossing—it's on the Internet already, I'm sure. Aren't you worried that the existence of vampires will be exposed to the public?"

Leif shrugged. "My own existence remains a secret. I will worry about it when and if I return."

"When," Gunnar emphasized, "not if."

"Come on, Leif," I persisted. "One or more of those vampire bodies are going to get kissed by the sun and go up in flames. That's going to be a big fucking clue. And even a semi-competent coroner is going to figure out that those bodies died a long time before last night. Admit it. You just made vampires real."

"I admit no such thing. They will blame fires on undetected flammable gases or fluids. And the coroner who suggests that those bodies are vampires or anything close to undeath will lose his job. Whatever they figure out will either be squashed or disbelieved by a public raised on a diet of science and skepticism."

I shook my head. "You must have a giant pair of hairy balls," I said, then added, "unless you don't. Say, Leif, do vampires have balls?"

Gunnar tried and failed to stifle a laugh.

"Atticus?" Leif said.

"Yes, Leif?"

"You have my permission to fuck off." Pretending I had never spoken, he proceeded to flesh out his hunting story, culminating in the dismemberment of the Memphis nest leader.

From Winkelman we headed south on State Route 77 and picked up a police officer anxious to pull over a speeding muscle car. Leif eased up on the accelerator and let Gunnar hold the wheel steady. He rolled down his window and leaned out, facing the rear. His gaze captured the officer's eyes and charmed him. Shortly thereafter, the sirens ceased their wailing and the police officer pulled himself over.

Leif pulled his head back into the car and spent a few vain moments straightening his windblown hair in the mirror, while Gunnar continued to steer from the passenger seat. I sniggered.

"You have something to say to me, Mr. O'Sullivan?" Leif asked archly.

"Please do not trouble yourself about your appearance, Mr. Helgarson," I replied. "I assure you that you look very pretty."

Gunnar chuckled and Leif raised his chin haughtily. "I shall ignore the jealous gibes of ugly men," he announced.

"He's talking about you, Atticus," Gunnar said.

"Your mom talked about me," I said, and the werewolf abruptly lost his sense of humor and growled. I smiled and kept silent after that, as did Leif. You can push a werewolf only so far.

We turned left on Aravaipa Road and continued for twelve miles, the last eight of which were covered in gravel. The Aravaipa Canyon Wilderness is not technically a forest, nor does it contain much in the way of oak, ash, or thorn, but its healthy riparian habitat is strong enough to support a tether to Tír na nÓg. More than two hundred species of birds, nine species of bats, and fish species native to Arizona live there, along with black bears, bobcats, desert bighorn sheep, and coatis. The trees are largely broadleaf species, a pleasing mixture of alder, willow, walnut, cottonwood, and sycamore, all lining the perennial flow of Aravaipa Creek. There are true forests with stronger ties to Tír na nÓg slightly closer to Tempe as the crow flies, but in terms of getting the hell out of town quickly, this was my best option.

The three of us climbed out of the Mustang, and Leif

left the keys in the ignition. I enhanced my vision for night and slipped off my sandals, carrying them in my left hand. The entrance to the wilderness was fenced off, but we vaulted it and began to jog toward the creek. The tabletop mesas on either side of the canyon held little in the way of wildlife; it was the bottom of the canyon that was rich in that regard.

"How far on foot?" Gunnar asked.

"About a mile in, we should be okay to shift," I said. "Keep a sharp ear out for pursuit, will you?" My senses couldn't begin to approach theirs while in human form. "I still don't think Bacchus gave up on us."

We loped easily through the night and I spoke to Sonora as I ran, informing him—or her, as Granuaile insisted—that I hoped to return soon.

Gunnar looked over his shoulder with about a half mile to go, and Leif did the same a second later. "He's coming," Gunnar said.

"No more jogging!" I said. "Leif, you're the fastest on two legs. Can you carry us?"

"I don't know where we're going," he protested.

"Straight down the canyon. I'll tell you when to stop, then you guys just throw rocks at him or something, keep him off us until I can shift us away."

Gunnar didn't like the idea of being carried, but he saw the necessity. We weren't going to stay ahead of flying leopards for very long. Leif picked us up easily in a fireman's carry over either shoulder, and then he lit out with his best speed. It reminded me of the violent ride on top of Ratatosk. Still, the vampire's best speed was short of a leopard's. We heard a roar behind us and then a victorious "Ha!" from Bacchus. Immediately afterward, Leif dropped out from under us and I went flying through the air, along with Gunnar, to land painfully against the trunk of a cottonwood. I scrambled to my feet and saw that Leif's legs were tangled in ivy—or perhaps grapevines. Bacchus was catching up and swooping down at us, his face a mask of the sort of frenzy he inspired.

Well, sanity was better than madness. I sent a message to Sonora through the earth: //Druid needs favor / Prevent rapid plant growth / My location / Now / Gratitude//

Gunnar was shucking off his shoes and jeans and going wolf. He didn't bother with the rugby shirt, deciding for philanthropic reasons it was best for everyone if it got destroyed in the transformation.

"Just hamstring the kitties," I told him while I was waiting for Sonora's answer. "Don't mess with the god." Gunnar managed a nod before his face elongated into a snout and his human expression was gone.

//Favor granted// Sonora replied, and I sent him my thanks. Bacchus touched down and unleashed his leopards with the Latin equivalent of "Sic 'em!" before leaping out of his chariot to follow behind. The leopards sprang at Leif, who was now disentangled from the vines that had tripped him, but he dodged out of way with vampiric speed and let them continue on. He stepped forward to confront the god of wine—who was notably bereft of his thyrsus and showing no sign that he'd had a pinecone stuck between his eyes an hour ago—while Gunnar advanced to meet the two leopards.

"Just chuck him back upstream, Leif; don't test your strength against his!" I shouted as Gunnar and the leopards collided in a mess of fur, claws, and teeth. Bacchus wasn't completely incompetent as a fighter, as evidenced by his stance as Leif approached, but neither was he used to confronting vampires with a thousand years of martial arts experience. Leif jabbed a couple of lightning raps to his jaw to set him back on his heels, then he spun and dropped the wine god on his ass with a kick to the side of the knees. While Bacchus was still down, Leif quickly grabbed him by the feet and yanked to deny him leverage for a kick, then spun him around in a discus toss, finally throwing him several hundred yards away up the canyon. He landed heavily in the rocky creek bed and probably broke something. Shame about that.

In the meantime, Gunnar had lamed the two leopards, but not without taking on significant damage himself. The good news was that he would heal and the leopards wouldn't be pulling Bacchus along to harry us anytime soon.

"Nice throw," I said. "Come on, let's go. It's just a little bit farther."

I gathered Gunnar's jeans and shoes and carried them with my sandals as Leif scooped me up again to continue down the canyon. Gunnar kept pace alongside now that he was in wolf form.

"Keep to the creek bed if you can," I requested. Leif obligingly swerved to take the requested course, which would allow me to keep a sort of jittery surveillance on Bacchus. The Olympian staggered to his feet in a fury and located us easily. He had one hand pressed to a spot on his lower back, but as I watched, he brought both hands around in front of him at waist height and slowly raised them, a clear gesture commanding something to rise from the ground—vines of some sort, no doubt. Thanks to Sonora's help, nothing happened. Leif ran unencumbered, and I chuckled.

Speaking in a conversational tone, I said in Latin, "Lord Bacchus, can you hear me? Nod if you can hear me."

Bacchus dropped his hands and nodded.

"You have never killed a Druid all by yourself, and you never will. Only with hordes of Bacchants and Roman legionnaires and the aid of Minerva have you ever managed to slay a single one of us. Your lackeys may get me eventually, and I know that I will never be able to slay you, but admit to yourself now that you, alone, will never prove my equal. The earth obeys *me*, son, not some petty god of grape and goblet." I switched to English for a postscript. "So suck on that, bitch."

Bacchus didn't bother to compose an intelligible reply. He merely roared his defiance and came after us. But he wasn't especially fast on his feet; he was no quicker than any mortal man, and he had hundreds of yards to make up.

"Find me a nice tree, Leif, anywhere near here," I said. Leif immediately steered us out of the creek bed and deposited me at the base of an impressive sycamore. Unlike the Fae, who specifically needed oak, ash, and thorn to shift planes, I could use any stand of timber that was sufficiently robust to connect to Tír na nÓg. It didn't matter if I used a sycamore or a sequoia; all I needed was a healthy forest.

Gunnar sat on his haunches next to us, panting and bleeding. "All right, both of you touch me and the sycamore at the same time." I looked at Gunnar to make sure he understood. He responded by rising on his hind legs and placing one huge paw on my chest, the other against the trunk of the tree. I needed skin contact, so I poked a finger of my left hand—the one holding the shoes and jeans—into his fur. Leif condescendingly put a hand on my head and the other on the tree.

I took one last look upstream to check on the wine god's position. He was sprinting somewhat spastically down the creek and not paying enough attention to his footwork. He slipped on a moss-covered rock and looked very mortal as he executed a spectacularly graceless face plant. I laughed, because I knew he could hear me and I wanted him to know I'd seen his humiliation. We still had plenty of time to shift.

Sensing that I was about to escape, Bacchus looked up from where he lay in the streambed. "Your insults will be paid in good time," he said in a voice of barely restrained fury. "I swear to Jupiter I will tear you apart myself, Druid. Your death is long overdue."

"Perhaps I deserve to die," I admitted. "But you don't deserve to live. Your very existence is nothing but a feeble echo of Dionysos. You are a weak copy of a better god."

I gave him no chance to respond, proceeding on the maxim that it's always best to have the last word. I closed my eyes, sought the tether to Tír na nÓg, and pulled us through to the land of the Fae.

Chapter 14

Werewolves are generally immune to any magic that's not Pack, but Gunnar came through all right. I neglected to tell him I'd been worried about it at all. The binding wasn't centered on him, anyway; it was centered on myself and what I wanted to bring along. He yakked up his dinner—which Leif and I pointedly did not notice—and he was fine.

When he was finished, I recommended he revert to human form before we shifted back to earth. I tossed his jeans and shoes to him and turned my back during the change so I wouldn't lose my lunch.

It was night in this part of Tír na nÓg, just as it was in Arizona. We couldn't switch right away to Nadym, because it was already after dawn there and Leif would sizzle away to greasy ash. Nor could we stay in Tír na nÓg; faeries wouldn't take well to Leif's presence, and even now they would be drawn to our location, sensing something wrong. We would shift instead to a forest about twenty-five miles north of Prague at Leif's request. He'd have a couple of hours before sunrise.

Gunnar got himself dressed and announced his readiness to go. Even with bloody scratches across his bare chest, he looked better than he did in that rugby shirt. He was healing quickly, but I could tell he'd lost something between the rapid changes, the fight, and the plane shift. He had one more to endure.

As before, Leif and Gunnar put one hand on me and another on the tree, then we shifted to a wooded hillside some distance from the wee hamlet of Osinalice in the Czech Republic. Gunnar was promptly sick again.

"I'll meet you at this tree tomorrow night," Leif said, wrinkling his nose. "It should be a simple matter for me to find it again."

"Where are you going?"

"I'm in Zdenik's territory," he explained. "I must pay my respects. Tomorrow night we will go the rest of the way. Please rest." He melted into the night until all we could see was his corn-silk hair, and then even that was gone.

"The shift was no better in human form," Gunnar muttered.

"Sorry," I said. "You're the first werewolf planewalker, so far as I know. There was no baseline data in the lore to predict how you'd handle it."

"What lore?"

"Druid lore."

"And now, I suppose, my sickness will be set down in your Druid lore?" He looked less than pleased at this prospect.

"You won't be named," I quickly assured him. "It'll be a footnote about werewolves in general. It will be an extreme caution, in fact, because if you get sick as an alpha, what might happen to a weaker wolf?"

Gunnar considered this, then nodded gruffly. Once again, his cuts were already looking better. Soon, I knew, there would be no evidence he'd ever been harmed at all. But there was a price to pay for that.

"I'm starving," Gunnar said.

"You want to eat as a human or a wolf?" I asked. "We

could hunt here, or go into town, get a mess of eggs or something."

"You speak the language here?"

"No," I admitted. "I don't know many of the Slavic languages. But they probably speak Russian or English. And we could always point at the menu."

"You have Czech money?"

"Nope. Just a few bucks in my wallet. It would be dine and ditch or work it off."

Gunnar curled his lip in distaste. "Let's hunt here, then."

I unslung Fragarach from my back and leaned it against the tree—a blue spruce, it was. I continued to strip and neatly folded my clothes as I went. Gunnar sighed and began to take off the jeans and shoes he'd just put on. I dropped to all fours and bound myself to the shape of an Irish wolfhound, then waited for Gunnar to complete his longer, more painful transformation. I took a good sniff around to lock the scent of the area in my mind, then I let Gunnar take the lead and trailed behind him.

Hunting was uncomfortable for us both, since he couldn't communicate with me via pack link and I couldn't form a bond with him like the one I had with Oberon, but we managed to find a small doe and bring her down before dawn. I left Gunnar to it and returned to the tree where I'd left my clothes and Fragarach. No raw venison for me.

I switched to my owl form briefly and did an aerial scout above the trees to figure out where the nearest diner was. I spied a likely spot five miles away in Osinalice.

A half hour's steady run with my sandals off brought me into town. It was a charming collection of timbered cottages, a few cocks crowing at the dawn, and a single road winding through its length, nestled in a narrow valley. There wasn't really a diner in a small place like this, just a bed-and-breakfast catering to ecotourists and writers eager to escape the oppression of modern cities. The innkeeper, who was also the cook, was a short, jovial, spherical man who spoke Russian and loved his business. He had food stains on his apron and a ready smile under a salt-and-pepper mustache. He cooked me a big breakfast in exchange for some work around the inn—degreasing the fryers in the kitchen and cleaning behind the oven, chopping some wood out back for the fireplace in their common room. His daughter was the hostess, and she flirted with me as I ate. She equated me with the road out of town, and any road out of that tiny, beautiful place was a good road to her. I reflected on the paradox of nature: Some people wanted to escape it and others couldn't wait to get back to it, never realizing that it said more about *their* nature than about nature itself.

The lodgers, who were eating breakfast communally in the dining room, tried not to stare at me and did a miserable job of it. Maybe they smelled the werewolf on my clothes, or the vampire—not consciously, mind, because their noses weren't that good. They might have smelled something a bit off about me, giving them a vague sense that I traveled with monsters as a matter of course. They made no attempt to speak to me.

I thanked the owner and his daughter and felt everyone's eyes on my back as the little bell on the door announced my exit from the inn. I crossed the single road in town and slipped into the forest. They'd make up stories about me in their minds, and that was fine. If my ephemeral presence in their lives made it a smidge more interesting for them, so be it.

I took my time returning to the tree marked with Gunnar's vomit. There was no hurry; until Leif returned, we could not proceed. I walked with my hands in my pockets, enjoying the feel of these woods. I hadn't heard from the elemental of this region in a long time, and I sent it a greeting and wished it well.

Near the rendezvous point, but far enough away that I wouldn't have to smell the acid remains of Gunnar's stomach, I assembled a rough lean-to—it's much easier to do when one can bind the branches together magically. I planned to indulge in a good day's sleep, since it was now my bedtime in Arizona, and the lean-to would provide shelter from aerial surveillance more than from the elements. Lacking a teddy bear or a pillow or even Oberon, I took small comfort snuggling up with Fragarach.

The forest floor was cold; snow would be coming soon . . .

Gunnar was sprawled nearby on his back when I awoke, his paws splayed comically in the air and his tongue lolling out to one side. He was snoring a bit. I wished I had a camera. One with a big flash, because it was past sundown. Something had woken me up—but, oddly, not the werewolf.

Turning on my faeric specs, I scanned the night without moving my body or creating any noise. I saw nothing and heard nothing. Maybe the pressure on my bladder had roused me, and nothing more. Still, I was convinced something was outside the lean-to, watching—perhaps waiting for me to stick my head out.

I wasn't going to give it the satisfaction. I'd prefer to wake up the werewolf instead and then exit while it was distracted with the problems that startled werewolves tend to present. Shifting the ground underneath him ought to wake him quickly. I placed my palm flat against the earth and was about to issue a command through it to disturb Gunnar's sleep when a voice spoke and did the job for me.

"Calm yourself, Atticus. And you too, Gunnar. It is I."

Leif stepped into view from behind a tree as Gunnar and I rose to meet him, a bit miffed by his entrance. This seemed to please him, judging by the smirk on his face. "Did you have a nice day?"

"Slept through most of it," Gunnar growled.

"That's what I always do," Leif said. "Sleep like the dead."

"How was Zdenik?" I asked.

"Impeccably tailored. Surprised to see me. Annoyed that I defended my territory so publicly. Gratified that I paid him proper respect. Shall we go on to Nadym?"

I released the bindings keeping my lean-to together and wandered off to relieve myself, then returned and pronounced myself ready.

"Can you shift us quickly out of Tír na nÓg?" Gunnar asked. "Perhaps I can vomit only once and pay for both trips at the same time."

"I'll do my best," I told him.

We shifted, and I spent as little time as I could in Tír na nÓg before hauling us east to the forest south of Nadym. Gunnar was violently ill immediately upon arrival. Leif and I stepped off to give him some privacy and save our noses.

Once Gunnar announced himself ready to proceed, we ran north underneath a clear starlit sky, arriving at the rendezvous point near midnight. Leif graciously offered to carry my sword and our clothes so that Gunnar and I could run in our shifted forms. We kept an eye on the sky above, watching for telltale signs of storm clouds gathering, but apparently the Norse were searching for me elsewhere. It made sense: They were expecting me to hide as far away as possible from Asgard, not to attempt a return trip. As the lake came into view, we spied a campfire licking at the night, setting the branches of a familiar tree on the shore into sharp relief. There should have been three people waiting for us, but I spied only two. Perhaps Leif had not managed to get hold of them all and tell them where to meet. Two elderly-looking men sat on either side of the fire, apparently unafraid of what might be lurking in the darkness outside its glow.

"I see we are the last to arrive," Leif said. Either he was expecting only two or he saw the third man somewhere. "Come. Shift to your human forms and I will introduce you." Gunnar and I shifted and dressed, and together we approached the fire. Leif hailed the two old men, and they turned toward the sound of his voice. Betraying no sign of arthritis or poor eyesight, they rose fluidly from the rocks they'd been sitting on.

One of the men was Asian, presumably Zhang Guo Lao. Wispy tendrils of white hair grew sparsely along his jaw and in a nimbus around his temples, reminiscent of half-formed clouds through which the sky is still visible. He wore traditional garb in the formal *shenyi* style, royal blue embroidered with a silver and gold chrysanthemum pattern, save for bands of sky blue at the collar, belt, and the edge of his sleeves. Though clearly advanced in years, he seemed faintly amused that we might think him frail because of it. I knew from experience that the loose folds of those clothes often disguised the true movements of shoulders and elbows, even fists. I would leave it to Leif and Gunnar to underestimate him; I was not deceived. His English, when he spoke, was quite excellent and only slightly accented. He bowed to us and said, "You honor me with your presence."

The other man was Väinämöinen. He gestured at my goatee and said, "Cute beard." His own was white and epically intimidating. I couldn't possibly call it cute; he could be hiding anything in there. There might be weapons or exploding powder pellets to help him disappear in a cloud of smoke, or there might just as easily be a family of starlings nesting in it. Beginning under his sharply bladed cheekbones, it flowed like an avalanche all the way down to his belly. His mustache was an even brighter shade of white than his beard, and it draped luxuriously over his upper lip, falling in thin tendrils on either side of his chin like ridges of fresh powdered snow.

His eyebrows were similarly impressive and snow white. They hung like rolled-up awnings over a prominent brow and deep-set sockets. His eyes were thus completely cast in shadow, pools of ink that were as likely to be amiable as angry. A black skullcap of the Finnish cut with earflaps on the sides was fastened with a bright red band around his forehead, giving the overall impression that he was a fearsome man to cross. He looked like an evil version of Santa Claus, lean and hungry and only liable to say "Ho-ho-ho!" when he was jumping up and down on your face.

He wore a tunic of forest green belted in black leather at the waist, and over this he wore a sturdy red wool cloak, clasped invisibly somewhere underneath his beard. A short sword rested in a scabbard attached to his belt, and he wore light-brown cloth breeches tucked into knee-high furred boots, which were cross-tied down to his ankles.

His grip was strong as I shook hands with him. "That hat is darling," I told him. If he wanted to damn me with faint praise, I had no compunction about doing the same. This was not a diplomatic mission. Besides, I had a feeling he was jockeying for baddest of the badasses.

Väinämöinen confirmed this when he turned to Gunnar and said, "What happened to your shirt?" as if it were more manly to be well dressed than to not care about the cold.

"It was astonishingly ugly," I explained, implying that at some point it had been destroyed and no one had mourned its passing. Gunnar glared at me as he shook hands with the Finn, but he let the comment stand.

Any additional efforts by Väinämöinen to proclaim

himself Manliest of Men were forestalled by the arrival
of a bona fide deity. An eagle swooped out of the night
sky—presumably from a perch in the tree above—and
shifted before our eyes to a heavily muscled thunder
god. It wasn't Thor; it was the Russian god, Perun, and
the third man I had missed.

His name—or some variation of it—still means "thunderbolt" in many Slavic languages today. His muscles
moved like slabs of architecture, sculpted yet not smooth;
the sharp lines of muscle were blurred by thick thatches of
hair, for he was impressively hirsute, with hair growing
even on the tops of his shoulders. His beard was full and
copper-colored; the tangles on his head were wild and full
of bravado.

His blue eyes crackled briefly with lightning, a much
more impressive version of the special effect they did on
the eyes in *Stargate*, and then he beamed merrily at all of
us. Suddenly I could see him in a Saturday morning car-
toon vehicle: He'd be Perun, the Happy Hairy Thunder
God.

He asked us in cultured Russian if he could speak to
us in that language. Looking at the blank stares on the
faces of Leif and Gunnar, I explained to him in Russian
that not everyone could speak it.

"English, then?" he said, his accent thick. We all nodded or murmured assent. "Is bad luck for me. Not my
good language." He shrugged off his misfortune. "I make
work."

Perun shook hands with everyone, delivering tiny
shocks to us all and chuckling softly at our reactions.
Then he held up what looked like stone straws.

"I bring gift," he said, and passed one out to each of
us. "I am not knowing English word for these. They are
shield for lightning."

Comprehension followed quickly. "Ah, they're fulgurites," I said—hollow tubes of lightning-struck sand,

superheated to smooth glass on the inside, rough on the outside.

Perun asked me to repeat the term and I did so. He practiced it a few times, then said, "Keep fulgurite with you always, protect you from Thor. Now his lightning no bother. See?"

Leif looked at his fulgurite doubtfully. "This will protect me from a lightning strike?"

"Wonderful!" Perun clapped and smiled at Leif. "We have volunteer for demonstration."

"I beg your pardon?" Leif said.

"Don't worry," I said. Perun raised an axe that he'd had strapped to his back into the air. I'm not sure where that had been when he was an eagle; I wondered if he'd teach me how he did it. "I think he means it works like a talisman."

"You may recall that the last talisman I had failed to protect me fully," Leif pointed out with some asperity. He spoke of the cold iron amulet I'd given him to protect from hellfire-throwing witches. "My flesh is highly combus—" At this point, a thunderbolt struck Leif square on the head. We saw the lightning travel down his body and dissipate into the ground. The crack of thunder startled us all, and I, for one, thought surely that Leif would keel over, a smoking, charred ruin. Curiously, though, he was fine. "—tible?" he finished on a querying note.

"Ha! You see?" Perun cried. "Better than shield. You feel no heat, no spark, yes?"

"It . . . sort of . . . tickled," Leif said.

Everyone grinned. "That is most extraordinary," Väinämöinen said. "Will you strike me next?"

Perun's answer was another thunderbolt from the sky. Not a hair on the Finn's face was singed. This time we all voiced our appreciation effusively. Perun seemed to glow with validation, and he proceeded to strike the rest of us with our very own bolt of lightning "for practice."

"Do these have a limit to their protection?" I asked, pointing to my fulgurite. "Good for only twelve strikes or something like that?"

"No, these blessed for all time by me," Perun assured us. "You safe from all lightning in future. Thor, Zeus, you name, no lightning bother you as long as you carry."

"Begging your pardon, exalted one, but do you speak of carrying it in a pouch or some other pack?" Zhang Guo Lao wondered.

"Eh?" Perun's brows met together like amorous hairy caterpillars. "No. Must touch skin somewhere. Hand, foot, backside, no matter. Place in pack, fulgurite protect pack, not you."

The enormity of the gift began to sink in, and we thanked him effusively.

"Is no big deal," he said, though it was clear he enjoyed the big deal we were making of it.

"Now that we are all here, I will cast a seeming," Väinämöinen announced. "We will not appear to be here to anyone who snoops around."

I rather thought it would have been a good idea to do that before the five lightning strikes in the same small area, but perhaps it would still be effective. "Pardon me if I'm being impertinent, but do you know if this seeming will deceive the eyes of Hugin and Munin, Odin's eyes in Midgard?" I asked.

The wizard's dark eye sockets swung around to regard me. "An excellent question. The answer is yes. I have had occasion to hide from him before." He strode back to the rock he'd been sitting on and withdrew a strange instrument from a pack there. It looked like the lower jaw of some animal, teeth still prominently attached, and wound tightly around these teeth were fine yellow strings.

"This is my *kantele*," he explained. "Made from the

jawbone of a giant pike and the hair of a fine blond woman." I was stunned speechless. What does one say to that sort of thing? "Who was the blond woman?" or "Why didn't you pick a brunette?"

Väinämöinen began to sing, and I flipped on my faerie specs to appreciate what he was doing in the magical spectrum. The normal bindings present in the air around us began to haze or fuzz over; he was cutting us off from the normal scheme of things, creating a pocket dimension. When he finished, his mustache raised slightly at the corners and I understood that he was trying to smile. "There. Has everyone eaten? We have something cooking," the wizard said, gesturing to a cast-iron pot hanging over the flames.

Gunnar indicated he'd eat anything, and we all moved around the fire. We stood until Perun and Leif secured a few more boulders for us to sit on; they may have competed to find the largest, heaviest ones nearby.

"It is a humble meal. A couple of hares, together with carrots and onions. We have no potatoes," Zhang Guo Lao said apologetically. "But it has been cooking since before sundown. We have added salt and pepper. It should be seasoned and tender now."

I smiled. "You guys seriously made a stew?" One of the things I've always enjoyed about twentieth-century fantasy novels is how bloody fast the heroes whip up a pot of stew from scratch over a campfire. To me that's more magical than slaying dragons, because it takes a good four hours to make a passable stew—often longer over a fire in winter—yet those folks in the books always seem to manage it in less than an hour, without explanation. Though it was still an hour past sundown in Prague, it was approaching midnight in Nadym, and the stew should indeed be ready to eat.

Väinämöinen and Zhang Guo Lao's packs were well stocked with cutlery and plates. Both were accustomed to spending nights in the open. Everybody chowed down—except for Leif. He drank a cup of my blood. Perun approved of the cooking but seemed wistful about the small portions.

"Is good. But next time, eat bear," he said.

No one seemed anxious to do the dishes; it was as if they had each become Hemingway Code Heroes (with all the concomitant chauvinism that implied), and they'd rather die than do "women's work" in front of all the other men. So I volunteered for the duty as a sop to their egos, and accepted their relieved thanks as I took everything down to the lake.

"Honored Druid," Zhang Guo Lao said, "I have heard few details from Mr. Helgarson beyond an assurance that travel to Asgard is possible. Please explain to us how this is so."

"I will shift us all there. Physically this is not an issue. Mentally it's a gigantic issue. I was able to shift my two companions here across the globe," and I gestured to Leif and Gunnar, "because I've now been acquainted with them for more than ten years. I know how they think. I know what gives them joy and I also know how to push their buttons. They are friends.

"But you are new acquaintances," I said, gesturing at the three sitting across from me. "I am unfamiliar with the essence of who you are. When I must hold Zhang Guo Lao and Väinämöinen and Perun in my mind, what are they to me but names? You are more than a name. You are experience and wisdom, wit and folly, hatred and sorrow, strength and weakness. You are motivated by different forces; you have different goals in mind. All this I must hold in my mind, so that when we shift to the Norse plane, I do not leave parts of you here."

"So we must tell you all of these things?" Väinämöinen asked.

"Not only me. You must tell us all. If we are to survive,

we must each see into the windows of our comrades' houses. We will open our windows by telling stories."

"Stories? What kind?" Perun wondered.

"All kinds. In America they call it male bonding, and that is an accurate term for what we must accomplish here. We need to be bound, mentally and spiritually, if I am to take us all physically to the Norse plane. So we will remain here until I am confident we can leave, and we will tell stories. I suggest that your first tale concern what you all have in common—that is, why you want to kill Thor. We can move on to lighter topics from there. Agreed?"

A general murmur of consent accompanied their nodding heads, but every visage scowled at the fire— imagining the Norse thunder god in it, no doubt.

"Who would like to go first?" I asked.

All five spoke at once, but four of them almost as quickly deferred when they saw Gunnar bristling, lest he begin to doubt that we thought him dominant.

Chapter 15

The Werewolf's Tale

I am probably the youngest being here, with only slightly more than three centuries to my name, but it seems I have hated Thor for longer than that—though he wronged me personally only ten years ago. It is strange how raw emotions can expand time or contract it. It is stranger still how a god can cultivate a reputation for being a friend to man when he is so often an enemy—for I know that Thor has done you all a great wrong, else you would not be here. I also know that we are not the only men in the world to whom he has offered injustice. I have heard whispers and stories, rumors of casual cruelties and petty behavior. It is, perhaps, his nature to be capricious and shockingly vicious, since his body is a bottle for extremely bad weather and his will makes for a weak stopper. His sense of right and wrong is no doubt somewhat storm-tossed.

Yet that is not an exculpatory condition. Werewolves contain ruthless predators within, and we must control our wolves if we wish to survive in the world. We must firmly adhere to pack law at all times and to mortal law where it does not conflict with pack law. Law is all that separates us from barbarism and the howling within; it is a necessary leash on our darker natures. The same should be true of gods. As we are subject to law and order, they should be also. We hear in tales that their justice is administered by a supreme god, if at all. But it is never commensurate to the crime, while the punishments they deal out to mortals are often excessive and eternal. I think it is time a god received his comeuppance.

To appreciate fully what Thor did to me, I must take you back to Iceland in the year 1705.

In that time I was a courier and peddler. I circuited the island in the summers, delivering messages and doing a little trade out of my pack, sharing news and providing some isolated farmers the sense that they were not alone in the world. Often they were just as glad to see me as I was to see them. I got free room and board for the gossip in my head, and they had the opportunity to reconnect with friends and relatives by entrusting me with a letter for a small bit of coin or provisions for my horse.

The visit I made to Hnappavellir farm that summer changed my life. Most of the household was out in the field; the only person at the farmhouse was a girl named Rannveig Ragnarsdóttir, nineteen years old and disaffected with rural existence. She had hair like summer wheat and a soft blush to her cheeks when she smiled. When I arrived, she was wrestling with a ball of dough in the kitchen, flour on her dress and completely unprepared for company. My presence flustered her as she tried to remember manners she'd learned long ago but had never practiced until now. I thought her completely lovely, and once we were seated with drinks and talking across a table, she thought my humble existence was somehow romantic and adventurous. The way she looked at me began to change after a few minutes; she became flirtatious, and I admit that I encouraged her. I had not known a woman's touch in weeks. Before long, she was suggesting a short excursion to look for lost sheep. She packed some dried strips of meat and some biscuits along with a blanket, then selected a mare from the stables and led me to what is now Skaftafell National Park. There was a special place there, she said, that I should see. It was a waterfall called Svartifoss that tumbled over black columns of volcanic basalt, which had slowly cooled and crystallized into hexagonal shapes. It was a place of dark, musical beauty, and after the sun went down she said she wanted to have me there. I let her.

There were few escapes to be had in Rannveig's life. Twenty people lived at Hnappavellir, most of them related, and there was nothing for a young girl to do in such a situation except be obedient. I was supposed to be a happy interlude, quickly enjoyed and long savored afterward, and I understood that and was grateful for it.

She was ravenous in her lovemaking, and I remember that she told me she wanted to do more than merely dwell on the earth; she wished that she could truly live. She and I interpreted this to mean that a nice shag under the light of a full moon sure beat the hell out of snoring through the night and then scrambling all day to bake the bread and keep the hearth fire burning. But that particular comment of hers was overheard and interpreted much differently.

The wolf who savaged us called himself Úlfur Dalsgaard. While we were locked in each other's embrace, he bit deeply into my hamstrings and then tore at Rannveig's calves. Utterly crippled and unable to flee or fight effectively, we thought we were finished. We half expected an entire pack to descend upon us, but soon enough we realized that there was only one wolf— a huge wolf, to be sure—and he'd backed off to watch us bleed.

I couldn't believe my eyes at first: There had never been any wolves in Iceland, but of course I had heard tales of them. This one didn't act like the wolves in stories. I didn't understand the behavior. We were wounded, bleeding, and scared, and that should have been more than enough encouragement for him to kill us, but he wanted us to stay there, nothing more. If we tried to drag ourselves away or call for help, he growled and lunged at us. We were being saved for something special.

"What does he want?" Rannveig asked me.

"I don't know," I replied. "But I don't think we have any choice but to wait."

"You think he's eaten our horses?" We'd heard nothing from them since we'd staked them perhaps a mile away and left them to graze—but that was not surprising, considering how close we were to the waterfall and the distance between us.

"No idea," I replied. There was nothing to do but wait and wonder if we'd perish from blood loss or from jaws at our throat.

Our answers came at dawn. When the sun outshone the pale glow of the moon, the wolf writhed and howled on the ground, suddenly overcome by a series of snapping bones and popping tendons and shifting, sliding skin. During this grisly metamorphosis, he could not pursue us, and Rannveig thought it a good opportunity to flee. She gathered her clothes, rose to her feet, and said, "Come on, I'm well enough to run," and I saw that her calves had healed very well in the hours before dawn. I looked down and realized my hamstrings were likewise remarkably restored, and this, coupled with the evidence of the transformation in front of me, explained the wolf's odd behavior.

"He's a werewolf!" I cried. "And he bit us during a full moon!" The stories of werewolves today vary greatly in their details, but at that time it was clear that they could add to their numbers only by biting someone during a full moon. The evidence pointed to a horrifying conclusion, but Rannveig had yet to realize it.

"Come on, Gunnar! Let's go now!" Rannveig said, already yards away.

"No, look, do you not see? He is a man!" I pointed at the twitching form on the ground, now clearly recognizable as human. He was a bit shorter than me but thicker and more muscled. His blond hair was cropped closely around his skull, but his beard was full. The twitching stopped even as I spoke and he stood before us, naked and unashamed.

"You said you wanted to truly live," he called to Rannveig in a mocking baritone. "So now I've given you the opportunity. Tonight, the moon will not be completely full, but it will be more than enough to trigger the transformation. You will become werewolves like me or die in the attempt. We will be Pack, and together we will live in the worlds of men and of nature."

"But I don't want to be a wolf!" Rannveig protested.

The man scoffed at this objection. "It's necessary only once a month after you establish control. Think of it as a menstruation, except you won't be the one bleeding."

"Why didn't you ask us first?" I said. "This is not a life I would choose."

"It's a life that chooses you," he corrected me. "I could hardly ask you while in wolf form. And you cannot appreciate what you're refusing until you've tried it. You will like being a wolf. Trust me."

"Why should I trust you?" Rannveig demanded. "You bloody bit me!"

"And you're welcome," Úlfur replied. "I know you'll get around to thanking me later."

"Thank you? For what? Turning me into a monster? For condemning me to hell?"

"You are concerned about hell?" He waved a hand at me and laughed. "This man is not your husband, am I right?"

Rannveig's face turned red. "God forgives weakness.

He does not forgive . . . abomination!" She shouted the last word and then hurriedly began to dress herself. I should probably pause to explain at this point that Rann-veig was a Lutheran—as was I, at the time, along with most of the rest of Iceland. But throughout Scandinavia, the Old Norse religion persisted among some individuals, as I believe it still does today. Úlfur, a Danish transplant, was one of those who still followed the old gods. (We had a steady trickle of Danish immigrants because Iceland was under Danish rule then, but Frederik IV largely ig-nored us, occupied as he was in the Great Northern War with Sweden.)

"It all depends on which god you're talking about," Úlfur said. "The Æsir are perfectly content with dual natures."

"You see?" Rannveig said to me. "He spouts pagan nonsense. He is damned, and now so are we."

Úlfur threw his head back and laughed heartily. "You are blessed, not damned. You will come to know this in time. Run with me under the moon and hunt, taste hot blood on your tongue—"

"Gah!" Rannveig covered her ears and ran away. She did not want to hear about hot blood on her tongue. I grabbed my clothes and chased after her. Úlfur laughed again and called after us.

"Run now if you wish! But don't be near any men when night falls, or the hot blood you taste will be human!"

Rannveig didn't slow down for half a mile. She hurtled as fast as she could to where we had left the horses, and I couldn't close the gap between us until we were nearly there. She was gasping and crying by the time we reached the spot where we'd staked them, and when we got there only one remained. The other was a mess of blood and bones and bits of skin and flesh.

"Oh, God! Oh, God!" Rannveig cried. "He ate my horse! Gunnar, he ate my horse!"

"Well, if it kept him from eating us, I'm grateful to the horse," I said.

She whirled upon me and started pounding my chest with her fists. They weren't weak punches either. She was letting loose with everything she had, fury erupting from her like a volcano. "How! Can! You! Be! Grateful!" she yelled, landing a blow with each word. "We are fucked! *Fucked,* you hear me? We heal like demons! We are no longer human! Our salvation is gone! Gone!" She dissolved into sobs and sank to the ground, clutching me. I knelt to hold her, but I did not know what to say. I could not tell her everything would be all right. She was going to have a hard time explaining to the men at the farm what happened to the horse. And if she truly turned into a wolf that night, everyone there would be in mortal peril. Rather than expose them to such danger— and to give us more time to concoct a tale if we found we could return—we decided to continue on my westerly path to Kirkjubæjarklaustur. That proved enormously difficult, because the remaining horse would not suffer our touch. It neighed in fear and reared up defensively whenever either of us approached, and we finally had to cut it loose and let it run away. It ran back in the direction of the Hnappavellir farm.

Seeing no other choice, we began trudging after it. A day without food or water we figured we could survive, and then we would make the farm by early the next morning. We did not see or hear from Úlfur all that day.

Rannveig and I were exhausted. We had not slept at all through the previous night and had been traveling all day. By mutual agreement, we collapsed together underneath a tree as the sun set. We both feared what was to come but no longer had the energy to waste worrying about it. I actually managed to take a short nap.

My awakening was the rudest possible. My skeleton snapped in a hundred places and knitted together again in alien shapes, organs squished and remade themselves, and you know those headaches you get between your eyes? They are worse than excruciating when there's a snout growing out of that spot. Being confined in human clothes didn't help the process along either.

Rannveig was enduring a similar transformation. Her cries and snarls of pain were even louder than mine, and I wasn't holding back. Our clothes eventually tore and the shifting stopped. The pain faded as we lay still under the tree, whimpering. I turned my head and saw much better than I ever had before. Where Rannveig had been, there was a light-gray wolf with white socks surrounded by shreds of Rannveig's clothes.

I got to my feet—all four of them—and took a deep breath. Smells I'd never known or perceived before flooded my mind. There was a burrow of wood mice somewhere nearby; their droppings littered the small stand of timber in which we stood. I could smell the lingering traces of my horse's fear on the trail back to Hnappavellir. Thinking of the horse made me realize how hungry I was. I needed to hunt.

Rannveig was up now, and she looked hungry too. She smelled the horse, and we set off after it together. I do not know how we communicated; there must have been something happening on an instinctive level, because as of yet we had no pack link.

Running felt good. It wasn't an all-out run but rather an easy lope. Rannveig ran beside me, and she seemed to be enjoying herself as well. I could tell we were getting closer to the horse. It was either slowing down or had stopped altogether with nightfall, unsure of the path. But as we grew nearer, we smelled and heard other horses and another smell on top of them: humans. I began to drool, and what was left of my own human thought drifted away as the wolf took over not only my body but the remainder of my mind. The next thing I remember is coming back to awareness with someone else's voice in my head.

<Good. You have eaten human flesh. Your wolf will be powerful now. It will be more difficult to control at first, but ultimately you will be strong members of the Pack.>

<What? Who said that?> I asked. I looked around and saw Rannveig nearby, her muzzle bloody. I could feel the blood on my own muzzle and smell the coppery scent of it. Another wolf sat calmly a short distance away. It was a wolf I recognized: Úlfur.

<You know me. I am your alpha. We are Pack.>

Rannveig came back to herself and processed what was going on. I didn't recognize the body we'd torn apart, but she did. She leapt back from it and yipped in alarm. Through the pack link, she screamed. <Nooo! It's Sigurd! We killed my brother! Gunnar, we *ate* my brother!>

He must have come looking for her. I turned to survey the scene; there was another body back along the trail. I didn't know who it was, because I'd never seen anyone at the farm besides Rannveig, but I suspected she would recognize him.

<I am sorry. Is that someone you know as well?> I asked. She wasn't paying attention. She was hung up on eating her brother and trying to vomit. I felt sorry for the men but didn't hate myself; I saw already that I had done nothing. These men were literally killed by wolves, not murdered.

<You are right, Gunnar,> Úlfur said, clearly able to hear my thoughts. <You did not do this. Your wolves did. Rannveig? Rannveig. Calm down.> I expected she would ignore him as she'd ignored me, but she calmed down right away. His influence as alpha was strong, and she tucked her tail between her legs and confined herself to soft whimpers.

Úlfur said, <Listen to me, both of you. We will head

north, to the other side of Iceland, and settle there. We will grow the Pack slowly and create a territory for ourselves, and we will prosper. When you turn back into humans in the morning, you will feel better. Stronger. You will never be sick again. And I will teach you to control the wolf so that, if you wish, he can be free only one night a month, instead of the three he wants, and you will never lose yourself in the wolf so completely again as long as we have the pack link.>

<We are damned, Gunnar,> Rannveig said.

<Perhaps,> I conceded. <But perhaps we may find a path back to salvation.> I wasn't sure I'd spend much effort looking for that path. I could tell already I would like being a wolf, and I wasn't feeling any of the horror she felt. <Who's the other man over there?> I asked again, now that she'd settled down a bit.

She padded over and looked at what was left of the face. <It's Einar. My grandfather. He was the owner of the farm. Oh, God, I can't believe this is happening.> She threw her head back and howled.

<It's not happening, Rannveig. It happened. And we didn't do it. It was an accident.>

<Don't act like no one is responsible! We fornicated out of wedlock, and God sent this thing to curse us. Now we've killed my brother and my grandfather!>

<I don't feel cursed,> I said.

<And you're one of those "things" now,> Úlfur added. Rannveig whined and lay down, covering her eyes with her paws in a very human gesture. Her ears were flattened and her tail tucked underneath her.

<Listen to me, Rannveig,> I said, my mind grasping the possibilities before us. <You told me you wished to truly live. Now you can. You don't need a husband or a brother to look after you. There will be the Pack, you see?>

<That's right,> Úlfur said. <We will go to Húsavík and

you can work in whatever way you wish. And when the moon comes, we will leave town and hunt the seals or the puffins or whatever suits us. In the summers we can go to the lake at Mývatn and enjoy the ducks.> There was little else to hunt in Iceland at the time. The reindeer herds from Norway didn't establish themselves until the mid-nineteenth century.

By the same token, there were no large land predators in Iceland. The most ferocious was the Arctic fox. No one would believe these men were taken down and savaged by Arctic foxes. When they were found, people would start hunting for whatever had killed them.

<We need to go,> Úlfur said. <Come. We can make Kirkjubæjarklaustur by tomorrow and get you some clothes. We will say you were robbed by brigands.> Úlfur was far better prepared for the change to wolf. He had a cache of clothes waiting for him, along with a pack of valuables.

<Brigands in Iceland?> I was incredulous. The reason I was able to travel alone as a courier and trader across the island was precisely because brigands couldn't make a living on the anemic commerce between settlements.

<Why not? Simply look miserable and they will believe you.>

Looking miserable wasn't difficult, since the transformation back to human was every bit as painful as it had been to wolf. The good people of Kirkjubæjarklaustur gave us clothes and food, and Úlfur bought us packs to carry supplies in for our long trek. We hiked cross-country between two glaciers to the north side of the island, sleeping in the open at night and fearing nothing. Rannveig spoke little to either of us and often wept at night. She did not want to be comforted.

We broke our journey for a time at Mývatn before continuing on to Húsavík. There we secured jobs on the coast; we could not join the fishermen or whalers for fear of being at sea when the full moon came around, so we found work elsewhere. We slowly became accustomed to being werewolves and added two more to our pack in Húsavík, another male and another female.

The plague hit Iceland two years later, in 1707. A quarter of the population died. I suggested to Úlfur that we grow the Pack a little bit more quickly than he intended, for every wolf would be safe from the plague and we would be saving lives as well as changing them. This was the first time I became aware of his deep-seated racism and outright bigotry. Úlfur agreed that saving lives while expanding the Pack was a good idea, but only for those of Scandinavian descent. Celts weren't allowed, nor was any other ethnic stock, and he'd prefer they be pagan as well. I did not understand the preference or the decree that consigned all other ethnic groups in Húsavík to a gruesome death.

When I tried to question him about it, Úlfur bristled and asked if I was questioning his leadership. I was second in the hierarchy, but the three other wolves in the Pack would often talk to me rather than to him. Rannveig, in particular, didn't talk to Úlfur unless she absolutely had to.

"Not your leadership," I replied, "only the reasoning behind your decision to exclude Celts from joining the Pack. I know of two sturdy men we could save from the plague at the next full moon." It was only three days hence.

"Celts would disturb the harmony of the Pack and sow dissension among us," he said, though I wasn't quite sure of what harmony he spoke. There was plenty of unrest and dissension as it was, even though our numbers were still in single digits at the time.

When we returned from our run under the full moon, those Celtic men were either dead or dying of the plague. It was a waste and a poor decision in my view, and it was the beginning of my discord with Úlfur.

"We could have saved those men," I said, and he snarled and cuffed me, sending me sprawling and turning my eyes yellow.

"The purity of species is pack law," he growled. "Never suggest again that we alter it." I thought he had a poor understanding of the difference between races and species, but I quelled the response in my throat and broke eye contact.

"As you wish, alpha," I said.

The next week I met a werewolf from another pack. His name was Hallbjörn Hauk. "I am the second in Reykjavík," he said, "under the leadership of Ketill Grímsson. You are the second for Úlfur Dalsgaard, are you not?"

"I am."

"I wonder if we may speak privately for a time?" he asked.

"There are few places we could go without the Pack knowing about it," I said. We were a small pack, but Húsavík was also a very small town.

Hallbjörn smiled. "I understand. I will be brief, then. Were you aware that Úlfur Dalsgaard used to be a part of the Reykjavík Pack and was cast out a little more than two years ago?"

"No, I was not. Why was he cast out?"

"He had ideas about racial purity that Ketill and others found distasteful. He would constantly denigrate or taunt pack members of differing backgrounds, including myself. I'm Anglo–Saxon on my father's side. Ketill told him to take his racial crusade elsewhere and banished him from Reykjavík."

"Why are you here?"

"To let you and the rest of your wolves know there is another pack in Iceland if you ever feel like moving elsewhere. You're welcome so long as you leave Úlfur's ideas behind. We are a motley crew."

"That's it? You came all the way here for that?"

"No. I'm also curious what you know about pack law."

"Úlfur makes it. The alpha's word is law."

"Of course. But what mechanism exists for a change of leadership?"

"I . . . what?"

"Say that someone in your pack disagrees with the alpha's word. It may be someone lower in the Pack, or it might be you. There might even be a majority of the Pack that agrees there should be a new alpha. What happens next?"

"I don't know."

Hauk snorted and shook his head, as if he'd expected such an answer. "Anyone may challenge the alpha for leadership at anytime. There's a fight. The winner is the alpha."

"What kind of fight?"

"The bloody kind. One wolf either yields or is wounded past the ability to heal."

"Interesting. Úlfur neglected to mention this particular pack dynamic to me."

"Guard your thoughts," Hauk warned. "If he hears what you're thinking through the pack link, you'll have a fight before you're ready."

"He can hear it now," I said. I called everyone except Úlfur to my house immediately for a meeting. He'd figure it out sooner rather than later, and either he'd show up to accept my challenge or he wouldn't. There were still people in Húsavík who could be saved from the plague.

Though it was the dark of the moon and our wolves were at their weakest, I announced my challenge to Úlfur through the pack link, then made the painful transformation of my own will and waited for Úlfur to arrive.

I will not dwell on the duel; it was short and brutal and I killed him in less than a minute. I did not realize my own strength until circumstances made it necessary for me to reach for it. But as he died, there was a small chill in the air that I did not remember or have an explanation for until many years later. I became alpha of the Húsavík Pack and then, later, alpha of all Iceland, after a dispute with Ketill Grímsson that has no bearing on this tale. My first act as alpha was to change pack law.

"When we recruit, ethnic heritage will not be a criterion determining a candidate's worthiness," I said. "Does anyone wish to question that decision or challenge my leadership?" No one did. They had supported Úlfur's replacement from the start.

My pack was twenty wolves strong when I moved us out of Iceland after the eruption of the Laki volcano in 1783. We came to the New World, and slowly we added to our numbers with wolves from many different backgrounds. Some of these left my pack and joined others, but many remained. Our largest jump in population occurred during the Spanish influenza outbreak of 1918. Until that time, I had not had many occasions to save lives through the gift of lycanthropy—which, as I was well aware, thanks to Rannveig, not everyone considered a gift. But during that time of terrible disease, I was reminded of the plague in Iceland and of our failure to save lives when we could. I was determined not to repeat that mistake this time. And so on the days immediately prior to the full moon that year, I instructed the Pack to keep their ears open for word of possible recruits. I wanted people who were without dependents to care for and who were on the verge of death. They also had to be dying at home in a rural area rather than in a hospital. We could not afford to give our existence away.

Few people matched my criteria, but wolves saved

eight people that year who otherwise would have died of influenza. None of them was Scandinavian.

There was a Native American man and a Mexican one, two Chinese women, a German teenager, a thin boy from India, a girl from England, and an immigrant from the Philippines who'd already lost the rest of his family to the virus. They were all lovely people and fantastic wolves. They enriched the lives of my entire pack, but especially Rannveig's.

She and I turned out to be very different wolves, you see. I was very dominant and she was quite submissive, despite her occasional flirtations with adventure. I could not take her for a mate, because she was incapable of behaving as an alpha, and the Pack would never accept such a submissive wolf in a leadership position. In fact, while everyone liked her, no one in the Pack wished to be her mate. So I was very glad for her sake when she fell in love with the man from the Philippines.

His name was Honorato, and he was finally able to relieve her of two centuries of misery. I am telling you, she was a new person once they paired off. Her earlier ideas about being damned faded, for how could such love be permitted to those who were damned? For the first time, she began to view her wolf as a blessing rather than a curse. If Úlfur had not chosen us centuries ago, she never would have met Honorato.

But Úlfur, though dead for hundreds of years, found a way to reach out and ruin her happiness from beyond the grave. That cold air I'd felt when he died—that was the Valkyries choosing him to join the Einherjar in Valhalla. I am sure of it. And there, while preparing for Ragnarok day after day, he must have distinguished himself enough to draw the attention of Thor. And once he gained that attention, he used it to turn a god into an assassin.

Ten years ago I took the entire pack on holiday in Norway. We visit someplace special every year, and since most of the Pack was of Norwegian or Icelandic background, they wanted to visit the homeland. We were to be there for a week, hunting and playing and indulging our wolves. On our third night there, the night of the full moon, the eight dear friends I'd saved in 1918—including Rannveig's husband—were struck down by lightning bolts. All the Scandinavian members of the Pack were left untouched. And I stress to you that we were not out in a storm. The sky was only partially cloudy, and I knew immediately that this could not possibly have been some accident of nature. My proof came when Thor descended in his chariot and spoke to me briefly. He took care to hover out of the Pack's reach.

He said, "Regards from Úlfur Dalsgaard, one of the finest Einherjar in Valhalla. He urges you to rethink your pack law regarding the recruitment of mixed races." And then he laughed at us as we snarled and barked at him, enjoying how powerless we were to confront him. He flew away without saying another word, leaving us to howl and mourn.

Rannveig, as you might imagine, was devastated. The howling she did that night for Honorato, her murdered husband, still haunts me to this day.

Thor is not part of my pack. He will never be part of my pack, nor can he have any voice in what pack law says or doesn't say. He had no business renewing a feud that I had justly settled long ago by sending Úlfur to Valhalla. And, from a human perspective, he had no business murdering people for any reason, much less for the color of their skin. There is nothing Úlfur could have offered him to make it worth his while, you see? He did it solely for his own entertainment. Can he therefore be called anything but evil?

Rannveig . . . well. She fell in battle two months ago
against witches armed with silver knives. Though I miss
her, I wonder sometimes if it wasn't a mercy. She was
suicidal after her husband's death. I think she would
have done it were it not for her wolf and her Lutheran
faith.

And now you see why I must go to Asgard. I cannot
kill Úlfur again—and even if I could, it wouldn't help,
since he learned nothing from the first time I killed him.
But I can kill Thor to avenge eight lives and one woman's
heart, and I will. Then, perhaps, I will not hear the howling at night.

Except for the crackling of logs in the fire, there was
no sound when Gunnar sat back down on his boulder.
I was thinking about the two werewolves that had
fallen in the battle against Aenghus Óg at Tony Cabin.
Their deaths had always been a touchy subject with the
entire pack, and now I understood a bit better why that
was so.

"I'm sorry about Rannveig," I said to Gunnar, breaking the silence, and he nodded sadly, though I wasn't
sure if he thought he was accepting an apology or sym-
pathy.

Zhang Guo Lao spoke up. "It pains me to hear that
Thor has treated you and your pack so abominably. I am
sorry to say it seems consistent with what I know of his
character."

"Is monstrous fuckpuddle," Perun asserted, and everyone turned to stare at him with equal parts amusement
and bemusement. "What? Is this not English word?"

I suggested that if it wasn't a word, it should be, and
the others agreed.

"I, too, have a crime to lay at Thor's door," Väinämöinen said after the levity of Perun's neologism faded.

"His feeble mind insists that his arrogant trespasses are somehow justifiable since he is a member of the Æsir. Any criticism levied against him is met with a thunder-bolt. Listen, and I will tell you how he violated a wonder of the world."

Chapter 16

The Wizard's Tale

Outside of Finland I am not widely known, and even there I am largely forgotten. Like so many other gods and folk heroes, I was shoved aside to make room for a new savior, who turned out to be a man with neither music, nor sex, nor any laughter, just a promise of paradise later in exchange for meek obedience now. I am not the son of yesterday's grouse: I could see that my people wished to swap me for something softer, and no matter how much I railed against it, no matter how much I struggled and strained, it wouldn't produce either a baby or shit.

The best thing for me to do would be to exit gracefully. So that is what I did: I sang myself a copper boat, packed my belongings, brushed out my beard, and my purpose held—like the Ulysses of Tennyson—to sail beyond the sunset, vowing to return one day when my people needed me. Someday, I thought, someday soon, they will tire of this pale, weak god, and then they will clamor for my homecoming. That was in the year of cone and helmet.

Now we are come many years forward, and still no one calls my name. I am tired of waiting. They will never shift back to my paradigm; my glory is centuries gone.

But in Asgard there is plenty of work for an axe.

I was bitter for a time, thinking myself cast away like the stale biscuits of a fortnight ago. But slowly, rising and falling with the swell of the ocean, a new rhythm emerged within me, a sense of the tide and what it washes away, and likewise what it brings to new shores. Music swirled from my *kantele* as the ocean waters swirled about my keel, and thus I sang myself into a finer state of mind.

I did not lack for food on my journey: I sang to the fish whenever I had stomach, and they leapt into my boat. Nor did I lack for company. I sang to the whales of sun and wheat and the animals of the earth, and they sang to me songs of currents and krill and ceaseless peregrination. More than this, they sang of old creatures still lurking in the depths, giant serpents that men sketch fearfully in the corners of maps.

Eventually I longed for land again and made fall on a green isle with clouds of steam rising from lakes of white water, spumes of spray erupting from the earth, each hotter than the anger of a wounded bear. Today this isle is called Iceland. There were Norsemen living on the western side, in modern-day Reykjavík, but I kept to myself on the opposite side, settling on the northern shore of a fjörd that later became the site of a town called Eskifjördur. A small shelter I built there, partly with my hands and partly with my voice, to break the wind's chill and keep my few treasures safe from the elements. This I did for solitude's sake, but not for misanthropic reasons. No, I so loved men that I shunned them to save them.

There were questions I harbored in my heart, but no man could answer them; there were sights I would see, but no man could show them to me; there were tales I would hear told and songs I would hear sung, but no man's voice could give them breath.

The whales, you see, had piqued my curiosity. There

were older things than I in the deeps, and it was with
them I wished to treat. I remained apart from men so
that if my embassies skewed awry from their intended
bent, no one but I would suffer the hammer's blow. And
after a month of fruitless attempts, in a gray twilight
brooding over a choppy sea, I finally drew a monster
from the deeps with nothing but my voice and my *kantele*.

I say "monster" only because that is what people tend
to call creatures that could eat men like hors d'oeuvres.
The surface boiled violently to herald its coming, and I
sang of peace and conversation and the pleasure of knowledge won and knowledge shared, and then it erupted from
the sea. It was a leviathan sheathed in blue-green scale, capable of swallowing a dragon ship whole, and it towered
above me to the height of six men, with far more of its
length remaining under the surface. It must have been supporting its body on the sea floor to raise its neck to such
an altitude.

Five bony ridges swept back from its head, and between these a membranous tissue grew and fluttered in
the wind, giving it the appearance of a crown. At the
time I thought it merely looked impressive, but soon I
learned that these were sensory organs that detected vi-
brations in the water. Its eyes were glossy tar pits twice
the size of my head, the better to see in sunless waters.
They found me standing on the shore, and the creature
bellowed a greeting, displaying foot-long teeth and a
black tongue. It had nostrils at the end of its snout,
which I quickly deduced were more for olfaction than
for breathing: Beneath its jaw and running some distance down its neck, gills flared and signaled it would
not remain above the surface for long. But it had seen
me, and I had seen it, and that was enough. It crashed
back into the cold water of the fjörd, but it did not leave.
After some thrashing about and repositioning of its

bulky length, the top of its head reemerged, so that I saw its obsidian eyes and the teal fan of its sensory crown. It spoke to me as the whales did, in a song unfathomable to most men, but as plain to me as your speech, or yours. So it is with all animal speech, and so it is that they can understand me. I played my *kantele* softly, and we spoke together.

<You are no fisherman,> it said. <What manner of man are you?>

"I am a shaman," I replied, "if I am any sort of man at all. A wizard, certainly. Some would say a folk hero. Some might say a god. But I am foremost a being of curiosity, and I am curious about you. What is your name?"

<I have no name in the tongue of men or gods. But sailors call me serpent. A monster.>

"What do you call yourself?"

<I have never thought it necessary to call myself, for I am always here. Do you ever call yourself?>

"No, but I have a name by which others call me."

<You have a name! What is it?>

"I am called Väinämöinen. Tell me, are there others like you?"

<There are the older ones. They taught me speech when first I swam the deeps, but now I am Curious and they will not speak to me until I am grown.>

"You say you're curious like it's a bad thing."

<Among my kind it is. It is our most dangerous time of life, when we seek knowledge of what lies on the surface. I will be Curious only a little while longer.>

"You are a child among your kind?"

<Only for a few more cycles of the sun. When next we harvest the blue whales, I will join the chorus of my people. They will sing to me my name and I will never rise to the surface again.>

"I see. How many of your people are there in a chorus?"

<I will make twelve. But there are other choruses in oceans far away. >

She—for the creature was female—asked me to build a fire, to see how it was done. She asked me where the lights in the sky were tonight, and I explained they were hidden by the clouds. She wondered why the clouds would do that. She wondered whether men had given names to the lights. She wondered how men got their names and how they kept them clean.

She told me the Remarkably Short Saga of Sheerth the Excessively Dim, He Who Sought the Secret Lair of the Giant Squid. She sang to me the Ballad of Moth the Valiant Born, She Who Fought the Sirens in the Grotto of Lime and Decay. She told me many secrets of the deep, such as the fate of fabled Atlantis; its gold and marble splendor serves the mermen now. There are treasures lying along the coasts of all nations, and off the coast of South America, sleeping gods of cold evil rest until the day they are called by men with dreams of power.

<Do you dream of power?> she asked. <Have you called me to destroy your enemies?>

"No, of course not. I am merely pleased to meet you and exchange knowledge of our worlds. We have much to teach each other before you earn a name in the harvest of the blue whales. What can I teach you? What would you know?"

We had long since spoken into deep night, with naught but a fire lighting the waters of the fjörd. Flickers of lightning played about the billowing skirts of clouds, and these flashes occasionally lit up the shore. The great creature's snout lifted up toward the low ceiling in the sky after a particularly bright display.

<What causes those flashes in the sky?>

I chuckled. "There are many explanations for those. One god or another is usually credited for them."

\<What do these gods look like?\>

"The god of the Norse is named Thor. He rides a chariot pulled by two goats—horned animals with four legs—and wears a large belt that doubles his strength."

\<Would that be he, there?\>

"Where?" I turned to look over my shoulder and saw a bright ball of lightning writhing in the sky. It centered round the head of a hammer, beneath which was a raised hand and a scowling visage wreathed in blond hair. The edges of a chariot and the horns of two goats were starkly highlighted. Nothing else could be discerned, other than that the thunder god was quickly approaching, intent on the two of us.

Fearful of his intentions, I frantically began to wave. "No!" I cried. "Wait!"

But Thor threw forward his arm, and the coiled lightning arced down to strike the magnificent creature in the eye. She screamed and reared up in pain, then plunged herself into the fjörd, more lightning bolts following her and burning holes into her scaled hide wherever it showed above the surface.

I dropped my *kantele* and proceeded to jump and gesticulate and call him the brain-dead spawn of a lackwitted shepherd, but to no avail. He kept hammering the poor beast wherever he could as she desperately tried to make it out of the shallow fjörd to the open sea. I ran to my hut and retrieved a spear from my small cache of weapons. This I quickly enchanted for true flight and hurled at the nearest one of Thor's goats. It spitted him cleanly and the chariot lurched violently to the side, spilling the thunder god into the sea.

This managed to secure his attention.

She who had sung to me was given a reprieve from the lightning, and I took up my *kantele* again to speak to her.

"Dive deeply and never rise again," I told her. "I am

so sorry." Nothing coherent came in reply, just a sense of agony and bewildered betrayal. I berated myself for not concealing us with a seeming, and for not acting more decisively to halt Thor before he could unloose the destruction of the skies upon her. Here was a terrible price to pay for our mutual curiosity. But she was still alive. Perhaps she would live if I prevented the thunder god from attacking further.

He thrashed to the surface, collecting more lightning to his hammer held high above the waves. I targeted him with my voice and sang a song to calm his rage. His remaining goat strained to land the chariot on shore, dragging both his dead companion and the chariot behind him.

I could not see the leviathan anymore, but apparently Thor had some sense of her location, for he struck out with clear intent at a certain swell in the ocean near the entrance to the fjörd, heedless of my song and immune to its spell.

A flare of pain lashed out from the sea and seized my mind, and I staggered backward. Then there was nothing, simply nothing.

After that I needed to sing a song to calm my own rage. The flood of it nearly loosed itself upon him, with no dam to stop it save my will; yet I knew that Thor could stand against that tide if anyone could, and furthermore I knew that I was woefully unprepared to fight him at that time. I had no defense against lightning. Instead, I did what I should have done earlier and cast a seeming over my presence to hide myself from his eyes. As Thor pulled himself through the water with powerful strokes toward the shore, I cast another seeming on my small hut and yet one more on my voice, so that when I spoke next Thor would not know from whence it came.

The thunder god emerged from the sea looking every bit as angry as I felt. He took the hammer from his belt, where he'd secured it during his swim, and shook it threateningly in my general direction.

"Coward! Show yourself! You who slew my goat! Answer for it!"

"Will you answer for slaying the leviathan?" I said. My voice boomed from every direction, and the thunder god spun, trying to locate me.

"I have nothing to answer for!" he shouted. "I did the world a service."

"Do the world another and slay yourself. That creature was harming no one."

"Foolish mortal! It was about to eat you!"

"We were speaking peaceably and you murdered it without divining its true intent. And I am not mortal."

His expression turned incredulous, then composed itself into a contemptuous sneer. "What are you, some sorcerer who keeps serpents as pets?"

I replied in the same tone, "What are you, a thick-headed, arrogant god who thinks immortality excuses all sins?"

The sneer left his face, which reddened as he shouted in a circle, making sure I heard him. "That creature was a spawn of the world serpent and as such was my rightful prey! I merely practice for Ragnarok. What was your purpose? Jörmungandr will not wait for any man's permission to attack Asgard, so I shall not stay my hand against those who would hasten its coming." He stalked over to his chariot and yanked my spear out of his slain goat before tossing it into the fjörd. Then, with a touch of his hammer, he resurrected the beast, who looked a bit wild-eyed but otherwise none the worse for having been dead.

"Witness the power I wield, whoever you are," he said. "I am life and death. Vex me further at your peril."

He waited for a reply, but I made none. The time to vex him further is now; it was not then.

Satisfied that he had cowed me sufficiently, he mounted his chariot and snapped the reins, flying back into the dark clouds that had concealed his approach.

From that day to this I have mourned the loss of my unnamed friend and cursed the name of Thor. He ripped from me the wonder of the ocean; he stole from all men the knowledge of a world they can never inherit. The Finns may no longer need an old wizard to watch over them, but Thor still needs to answer for his callous murder.

I have salted my hatred and cured it, stored it in a dark cellar of my mind against the day when I could let it be my only nourishment. The day is finally come, and I will tear into this meat and savor its taste.

Väinämöinen's last words were a guaranteed applause line with this crowd. Perun suggested that it called for a toast. He pulled a bottle of vodka from somewhere and started pouring. I joined in, more out of appreciation for his lyricism than from any bloodthirsty sentiment against Thor. What had stunned me from the moment he described his unnamed friend was how it recalled what Odysseus had told me in Hades—I hadn't been lying when I told Granuaile that the sirens had spoken to him of hasenpfeffer and sea serpents. What they'd said, essentially, was a bunch of rubbish to the fabled king of Ithaca, but to me it all made perfect sense. They had sung to him a series of prophecies that were far more accurate than anything Nostradamus spewed forth.

That was the attraction of the sirens: not promises of power or riches, but bewildering, tantalizing prophecies that made men leap from their ships to go ask the crazy bitches what the fuck they were talking about. Or, if that didn't work, then they leapt when the sirens said they knew what would happen to the sailors or to the sailors' families. Odysseus lost his shit and demanded to be freed from the mast when they sang their prophecies about Penelope and Telemachus.

Odysseus never saw any of their prophecies come true, but I did. He related to me what they said—word for word, because they were burned indelibly into his memory—and they were creepily accurate. They'd predicted the Black Death in Europe and the breadth of the Mongol Empire. They said things like, "The red coats will be defeated in the New World," and "Two cities in Asia will perish under clouds shaped like mushrooms." They added that "A man with a glass face will walk on the moon," and "People will never get along in Jerusalem." Only one of their predictions hadn't come true yet: "Thirteen years from the time a white beard in Russia sups on hares and speaks of sea serpents, the world will burn."

Cue the shivering violins. Had I just witnessed the beginning of a final countdown? Was Väinämöinen the herald of the apocalypse? It occurred to me, rather uncomfortably, that if this final prophecy of the sirens came true, it would be shortly after the time Granuaile completed her training and became a full Druid.

Correlation does not imply causation, I reminded myself. Maybe the sirens were talking about global warming.

Perun was growing more convivial the more he drank. He was pounding two shots of vodka to every one of ours. Aside from getting happier, he showed no other effects of inebriation. Perhaps this was one of his godlike powers.

"Is time for my tale, yes?" he said, rising smoothly to his feet and grinning amiably at us. "You maybe thinking, Perun just jealous of Thor. He does not want to share sky. But you would be wrong!" He pointed a finger at me and then waved it around clockwise to indicate everyone. "Plenty of sky for all gods. Plenty of men

and women to make worship, plenty of vodka—hey."
He halted, raising his eyebrows at us and holding up his
bottle. "You want more?" No one took him up on the
offer, so he shrugged and poured himself a shot.

"I drink alone, then." He tossed it back, winced appreciatively at the burn in his throat, and exhaled noisily.

"Ahhhh, is good. Good, very good. Now, listen like
thieves."

I looked at him sharply to discern whether he'd inten-
tionally alluded to an INXS song, but he appeared unconscious of making any pop culture reference at all, and
no one else seemed to recognize it.

"I tell you what happened. But I tell it short, yes? English is no good for me."

Chapter 17

The Thunder God's Tale

Americans say all men created equal. These words very good. Make men feel special. They know is not true, not really, but they always *say* is true, and they point to these words and say, Ideas like this make us strong. They turn mouse into bear. They turn dog into bear. Everything can become strong like bear if you think with American brains. But if everything is bear, what do bears eat?

Americans want magic, perfect world. But these places only seen in movies. People never equal, same as animals never equal. There is always predator and prey. Little fish make dinner for big fish, yes? And there is always bigger fish.

Is same with ideas. Exact same. Small ideas eat up by big ideas. Big ideas stay for long time in brains of men. Small ones forgotten; is like little fish eaten up by big fish.

Gods are big ideas. They stay for long time in brains. They walk on earth or live in sky or water or under ground. But even gods can be eaten by bigger gods.

I was eaten by Christ. You see? Christ ate many gods. I mean he ate me as idea, not as flesh. He ate me and other Slavic gods. He ate Celtic gods and Greek gods, Roman gods and Norse gods—even Väinämöinen here—and took their places in brains of men. Some of those old gods are dead now. Men have forget—no, forgot—them.

But I am not gone from all brains yet. There are some who remember me. There are some who still worship. I will not die until they forget.

Yet I am weak like kitten. Not strong like days before Christ came to my lands. And reason is Odin and Thor.

At first I think only Thor did this. Later I think Odin ask him to do it. Thor comes to me and say, "My people build me finer statues than yours. They love me more than your people love you. Nothing is finer than statues and stone tributes."

He shows me his statues in Sweden. He shows me his tributes in Norway and Denmark, and they are fine indeed. I become envious. I become jealous. I ask my people to build me stone tributes. Wooden ones too. Not only for me but for my pantheon. This is how you show love for me, I say. And so my good people do this, and soon I have monuments and statues better than Norse ones.

But later I see truth. Is hard to write on stone. So hard that it is better to write nothing at all. And any writing that goes on statues gets worn away by time. So then Christ comes with his reading monks and their printed word, and idea of Christ remains and grows while idea of Perun washes away in rain and wind.

This is how gods are strong today. Christ, Allah, Yahweh, Buddha, Krishna: They have pages and pages of words about them. These words travel everywhere to bring idea of them to new generations. I have stone statues that travel nowhere. If lucky, I get half hour of man on History Channel asking who I was in deep voice.

Odin saw this coming. He sent Thor to me to trick me into slow death. Then he sent Thor to Iceland to have their skaldic poets write *Eddas*. Centuries later, when it is too late, I see what happen. Norse remembered because of *Eddas*. They still weaker than before Christ, but much stronger than me. Because of words. Because now children in many parts of the world hear about them. And so they are bigger ideas.

What can I do now? If I appear to men and say, I am Perun, I am a god, they will say, No, you are just very scary hairy man. This has happened. A man in Minsk said to me, Put down that axe and I will give you brush for hair.

If I say to men, Look, I control thunder, they say, No, that is natural force. Is science. Or coincidence. Magic does not exist. Gods do not exist. No belief, you see, is as strong as their disbelief.

And besides, they say to me, even if gods are real, you cannot be god of thunder. That is Thor.

You see what Thor has done? Among all thunder gods in world, he is now supreme in minds of men. He has done this with words and by tricking me. He has stolen my thunder, as saying goes.

And not only mine. I pay visit to other thunder gods. Shango in Africa, Susanoo in Japan, Ukko in Finland. All of them get visit from Thor, and Thor say to them, Oral tradition is best, or carve this in wood, or scratch this on rock, and you will be remembered. But none of them remembered now like Thor, except Olympians.

Zeus and Jupiter doing fine. Much written about them by their people. Thor and Odin doing very well. And I think they see this time coming long ago. Old One-Eye throws runes, or he talks to Norns, and he sees what he must do to remain strong in age of science. He sees that he must make idea of Norse become bigger than ideas of Slavs or Celts or other peoples. And he sees he can do this with words instead of spear. He sends Thor out to world, statues and carvings get made, and many gods of world fall prey to bigger ideas.

Their words—their lies—have made me little fish. But

I am still fish with sharp teeth. They owe me blood. My axe will take it. Is all I have to say.

The lightning flash in Perun's eyes was not so friendly by the time he finished his tale. I thought his self-assessment was remarkable for a god. I could not imagine the Morrigan, for example, frankly asserting that she was a little fish. Flidais would never contemplate the possibility that she might be prey; she was always the predator. Perun's ability to do so spoke of a certain realism spawned by many painful hours of reflection. His seeming good humor most likely masked a terrible rage.

I checked the magical spectrum to see if the stories were doing the trick, and it appeared they were. There were bonds forming between the men who had told their tales, gossamer threads of camaraderie twining between their auras. To those who hadn't spoken yet, the bonds flowed only one way. Weakest of all, however, was my own bond to them. Thor had never done anything to me personally, so I couldn't relate to them in this way. I'd bond to them later through different tales, some other shared experience that would make us brothers.

There were two left. Everyone looked at Leif, but he stared at Zhang Guo Lao and nodded at him, indicating that the alchemist should go next. The ancient immortal returned the nod, acquiescing, and cleared his throat delicately.

"If leisure serves, I will offer my experience now," he said.

There were replies of "Aye, Master Zhang," and "Please, sir," and "Excellent." The immortal Zhang Guo Lao rose and bowed to us, then began his tale.

Chapter 18

The Alchemist's Tale

Begging your forgiveness for this poor, simple tale; it is a trifling matter only and not weighted with portent and substance like the adventures you have shared with me.

In elder days I walked the earth as a simple man, learning the mystery of the Tao. Through study and application I conceived the Elixir of Immortality; through battle and experiment I won reputation; through legend and worship I acquired godlike power. Wisdom eludes me yet, but foolishness I captured long ago and to this day it is my constant companion, though many people consider me wise.

Throughout China I am known for riding upon a white donkey. My portrait, sketched many times, always shows me astride my companion. This ass was a singular creature; he brought me much fame. He carried me for thousands of *li* every day, and when I arrived at my destination, I folded him up like a work of origami and put him in my cap box. When I was ready to travel again, I would squirt water from my mouth upon the paper donkey and it would expand and grow to its normal size.

It was in this very part of the earth where I met Thor seven hundred thirty years ago. I was making camp for the night, about to fold up my donkey for the night, when he descended from the sky in his chariot pulled by two goats. Though the night was chill, he wore a fur wrapped around his hips, secured by a belt, and nothing else save a pair of fur boots laced up with rawhide.

We exchanged greetings. He did not speak Mandarin and I did not speak Old Norse, but we both knew a third language, Russian, and we communicated brokenly in that, happy to have the practice. He smiled and was very charming. I invited him to join me for a humble dinner of fish broth and vegetables.

"Why content ourselves with meager fish when we can feast on our animals?" the god asked.

"I cannot eat my own ass," I said, though I thought it should be obvious to him. "He carries me wheresoever I wish."

Thor shrugged. "I need my goats to pull my chariot. That doesn't stop me from eating them whenever I get hungry."

"You must have a very large herd of goats to indulge in such wanton consumption," I said.

"Not at all. There are only these two."

"Will you not be stranded if you eat them, then?"

He brandished his hammer. "No. I simply touch them with this, and they are resurrected from their bones."

"Surely you jest."

"Nay, I am in earnest. See for yourself." He slew his goats with two quick strikes of his hammer, and then he gutted them and cooked large pieces of them over my fire. We ate until we were full, but I kept looking at the sad remains of their bodies lying on the ground. When we had finished, Thor stood over the carcasses of his goats and softly, even tenderly, touched them with his hammer. Immediately they sprang back to life, healthy as when they'd arrived, formed out of nothing more than skin and bones. They seemed content to graze nearby for the rest of the night.

"Remarkable," I told him. "I have never seen such doings."

"Efficiency," Thor said. "It makes traveling much simpler. Where are you bound?"

We spoke of our travels and traded tales of faraway cities. He was affable and polite, and for that evening I enjoyed his company. When I folded up my donkey for the evening, he looked like a fish gasping for air.

"I am truly astonished, Master Zhang!" Thor said, his eyes following me as I carefully stored my donkey in my cap box. "What a novel way to stable your beast! But does that not make it easier to steal?"

"This box never leaves my possession during the night. It is very secure. And, besides, stealing it would prove no advantage. To everyone else save me, it is nothing more than a worthless piece of folded paper."

He stayed the night with me on the other side of the fire, and in the morning he asked if he might travel with me some distance, since my company was so refreshing. I agreed, for to have a well-traveled companion is no small comfort on a long journey. We spoke of novelties to be found in various corners of the earth, each cataloging future adventures to seek, courtesy of the other's advice.

When it came time to camp again and think about cooking dinner, Thor suggested we try something different. "I have been eating goat for far too long. I'm in the mood for something new. Why do we not eat your donkey? I will resurrect him tomorrow."

"Oh, no, I could never do that to him," I said, holding my hands up in protest.

"He won't remember a thing," the thunder god assured me. "Look you, my goats show no fear of men or gods, though I kill them every day when I travel. They are every bit as strong as the day they first became mine. The entire process will be painless. Please reconsider as a favor to me, your guest."

We were not at my home; we were merely traveling together. I did not think the customs of hospitality applied in this case. Still, I did not wish to be rude or give the impression of stubborn selfishness, and soon I had granted him permission.

He swung his hammer down onto my dear donkey's skull, and the animal was dead before he hit the ground. We ate—but I will not relive that for you.

After we finished eating, I requested that he resurrect my donkey as promised.

"Of course, I will do that shortly," Thor said, wiping his greasy hands on the furs he had wrapped about his loins. "But if you will be patient a moment longer, I urgently need to relieve myself." He gestured toward the woods and walked off behind some underbrush to answer the call of nature. I, too, felt the call, so I walked in the opposite direction and found some privacy of my own.

Imagine my surprise and horror when I came back to the campfire, only to see the thunder god rising into the air in his chariot, his cold laughter falling down on me like stinging sleet. "Thanks for the meal, fool!" he called, and I knew then that I had been gulled. He left me there, stranded in Siberia with the bloody remains of my donkey, a victim of my own good manners.

I have never known such humiliation. To be tricked and preyed upon by a lout such as he—the impossibility of it beggars my imagination, while the reality of it galls my conscience. My shame feeds my rage, and my inner peace has left me, seeking shelter elsewhere until my turmoil is spent. Even now, sharing this with you, I tremble with anger. Ever since that time, I age quickly and must drink ever more elixir to keep myself alive. I would have respite from these feelings. I would have a reckoning. I have imagined our confrontation almost daily for hundreds of years, and my chest aches with the need to pay

him for the injury he dealt me. I am not afraid of his
hammer. He will never be able to touch me with it, and
he will find that he cannot use it to effect his own resurrection.

Leif made some throat-clearing noises. Vampires were
not afflicted with an excess of mucus in their esophagi,
so this was purely an effort to politely call our attention.

"If there be no objections," he said, "I would like to
begin my tale presently. The earth still spins on its axis
and dawn approaches. I would like to finish prior to that
with some time to spare."

We were all immediately attentive and deferential. It
was Leif who had pushed most strongly for our expedition, and, as far as I could tell, he'd been longing for it for
a thousand years. The bone he had to pick with Thor
must be the size of a whale rib, and I'd never before heard
precisely what it was.

Chapter 19

The Vampire's Tale

I met Thor once a thousand years ago, when I was still human. Since that meeting, my every action has been calculated to bring me closer to meeting him again.

I was a colonist of Iceland in early times. A proud Viking man, carving out sustenance from the raw earth, and faithful to my family and my gods. Though it galls me to say it now, when I was human I gave to Thor all honor and obeisance. I wore this hammer necklace every day. I praised him, and Odin, Freyja, and Freyr—all of the Norse. And I hoped one day I would feast in Valhalla and be served mead by the Valkyries, take my place among the Einherjar, and fight in Ragnarok, at the end of all things, against the children of Muspell. All that was in another age, but there I must return if you are to know how I come to be here today.

My wife was named Ingibjörg. Together we had two sons, Sveinn and Ólaf. I fished, kept some sheep, and even turned the earth with my hands.

I was considered a candidate for the Althing. I had seen the New World with Leif Eriksson and returned. I might have extended my acquaintance with the famous explorer, except that he converted to Christianity and insisted that all his men do the same. Nevertheless, I was well traveled and my sword had sent seven and twenty men to Valhalla. Every new accomplishment swelled my ego, increased my fame, and added to the stories I could tell over a tankard of ale in a tavern. I am sure you know how drunken conversations can turn bawdy and even bizarre in the space of a few seconds. Someone will crack a joke, someone else will riff on it, and before you know it you are talking about ridiculous things you would never consider when sober, such as the possibility of breeding blue cows or making weapons out of puffin bills.

One such conversation set me on the path that brought me here.

I was drinking mead on a chilly spring evening with two friends and two strangers. Strangers were common enough near Reykjavík; someone was always sailing in from somewhere. These particular two were big, hulking men, even larger than me, blond and blue-eyed and fresh from raiding and pillaging the coast of Ireland. All of us had been raiders at some point, and to many people we were the scariest things in the world. Naturally, we were scared of something else, and that night we were trying to frighten one another. I mined the stories told on dragon ships, mutterings in the dark that hardened, seasoned men found terrifying. Some were about men who turned into wolves on the full moon. Others were about degenerate creatures that ate the flesh of the dead and took on the form of the one they last consumed. And some that I had heard, more than once, concerned beings who drank blood and lived for centuries. They had inhuman strength and speed and could tear a berserker apart in seconds without shield or sword. But, more than this, they possessed a cold intelligence. They were the power behind the Romans, the tales said. They were slowly moving north and would eventually come to Viking lands; judging by a few mysterious deaths, a powerful one had supposedly established itself in Prague, the capital of Bohemia. The term today is *vampire*, but that is a modern word applied in the last few centuries. There were different names used back then: *revenant* or *diable*, in French; *blutsauger* in Germany; in Bohemia we were *chodící mrtvola*, a walking corpse. Every so often, the legends said, these creatures made others like them, damning men's souls forever with evil so foul that they could not stand the kiss of sunlight on their skin.

"Would it not be grand to be immortal?" I said to the men crowded around a wooden table. "Think of what treasure could be hoarded. What influence one could wield. Think of the lands one could visit if only there were time enough to do it."

"You would do this if you could?" one of the strangers said. He carried a large hammer instead of a sword, and I remember thinking at the time that it suited him. "If these creatures truly exist, you would sacrifice your humanity?"

"Well, not now, of course. There is my family to think about. In a younger, more reckless time of life, however, I would leap at the chance."

"Truly? You would give up Valhalla, the food and drink of Odin's table, for what? A sunless, bloodsucking existence on Midgard?"

"You are leaving out the part where I would be incredibly strong and live for centuries." My companions thought this rejoinder was particularly witty and laughed. Everything was funny when you had drunk enough mead.

"Fine." The stranger spread his hands. "I grant you your own definition. But you would prefer this to the glory and honor of becoming one of the Einherjar?"

"Again, I cannot say yes now. I have responsibilities to my family and my community. But if I were just starting out again, nothing holding me back, then why not?"

The stranger sat back in his chair and glared at me. "Why not, indeed?" He looked at his companion, who had lost one of his hands in battle. There was an unspoken query on the first stranger's face, and the one-handed man answered it with an indifferent shrug.

One of my friends tried to change the topic to dragons, but the first stranger interrupted him. "Very well, it is decided. You are Leif Helgarson, are you not?"

I blinked in mild surprise. I could not recall introducing myself or either of my friends introducing me. We had merely begun talking with these strangers in the way veteran warriors will, ready to share laughs but not names unless we planned on seeing them again.

"Yes. Who are you?"

"I am Thor, god of thunder."

My companions and I thought it was a fine joke and laughed in his face. He did not smile, however, nor did his one-handed companion.

"You say you would become one of these creatures if you had nothing to hold you back," he said. "My gift to you is freedom to pursue this dream of yours. You are free of your familial obligations, Leif Helgarson. Now you can follow through on your boast and become a blood-sucking immortal. I dare you."

"What are you talking about?" I said.

One of my friends chimed in. "I want whatever that guy's drinking."

"Your family is dead," the stranger insisted. "Nothing is holding you back."

All laughter ceased. "That is not funny."

"I do not jest," the stranger replied.

"My family is well. I saw them this morning."

"Lightning can strike at any time, and it struck a few moments ago."

I wanted to crunch my fist into his face, but if I wished to join the Althing my fighting days were over. I would profit nothing from starting a brawl. So I roughly excused myself instead and left the tavern, a bit unsteady on my feet, and discovered that a storm had rolled in while I'd been drinking. I had some trouble mounting my horse but eventually succeeded. I hurried home in the rain, telling myself that I was being silly, that could not have been Thor, it was just a big bastard with a hammer.

My dread mounted in equal measure with my denial as I rode. That was never Thor. But what if it was? What if a careless moment of drunken braggadocio had doomed my family?

You may imagine the desolation I felt when I burst through my door and found my wife and sons strewn limply about the lodge, their lives burned away. My heart became ash and I tasted nothing but bile.

Guilt and grief: My throat closed with it, choking me and letting nothing but animal cries escape. I sank to the floor, weeping for them and telling them, when I could manage, that I was so very sorry.

Sometimes I cheer myself by thinking perhaps they went to Freyja's hall, Fólkvangr, for they did nothing wrong. But that would have been a mercy of the gods, and Thor was anything but merciful. More likely they went to Hel, a sunless, cheerless realm, because I, in a fit of inebriated bombast, laid claim to powers beyond my ken.

I built them a funeral ship and sent them to sea aflame. No land has been green for me since that day. It is all a waste, all emptiness. Inside me an emptiness grew as well, a black gnawing void that threatened to eat me and give Thor his victory. But I fought against this: I filled that emptiness with rage and discovered that my rage was as boundless as the emptiness. And so I did not break. I had my purpose: become an immortal and kill Thor. He had dared me.

And, in truth, it was the only way I could see to even challenge him. What cared I for damnation? I was already damned. But immortality, strength, speed—these I would need if I were to ever avenge my family, and I vowed to do so at any cost.

I left my farm, traveled to Reykjavík, and hired myself on the next boat to Europe. By a bit of mercenary work here and a bit of banditry there, I made my way back to the North Sea and thence up the Elbe to Hamburg. This was in 1006, well before the Polish King Mieszko II burned Hamburg to cinders. With some inquiry and patience, I found work as a sword arm to a merchant who wished to trade upriver with Prague. He was anxious to establish ties with the court of Duke Jaromír, part of the Přemyslid dynasty in Bohemia. He taught me some of the language during the trip, but it was practically useless. He did not know Old Norse, and my German was terrible at the time, but I kept at it because I knew I would need to ask questions of the locals if I were to find this blood-drinking immortal who had supposedly settled in Bohemia.

We turned up the Vltava River to get to Prague. It was not then the beautiful city it is today. Like all other medieval cities, Prague was dirty and mean and full of the illiterate and diseased. I myself fit that description fairly well. There was a thriving slave market in the city, which was a trade center for the region, with many merchants basing their operations there.

Once I'd helped to unload the German merchant's cargo, I got a job at the docks guarding warehouses; it was boring work, but it kept my belly full and paid for a room while I learned the language. Eventually, when snow began to fall, I started to frequent the taverns and ask questions. Sometimes my questions were met with drunken amusement and were openly mocked. To these places I never returned. In other places, my questions were met with stony silence or a curt warning that such things were not spoken of there. I was kicked out of one establishment for daring to ask. I noticed that these places were all located near the old Přemyslid fortress on the west side of the river—it's the Hradčany Castle now, but English speakers simply call it Prague Castle.

For two months I made a nuisance of myself. I had met every drunk in the town and many occasional drinkers besides and learned nothing of significance. I was about to give up and try elsewhere—Rome, I heard, was the place to go—when a small man, richly dressed with a high collar underneath a gray squirrel cloak, sat down next to me in a tavern on the west side. His dark beard was trimmed into a thin line around his jaw, but his mustache was thick and groomed. He spoke the Bohemian language, but he had a foreign accent that I could not place. The barkeep served him quickly and nervously and scampered away. He did not want to overhear our conversation.

"You are the northman who has been asking questions about blood drinkers," he said. It was not a question; it was identification.

"Who are you?" I asked.

"I am no one of importance. I represent a gentleman— a scholar—who may be able to answer your questions. Would you like to meet him?"

I peered at him suspiciously. "Is this an invitation to my death? I have seen people frown at me and heard the muttered oaths. The Christians, especially, do not like me speaking of this. Are you one of them? You have a group of men outside ready to silence me forever?"

"Hardly," the small man snorted. "This gentleman merely wishes conversation. I think you might survive."

"Why does he not come here and talk to me? Tell him where I am."

"He already knows where you are. That is why I am

here. You must forgive him; he is somewhat of a recluse. He is obsessed with converting his scrolls to books. Have you heard of these?"

"Yes, I have seen books. The Christian monks and priests have them."

"Precisely. But they have only one book, do they not? My employer has many in his library and is making more. He has learned how to make paper from the Arabs, who learned it from the Chinese. Now he employs the literate in copying his scrolls and turning them into books."

"Why not simply copy the scrolls?"

"Books are sturdier. Easier to travel with. Are you able to read?"

I shrugged. "I know the word *tavern* in three languages. That probably does not count."

The small man chuckled. "No, but that is a good word to know. Perhaps there is much you can learn from my employer. Will you not return with me to his study?"

"This is not an ambush?" I asked again.

He finished his drink and toyed with his mustache before answering. "I will not raise a hand against you. Neither will anyone I've employed, nor anyone my employer has hired. Good enough?"

"What about your employer?"

"I cannot speak for him. He is a . . . violent defender of knowledge, shall we say. But I believe he merely wishes to speak with you. That is all I can say."

"Hmm. What is your employer's name?"

"He will give it to you if he wishes."

"Very well. I will go with you." We settled our tabs with the barkeep and walked into a softly moonlit evening in the Little Quarter. The small man did not offer light conversation but kept silent. I kept my eyes moving and a hand on my sword hilt. After three blocks we stopped at the gate of a walled compound. The guards there recognized the small man.

"I have brought him," he said, and the gates were opened. Beyond them was an impressive house—impressive for the time, anyway—its façade lit by torches in the brick courtyard in which we currently walked. There was a fountain. Flower beds. Architecture. This bookbinder was a wealthy man.

My guide led me into a candlelit foyer. The floors were marble and covered with Persian rugs. Tapestries hung on the walls. It was the sort of wealth one saw only when raiding a monastery, and it exceeded anything in my personal experience. I caught but a few glimpses of the rooms on that floor, because the mustachioed man led me down a flight of stairs into the basement. There was a hallway with periodic candle sconces and several doors that I could see. We stopped at the first one and my guide knocked.

"Come," a voice said from the other side.

We entered a room lined entirely with bookshelves. Of course it was a library, but I had never seen such a room before. A long worktable scattered with loose pages, scraps of leather, and strange tools led my eyes to a pale man standing at the end of it. Though it was winter and quite chilly in the basement—and I was grateful for the warmth provided by my cloak—this man seemed unaffected by the cold. He wore rich purple silk imported from Asia; the fabric was new to me, but I recognized immediately that it was far superior to linen and wool. He was examining a book he'd apparently just pulled from a wooden vise.

"Ah, you must be the northman. Magnificent," he said.

"You must be the mysterious scholar," I replied. "I am Leif Helgarson."

"It is my pleasure to meet you." He placed his book gently on the table and inspected me frankly. "Tall, blond, and Viking. Excellent."

I could have noted at that point that he was none of these, but I had no wish to be rude. Yet. "And what shall I call you?" I asked.

He paused to consider, communicating that any name he gave me would not be his true one. "You may call me Björn."

"That is not your name."

"No. It is what you may call me. My name has a high price."

"You paid nothing for mine," I said.

"Untrue. You have cost me much already with your ceaseless pursuit of a blood drinker in Prague." He shifted his gaze to my guide. "Thank you. You may leave us." After the unnamed servant closed the door behind him, the unnamed scholar smiled thinly and resumed. "Tell me, Mr. Helgarson, why you are so keen to find a creature who drinks nothing but blood."

"Are you such a one?"

He waved my question away. "More about me later. Tell me about you. Your curiosity has piqued mine."

There was no point in crafting evasions. Either he could help me or he could not. "I have heard that these creatures possess great strength and long life. I need that to avenge my family. Thor killed them, and so he needs killing in return. But I will never be successful without the time and means to do it."

"You want to kill a god?" he said, raising an eyebrow.

"Not just any god. Thor."

"And thus you want to become one of these creatures?"

"Yes."

The scholar studied me and rolled his tongue around in his mouth. Abruptly, he laughed. "That is a new one, I must admit. I give you credit for novelty. So you are not a Christian?"

"No."

"Are you aware that the Christians believe these creatures to be damned—or even demons?"

"Yes."

"Because you know that you must die to become one of these creatures and then hope you rise from the dead?"

"I have heard that, yes."

"Tell me, Viking, what would you suffer for the cause of vengeance? What atrocities would you commit in the name of revenge?"

I paused to consider. "If it brought me closer to my goal, I suppose I would suffer anything, commit most any crime."

"Most any?"

"I have . . . no stomach for harming the young."

This brought a wry smile to the scholar's face. "Because they are innocent?"

"No, it is not that. I have killed innocent men and women along with the corrupted. Whatever they are when their doom falls, they are what the Norns have made them, and I am merely the instrument of their end. But children . . . are incomplete. I suppose the Norns do not wish to finish the ones who die, but then, neither do I, if you see what I mean."

"Interesting. You dislike leaving things undone."

"Precisely. And slaying Thor is something that must be done."

He said mockingly, "Do not the Norns have something planned for him? A battle with a serpent, I believe?"

"I will figure something out. But, first, I need time."

"So single-minded! You wish to subvert fate to your own will. That will truly take some figuring. I can see that you have trained your body to dominate others with the sword. Can you train your mind to dominate with the word?"

"What do you mean?"

"I am asking if you would be willing to learn how to read and write."

"What purpose would that serve? I am not going to write Thor a letter."

"It would serve many purposes, but primary among them would be your survival. Let us suppose that you become one of these blood drinkers. The long life and strength you speak of would have to come at a steep price, or else such creatures would be everywhere, would they not?"

"I suppose that makes sense."

"Excellent. So what price do you think these creatures might have to pay?"

I frowned. "They never see the sun again."

"Correct. What else?"

This question earned my host a noncommittal shrug. "I suppose there is the damnation to worry about if one is Christian. But I am not worried about this."

"No, there is something more you are missing."

"What?"

The scholar sighed and, instead of answering, said, "Let us sit. My manners have escaped me. Are you hungry? Thirsty?"

"I could do with a drink, thank you. Ale or mead or whatever you have."

We left the basement library and bookbindery and returned upstairs. The scholar—for I refused to address him as Björn—asked a servant to bring a drink to the sitting room. It contained four chairs and a fireplace but no windows. There was a fire in the hearth, but the smoke was traveling up into an unseen hole rather than filling the room. My host saw my puzzled stare and explained.

"Ah, the smoke is traveling up a device called a chimney, where it exits above the roof. Wonderful innovation. We can enjoy the fire's heat without suffering its smoke. Every house will have one eventually, you will see."

He offered me a chair and took the one opposite. A handsome young woman brought me a tankard of ale. I thanked her, and my host waited for me to sample it and offer my compliments.

"Before I answer the question, I hope you will not think me rude for asking—what do you do for a living?"

I thought he already knew the answer, but I gave it anyway. "I am a guard at the dockside."

"I am in need of guards here. You have probably noticed that I have significant assets that need protection. Would you consider working for me? I would pay more and you could live here in the bargain, free of charge."

"I will consider it."

"Why does it require thought? It is clearly a better offer."

"I still do not know who or what you are. You tend not to answer the most basic questions. You always change the subject."

The pale man in purple silk smiled. "I believe I like you, Mr. Helgarson. You are no fool. But verbal dexterity is a skill you should cultivate."

"You are doing it again."

His smile grew wider. "Yes. But we were speaking of prices. The knowledge I have gathered regarding these creatures was bought at a very steep price. Like my name, I do not give it away for free."

"What do you require?"

"Your loyalty. Work for me—under the terms I described, at a higher rate of pay and living here—and never repeat what I share with you."

"Done."

"Will you swear in blood?"

It seemed an odd question, especially in relation to the nature of my quest, but I could see no benefit to refusing. "Yes," I said.

Before I had time to take another breath, he was

latched onto my neck and draining me. I tried to push
him off, but his grip was iron, and I could no more move
him than I could move the stars. I punched him in the
kidney and it was like punching a pillar of stone. However, my continued struggles must have finally irritated
him, for he struck me sharply in the gut and deprived me
of breath.

He withdrew and returned to his chair as my vision began to darken at the edges. I tried to rise from my chair
and run but discovered I was too weak. "Now you know
what I am," he said, his fangs clearly visible where none
had been before. "I am the thing you would become.
Learn to read and write several languages first, and prove
your loyalty and discretion. When you are ready, pledge
your service to me for three hundred years, starting from
when you first rise from the grave, and I will grant you
life after death. I will also answer your questions and tell
you my name. Then, only then, may you pursue your
personal vendetta. Does this sound acceptable to you?"

"Define several," I managed.

He laughed, my blood thickening in his throat. It
sounded like caramel. "You still have the strength to spar
with me? You are unusually robust." He sat and faced
me, an amused and bloody half grin on his face. "Let us
say three." He ticked off the names on his fingers. "Greek.
Latin. German. And as for this Bohemian tongue, you
already speak it and that is good enough. I will not have
you write anything in it."

"And if I refuse?"

"You will never leave here alive. Your survival depends on literacy, as I mentioned before. If you agree but
then attempt to betray me, as others have done, you will
die. I demand complete loyalty."

"These other people here—they all wish to be like
you?"

"Every one."

"Will you . . . turn them all?"

"An excellent question. The answer is no. Some will betray me. Some will get killed in the normal course of living in Bohemia. And some will never live up to their potential."

"So if I do not learn Greek, Latin, and German, you will kill me?"

"You are quick," he said. "Come, you are still losing blood and soon you will be too weak to recover."

"I agree to these terms."

As before, he moved too quickly for me to follow—especially with my vision fading. I felt his cold hand on my neck and then nothing; I woke up later on a mattress stuffed with feathers, weak but alive. That was in the last month of 1006. In 1010 he told me his name was Zdenik and turned me into a vampire. He told me all the secrets of our kind, of course, though I may share none of them with you.

I served him for three hundred years. I killed for him—not mere humans but sometimes witches or ghouls and the odd lone werewolf. I helped him defend his territory from other vampires and learned how to manipulate the wills of men. The Vikings were right to fear us; the things I did were terrible.

Finally freed from his service in 1310, I returned to the north and searched for ways to get to Asgard. I consulted Norse pagan wise men throughout Scandinavia, and all said I must cross the Bifrost Bridge to get to Asgard or be sent there by the Valkyries to Valhalla. It was another plane of existence, they explained, and the full cruelty of Thor's crime became clear: Even though I now had the strength to confront him, I could not muster the power to reach him.

Eventually I refocused my search on planewalkers. There are remarkably few of them, and most of those can travel only to certain planes. The only ones who have complete freedom to go where they wish are the Tuatha Dé Danann—and Druids. But the Tuatha Dé Danann rarely leave Tír na nÓg. Their progeny, the Fae, are limited by their need to use oak, ash, and thorn to shift. I thought all was lost. But I ran across the goddess Flidais in the eighteenth century. She refused to take me to Asgard, but she told me one Druid still walked the earth and, if I could find him, perhaps he would take me.

"Where do I find this Druid?" I asked.

"I do not know," said the goddess of the hunt. "He is in hiding, and he has shielded himself from divination somehow. I think he moves around in tropical zones and deserts, where the Fae cannot find him easily. Probably somewhere in the New World. Do not get frustrated; he's older than you and has no intention of dying soon."

That is when I came to the New World. I picked a desert in the southwest of the continent and waited. It was a long, mind-numbing wait, but it proved to bear fruit, for the Druid finally appeared, did he not? I could not simply charm him and force him to bring me here; he is well defended against such intrusion. I had to charm him the way humans do it: I befriended him and earned his trust. Soon we will shift to Asgard, and my millennium of suffering will end one way or another.

I have paid with centuries of anguish for one night's drunken boasting. I have endured much for the sake of revenge. But when I get my chance, friends, I will be swift. I will not gloat over the thunder god or try to make him suffer. The point is not to cause him pain but rather to end mine. No matter how quickly Thor dies, it will be too late for my family.

Chapter 20

Well, that was revelatory. When I met Leif shortly after moving to Tempe, I never suspected then, or at any point afterward, that he'd been waiting for me there. For centuries. Or that, for him, all our professional and personal acquaintance was nothing more than a prelude to pursuing his own vendetta.

I felt hurt for the space of a mouse whisker—"He used me!" a tiny voice said—but then I laughed at myself. He was a *vampire*, after all. To them, all other creatures are to be used as they see fit. Leif had fooled me into thinking that he was different.

But I was not the only fool. The expression on Gunnar's face told me he was thinking similar thoughts. The question was, did this new information change anything?

Leif had given his word and followed through on it. I had given mine, and that is no small matter for one of my generation. People today make promises, break them blithely, and then excuse themselves by saying "I tried" when in truth they did not. For people of the Iron Age—my age—a man's word was the foundation of his reputation, the underlying architecture of his honor, the bedrock of his identity. Even though I often lie—a very different thing—I never forswear myself. I couldn't get around that. Or the fact that Thor could use a good killing.

But, thanks to Jesus, I had my doubts that slaying

Thor would be an unequivocally good idea, even though all evidence suggested he might be an unmitigated asshole. The function of assholes in the world, just like the asshole we all have, is to spread shit around. They are loathsome and dirty and smell extraordinarily bad, but they are also vitally necessary.

That thought led me to consider the nature of vampires. Were they vitally necessary? What niche did they fill in the scheme of things?

Despite the impenetrable curtain Leif had drawn over his undead secrets, I knew something about vampires he'd probably rather I didn't know. He couldn't hide it from me, because I could *see* it.

Normal people churn with life and their bindings to the earth; the activity of their minds and their relative health is clear from their auras, which suffuse their entire being. Vampires are different in that there are only two clear areas of "being" at all. There is activity in the center of their rib cages, and there is activity directly behind the eyes, a dull red pulsing glow like coals in a fire. The rest of them comes across as nothing more than a sterile yet ambulatory collection of carbon, calcium, and iron, though they do have thin gray auras around their heads and torsos.

Those red lights, whatever they are—the dark magic of vampirism Leif refused to explain—they are fail-safes of a sort. I think of them as resurrection engines. That's why you can't just stake a vampire in the heart and assume you're done; you have to cut off the head as well to prevent regeneration, because if someone removes that stake, it'll heal up and the vampire will rise again. Even then, if you cut off the head and remove the stake, the heart will grow a new head eventually. You'll have a thin and wasted-looking vampire, but it will be tremendously hungry and feed incessantly until it gets back to full strength.

Theories in Druid lore speculate that vampires are completely alien, or else demonic symbionts brought to this plane long ago. It mattered little to me which was true, because the upshot of it was that I could do whatever I wanted to vampires. As far as the earth is concerned, vampires don't exist as sentient creatures. They are simply collections of minerals and elements that have yet to be reabsorbed, and as such I could unbind them whenever I wished. Druids have absolutely no *tabus* against using our magic on the dead—it's only the living we can't mess with.

My private theory about the downfall of the Druids—which I didn't share with Granuaile when she asked, except in passing—has quite a bit to do with vampires. In my opinion, Caesar was simply a sword wielded by the hands of vampires in Rome. There was (and still is) a well-known nest there, and I think they were working behind the scenes, pushing the Senate to have Druidry wiped out. The young vampires wanted to expand northward and carve out territories of their own, but the continental Druids in Gaul were preventing that expansion by unbinding the vampires on sight, turning them into a mush of protoplasm and then setting the mess on fire to prevent any chance of resurrection.

I would have done the same to Leif when I first met him, if Hal had not introduced us and taken care to warn me ahead of time that he was very nice for a dead guy. Though I was aloof at first, gradually I realized that Hal was right and I came to enjoy Leif's company—even considering him a friend. I was not sure anymore if Leif's regard for me had ever been genuine.

His tale also made me wonder if he knew what I could do to him if I so chose. He became a vampire after the fall of the Druids, and most likely his maker, Zdenik, had as well—though I was basing that guess entirely on his ethnic name and the conjecture that vampires had not yet penetrated into Bohemia by the sixth century. But Zdenik had probably been made by one of the Romans, and they could have told him what Druids could do, and he in turn could have told Leif. I suspected that asking Leif about it would be wasted breath, so I cleared it from my mind. Something else leaped in to occupy it, a horrible gestalt that had been bubbling up to the surface all the while.

Leif knew I'd have doubts after he said those things, and he also knew with full certainty that I'd take him to Asgard anyway. Why?

The chilling conclusion I reached was that I *had* given Leif my word, and any creature capable of waiting for centuries to get his revenge would not hesitate to use any leverage he could to ensure I followed through. Any creature capable of suffering what he had suffered would not blanch at inflicting a bit of suffering on others. He knew who my loved ones were. He knew where they lived.

Almost as soon as I thought this, I rejected it as unworthy. No one could be so Machiavellian. Not even Machiavelli.

And the simple solution—to unbind him like any other vampire and have done with it—was not so simple, aside from being completely dishonorable. He had drunk gallons of my blood; it was part of him now. If I unbound him, might I do some damage to myself in the process? I had no way of knowing. There was no precedent for this. And now was not the time for figuring it all out, because people were staring at me and I wasn't sure why. Had I been thinking aloud?

Zhang Guo Lao cleared up my confusion by politely inquiring if we had bonded sufficiently for a trip to Asgard.

"Oh. We have made excellent progress," I replied, extremely relieved that this was all he wanted to know. "But more must be done, I'm afraid."

"Tomorrow night, then," Leif said, standing up and nodding at me, his face inscrutable. "I wish you all a good day."

"Rest well," Gunnar told him, and the others expressed similar sentiments. Leif bowed to us and left the circle of firelight, off to find someplace to hide from the sun.

Gunnar and I took a walk around the lake after dawn, when Leif was truly asleep.

"Are you still going through with it after that?" he asked with no preamble, sure that I would take his meaning.

"Leif seems certain I will."

"Yes, he does. I don't know what game he's playing. I'm hoping it's the kind where we're on one side and the Norse are on the other."

"As opposed to what?"

"Every man for himself."

"Ah. Well, I can't speak for him or what side he's on. But I'm on your side," I replied, and then tossed my chin at the other members of our party. "And I'm on theirs too."

The alpha squinted at me. "So you don't think we need to do anything?"

"Not right now. Let's see what happens in round two."

That began almost as soon as Leif rose after sundown. He asked me to talk with him a discreet distance away from the night's campfire. Gunnar asked a question with his eyes, and I shook my head ever so slightly. He let us go alone.

We walked in silence along the lakeshore for perhaps a hundred yards, hands in pockets and staring at the ground. Leif seemed to be waiting for me to speak first, but he was the one who'd asked if we could talk. Finally he stopped and I stopped too, turning to face him.

"You have had the day to grow angry with me, and yet I still find myself here, head on my shoulders and with a stake-free chest," he said. "You are a good man, Atticus."

"And you are a charming vampire."

He nodded ruefully. "I deserve that. I understand, I do. But I hope you realize that I did not make some kind of Freudian slip last night. I confessed it very purposefully."

"For what purpose?"

"Complete candor between us."

"How refreshing. Why tell me now?"

"Because that is what friends *do*, Atticus. It is true that when we first met I was playing a part. You had something I wanted, and befriending you was the only way to get it. But in that long process—our physical and verbal sparring matches, your attempts to modernize my language, actually fighting side by side—I discovered that I genuinely like you. And for several years now I have not had to act."

I shook my head. "I'm sorry, I'm having difficulty believing that. Occam's razor suggests that the simplest explanation is the correct one. And the simplest explanation is that you are a manipulative bastard like every other vampire."

"Atticus, *I had no need to say anything*. You were going to fulfill your oath anyway. The simplest explanation for that—the *only* explanation—is that I wanted to say it, to give you my trust and pay you this compliment, to tell you freely that I value your friendship, I will not betray it, and I will hold nothing back from you again. I am tired of all my secrets."

I still had my doubts, but that was clearly what he had wanted to say to me, and he expected me to buy it.

Maybe I would later; his actions would prove him true or false. My best move was to accept his explanation and be wary. Perhaps he was truly being genuine with me, but there was no way I could fully trust him again, and I'd have to act the friend from now on.

"You wish to share your secrets?" I asked. I tilted my head and smirked. "Vampire secrets?"

Leif raised his hands by way of qualification. "Only with you. No one else can know."

"So you're saying I can ask you anything right now about vampires and you'll answer it truthfully?" I was grinning.

He dropped his hands and sighed in resignation, believing he knew what was coming. "Go ahead," he said dully.

"Tell me everything you know about the whereabouts of Theophilus."

I caught a brief flash of genuine surprise. He'd thought I was going to ask him whether vampires poop or something unimportant like that. Why should such things matter? There were far weightier questions on my mind. If this mysterious Theophilus was truly older than me, then he'd probably know who was behind the old Roman pogrom against Druids. He might turn out to be the one behind it himself. Such a creature was worth seeking out.

"And no equivocations," I added. "I want your best guess at where he is right now and how to make contact with him."

"Do you intend to end his existence?" Leif asked.

"Not unless he gives me cause. I merely wish to chat."

"He will wonder how you found him."

"I'll tell him I guessed."

"He will know it is a lie. The quickening of your pulse, the tiny chemicals escaping from your skin, analysis of your expression—he will know someone told you and demand you reveal your source."

"He can demand all he wants. He cannot take the information from me by force, Leif. You know this."

"I do not," Leif said, shaking his head emphatically.

"What do you mean? He's telepathic?"

"I mean I sincerely do not know. I have never met him. My information on him is vague and extremely suspect."

"Whatever. Bring it," I said. "He'll never know from me that you ever spoke a word."

Leif flared his nostrils and exhaled heavily through them, frustrated. "He is said to divide his time between Greece, Vancouver, and a small tropical town in Australia called Gordonvale. He follows the clouds."

"I beg your pardon?"

"He wants overcast skies. He is supposedly so old, so powerful, that he is capable of walking abroad in daytime for brief periods if it is not full daylight."

My eyebrows crept up my forehead. "Can you do this?"

"No. It takes a tremendous effort for me to remain awake past dawn, even in a sunless basement."

"Hmm. You mentioned Greece. In what part of Greece?"

"Thessaloniki."

I frowned. "That is not an especially overcast city."

Leif shrugged. "My own private theory is that he is from there originally."

That fit with his Greek name, anyway. I kept firing questions at Leif and watching him carefully for signs of prevarication. If he was lying, he was deucedly good at it. Whether they turned out to be true or not, they were leads, at least, something to pursue in the very coldest of cases. And his seeming candor allowed me to hope that perhaps he truly wished us to be friends.

We spent that night and the next telling stories of our respective pasts—sometimes jokes that didn't make any sense when translated to English, sometimes adventures in distant lands and in cultures that have long since faded. We tried to top one another in The Weirdest Shit I Ever Ate contest (Väinämöinen won). Zhang Guo Lao pulled out his fish drum and tried to play something along with Väinämöinen's *kantele*, but it turned out to be a clash of musical styles that's best forgotten, sort of like Indonesian Folk Death Polka.

Leif didn't ask to drink any of my blood, and I didn't offer. Neither did anyone else. He seemed no worse off for it, so he clearly didn't need to drink every evening.

After the third night of storytelling, I examined the bonds between us and saw that they had strengthened considerably. I felt I had a good grasp of who these men were now.

"Gentlemen, I believe we are ready," I told them. "Tomorrow night, we will go to the Norse plane."

Chapter 21

Getting five men to simultaneously touch me and the root of a tree was vaguely akin to a game of homoerotic Twister, and I almost giggled—especially since their expressions practically broadcast that they were asking themselves, "Is this gay?" That would have lost me major testosterone points, though, so I firmly refocused my mind on the task and pulled us through to the Norse plane.

This time, the Well of Mimir was being watched. An eagle let out one of those "Ee-yaahh!" cries that now remind me of the title music to *The Colbert Report*, and we all turned our heads to find the source.

"That's no bird," Väinämöinen said after a second's hesitation. "That's a frost giant." His magical vision was as good as mine, if not better. When I looked at the eagle's aura, it didn't look like a bird of prey. It looked like a huge biped in ice blue. "You're up, Atticus."

I'd been elected to do all the talking, if any were to be done. Väinämöinen spoke Old Norse, but Leif spoke it better, so the vampire would act as translator to the rest of the group.

"Greetings, noble sir. May we speak with you?" I asked the eagle. "We have come to Jötunheim to have words with Hrym, if that is possible."

The eagle leapt from its perch and turned into a towering giant, shaking the earth and sending sheets of snow into the air as it landed. He was twelve feet tall, with skin a few shades lighter than the blue people in *Avatar*. His beard had real hair, but it was sheathed in ice, as were his eyebrows. His tangle of dark hair was tipped with highlights of white frost. Despite his obvious cold, he wore nothing but a fur about his loins, which made me wonder: If the frost giants figured out that a fur would keep their privates a bit warmer, why didn't they figure out that *more* furs would keep the rest of them warm? Did they never worry about hypothermia? Considering their elemental nature, they were most likely immune to it, and their scant clothing and shivery appearance was calculated to cause hypothermia in all who gazed upon them.

"Who are you?" he demanded. His voice was like barrels rolling down a dock.

"No friends to the Æsir," I assured him, thinking that was probably more important than our names. I offered those next, and since he had yet to squash us into jelly, I thought relations were proceeding remarkably well.

The frost giant fixed Perun with an icy glare (what other kind of glare could he possibly deliver?). "Graah. I do not like thunder gods. Do not trust them. What words do you have for Hrym?"

"We can end the tyranny of the Æsir tonight, or the next, or whensoever the frost Jötnar choose. Odin is vulnerable, and he knows it not. Thor is crippled, yet he knows not how. Freyja is there for the taking. The Norns are dead. All of Asgard is a fruit waiting to be plucked if Hrym feels hungry."

The giant laughed like someone with severe respiratory symptoms. "Mrr-hhr-hwauugh! What nonsense is this? You think scrawny snacks like you can defeat the Æsir?"

There is no use in bandying words with the muscle-bound and oafish. They communicate physically, and that is the only way they can be reached. I turned to the immortal Zhang Guo Lao and spoke to him in Mandarin. "Master Zhang, I believe he needs a brief lesson in manners. Perhaps you could show him how to speak on our level."

A flicker of a smirk played under the wispy mustache of the ancient alchemist, and he afforded me a brief bow. He shrugged off his pack and set his fish drum aside, drawing out one of its iron rods.

"Allow my comrade to show you a glimpse of our power," I said to the giant, switching back to Old Norse. "Perhaps you will be willing to hear more when you have seen what we can do."

"Hrrgh!" the Jötunn snorted. "What can this old man do? Fart on me?"

I hope I never get taken down by a fart the way Zhang Guo Lao took down that frost giant. He swung a high kick to the giant's kneecap to begin with, just to let him know he was serious. The giant bellowed and kicked spastically at Zhang with the same leg. Zhang grabbed on and then leapt up at the giant's face, somersaulting until his spread legs approached the giant's throat. These he locked around the giant's neck, then hung upside down, and the giant's eyes widened in surprise: How'd he get saddled so quickly with an old-guy necklace? His massive hands moved toward his chest, obviously intending to grab Zhang and yank him off, but Zhang wasn't merely hanging out. While performing a sort of extended crunch, he used his iron rod to administer surgical blows to various pressure points on the giant's chest and neck—*thup-thunk-thak-thunk-thup*. After the last one, the giant's hands stopped moving. He was paralyzed from the waist up. Zhang, still hanging upside down, relaxed and spread his arms wide in a sort of "ta-da!" gesture. I led our group in a round of appreciative golf claps. The giant slowly processed what was happening and staggered about, trying to get his upper body to move. When he lurched back a step, Zhang bent at the waist until he could grab on to a couple of beard-cicles. Then he allowed his feet to slide from around the giant's neck, planted them against the giant's collarbones, and sprang backward as if he were participating in a high dive competition. After a bunch of twists and flippy thingies—I'm not a gymnastics expert—he landed gracefully on his feet, if somewhat deeply in the snow. The frost giant fell backward in a markedly graceless fashion, propelled by Zhang's kickoff. Unable to windmill his arms for balance, the giant roared his frustration all the way down and crunched loudly (and wetly) into the snow.

I looked at Leif. "If we hadn't been here, would he have made a sound?" Leif snorted once in amusement but made no reply.

Back to Mandarin. "Master Zhang, I am assuming, since he can obviously make noise, that he still has the ability to speak?"

Zhang Guo Lao nodded once. Together we walked through the snow to the frost giant's head.

"Please forgive us for this small demonstration of our power," I told the Jötunn. "I assure you that no permanent damage has been done and we will release you shortly. May I have your name, old one?"

"I am Suttung," the giant growled. "Release me from this foul magic now!"

"Not before we have your pledge to offer us no violence and take us to Hrym."

"You tricked me!" He thrashed about in the snow, trying to get up but finding it impossible to do with only his legs. I let him give it a good try, then spoke again when he subsided in angry frustration.

"I disagree. We told you we know how to bring down the Æsir, and you refused to believe. It was quicker to show you rather than simply tell you. May I have your assurance of safe conduct?"

"Graah. I suppose I must give it, or else I will lie here like dead wood."

"And you will take us to Hrym?"

"Yes. He will spit you and roast you with rosemary, and we will all sample your flesh tonight. Tomorrow you will be shat out in the snow."

"Your diplomacy is bold and edgy, sir. I would not call that safe conduct. Still, I suppose you cannot speak for Hrym. Master Zhang, he has given his word. Please release him." I said that in Old Norse for Suttung's benefit, then repeated the last sentence in Mandarin. Zhang nimbly flipped himself onto the Jötunn's chest and poked him again in various places. After the last one, Suttung's arms spasmed and he slammed them forcefully into the snow, levering himself to a sitting position. Zhang performed some acrobatics to get out of the way and nailed another perfect dismount.

Suttung stood and spent a few moments reassuring himself that everything worked the way it had before. When he was satisfied, he examined Zhang more closely, trying to spot what he'd missed earlier—that this seemingly frail old man was truly quite dangerous. He likewise favored us all with suspicious glares—frosty, of course— wondering what powers we might possess that could destroy the Æsir.

"Graah. Follow," he finally said, and turned east, dragging his massive feet to plow a trail through the snow for us.

The village of the frost Jötnar was two hours' march through the biting cold. My jeans and leather jacket were not up to handling it, to say nothing of my sandals, so I was forced to beg a blanket and snowshoes from

Väinämöinen, who gave them to me with an expression that clearly said he thought I was a dumbass. Chilblains I could heal; it was frostbite I worried about. The other members of the party seemed acquainted with such cold—or at least better prepared for it.

Perun walked beside me and thumped his chest, which was covered in matted curls. He wore a fur cloak, but his thin shirt was open in front and his personal fur was on prominent display. "You see? Hair is good for place like this. Is stupid to shave."

"Would you give the same advice to a woman?" I asked.

"Of course! Hairy woman is good. Give me beefy, hairy women."

"I'm fresh out. But, hey, you know, that sounds like a spectacular band name. Beefy Hairy Women. Think of the logo and merchandising possibilities. Could be trend-setting."

Perun looked distressed. "We should speak Russian. I not know what you mean." We switched to Russian and chatted amiably in Suttung's wake. Perun was excited about the possibility of seeing the giantesses, who might indeed be both beefy and hairy. I deduced from this that he had not enjoyed an amorous encounter for some good while.

The frost Jötnar did not live in caves or primitive huts but rather in solid blocks of carved ice insulated with snow. In some cases, the snow was hardpacked and carved into attractive patterns around the windows and along the bases. They had steep roofs and chimneys and very tall doors.

There were no heaps of human bones in the street or evidence that the giants regularly shat in the snow. The village was remarkably clean, in fact, almost artistically so, without any of the squalor or refuse that one might expect from people fond of saying *graah*. There was a large communal fire pit in the center of the village, but it looked like it had not been used in some time. Perhaps, I reflected, all the human bones were buried in the snow, along with the missing squalor and refuse.

Everyone seemed to be enjoying a quiet night at home. The snow-lined main promenade was deserted, but orange glows from inside the houses and chimney smoke spoke of warm fires inside. For all of its idyllic appearance, however, the giants' village did nothing to put our party at ease. We were half expecting an ambush.

"Where is everybody?" I asked Suttung.

"Graah. Hiding from Odin's spies. Hugin and Munin have been visiting too often the last few days."

How very interesting. Had they perhaps been looking for me there? "We should probably get indoors soon. It would not do to have them see us now."

"We are here." Suttung stopped in front of a house no larger than the others, marked by nothing spectacular to set it off from any other house. Granted, all of the houses were huge, but there were no special ice carvings around this one's door; no skulls on a spearhead; no helpful sign saying that the chief was in. My ambush alarm went off and I checked our surroundings. Leif and Gunnar and Zhang Guo Lao also set themselves facing outward, watching for incoming attacks. Perun and Väinämöinen looked unconcerned. But no cadre of camouflaged giants appeared with spears in hand; no frozen Nordic zombies leapt out to snack on our brains.

Maybe Hrym wasn't the chief right now. I'd asked Suttung to take us to him specifically because he was the giant who was supposed to lead all the frost Jötnar in Ragnarok. As such, I figured his word would carry some weight with the others.

"This is where Hrym lives?" I asked.

"Yes. You'd better hope he's not hungry." Suttung pounded twice on the door before swinging it open. I can't speak for anyone else, but I expected to see Hrym sitting on a massive ice throne and holding a spear in one hand while a polar bear lounged at his feet, keeping his toes snuggly and warm. In his other hand he'd have a colossal tankard of mulled cider or maybe some honeyed mead. Some sort of chamberlain figure would be waiting attentively behind the throne, and there would be servants and courtiers and a long table set with meats and cheeses and freshly baked loaves of bread.

Instead, we saw two giants squelching noisily in what I cannot help but call a monstrous fuckpuddle.

Chapter 22

There are some sights that, once seen, can never be unseen. They replay themselves on a loop in your mind's home-theatre system with Dolby surround sound until you're so desperate to be rid of them that you'll resort to other loops simply to dislodge them for a while.

The long table I'd been expecting to see was actually there. Hrym had mounted his partner on top of it; they'd made little effort to clear away the trays of food or the spilled tankards of mead, and they were completely oblivious to the fact that they were now humping in front of a live audience. I am not sure they would have stopped for our benefit in any case.

"Graah," Hrym said. *Slap-slap-slap*.

"Graah," his partner said. *Slap-slap-slap*.

Suttung did his best to close the door again both quickly and discreetly, but the damage to my psyche had already been done. Recognizing the danger, I closed my eyes and began to sing: " 'The farmer in the dell, the farmer in the dell, hi-ho the derry-o, the farmer in the dell. The farmer takes a wife'—oh, bugger, that won't do at all! Help me, guys, help me, I need a different song!"

"What are you on about, Atticus?" Gunnar asked.

"I need a vastly irritating, mind-numbing song to sing that will prevent me from reliving what I just saw. I have an intense need to forget it."

"Oh, excellent plan. I'm with you," Gunnar said, every bit as disturbed as I was. "How about 'El Paso' by Marty Robbins?"

"That's good, it's a catchy tune, but it won't reduce us to catatonia quickly enough."

"I have it!" Väinämöinen said, unexpectedly chiming in. " 'It's a Small World, After All.' "

"That's perfect!" I cried. "That's just the tonic we need in a land of giants! Everybody, on three." Soon the six of us were singing the execrable song with all the gusto at our disposal, a bit wild-eyed and panicked in the snow. Perun and Zhang Guo Lao weren't familiar with it, but they learned quickly and joined us the second time around.

Suttung the frost Jötunn stared at us in perplexed silence, embarrassed at his faux pas and half convinced that we were all mad.

Chapter 23

Before our neural ganglions dissolved completely into mush, we were saved by the arrival of a black bird in a black sky. Leif's superior night vision spotted it first, and it was a welcome distraction from the twin traumas of bearing witness to Hrym's marital exercise and singing the most soul-destroying song ever written. There was some small illumination coming from various fires within the ice houses, which kept it from being pitch dark.

"Maybe is Hugin and Munin?" Perun wondered aloud.

"It cannot be. There is only one of them," Väinämöinen said.

"What is it, then?" Gunnar asked.

"Perhaps it is simply a bird," Zhang Guo Lao said.

Leif shook his head. "No, its blood smells wrong."

"Oh, bollocks," I breathed, realizing who it must be even before the crow swooped down and shape-shifted into a milk-white naked woman. "It's the Morrigan." She'd followed me to the Norse plane. Like Druids, the Tuatha Dé Danann could travel anywhere, but they usually confined themselves to the Irish planes and earth out of courtesy to other pantheons.

Her eyes glowed red as she approached, seemingly unaffected by the cold. I stole a quick glance at Suttung to gauge his reaction, and he appeared impressed and perhaps inclined to ask if the lady was spoken for. If he was smart and thought it through, he would realize that a woman with glowing red eyes will always speak for herself, and it would be best to keep his mouth shut.

"Siodhachan Ó Suleabháin," she said with spine-tingling minor chords in her voice, "I must speak with you ere you proceed with this madness."

I shivered uncontrollably. Freezing cold plus the Morrigan's voice will do that to a guy. "Right. Of course. Let's, uh, go speak. Guys, you think maybe you could get a fire going while I'm gone? I'll talk to Hrym when I return. I mean, if he's ready to talk." I shivered again.

They all assured me a fire would be no problem, don't worry about a thing, see you soon, Atticus. The Morrigan and I walked west together, out where no one would be able to overhear us.

"You are poorly dressed for this climate," the Morrigan began, still utterly undressed herself.

"Yeah, might you have a thermal blanket in one of your pockets?" I asked.

The Morrigan continued as if I hadn't spoken. "It suggests how poorly planned your entire adventure is. This is most unwise. Surely you realize I cannot help you in Asgard? Even here, in Jötunheim, I cannot protect you. If you die, the Valkyries will take you wherever they wish."

"Yeah, about the Valkyries. Turns out they can't choose me to be slain."

The Morrigan turned her head sharply and looked at my face to see if I was teasing her. Deciding I was serious, she asked, "How do you know this?"

"I ran into them about a week ago and they tried to snuff me. My amulet turned cold but otherwise nothing happened. I came out ahead in that battle and I'm going back for round two."

"You'll fight them directly?"

"I don't know. If they come after me, it's possible. I'm not really interested in the fighting. I'm more interested in keeping my word to Leif, and that's all about getting him to Asgard. I'm sure you wouldn't advise me to become an oath-breaker when I have made an oath to you."

"Then why are you here talking to the frost Jötnar?" she asked. "You did not promise Leif you would recruit them, did you? Or promise to bring these other hangers-on? Drop the vampire off and be gone. Leave these other men behind."

"Morrigan, Thor is completely bereft of nobility. You should hear what he's done to those lads. He's a total choad-chomper."

"He is what?"

"Never mind. Look, the more guys I bring with me, the more likely it is that I get away. I'm just going to let Leif take his shot and see how it turns out. If Thor kills him, we leave. If he kills Thor, we also leave. We're not sticking around to lay waste to the entire plane."

"There will be dire consequences in either case, Siodhachan."

"I've already had this conversation with Jesus, and I'm still following through. The way I add it up, the consequences will be dire if I don't. What have you got to add to that?"

"I'm not privy to your conversation with the Christian god. But I have foreseen your death in a vision."

I had to stop. You can't keep walking casually when someone says they have foreseen your death. "Here or on earth?"

"On earth."

I frowned. "Aren't you supposed to have my back there?"

The red in her eyes faded. "Yes. But I foresaw your death anyway. It was . . . unsettling."

I'll say. What had she been doing in that scenario?

"Well, I promise to be extra paranoid when I go and super turbo paranoid when I get back. But I'm going, Morrigan."

"I know you will go. I simply want to minimize the impact you will have."

"Impact on what?"

She chose to ignore that question. Instead, she stepped closer to me and waited for my eyes to meet hers. "Siodhachan, some of the Valkyries . . ." Her mouth twisted and she broke eye contact as she searched for words. She couldn't say they were her friends. ". . . I know them," she finished.

"Well, that may be. But every one of them tried to choose me for death, and then I made them look stupid and ineffective. If we meet again, they're not going to want to do Jell-O shots off my tummy, you know?"

"I can imagine their anger at you," the Morrigan said. "And I know better than most that you cannot promise me anything about a battle. I have merely come to advise you that this is a situation where fulfilling the letter of your oath would be wiser than fulfilling the spirit or intent."

I smiled wryly at her. "Don't you find that to be wise in every situation?"

"I often do, yes."

"That is a difference between us." Something the Morrigan said earlier came back to gnaw at me. "Did you say you saw my death in a vision?"

"It was a lucid dream, yes. Not an augury or casting of the wands. It happens sometimes."

"Any of those ever wind up not coming true?"

"No." Her lips pressed tightly together and she would not look at me.

"And you're sure it was me, not some other handsome rake with a faerie sword?"

"There aren't many faerie swords around. Or red-haired Druids wielding them. I'm positive."

"Ah, well then. I've had a pretty good run, whenever it comes—don't you think? It would be ungracious of me to complain." I wasn't going to ask her precisely when, where, or how I was going to die. I didn't want to know, and she might not have the answers. I sighed and watched my breath crystallize in the dark. "Say, do you ever go up to people and tell them, 'Congratulations! This is going to be an awesome year for you in many ways, but especially because you *won't* die this year'?"

"No," the Morrigan said, "that never occurred to me. It seems frivolous."

"You might enjoy it. People might take a liking to you. Especially if you shag them afterward and they know that they're going to survive the encounter."

The Morrigan chuckled. "Are you trying to hint that you would like to enjoy my favors, Atticus?"

"Oh, no," I said with a snort, trying to keep my tone light when I was actually terrified by the prospect. The Morrigan is stunningly beautiful, but she makes love the way linebackers love quarterbacks: The last time I'd "enjoyed her favors," Oberon thought I'd been on the losing side of a street fight. "I cannot spend myself now if I'm going to battle shortly. And, besides, I have an alliance to make with the frost giants. How's the amulet coming?" I asked, to get her off the subject completely.

"Slowly, but I believe some progress is being made. I've found an iron elemental who will speak to me. I gave it three faeries to eat, and I think it might answer me more quickly the next time I call it."

"That's excellent, keep it up," I said.

The Morrigan purred with the praise and stepped close to kiss me farewell. She yelped when she pressed against my chest. "You're bloody cold!" she said.

"And you're not? You're standing bare-assed in the

snow and you're telling me you're all warm and toasty?"

"Raise your core temperature, you fool!"

"Oh." I nodded as if I knew what she was talking about, but she kept staring at me expectantly, waiting for me to obey her command. So I was forced to say, "Um, how do you do that?"

She slapped me across the face. For the Morrigan, that wasn't even a mild rebuke. She was just making sure I was paying attention. "How have you survived all this time without knowing that particular binding?"

"With many layers of warm clothing, like everybody else."

"Where are these layers now?"

"Elsewhere, regrettably."

"You can bind your sight to the magical spectrum, I hope?" the Morrigan asked. The question was fairly insulting, since it was one of the first bindings all Druids learned. But it was a lengthy one, unsuited for stressful situations, and I had simplified the casting of it long ago.

"Yes, that's what this charm is for," I said, pointing to one on the left side of my amulet. Using a charm was like clicking on an icon to launch an application. They were shortcuts that freed me of the time and concentration necessary to craft the bindings from scratch each time. On the left side, I had charms for camouflage, night vision, healing, and my faerie specs, along with one other. On the right were the charms I used to bind myself to animal shapes, plus the bear charm I used for magic storage. I turned on my faerie specs and said, "Show me how to raise my temperature."

The Morrigan showed me and taught me the words for the binding. It turned out to be adjustments to the thyroid and hypothalamus so that my metabolism increased, burning more fuel in my cells and thus releasing more heat, while simultaneously preventing my blood vessels from restricting due to cold air on the surface of my skin.

"You will need to eat a bit more to maintain this," the Morrigan explained, "and do not forget to readjust these when you return to warmer weather or you will never stop sweating."

"Thank you, Morrigan. This is very helpful," I said, already feeling myself warming up. "And delivered to me entirely without pain."

The Morrigan sucker-punched me hard in the face, sending me sprawling in the snow and breaking my nose.

"You spoke too soon and with entirely too much sarcasm," she said. "We could have parted with a kiss. Remember that. And remember that I advised you not to fight the Norse. Consider it well." She spread her arms and they blackened; her legs rose from the ground and also turned black as her body bound itself to the form of a crow; and she flew west toward the root of the World Tree, where she could shift away from this plane, leaving me to bleed and regret my choice of words.

Chapter 24

When I returned to the center of the village, nose knitting and blood washed away with a handful of snow, a blessedly clothed Hrym had joined Suttung and my companions around the communal fire pit. Someone had produced some dry wood from somewhere, and now a cheerful blaze from a few logs of northern pine illuminated the scene. Some other frost giants were standing around, curiosity driving them outside, making my friends look like Halflings. I surveyed the tableau with my faerie specs and saw that Väinämöinen had taken it upon himself to cast a seeming over the area, shielding us from the sight of Odin's spies.

The frost giants had interesting auras; the white noise of their magic was elemental and limited to ice, of course, but over that I saw colors of curiosity and mistrust and even anger over our presence. I could have been misinterpreting what I was seeing, however, since I had no baseline experience with frost giants.

Hrym was taller than Suttung and much broader in the chest. Reminiscent of a growling heavy metal singer, he had studded black leather bracers on his wrists. He also had a fine fur cloak draped around him, which marked him as the chief and a little more sensible about the cold. I'm not sure he ever got to finish his business with his partner, though; the expression on his face combined with the tone of his skin suggested that he might be feeling a bit blue.

He was grimacing down at Leif, who was trying to explain something in Old Norse, when one of the other giants directed his attention to my approach. He sized me up with his cold eyes and did not seem to be impressed. He had a beardcicle thicker than my neck and longer than my torso.

"You are the Druid?" he said.

"Aye. Call me Atticus."

"I am Hrym," he said, and thus the pleasantries were concluded. He pointed at Leif. "This dead man tells me you can get to Asgard without crossing Bifrost."

"It is true. I have already done it."

"He tells me the Norns are dead, as is the great squirrel, Ratatosk."

"Also true. It is why Hugin and Munin have been so active recently. They are looking for me."

"Graah. Those cursed ravens always hound me. They know I will lead the frost Jötnar to the final battle."

"Have you thought that the final battle may not occur as foretold anymore, now that the Norns are dead?"

The Jötnar all looked at one another to see if any of them had thought of this. It was clear they hadn't.

"The prophecy can outlive the prophet and still come true," Hrym finally said.

"Graah," the Jötnar chorused in agreement, nodding their heads at Hrym's nugget of wisdom. A few of their beardcicles snapped off at this unexpected activity.

"Sleipnir is dead as well," I said. "Does that not change the outcome of Ragnarok?"

"No," Hrym replied. "In some tales Odin rides Sleipnir to confront the wolf Fenris. In others he does not. Nothing is changed."

"But without the Norns to spin their fate, the lives—and deaths—of the Æsir can be changed. We can change the outcome now."

"You wish to begin Ragnarok now?"

"No. We wish to bring justice to Thor for his many crimes against humanity and the Jötnar. We ask for your aid in this."

"Why should we help you?"

"You will remove your oldest enemy."

"Jörmungandr will remove him for us," Hrym said. "All we must do is wait."

"For how long? The frost Jötnar need not cower any longer in Jötunheim. Help us slay Thor, and the spoils of Asgard will be yours to take. The goddess Freyja, for example, will be among the spoils."

"Freyja!" Suttung exclaimed. All the male frost giants took up the name in a sort of horny echo. It was like walking into a nerd party and shouting, "Tricia Helfer!" or "Katee Sackhoff!" I checked their auras again and the males were turning red with arousal. The women were rolling their eyes and trying not to vomit. It let me know that their auras could be read reliably like human ones.

"There are other gods to contend with before that can happen," Hrym pointed out, justifiably so. "Freyja will not fight without her twin, Freyr, in attendance. If Thor goes to fight, Týr will probably tag along. Heimdall, maybe Odin himself, will oppose us, to say nothing of the Valkyries and the Einherjar. We are a mighty people, but we have learned the hard way that we cannot face the combined might of Asgard alone."

"Excellent points. Allow me to remind you that you won't be alone—you'll have us—and the Einherjar should not be a problem. We're going to show up on the opposite side of the plane from them. You cause lots of freezing and suffering as soon as we get here, and the Æsir will send out those who can respond the fastest—which means those who can fly, right? So we can expect Thor, Freyr, Odin and the Valkyries, and anybody else who can hitch a ride with them. They can't bring all the Einherjar with them. We strike fast, kill Thor, and take Freyja, then leave. The Æsir will be crippled and—"

"Graah!" Hrym broke in. "How can you prevail against Thor? His thunderbolts will destroy us all."

"Oh. Perhaps you have not had time to be introduced to our companions. We have our own thunder god." I turned to Perun and asked him quickly in Russian to produce more of his fulgurites. "This is Perun," I said to Hrym. "With his help, Thor's primary weapon will be neutralized. The Æsir are unlikely to have similar protection, because they've never had to deal with it before. Our attacks will be unlike anything they have seen or prepared for. None of your people can be struck down by cowardly attacks from the air. If the Æsir are to defeat you, they must do so by force of arms, and surely the people of Hrym can acquit themselves well in battle."

"Beware of tricks, Hrym," one of the females said. "This could be a snare to draw you into the Æsir's clutches."

"See for yourself, lady, that I speak truth. Here," I said, tossing her my fulgurite. She caught it and regarded it quizzically; she had probably never seen sand before. I signaled to Perun to let her have it and held my breath. I wasn't sure that Perun's powers would work here on the Norse plane—but they did. A lightning bolt struck the giantess, and the frost Jötnar dove for cover. "Graah!" they shouted.

But then they looked back at the woman and saw that she was laughing at them, completely unharmed.

"You see, Hrym? You can finally give back some of what you've been getting from the Æsir. There is no need to wait for Ragnarok. This can happen tomorrow." Perun was busy passing out fulgurites to the frost Jötnar and grinning hugely at them. He was growing beardcicles of his own due to his proximity to the giants.

Hrym still had his doubts. "Is this real lightning you call down from the sky?"

I translated for Perun, and he promptly destroyed someone's ice house to prove that he was using one hundred percent real fucking lightning. One of the Jötnar bellowed in outrage, but Hrym found this amusing and laughed like he was trying to clear wet cement from his throat.

"Very well, tiny man called Atticus. You may tell me more of your plan. How precisely do we bring the Æsir low?"

I told him.

Chapter 25

The frost giants needed no convincing that Thor needed killing. He'd slain the family members or ancestors of everyone in the village, so once they were convinced they had a hamster's chance in Hel of surviving, asking them to come along was like asking a starving man if he'd like a bucket of chicken. Still, we did not get the entire village to join us; we got twenty, all of whom could shape-shift to eagles, and some of them came from other villages a short distance away. They were called during the day while Leif slept, and we all did our best to prepare for the night ahead by catching what sleep we could. Perun gave me a new fulgurite to replace the one I'd given to the giantess.

When the sun set that evening and Leif pronounced himself ready to get his revenge on, Hrym offered to carry us to the root of the World Tree, since we were so bloody slow in the snow.

Druid's Log, December 3: "Hitching a ride on a frost giant's back is both entertaining and eco-friendly." First, the greenhouse-gas emissions are almost nil; you get to hear all about the many splendid beauties of Freyja; the wind noise is minimal, aside from the occasional *graah*; and since you don't have to steer, you can simply enjoy the scenery from ten feet above the ground. On the downside, they smell like ice cubes made of sweat instead of water.

We were traveling in a valley between cragged sweeps of glacial mountain ranges, which I'd failed to notice while shivering in Suttung's footsteps the night before. It was probably a lovely meadow in the summer—if summer ever truly came to this part of Jötunheim—but under recent snowfall it was a cobalt blanket gently undulating to the night horizon. Stands of evergreen timber, drooping with heavy snow, bracketed us on either side like mute and shivering spectators. A wolf howled off to the south, and Gunnar looked a bit wistful.

Once at the root, we hopped down from the frost giants' backs and they shifted to eagles—bloody big ones. They launched themselves straight up, following the root to Asgard. Long ago, Hrym told me, young Jötnar tried to climb the root to see if there might be a way to Asgard, but none ever returned. Ratatosk slew them, perhaps, or else the Norns did. Now there was nothing to prevent them from taking advantage of Ratatosk's passage to the plane.

Perun was going to provide transport for the rest of us. I could have shifted to an owl and joined the frost Jötnar, but I wanted to hold on to my clothes for a bit longer. Väinämöinen and Zhang Guo Lao deposited their packs at the base of the root, to be picked up on the return trip. I slipped my wallet and cell phone into Väinämöinen's pack, because rule number one of committing naughty shit is that you don't take ID with you.

"You have arms out to sides, legs together," Perun said, demonstrating with his own wingspan. We all did as he instructed, but Gunnar in particular looked tense, and his yellow eyes indicated he was struggling to keep his wolf under control. It was a control issue, period, because Perun was going to fly us up there. Thunder gods have to be able to push storms around, so summoning sufficient wind to carry us up the trunk was no problem for him. Keeping all six of us from twisting away unpredictably in the winds was a bit tougher. Imagine an extremely turbulent airplane ride without a seat belt. Or a barf bag. Or a plane. The first half mile was rough on us all, but Gunnar suffered especially, because wolves don't like to fly.

During the flight, Väinämöinen's beard flew up around his face, completely hiding it, and a steady stream of Finnish curses could be heard from behind the white curtain of hair. My earlier suspicion that he had weapons hidden under his beard was confirmed: Strapped to his tunic at the top of his chest were seven thin sheathed blades suitable for throwing. Four hilts could be drawn from the right, three from the left.

Perun was finally able to stabilize us and we flew steadily upward. He pushed himself ahead of us, the better to direct the winds at the top of the root, where we'd have to duck into Ratatosk's hole and then rocket up the chute that would give us egress to the Plain of Idavoll. He gradually strung us out underneath one another in a tight little wind tunnel, which would also facilitate our travel up the root's throat.

The plan was simple. Once on the Plain of Idavoll, we were going to follow the immortal strategy of Ehhy Calvin "Nuke" LaLoosh and "announce [our] presence with authority." Perun would send thunderstorms toward Asgard, and everyone would yell at Thor for failing to control them. He'd get angry over the loss of face and come barreling out to investigate the source of the trouble. Meanwhile, the frost giants would send shivering ice storms at Fólkvangr, and Freyja would harness her kittehs to ride out and put a stop to it. There would be no long march on Asgard to attack fortified positions. They'd come to us. That was the plan. It was simple, playing to our strengths and preying on the enemy's weakness. What could go wrong?

One word: Heimdall.

He was lingering around the roots of Yggdrasil instead of tending to Bifrost—probably as a result of my nighttime raid for the golden apple—and must have thought it odd when twenty giant eagles came flying out of Ratatosk's passage to Jötunheim. Thus, when we emerged from the hole directly behind said eagles and Perun let us drift down to the new-fallen snow around the trunk, there was already blood staining it. Heimdall had cut down two of the frost giants as they shifted to their bipedal forms, but the rest had shifted successfully and were converging on him. He didn't see much hope of getting out alive, and he spied us landing and realized we weren't friendly tourists either. So the bastard whelp of nine mothers put a horn to his lips—Gjallarhorn, specifically—and blew for all he was worth until the giants smooshed him to paste with colorful, juicy noises.

Hrym's people considered this to be a wholly positive turn of events, and they laughed uproariously at the pulped remains of the god. Stomping Heimdall into a bloody smear was tangible, immediate proof that we could change the future and that Ragnarok would not play out according to the prophecy of the Norns. Heimdall was supposed to have killed Loki on the Field of Vigrid and be killed in turn. He was fated to be the last of the gods to die; instead, he was among the first.

But I thought their celebration was misplaced. Gjallarhorn was supposed to warn everyone in Asgard that Ragnarok had begun, and now everyone who could grab hold of something pointy would come running to the source of that magical call—including the berserker hordes of Einherjar.

"Look to the west, Leif. That's where they'll come from. I need to see if I can find Moralltach," I said.

"Which way is west here?" he asked, and I realized that he'd probably become disoriented during the flight up, and the stars weren't the same as ones we saw on the plane of Midgard in any case.

"That way." I pointed, indicating the mountain range that surrounded Asgard.

Leif started shouting in Old Norse and then repeating himself in English to get everyone facing west. He had Hrym and Suttung erect a wall of ice behind us so that we couldn't be easily flanked from the other side of Yggdrasil, and he asked Väinämöinen to cast a seeming over us so that Hugin and Munin couldn't scout our forces. I liked that spell because it targeted an area rather than me specifically, so my amulet didn't shut it down.

Once standing uncertainly over a spot that seemed close to where I had cached Moralltach for later retrieval, I had to dig down through two feet of snow to reach the half-frozen earth. The storm that had brought this snowfall must have hit shortly after my last visit. I was so very glad the Morrigan had taught me the core-temperature trick, because the ground was still bloody cold when I put my bare feet on it. The tattoo on my heel renewed the strained connection I had with the earth on this plane, and I used it to search out the cold bite of iron that would indicate the presence of a sword. It bit me, blessedly, after only a few seconds' searching; Moralltach was three feet to my left. That required more digging through the snow, but it was worth it. The frozen earth cracked and groaned as it parted under my command and yielded Moralltach back to my hands with no time to spare for inspection.

"Atticus!" Leif called. "He's coming with the Valkyries! I need you up here!"

Gods Below, that was fast. Heimdall's horn had brought the cavalry at top speed. I wasn't ready yet. I was supposed to be point man when Thor showed up, but here I was yards behind and still clothed.

I stripped hurriedly and ran to join the others, carrying both Fragarach and Moralltach with me. It occurred to me, somewhat manically, that running naked through the snow was a holiday tradition at some college campuses, and I should have participated in order to train for this frantic moment. The snow slowed me down as my feet sank into it, and I biffed it twice in my hurry to advance to the vanguard.

The reason for my hurry was that I had the only proven dodge to Norse targeting spells. Thor's hammer, Mjöllnir, had the same targeting spell on it that Odin's spear did. Plus, Odin and the Valkyries had doubtless described me to the other gods—perhaps as "red-haired, naked, and mad"—so I wanted to make sure Thor saw me as described. Since I was the slayer of Sleipnir, he'd want to wipe me out fast to earn brownie points with Odin.

Secondarily, we couldn't let the Valkyries target the rest of the group; aside from Leif, who was already dead, they could choose the lot to die somehow and never leave Asgard alive. Though I bemoaned the necessity, I had to take the Valkyries out, no matter how much it would displease the Morrigan to lose her BFFs. I hoped that would be the extent of my participation in this battle.

"Väinämöinen, contract your seeming!" I shouted as I tossed Leif the sodden scabbard of Moralltach. It had most likely suffered some water damage, but hopefully the ice had halted the beginning stages of rust from progressing too far. I drew Fragarach from its scabbard and tossed the latter into the snow, not caring if I found it later or not.

The Finn's seeming sloughed off me palpably and I picked up speed, surprised that his illusion had slowed me down. I ran perhaps another ten yards and stopped, a bit out of breath because I couldn't reach the earth through the snow and I didn't want to draw on the power stored in my bear charm until necessary. Thunderclouds were rolling in rapidly from the west. Thor was certainly there, but my eyes were not the equal of Leif's, even with night vision, and I couldn't pick him out yet. I couldn't see the Valkyries either. I didn't know what their visual range was, but thanks to Väinämöinen's seeming, they should see nothing but me for the moment.

"Leif," I called back to him, "where are the Valkyries in relation to Thor?"

"Eight o'clock, slightly behind him," he replied. "V formation."

"Väinämöinen, do your voice thing now!" I shouted.

Voice thing, I'd decided, was a technical term. There was no way I could make Thor hear me from this distance, but Väinämöinen had the pipes to do it. He could whip out that *kantele* of his and whisper creepy, flirtatious things to a Harajuku girl in Tokyo if he wanted. And even though I was probably thirty yards or so in front of him and to his right, he could make it seem like I was the one saying it. Thor had never heard me speak before, so he'd have no clue he was being duped. Leif and I had coached the Finn in precisely what to say in Old Norse to turn Thor murderous, and Väinämöinen recited it flawlessly, his voice booming across the Plain of Idavoll:

"Thor, Goatfucker, Violator of All Animals Great and Small, come and face your doom! Jörmungandr is a worm compared to me! I have slain Sleipnir and knocked Odin on his ass! I have slain the Norns, and now your fate is in my hands!"

Yep. That did it. My amulet turned frosty in a familiar way as the Valkyries once again tried to choose me for death. It's funny how something like that will sweep away your moral uncertainties. Regardless of the wisdom of coming here at all, right now it was kill or be killed. A lightning bolt arced down from the sky and plunged through my body, and I felt no more than a tingle, thanks to the fulgurite Perun had given me. It was strung on my charm necklace now, resting on the back of my neck. I laughed, and so did Väinämöinen in the same loud voice. We wanted to make certain Thor knew his lightning was ineffectual. I was promptly struck seven more times by lightning, each as harmless as the first. We'd anticipated this too, and Väinämöinen spoke the appropriate line, choked with laughter:

"Stop it, Thor, that tickles!"

That was calculated to make him throw his hammer at me. Leif and I knew from experience how the male psyche works: If one weapon doesn't work, switch to something else and try to shove it sideways through an orifice far too small to allow for comfortable entry.

The clouds above exploded with Thor's rage, and I dimly heard Leif cry behind me, "Get ready, Atticus! Here it comes!" I could see a pale smudge against the clouds now that must be Thor in his chariot, but Leif could already see him in Hi-Def. "Now!" Leif shouted, telling me that Thor had thrown his hammer and that target lock was acquired.

That was my cue. I tossed Fragarach into the snow and leapt after it, triggering the charm that bound my form to a sea otter in the process. Mjöllnir's targeting spell was dissolved in that instant, and simple physics held sway on the hammer now. A couple of cute otter hops brought me to my sword and I switched back to human.

"Come on, Leif!" I shouted as I picked Fragarach out of the snow.

The vampire was already out of the Finn's seeming

and paces away by the time I'd finished speaking. He had Moralltach gripped in his right hand and a savage grin on his face, fangs out.

"It's hammer time," I said, and then winced. "Sorry."

"For what?"

Mjöllnir plowed into the snow in front of us before I could explain the brief popularity of MC Hammer.

Mjöllnir has a spell on it that Odin's spear, Gungnir, does not: It's enchanted to return to the hand of he who throws it. We were counting on it.

"Grab on!" Leif said, and I promptly dropped into the snow and wrapped my left arm around his right leg. Leif reached out with his left hand and grasped the handle of Mjöllnir, which, after contact with the earth, was already turning back in Thor's direction. We were abruptly yanked skyward, wrenchingly so, and gaining speed. But we were headed toward a Grade A asshole who had no idea that a crime he'd committed ages ago was finally coming back to haunt him with a thousand years' violent interest.

Thor wasn't going to be my business; I was after the Valkyries. Twice now they had tried to snuff me without so much as a verbal challenge, and I knew they'd do the same to the rest of the party if I gave them the chance. The problem was, there were twelve of them on flying horses and only one of me, and I was hitching a ride butt naked on an airborne vampire's leg, with nothing more than a sword. Soon the vampire would engage in battle with a thunder god, and I had to be gone by then.

My aura was the problem. If I laid hands on Mjöllnir, my amulet would most likely snuff the return spell and all other magic and leave us with a regular hammer. That would deny Thor a powerful weapon, but it would still leave us with twelve airborne Valkyries who would doom our entire party as soon as they spotted us. Curiously, though we could be shortly facing the entire host of Asgard, it was the Valkyries we feared the most, because they could choose the slain. Therefore, Gunnar had suggested this more risky stratagem during the previous night's planning session with the frost giants. Thor's death was the ultimate objective, but killing the Valkyries before they could pronounce sentence was the top priority.

I had a single glimpse of Thor before I had to direct my attention elsewhere. He was not the clean-shaven man Americans were used to seeing in comic books. A gnarly blond beard covered his jaw but did not extend down to his neck. There was no winged helmet, or any helmet at all. He had a thin strip of rawhide tied around his forehead to keep his long hair out of his eyes. He wore a mail shirt and a red tunic over it, belted with Megingjörd, which doubled his already prodigious strength. Járngreiper, his iron gloves, clutched the reins of his chariot as if he imagined they were our wee, stringy necks. His face was so red it practically matched his tunic; it was scrunched into constipated fury. He could not believe I was still alive and bringing a friend to the battle. As he watched us approach, he dropped the reins and hoisted a shield from the side of his chariot and secured it to his left arm.

My time was up. If Leif was to have a decent shot at Thor, he couldn't have me hanging on to his leg. The Valkyries were riding behind Thor and below him to his right, as Leif had described. The steep ascent of Mjöllnir to Thor's hand was bringing us to eye level with them. Once we reached that level, I tossed Fragarach high into the air and triggered my owl charm. I let go of Leif's leg and shifted, flapping madly after my sword. Leif continued on toward Thor, and the Valkyries were now on course to fly underneath me. I saw gravity taking hold of Fragarach and slowing its ascent, allowing me to close the gap between us at the zenith of its journey. I switched back to human form, snatched the hilt out of the air, and fell naked and screaming onto the Valkyries below.

The shouted warning from the trailing riders was too late to save the second Valkryie on the near side of the V. I sliced through her skull and spine with nothing more than the force of gravity, Fragarach sliding through armor and flesh like scissors through silk. The halves of her body sheared away to either side and showered me in blood. When my feet landed on the flanks of her horse, I knelt and launched myself back up, somersaulting backward and twisting to meet the next Valkyrie in the formation. Thinking it might protect her, she'd raised her shield, but she hadn't had enough time to process what my sword could do. I slashed through both it and her torso, again springing off her horse's back to meet the next opponent. This one was far smarter. She just got out of the way, yanking her mount up and to her left, past my reach. I began to fall, and I twisted around to assess the situation. Two down, ten to go, formation broken and pursuing me. Whoops, make that nine! A thunderous impact and a flash of steel across my vision showed me a Valkyrie hurtling to earth with a vampire latched on to her neck, her horse plunging fatally to earth with a broken wing. Somehow, Thor had tossed Leif away to let the shieldmaidens of Valhalla tangle with him. But they were no better equipped to deal with an ancient vampire than the god of thunder was.

Twisting again to face the approaching earth, I let go of Fragarach and shape-shifted once more to an owl, breaking my fall and landing safely next to my sword in the snow. Leif and his victim impacted sickeningly fifty yards away, and he immediately leapt defiantly to his feet and roared at the sky. Four Valkyries dove in his direction, five in mine. I shifted back to human form and retrieved Fragarach, drawing on my bear charm to quicken my speed and magnify my strength. The charm was nearing empty; all the shifting had taken its toll.

The first Valkyrie came at me in an airborne cavalry charge, thinking to ride me down, but I sprang out of the path of her blade to take on the one who would inevitably follow, because it's always the two in the old one–two you have to worry about. The second one was bearing down hard and descending to snow level, counting on her horse to trample me to fleshy bits of mincemeat. Well, I had my Irish up, so I wasn't going to dodge this one. I bellowed incoherently, charged directly at the steed, and led with my left shoulder. My magically boosted strength slammed into it at the base of its neck and stopped it cold, flinging the astonished Valkyrie ass over teakettle to land awkwardly in the snow. The horse staggered backward, flapping its wings to keep upright. My left shoulder popped painfully out of its socket, and my collarbone shattered on impact, but my right arm— the arm with Fragarach clutched at the end of it—still worked just fine. I turned and chopped off the Valkyrie's arms before she could rise from the snow, Fragarach's power to cut through armor again aiding the process. She shrieked and writhed as her lifeblood squirted from her shorn shoulders, and it was precisely the music I needed. Her companions would rush in, their need to render aid and pay me back giving them a sort of tunnel vision.

Four cursing Valkyries landed and dismounted, spreading themselves to surround me, swords drawn and shields raised. One of them pointed at my naughty bits and laughed.

"Hey, you know what?" I said. "It's damn cold out here. And those wings on your helmet look fucking stupid."

Leif, I saw, was beset by three more of them, having ripped out the throat of the fourth. He was probably in better shape than I; both his arms still worked. As my adversaries gathered themselves to charge me, I shouted in Russian, "Perun! Help now!" and prayed to Brighid that he heard me.

The Russian thunder god could not have revealed himself earlier and allowed the Valkyries to lay a death curse on him. I wasn't sure this would work, because Thor might have given them some sort of protection, but it was worth a try. Now that all their attention was fully engaged by a Druid and a vampire, Perun could let loose. Seven thunderbolts lanced down from the sky to slay the remaining Valkyries, and as their smoking corpses fell limply into the snow, Väinämöinen laughed again, a creepy Vincent Price job that echoed under the ceiling of clouds. He banished his seeming and revealed our entire force to the pompous Æsir asspudding floating in the sky.

We gave Thor a few seconds to absorb it all. The Valkyries were all dead, wiped out in less than a minute by three members of a strange, unforetold force that numbered two dozen. And, by virtue of being the first on the scene, he now had no help whatsoever.

"Perun, fry his goats," I called. Two more thunderbolts cracked in the sky, and Thor howled in rage and surprise as his ruined chariot plunged down onto the Plain of Idavoll, led by the charred black carcasses of his rams.

Chapter 26

"Last one there's a rotten egg!" I said, and the boys were off. It was an interesting footrace. I think Leif would normally have won on a flat surface, but Gunnar in wolf form was able to bound nimbly across the snow while Leif had to fight it with every step. Väinämöinen, Perun, and Zhang Guo Lao didn't stand a chance, though the latter did his best with some superhuman leaps that would require wire work in the movies. The frost giants just stood there and watched the tiny people go after Thor. Aside from losing two of their number at the very start, they'd been very entertained by the visit to Asgard so far.

If Thor had been smart, he would have thrown his hammer at someone else. Nobody else could avoid the tracking spell on Mjöllnir, and he'd instantly regain his confidence. But his beloved goats were dead, and even his dim bulb of a brain could figure out that, if he resurrected them, Perun would simply strike them again. For an instant I thought he was going to let his hammer fly at Gunnar, because he whirled it around impressively as a precursor to a throw, but what he did instead was throw it without letting go—he targeted some point far in the distance and let Mjöllnir drag him through the air by the handle, the same way it had borne Leif and me to his position in the sky.

"Mrrh-hugh-huuaaagh!" Hrym laughed and pointed. "He's flying away to go get his daddy." The frost Jötnar all joined in the laugh and began to speculate about when or if he'd come back for more and whom he'd bring with him next time.

The only one of us that could chase him at this point was Perun, who couldn't hope to overtake Thor before he reached help. The remaining flying mounts of the Valkyries, having nothing better to do, flew back toward Asgard without their riders.

"Coward!" Leif shouted after the diminishing god in the sky. Gunnar howled.

"Hey, Leif, a little help here, maybe?" I said in a normal tone. "Shove this back into its socket?" The vampire had no trouble hearing me from fifty yards away. He turned, located me, and ran to my aid. The adrenaline was wearing off, and my body was thinking about going into shock.

"Hmm," he said, braking abruptly in front of me and examining my arm. "You've broken a bone as well."

"Right. Socket first, then set the bones, and I'll knit from the inside."

"Ready?"

"No, wait. I need to touch the earth before we do this. I need more juice."

Leif efficiently cleared away a hole in the snow and I stepped into it, drawing on the earth's power and dulling the nerves in my shoulder.

"Okay, do it," I said. He grabbed my arm and shoved it back into its socket with an audible, crunchy pop. Then he took hold of my splintered collarbone at the first break—there were three—and held the pieces together until I could get a rudimentary binding in place. "Next," I said, and he moved on to the next break, and then the last. "Good enough," I said, placing Fragarach down carefully and then lying on my right side so that the maximum surface area of my tattoos could touch the earth.

Leif watched me in silence for a full minute to make sure that lying down wasn't a prelude to performing something tactically brilliant. Then he said, "You're just going to lie there until he comes back?"

"Hey, you're pretty smart for a dead guy. What happened up there? I got you your shot and you blew it."

Leif grimaced. "No denying that. I shattered his shield, but he knocked me away with a hammer blow before I could take another swing."

"That must have given you an ouchie."

"He crushed my ribs," he replied, grinning. "But that Valkyrie healed me up nicely. Their blood is powerful. First full meal I've had in days."

"Good. You're going to need it." I sighed. "Our surprises are all spent now, Leif. Nothing will be easy when Thor returns, and our best chance to get out of here unscathed is gone." Leif nodded but said nothing.

Gunnar joined us, barked once by way of greeting, and lay down against my back. He was trying to keep me warm, and it made me smile. Though he'd never admit it, Gunnar was treating me like a surrogate pack member. I could tell he missed them. I hoped he'd make it back. He would if we left now; we all would.

"Leif."

"Hmm?" He kept his eyes on the skies for Thor's return.

"I need to tell you something. Complete candor."

He looked down at me, interested. "What is it?"

"I've been visited by two different gods. You saw the Morrigan, and the other one was Jesus. They tend to be pretty fucking good at seeing the future."

"Yes?"

"They both said killing Thor would be an extraordinarily bad idea."

The vampire's expression hardened. "So?"

"So let's get the hell out of here and call it a victory."

"Victory? We have won nothing!"

"Heimdall is dead, plus twelve Valkyries. That's the blood price of your family times four. You've made your point and we're all still alive. Let's quit while we're ahead."

"We are *not* ahead. You do not keep score properly. The only death that counts is Thor's."

"What about my death? Or Gunnar's, or the rest of us? Will those count? Because the odds of us dying are pretty high if we wait for Thor to come back with the rest of the Æsir."

"Go, then, if you want, but leave me here."

"You know I won't do that." Hal would never speak to me again if I left Leif behind. "We all need to go."

Leif knelt next to me in the snow and said in low, intense tones, "A thousand years, Atticus. I have been waiting for this, needing it and wanting it, for a thousand years of sunless existence. Against that you put the ten years I have known you. Friend that you are to me, there is no argument you can make that will swerve me from my course. And I doubt seriously that you could sway any of the others with this talk of the future. If they have a fraction of the feeling I have, then the only future they care about is the one where Thor is dead. Nothing else matters."

Gunnar whuffed a small breath of agreement and nodded his head. I sighed, defeated. Revenge and rational thought never sleep together.

"Surviving matters," I said, my last salvo in a lost battle.

"Right," Leif said, happy to agree to anything that did not involve leaving. "So use that head of yours and help us out with that. Ought we to do anything while we wait? What if he does not come back at all?"

"Oh, he'll come. The frost giants can send ice storms toward Fólkvangr as we planned. And Perun can do his thing too if he wants. Maybe draw straws to see who's going to take on Týr, because he'll show up for sure." The Norse god of single combat might have only one hand (the great wolf Fenris having chewed the other off ages ago), but he could still wreak plenty of ruin with it. "And have Väinämöinen put us under a seeming again. We don't want Hugin and Munin to scout things out and give Odin a chance to war-game us. Let him deal only with Thor's verbal report."

I got almost a full hour of healing in before a cry went up that the Æsir approached. The collarbone was still fragile, but the shoulder joint worked fine and the muscles around it were solid, if a bit bruised and stiff. When I rose to my feet, the stars were gone from the western sky, blotted out by thunderheads that roiled with the barely contained fury of Thor. Gunnar rose too and stretched.

The massive trunk of Yggdrasil still loomed to the north, a gray wall that secured our right flank, though it was a football field away from where I stood. Gunnar and I were on the far right of our company, and the rest of the group was spread out to the south, scanning the western sky.

Even with night vision, there wasn't much for me to see except for a bright point of light that was probably the boar Gullinbursti. Forced to rely on Leif, I asked him what he saw.

"Odin and Freyr for certain. The lady with the cat chariot must be Freyja."

Saying that in hearing of the frost Jötnar was a mistake; they became extremely animated and repeated her name like fanboys, some of them even jamming their hands down their furs.

Leif continued, raising his voice to drown out the randy chorus of the giants. "I count three others."

"Including Thor?"

"No. I do not see Thor."

"Six of the Æsir but no Thor? Something's up."

"I should like to take this opportunity to name you Sherlock and point out that there is no shit."

"What? Leif, no. You said that completely wrong. You're supposed to say, 'No shit, Sher—'"

"Incoming!" Leif interrupted me. "Odin's spear! I cannot tell who has been targeted from this distance."

"Gods Below," I breathed. "How can he target any of us? Aren't we under a seeming right now?"

"Aye, we are," Väinämöinen confirmed.

"It might be proof against Hugin and Munin but apparently not against Odin himself." I shape-shifted to a hound, then back again in case it was aimed at me. Taking Fragarach with me, I drifted to the left and watched the phosphorus glow of Gullinbursti grow brighter. He was so bright that he was lighting up the puffed blanket of clouds above.

"Oh, bugger, the clouds!" I said. "Thor's above the clouds!" I got no response, for that's when Odin's plan hit us. The long flight of his spear ended through Väinämöinen's chest, throwing the Finn backward ten yards and spilling him dead into the snow. His seeming dissipated with his death, and now our exact positions were revealed to the Æsir. How Odin had known to target Väinämöinen was anyone's guess, but it was clearly the linchpin of his plan.

"One of the Æsir is an archer," Leif said. "Arrows incoming. That must be Ullr."

"Take him out, Perun!"

"*Da!*" The happy hairy thunder god grinned, and lightning lanced down from the sky, but nothing happened except for a frost giant taking an arrow in the throat.

"They're ready for it this time," I said. "They learned

from their mistakes. They're protected like we are. You'll have to make do with your axe. If you see either of Odin's ravens, take a shot." I hurried over to the frost Jötnar as another arrow found its mark, albeit not fatally. "Hrym! Suttung! Can you do anything about that archer? Wind or ice or something to throw off his aim? He'll just pick us off otherwise."

"Graah," Hrym said. "Hrrrrgh," he added, and a long ice club grew from the palm of his right hand, sort of like an extreme beardcicle. The other frost giants followed suit, condensing and freezing their own clubs, then they pointed them in concert in the direction of the Æsir. Shortly thereafter, a curtain of snow was thrown up perhaps a hundred yards in front of us, violent tempests in miniature that were sure to throw off anything flying in our direction—including winged horses and chariots and giant shiny dwarf-made pigs, as well as arrows.

"That's good," I said, "but keep an eye on the sky above. Thor is up there above the clouds, and he'll try to drop in on us soon." I moved back to the body of Väinämöinen to retrieve Odin's spear. The cold iron touch of my hand on its shaft did nothing to deactivate the targeting runes on the spearhead, so I had a surefire kill shot here. But using it would mean giving the Æsir a chance to throw it at us again.

The Finnish wizard looked surprised, his eyes open in an unblinking stare, focused on the spear sprouting from his chest. I closed his eyes and hoped that his soul, wherever it was, felt content with his brief contribution to the battle. I was not content, I would have liked to hear more of his stories, and more of his songs. I would have liked for him to feel he'd done right by the sea serpent he championed. And I would have liked time to mourn him properly, but the demands of battle meant I had to move on quickly if I wanted to live through it.

I hefted the spear in my left hand, deciding to hold it in

reserve. Perhaps the ideal moment to use it would present itself. In the meantime, the Æsir wouldn't be able to pick it up without dealing with me first.

Unfortunately, picking it up proved to be their plan precisely. Leif's shouted warning saved me. I jumped frantically to my right and barely avoided Thor's hammer, which fell from the hand of the thunder god, directly above. The earth shook with his blow and toppled our entire party to the ground, and a white splash of snow exploded from the impact, stinging me as I landed nearby. Before I could gather my arms and legs together, Thor was already back on his feet in the small crater he'd made. He had a new shield, I saw, and a new outfit of armor that indicated he was taking us a bit more seriously. The mail shirt was still there underneath, but he had a sleeveless tunic of lamellar armor over it now, made of red-dyed hardened leather. His bracers and greaves were also hardened leather, albeit the normal brown color, and he had nothing of substance over his thighs save for a mail skirt. He wore a cap helmet with a nose guard, but no ridiculous wings or horns sprouted out from the sides of it. His blue eyes blazed from underneath as they locked on mine.

"Vengeance for the slain!" he cried in Old Norse, and then he charged, hammer cocked to pound my brains to tapioca.

"Yeah, that's what this is all about," I said, scrambling backward in a graceless crabwalk. All I could hope for was to get out of the way again; there was no question of parrying or striking back when I was so off balance, and parrying a war hammer is damn near impossible in the best of situations. My situation—lying naked on my back in the snow—was therefore less than optimal.

The fire in Thor's eyes cooled a smidge as he realized this wasn't a one-on-one duel: He was now in a free-for-all. He took his eyes off me and raised his shield in time to get bowled over by Leif. They tumbled past me in the snow, the vampire hissing and the thunder god roaring, and that gave me enough time to gain my feet and worry about who else might be on the way. Gunnar was coming hell-bent for Thor, and so was Zhang Guo Lao. So eager were they to pile on that they didn't see what was coming hell-bent for them. The Æsir had flown through the frost giants' curtain of snow, and now they had all picked a target. "Behind you!" I shouted, hoping they would realize I was speaking to them both, but only Zhang Guo Lao took heed. He turned and set himself, an iron rod in each hand, and neatly redirected the attack of Týr, who leapt at him from the back of his winged horse. Týr was armored in a similar fashion to Thor, except the leather of his lamellar tunic had been dyed blue. He was fighting left-handed, of course, shield mounted on the stump of his right arm.

Gunnar took a boar tusk in the gut. Gullinbursti gored him from behind, the great tusk sweeping under the werewolf's hind legs and catching him in the soft underbelly. Gunnar yelped as he was tossed high into the air, blood and maybe intestines trailing beneath him. The sheer wattage output from the dwarf-made boar was blinding with my night vision on, but the silhouetted figure on its back could be none other than the god Freyr. He was raising a sword to cut through Gunnar as he fell back to earth. I'd been hoping to sit out this part of the battle, in the faint hope that nonparticipation would ward off whatever bad karma would accrue here; the words of Jesus and the Morrigan still rang in my ears. But I couldn't stand by and let Freyr chop Gunnar in two.

I'm not much of a lefty, but the distance was short and either the runes would work or they wouldn't: I hurled Odin's spear as quickly as I could toward the god and hoped it would be in time. It caught Freyr under the arm and threw him off the back of Gullinbursti, as his sword cut shallowly into Gunnar's flesh on the right side of his rib cage. The werewolf plunged snarling into the snow, not done yet but grievously wounded. The huge golden boar—the size of a conversion van—charged past me, and I raked Fragarach along its right side as it hurtled by, eliciting a startled scream from it. It struggled to slow its rush and pivot around to make another pass, and I took the frantic second this afforded me to check the field.

Leif and Thor were still entangled, as were Zhang Guo Lao and Týr; the other four Æsir had plowed into the frost giants, and several large blue corpses lay in the snow. I recognized two of the Norse by sight—Odin and Freyja. Odin wore the same spectacled helmet I'd seen him wear before, but the simple reindeer tunic over mail was gone. His leather armor was articulated with broad lames, tooled with Nordic runes, and doubtless enchanted to be as strong as plate without the heaviness or movement restrictions of metal.

Freyja, for her part, was not quite as hot as I had expected. In fact, I wasn't sure at first why the frost giants were so taken with her. She was fair, to be sure, but not excessively so. I could walk on a beach in Rio or the south of France and find dozens of women with more sizzle in their bacon. She was blond, her hair gathered in two long braids and falling out of a helmet wreathed in flowers. Over mail and a green leather cuirass she had draped a white cloak, fastened at the right shoulder with a brooch. Her belt was slim and golden, and thin flowering vines trailed down from it, resting on top of a green lamellar skirt. It was an odd juxtaposition of images, but she was an odd deity, equal parts fertility, beauty, and war. I think the fertility and war must have appealed to the frost giants every bit as much as the beauty—and the influence of war, no doubt, colored her appearance somewhat. Her jaw was just a bit too square, too mannish, to be called truly beautiful in my eyes. She worked for the frost giants, though.

At a guess, one of the other Æsir might have been Odin's son Vidar; his armor was a gloomy black studded with steel, and he had no beard on his chin. The last one, with the bow, was most likely Ullr, and he had parted his brown beard and braided it. Perun was attempting to reach Odin, but Ullr was behaving like a bodyguard and firing arrows at the Russian as fast as he could nock them. Some of these Perun had either dodged or swatted away, but I saw at least two shafts sticking out of his left arm.

That was all I could take in with a frenzied glance around, because true battles don't allow for leisurely vistas and the taking of tea. They are quick and savage and likely to end abruptly for all concerned.

I was likely to end abruptly if I didn't move. I was currently standing between a wounded boar and a wounded werewolf, either of which could churn me to gravy. Fragarach was going to be useless if I had to face Gullinbursti head-on. Even if I poked him between the eyes, he'd run over me on sheer inertia.

I waited until the boar had a good head of steam, then I tossed Fragarach toward the fallen body of Freyr and shifted to a hound. I sprinted after my sword, and the boar swerved to pursue me. He was faster than I was—but not faster than Gunnar. The snarling werewolf took advantage of the angle I'd provided and leapt onto the boar's back, his claws digging savagely into the creature and knocking him off my tail. The boar squealed and tried to buck the werewolf off, but Gunnar was all tooth and claw and methodically tore chunks out of the beast while ropes of intestines kept sliding out of his own belly.

A cheerful bark welled in my throat as I saw Gunnar

rip huge, vital, pulsating things out of the boar—those had to be important. But it turned into a whine as the boar toppled fatally to the earth with a final peal of anguish, crushing Gunnar underneath his massive bulk in the process. I ran over to where he fell, ready to shift back to human form to try to lift the boar off my friend, but Gunnar was undergoing the shift himself—his final one, bereft of pain for this time only. Wounded beyond his wolf's ability to heal, he expired, and his face smoothed with a peace he'd never possessed in life.

I tried to scream "No!" but forgot I was a hound. It came out as a strangled yip.

I've had friends die on the battlefield before—more than that, for my wife, Tahirah, died on the battlefield—and it always has the same effect on me. There is a quick stab of sorrow, but it is quickly shunted to the back of my mind until I have leisure to indulge it; my Celtic rage is kindled to white-hot temperatures in the meantime, which only the blood of enemies can ever hope to quench. Gunnar's passing flipped a switch inside my head, and I turned into the Celtic warrior—a fearless, unreasoning creature that kills until he cannot kill anymore. A red haze clouded my vision and spittle frothed from the sides of my mouth, as an inchoate roar swelled from my lungs.

I sprinted to the body of Freyr and shifted back to human once I reached him. He was dead, Gungnir having done its work, and I yanked the enchanted spear out to employ it further. I searched eagerly for new targets, but all were partially blocked by allies—until I looked up. There I spied two enemies circling above the mêlée between the few remaining frost Jötnar and the Æsir: Hugin and Munin. I had no clue which was which, but if Odin's unconsciousness could drop them from the sky, could the death of one or both ravens drop Odin? Time to find out. Choosing one, I hurled Gungnir with all the strength of my right arm and watched it fly. It bent in the air like a well-struck football will swerve toward the corner of the goal, heading for its target with infallible accuracy. It spitted the bird through the breast. When the raven fell spiraling to the snow, Odin seized up in the midst of swinging a blow at Hrym and allowed the Jötunn to bat him away powerfully with his ice club. The one-eyed god flew like a sack of bones through the air, and his journey attracted the dismayed attention of Freyja, who called out and broke off her own attack, wheeling her chariot around to render assistance. She forgot entirely in her haste that frost giants have very long arms. Suttung snatched her out of the open back of her chariot and instantly caused a sheath of ice to freeze her from head to toe; she was a goddess Popsicle. The chariot, pulled by Freyja's cats, flew on toward Odin.

"Graah!" Suttung bellowed jubilantly, holding his prize above his head. "I got her!"

"Father!" the Æsir in black cried, confirming his identity as Vidar. He disengaged from the giants more successfully than Freyja had and rushed to the allfather's aid. This would have been the best time to sound a retreat and get out of there while we still could, or at least help Leif or Zhang Guo Lao or Perun with their Æsir deathmatches, but instead I scooped up Fragarach from where it lay in the snow and chased the son of Odin, all the warnings from Jesus and the Morrigan forgotten now that I had taken leave of my reason.

I really should have heeded those warnings.

Something punched me hard in my left side as I ran, knocking me off my feet to tumble gracelessly in the powder. Pain followed shortly afterward, and my arm swung into an arrow shaft underneath my ribs. I couldn't breathe for the excruciating agony this caused, but I understood what had happened. Ullr had taken a shot at me instead of at Perun, knowing an easy target when he saw one. I drew on the magic in my bear charm to squelch the worst of the pain and staggered to my feet, twisting around in time to see Perun cleave the bastard in two with his axe. That relief allowed me to gasp in a lungful of cold air, but my will to fight on left me when I exhaled. Reason returned: Let Vidar tend to the broken body of Odin, I thought, and I'll tend to my torn intestines.

I was a bloody mess inside, and it was only going to get worse. The tip of the arrow hadn't gone all the way through, and it would have to before I could snap it off and remove the shaft. Perun, looking around for another foe, spotted me floundering in the snow and I waved him over weakly. He had three arrows in him, all on his limbs on the left side. The two I had spotted earlier were still in his arm, and a third was lodged in his thigh, causing him to half-limp, half-hop to me. The five surviving frost giants were huddling together to admire the frozen Freyja, still clutched triumphantly in Suttung's hand.

Two vicious battles continued as Perun made his way to my side. Týr was discovering that he had no way to anticipate the drunken boxing moves of Zhang Guo Lao. His thrusts whiffed through the air or caught nothing but the voluminous material of the immortal's robes, and it was all he could do to keep his shield in front of Zhang's attacks.

Farther away, almost all the way back to the wall of ice the Jötnar had erected upon our arrival, Leif's duel with Thor raged on. Considering Leif's speed and skill with swordplay, I would have thought he'd have finished it one way or another. But Thor was lightning fast himself—go figure. And that new shield of his was holding up very well compared to the first one; there was probably an enchantment of some kind on it.

Perun ducked under my right side and draped my arm

around his hairy shoulders. Together we limped back toward the root of Yggdrasil.

"Is Odin killed?" he asked.

"I don't think so. I got one of his ravens, so he's currently functioning without thought—or maybe it's memory." The remaining raven was circling over the spot where Odin fell. Vidar was bent over him, trying to get him to respond. "Plus whatever it feels like to have Hrym tee off on you with an ice club."

The Russian thunder god laughed. "Is good enough for me, then. For wise one to be crippled in mind is fate worse than death."

"We have to get out of here," I said. "If the Einherjar or more of the Æsir arrive, we won't make it." Two of us and fifteen of the frost giants were dead. We could have left with only two frost giants dead, with Väinämöinen and Gunnar still alive; the thought made me want to weep.

"*Da*. Is truth. But Thor still lives and fights."

"Leif could probably use our help."

Perun chuckled wryly. "I do not think we help much at this point."

Leif was now trying to get past the shield by circling around the thunder god. All he needed was one good strike against Thor for Moralltach to do its work. Unlike Fragarach, Moralltach couldn't cut through shields or armor, but its power was to kill with one blow. Lopping off a pinky, a flesh wound to the calf, a pound of flesh from the forearm, it didn't matter: All were fatal wounds when Moralltach delivered them. At least, that was how it was supposed to work. I'd never seen it work like that, because when I decapitated the Norns with Moralltach, its magic was redundant. But Thor was pivoting easily to meet Leif's blows. Occasionally he lashed out with his hammer, but Leif was never there.

That told me my friend was a fraction faster than the

thunder god. Leif hadn't figured out how to get around that shield, though. He needed to try something new. Even as I thought this, his blurred circle around Thor came to a halt and he squared off perhaps ten yards away from the thunder god's shield. A human's chest would be heaving for breath at this point, but Leif was perfectly still, a statue of a pale blond ninja in a field of white. His booted left leg was bent in front of his right; his right arm was cocked to the side, with the hilt of Moralltach held at ear height, its blade a cold blue gash in the dark above Leif's head.

A silence fell on the plain. Zhang Guo Lao flipped backward three times to put some distance between himself and Týr, holding up his hands in a clear signal to hold. The warrior god held. The frost giants tore their gazes from Freyja and stopped grunting long enough to listen.

"Do you know who we are, thunder god?" Leif said into the silence. I translated the Old Norse for Perun's benefit.

"I care not!" Thor sneered.

"That is precisely why we are here. You are a careless, thoughtless god wrapped in protective myths of goodness. You are a slayer of innocents. You killed my family a thousand years ago and dared me to become a vampire. You probably do not even remember, do you?"

The thunder god's voice rang with icy scorn. "No. Why should I remember a moment's amusement from a thousand years ago?"

"Amusement? My family's death was amusing to you? It is as I thought. Come on, Thor," Leif said, beckoning to him with his left hand. "Your destiny awaits."

He wanted Thor to charge, thinking he would gain some advantage by it, but I could not see any. Thor bellowed and rushed him, shield and hammer held high. Leif remained immobile, and as I watched the headlong progress of Thor, Leif's plan became clear to me.

"No, Leif," I breathed.

In order for Thor to follow through on his hammer blow, he'd have to lower his shield and rotate it to his left side. For the space of a split second, his left shoulder would be unguarded, and Leif wanted to take advantage of it. But, in so doing, Leif could not avoid the hammer.

Their collision was a blurred, dull explosion of crunching bones. Thor's hammer burst Leif's skull apart like a watermelon, and he collapsed to the plain without a head. Thor remained standing.

"Ha!" he shouted. "Who has met his destiny? Not I!" But then his shield dropped and he turned to face the spectators. Moralltach was lodged in the muscle above his collarbone, between his neck and left shoulder. It had missed the brigandine and successfully parted the mail; Thor had worn no gorget. It was bleeding well but not gushing by any means. Thor dropped his hammer and wrenched the sword loose with his right hand, tossing it away from him.

"Ha!" he said again, and bent to pick up Mjöllnir. But his face, flushed with victory, darkened to a frown. The skin around the wound began to blacken, and then it spread quickly to his neck and down his arm like an oil spill.

"Eh? What sorcery is this?" the thunder god growled. Those were his last words. The malignant rot reached his heart and perhaps his spinal cord as well, withering them and snuffing out his life. He fell face forward, already dead, the putrefaction continuing to turn him black and greasy.

It was Fae sorcery, of course. A moment of stunned silence settled across the snow as the onlookers absorbed what had happened.

"No!" Týr shouted, breaking into a run toward Thor, his unfinished duel with Zhang Guo Lao forgotten. "He cannot die! He was supposed to slay the world serpent!"

Týr had just made himself vulnerable by giving in to his emotions—the same way I had a few moments ago. The emotions were still there and they wanted all my attention—grief for Gunnar and for Leif and for my inability to stop any of this from happening—but I firmly held them in check and concentrated on damage control. "Hey, Perun, we have to do something about Týr. See if your lightning works again. Thor's dead, so perhaps his protection is gone. But don't kill him."

"Is good idea," he said, nodding. "I give him baby bolt." Týr howled as a lightning strike shot through his body, scorching his skin and sending him into an epic flop-and-twitch.

"Excellent. Now can you get a wind to fly us over there?"

"I think yes," he replied, and I stifled a grunt of pain as the sudden lift tugged at the arrow in my side and we awkwardly flew to the gory aftermath of the duel. The frost Jötnar were walking over to confirm Thor's demise, and Zhang Guo Lao was casually paralyzing the helpless Týr with his pressure-point technique so the Æsir could bother us no more. Once past them, I had eyes only for Leif—my magical ones.

The mess of his head was splattered across the snow, not a single bone of it left intact. Thor's hammer had pulverized it down to the neck. But the red ember of vampirism still glowed faintly within his chest. If he didn't drain out completely, there was still a chance he could recover.

My bear charm was nearly out of juice thanks to multiple shifts and the strain of keeping myself from lapsing into shock and worse. I'd need to touch the earth if I wanted to do much more than keep from passing out. I nearly did when Perun set us down next to Leif's body; it might have been a swoon.

"Hrym, could you clear some snow away right here

so I can touch the ground?" I asked as the giant approached.

"Graah," he affirmed. He pointed his ice club at the spot I'd indicated and the snow lifted away, piling up at Leif's feet.

I stepped onto the frozen ground and felt the energy waiting for me there. "Thank you," I said. Magic flowed up through my tattoos, enough so that I could dull the pain, stabilize the trauma, and keep functioning. Dealing with it properly would take time I didn't have right now. "I'm sorry for the people you lost today," I added.

Incredibly, the frost Jötunn responded with an indifferent shrug. "We lost some but won much today. Thor is dead. Ullr and Heimdall, Freyr and the Valkyries too. Odin is an empty shell. And we finally have Freyja. Usually we win nothing."

"Oh," I said, unsure of how else to answer. Hrym's tally of the dead brought home to me how much trouble I was in—and I meant beyond the arrow lodged in my guts. Once news of this battle spread throughout the world, a whole lot of supernatural folk besides the surviving Norse would be looking for me.

"You were true to your word, tiny Atticus man," Hrym said. "I will tell my people this. We go now."

"Right, yes, don't let me keep you," I said. The frost Jötnar dropped their clubs and shape-shifted into giant eagles. Suttung, bringing up the rear, gripped the frozen Freyja in his talons as they lifted off and flew toward Ratatosk's hole in the root of Yggdrasil. I felt sorry for her as I watched them go. I knew I'd promised her to them to secure their help, but I never thought they'd actually take her alive and return to Jötunheim safely. I didn't like to think what a tribe of horny giants would do to her once she thawed out.

I wasn't the only one who felt this way. A streak of gray flashed in front of my eyes, a feline yowl split the night air, then Suttung screeched as said streak slammed into his underside. He dropped Freyja and began to circle around, as did the other eagles, to see what had attacked him. It was Freyja's flying cats, still harnessed to her chariot, one of the craziest conveyances in all mythology. They had the same agility and speed in the air that normal cats have on the ground, and they swooped underneath Freyja and caught her in her chariot as she fell. Some of the ice shattered on impact, and the goddess broke through the rest on her own, urging her cats to flee.

Those were some pretty smart kittehs. They wouldn't have stood a chance against the frost Jötnar in bipedal form, but the giants couldn't bash them with ice clubs as eagles or whip around any elemental magic. All the cats had to do now was outrun the eagles in the air, and I thought their chances were pretty good. They flew southwest toward Freyja's hall, Fólkvangr, with the eagles screaming after them.

I shook my head to clear it and turned my attention to Leif. Part of me thought it might be best to leave him here. The Norse might be comforted knowing that Thor's killer was also dead. But I doubted it.

On the other hand, there was no doubt that I had put Hal in a terrible position. The one thing he'd asked me to do—bring them both back alive—I couldn't deliver. He'd feel betrayed, no doubt, and I already felt guilty beyond words and terrified of facing him. But perhaps, if I got extremely lucky, I could do something to save Leif. Sort of.

Peering through my faerie specs, I sealed up all the leaking vessels in his neck with a binding so that he'd lose no more blood. Whatever that red glow in his chest was, it needed blood to survive. That was the easy part. The hard part would be figuring out how to bring in new blood, new energy, without any fangs or a head to keep them in. If left alone, the vampire would eventually grow a new head, but would it still be Leif, or would it simply be an unthinking, bloodsucking monster? Vampires of that sort tended not to last long. They killed too many humans, and other vampires destroyed them to keep their existence a secret.

There was no charm I could use for what I wished to do. I had to laboriously speak the bindings from scratch and improvise much of it, because I'd never tried anything like it before. Slowly, as Perun and Zhang Guo Lao stood sentinel nearby, listening to Týr curse impotently at us in the snow, I bound as much solid matter as I could back together. There were some chunks of brain here and there, carbon and calcium fragments that used to be his skull, and strands of hair as well. All of these I bound together in something resembling a head shape, a sort of grotesque mockery of Leif that looked like the head of a primitive voodoo doll. There was no question of me sculpting it back to any semblance of Leif's actual features or re-creating the complexity of bone and tissues he needed. I was simply trying to give the resurrection engine in his chest as much material to work with as possible, so that Leif would have a fighting chance to come back as some shadow of his former self. Once the head and a rudimentary neck were assembled, I attached them to the stump atop his shoulders, sealed it all around, and then reopened the vessels inside so that the blood could flow into the head and the vampire could begin the work of rebuilding itself.

"That's all I can do," I said, sighing. The lump of matter that used to be Leif's head looked ridiculous on top of a black leather jacket, and smaller without all the fluid, but it was the limit of my capabilities. My old archdruid had taught me only the theory of unbinding a vampire's component parts, and I hadn't actually had to do it until centuries later. No one had ever taught me

how to put a vampire back together again or even discussed it as a hypothetical necessity. I don't think anyone else would have considered it a good idea. I wasn't
sure it was a good idea either; it was more of a desperate
attempt to salvage something positive out of this blood-
bath. If Leif could come back from this and prevent a
vampire war in Arizona, that had to be good.

Perun curled his lip in uncertainty. "This will work?"
he said.

"I have no idea. I hope so. But we haven't escaped yet.
We need to leave now."

"Is good plan." He clapped me lightly on the shoulder.
"I like."

Chapter 27

There were still three of the Æsir scattered about the field. More would be coming soon but probably not before dawn. Heimdall's horn had called everyone. Frigg, Odin's wife, would no doubt appear to take charge of her husband's care. If anyone could restore him, she could.

I needed to see to my own care, but I couldn't do it safely in Asgard. I needed to get back to Midgard or one of the Fae planes, where I wouldn't be disturbed, because once I started this sort of healing I'd probably fall into a trance. First, there were things to do and words to speak. We collected my swords and Odin's spear—I figured it was mine now—and placed them against the root of Yggdrasil, along with the bodies of our fallen. Perun's strength, like Thor's, was Herculean, and he was able to drag Gullinbursti off Gunnar using only his right hand, even wounded as he was.

After that, Perun and I limped and winced our way over to the paralyzed and cursing Týr, while Zhang Guo Lao accompanied us in serenity. He had acquitted himself remarkably well, accomplishing his revenge and suffering nothing but a bruise or two from his extended duel with Týr. He'd been sipping on his elixir to restore himself.

It took Týr a good couple of minutes to shut up long

enough to listen to us. He thought we were there to finish him off, so he wanted to make sure he cursed us good
before he went to Hel. The thing about uttering death
curses is, they don't work unless you follow through and
die, and we had no intention of killing him. When I finally convinced Týr we meant him no harm, he glared at
me while Perun kept an eye on the west. Vidar hadn't
moved from Odin's side, and the remaining raven still
circled above. Neither Freyja nor the frost giants had returned from the southwest.

"Your worthy opponent will release you from paralysis
in a moment and you will be free to leave," I said to Týr
in Old Norse. "If you attempt to attack us once he does,
you will be slain. I want you to return to Gladsheim and
report what happened here today, but, more importantly,
I want you to know *why* this happened. We came for
Thor and Thor only, but of course he was too cowardly
to face us alone. His centuries of carnal, bloody, and un-
natural acts, his casual slaughters, have brought this day
of reckoning upon you all. Should we kill all the Æsir and
the Vanir too, it would not be sufficient blood price for
Thor's villainy. If you have even a passing knowledge of
his activities on Midgard, you know this to be truth." I
suspected he did. The one-armed man with Thor in Leif's
tale had probably been Týr.

"Who are you?" Týr asked. He saw me standing there
with an arrow in my side, apparently unconcerned by it,
but in truth the effort of keeping myself together was
very taxing. His question was too good a straight line to
pass up, though.

I preened. "I am the immortal Bacchus of the
Olympians. I represent a consortium of individuals who
had scores to settle with Thor. That includes the dark
elves, who showed me how to get here without using
Bifrost. You really should have been nicer to them in the
old days."

I doubted that would hold up under scrutiny, especially if the frost giants ever talked, but one could always hope the Norse would swallow it for a time. It would give me a head start on hiding and give Bacchus a headache. I turned to Master Zhang and asked him in Mandarin to release Týr from his paralysis but to be on guard afterward. He lunged forward, causing Týr's eyes to bug out, and struck him in five places with one of his iron rods. He didn't bother to do it gently. Those hits were going to leave marks.

We backed off and Týr leapt to his feet, death in his eyes. His shield and sword were still in the snow, so perhaps he thought we'd wrestle.

"Go in peace and see the sunrise," I said, "or a bolt from the sky will strike you down where you stand."

He took his time thinking about it. He really wanted to come after us, but eventually he counted and saw that we were three, he was only one, plus there was the lightning thing. He took a few steps back, hurling insults he thought were dire, like "craven weasel puke" and "maple-flavored whale shit."

A muttered request to Perun lifted us in the air back to the root. There I picked up my swords, and Zhang Guo Lao graciously agreed to carry Gungnir for me.

We took one last look at the southwestern sky. No eagles flew there. I hoped the frost giants were not so stupid as to follow Freyja all the way to Fólkvangr.

"Let's go, Perun," I said. "Hrym and his people can find their own way back to Jötunheim."

As he had done on our trip up the root, Perun summoned tightly controlled winds to carry us—including the bodies of Leif, Gunnar, and Väinämöinen—through Ratatosk's tunnel. On the way back down, I finally let the emotions I'd been repressing out. Anger and guilt for myself, grief and regret for Gunnar and Leif, fear and uncertainty about what consequences this would hold in the future: All of it came roaring out of my throat and eyes and was consigned to the wind.

I'd kept my word and my friends had avenged themselves, but I doubted the Tempe Pack would thank me for losing their alpha. I don't know what I could have done differently, once the battle started, to save either of them; I just kept returning to the idea that I never should have taken them there in the first place. My word would have been worth nothing and they'd have hated me, but they'd both be alive. Now my word was still good but they were dead (or as good as dead). How was this any better? I'd cocked everything up so badly, and Hal might never forgive me. He was alpha now and Leif was out of commission for who know how long, perhaps never to regain his old personality. There would probably be a vampire war anyway, despite my efforts to give Leif a chance at coming back.

At the Well of Mimir, we wasted no time, because we had only a few hours of darkness left. We retrieved the packs we'd left behind—I checked Väinämöinen's to make sure my wallet and cell phone were still in there—and clustered around the root. We had some difficulty arranging ourselves, since three of our party were dead, but I pulled us through to earth and breathed a heavy sigh of relief—at least as heavy as I could with an arrow in my side. Our campsite was undisturbed, and there were no signs that anyone had visited the area since we'd left.

"All right, I've stalled long enough," I said, wincing. "Perun, if you push through my one arrow and break off the tip, I'll do all three of yours."

"Is deal," he said. "Ready?"

"One thing. Can you tell if it's going to come out where my tattoos are on the right side?"

He and Zhang Guo Lao both examined the angle of the arrow and determined that it would come out slightly in front of them on the stomach side.

"Good, that makes things a bit easier," I said. The tats renewed themselves as part of my skin whenever I took my Immortali-Tea; they looked new instead of two thousand years old. But if they were torn completely, I'd need to get them touched up, and at this point that meant going to one of the Tuatha Dé Danann. No thanks.

Feeling the comfort of the earth underneath my feet, I asked Zhang Guo Lao if I could use one of his iron rods. He handed it over and I put it between my teeth, at which he blanched. Who knew he was a germophobe?

"Okay." I nodded at Perun. "Do it."

Yes, I cheated and dulled my pain receptors. You would too. I still felt a blazing stab, and the unspeakable discomfort of things tearing inside cannot be ignored, pain or no pain. This wasn't simply hemorrhaging tissue; there were gastric acid and other toxic fluids loose. Without the earth's help, it would have been a mortal wound.

We weren't finished. Perun snapped off the arrowhead and I felt the twinge of it through my core. He did his best to clear away any splinters, and then I bit down hard on the iron rod as he yanked the shaft back through me.

Thank the Gods Below I didn't have to deal with this while stranded on cement somewhere. The earth gave so much to me, and as I used its energy to bind my insides back together, I was reminded again that I still needed to help the earth heal itself in the Superstition Mountains. Every moment that it gave of its substance to help me renew myself only increased my debt.

After an indeterminate time, I became aware of an ache in my jaw and realized I still had my teeth clenched around a rod of iron. My companions were staring at me. I withdrew it from my mouth, now a bit slobbery, and offered it to Zhang Guo Lao with my thanks.

"Consider it a gift," he said, a trifle horrified. "I will get a new one."

I thanked him again and refocused on my healing, closing my eyes. When I opened them again, Perun's arrows had been removed, and he was urging a giggling Zhang Guo Lao to have just one more shot of vodka with him as they sat on the boulders around the fire pit. And it was daytime.

"Where's Leif?" I said. "Guys? Where's Leif?"

"Druid speaks!" Perun gushed, throwing his hands up in the air. The growth underneath his arms was nearly as full as his beard. A gigantic smile split his hairy face, and he said, "We should have drink!"

"Honored Druid," the immortal Zhang Guo Lao began, waving at me. He must have been deep in his cups, for this action caused him to slip off his boulder and fall backward, feet in the air. This set off Perun and he nearly fell over himself.

"Guys? Seriously. Where's Leif?"

"Is fine," Perun managed. "Is safe. We bury him behind you." He pointed, and I turned to see three grave-shaped mounds of dirt. Perun's voice was sober in my ears, hilarity gone: "We bury others also. Is okay?"

I wasn't sure how I felt about that. "You buried Gunnar?"

"Da. You sleep standing up, could not wake, so we make us busy."

Zhang Guo Lao raised himself up to a sitting position and waved for my attention. "Honored Druid, I have a question."

"Yes?"

"I have a question," he repeated.

"You said already," Perun pointed out.

"Thank you for your attention. My question is this: When are you going to put on some clothes?"

I looked down and realized with some embarrassment that I'd left my clothes back in Asgard. It was precisely the reaction they'd been hoping for, and they clutched at their bellies and roared with unbridled mirth.

Chapter 28

Zhang Guo Lao took his leave near midday and walked east with his pack and fish drum. He offered to donate a robe to me before he left "as a public service," but I found a spare set of clothes in Väinämöinen's pack that would serve—a simple pair of pants and a tunic that I tied up with a length of rope, since I didn't find a belt.

Perun agreed to help me transport Leif and Gunnar back to Tempe. We would have done something for Väinämöinen had we known where else to take him, but in the absence of better information, he had found his final resting place. We took turns saying a few words for him—inadequate for such a life—and bid him a somber farewell.

"Why do you think the Norse have not come here yet?" Perun asked. Now that it was just the two of us, we spoke Russian, in which he was far more fluent than I.

"They have funerals to conduct and a severe leadership crisis at this point," I said. "And perhaps an identity crisis to deal with as well. Many of them have dedicated their very long lives to preparing for Ragnarok. Now they have undeniable evidence that it won't happen as prophesied."

"Yes, they will need a new purpose," Perun said. "I see."

"Beyond that, they have to use Bifrost to reach Midgard. They can't shift planes the way I can. But since I blamed the dark elves and Bacchus, the Æsir will probably bother them first."

Perun chuckled. "That was good. It will give us time to hide."

"You're going into hiding?"

"Yes, for long time."

"Thunder gods don't hide."

The Russian shrugged. "I am not like Thor. I have the Russian depth of character. And I like to help people, not hurt them. Usually I help with vodka. You want some?"

"No, thanks, I don't think that would be wise right now. I have a delicate digestive system at the moment."

He beamed at me. "I will help some other way. Sleep and heal more. I will watch."

Grateful for the chance to continue my recovery, I stretched out on the ground and dropped back into a healing trance. I still had a long way to go and I'd be on a liquid diet for a while, but nothing was leaking anymore and the acid was neutralized. I'd done very little about the wounds on the outside or the torn abdominal muscles, partly because they weren't immediately dangerous and partly because they'd provide me a bit of safety when I had to face Hal. He had to know already that Gunnar was dead, because the alpha magic would have settled on his shoulders by now.

Perun woke me at sundown, and I felt much better inside. I might be able to concentrate on the muscle walls soon and devote some attention to a weak collarbone.

I asked the earth to move aside from the bodies of Gunnar and Leif. Leif didn't look any better, but neither did he look any worse. Perun and I levered them up to a standing position, then the Russian summoned winds and bore us south to the forest where I could shift us to Tír na nÓg. Once safely on the Fae plane, I did not wish to waste another day shifting only part of the way for Leif's benefit. It was morning in Arizona, so if we wanted to travel there immediately, we'd need a way to protect his body from the sun. The solution was to build a coffin without any nails.

Trees are plentiful in Tír na nÓg. The trick is to find one that isn't vital to shifting planes through some tether or other. We had to walk a mile before I found a young ash tree suitable for harvest. Perun laid about with his axe, cut rough planks, and I bound them together magically, making sure that there were no gaps for sunlight to leak through. We built one for Gunnar too.

Once ready, we shifted all the way back to the Aravaipa Canyon Wilderness.

"I have never been here," Perun said, looking at the stream and the bare sycamores along the bank with pale, fingerlike branches scraping the sky. "It is beautiful."

I agreed and cast camouflage on both of the coffins and us. Once we got to populated areas, people would probably feel the wind of our passage and see a blur overhead, but I couldn't bring myself to get too concerned; I figured they'd blame it on aliens or secret military experiments or the mushrooms they ate and that would be the end of it. But I was careful to cast this using magic stored in my bear charm and not draw anything from the earth. I had a theory that the Hammers of God could track those draws somehow and thus pinpoint my location. It would explain how they knew about most of my activities—but not how they had found me at Rúla Búla. That mystery aside, I was going to be operating on a reduced magic diet as a general policy now that I was back in Arizona. There would be too many people—and perhaps too many gods—looking for me here, and I didn't want to give them any clues.

"Where are we going?" Perun asked.

I didn't want to fly back to Tempe under these circumstances. Any magic, including Perun's, was likely to draw attention now. So I named a town about seventy miles from Tempe and hoped I could arrange a ninja operation from there. "A copper-mining town called Globe, northwest of here. I know the perfect place. You can drop me off and I'll buy you a Big Boy."

"I am not fond of children."

"Don't worry, it's a drink."

We reached Globe a little after eleven in the morning by riding the winds, and I directed Perun to an alley behind Broad Street downtown—specifically the alley behind a sports bar called the Huddle. It wasn't an urban alley full of rats and moldering dumpsters but rather a wide sort of throughway with parking and a couple of trees. Asphalt laid down decades ago was deteriorating, crumbling to gravel and allowing weeds to poke through.

The Huddle had a back patio constructed specifically for smokers; it faced an unused parking lot on the other side of the alley, currently fenced off with chain link. A single trash can sat in front of that fence, enjoying the shade of a willow acacia tree. I had Perun set us down there, and we stacked the coffins on top of each other about five feet away from the trash can. No one saw us do this, because the Huddle isn't full of smokers at eleven in the morning. The smokers tend to come out at night.

"I need to make a couple of calls in there," I said, gesturing at the back entrance of the bar, "and then we can enjoy our Big Boys." I'd chosen this place precisely because it had a back entrance; those come in handy sometimes.

I dispelled our camouflage but left it on the coffins. After a bit of conversation, Perun was convinced that he didn't need to wear his fur cloak into an American bar around lunchtime. Besides, we were in Arizona now: It was sixty degrees outside in December. He removed the fur to reveal another layer of fur underneath—his own hairy arms and shoulders sprouting from his thin sleeveless shirt. I grinned as I camouflaged his cloak on top of the coffins. Americans have a visceral fear of body hair—a fact exploited by hippies, bikers, and construction foremen—so Perun's appearance would likely scare everyone in the bar, including the bikers.

After I reminded Perun to speak English again, we entered the Huddle and I threw a wave at Gabby, the owner. She had a quick smile, a ready laugh, and the supreme confidence that she could handle anything. I watched her size up Perun, who was probably two feet taller than she was and weighed twice as much, and savored the moment when I saw she had decided she could take him, even though he was holding Odin's spear.

"Hey, Atticus, it's been a while. Good to see you again," she said. My familiarity with her and her place of business was based on several hunting excursions I'd made in this vicinity with Oberon. She pointed at our weapons. "You need to put those behind the bar."

"No problem." I carefully leaned the swords and spear up against the bottled-beer fridge.

"What'll it be?"

"Two Big Boys full of Bud." She had a fully stocked bar, complete with a large mirror behind it, but most people came in to enjoy the thirty-four-ounce frozen mugs of beer. Perun and I pulled up stools and avoided eye contact with the locals. They were staring at us and trying to decide if they'd pick a fight if Gabby weren't around. After a minute I felt their eyes slide away, probably because they reasoned that anyone as aggressively unshaven as Perun was thoroughly dangerous.

Gabby gave us our beers and Perun eyed his uncertainly. "This is Big Boy?"

"Correct."

"Is not vodka," he observed.

"Right. You're in an American bar, so to fit in you have to drink this."

Perun glanced around the bar at the other patrons, who were mostly wearing jeans and T-shirts and shaved responsibly. "Do you really think I can fit in here?"

"Not a chance. But it's your duty to make the effort. Cheers." I clinked his mug and started chugging. Perun took a few cold swallows and then set down the mug abruptly, shuddering as some of it dribbled down his beard.

"Americans *like* this?" he asked.

"They say they do. Bestselling drink in the States."

"Should I give them my respect or my pity?"

"It's a dilemma, isn't it?" I said. "Hey, Gabby, mind if I borrow your phone?"

I had my cell phone, but there was no way I was going to turn it on at this point; it was most likely dead anyway. Gabby handed the bar's phone to me, and I punched in a memorized number while Perun took in the sights of the bar. There was plenty to see, starting with the mounted jackalope wearing a pair of sunglasses near the bottled-beer fridge. There was also a mounted javelina head staring at us with glass eyes, because dead animals are practically mandatory objets d'art in Arizona bars. The centerpiece of the place was a pure carven teak sculpture of an Indian motorcycle, resting on an old bartop that was hung from the ceiling by chains. Two pool tables in the back room were currently awaiting players, and an old Lynyrd Skynyrd song moaned on the jukebox in the corner opposite the bar.

A puzzled Granuaile answered her cell phone, not recognizing the number calling her.

"Hey, it's me, back safe," I said. "No names, okay? Are you in town yet or are you still working on the Verde River thing?"

"I got back a few days ago."

"Great. I need you to come pick me up at the Huddle on Broad Street in Globe as soon as possible."

"I'm bartending," she said, by which she meant she was at Rúla Búla. "Just came on shift."

"Time to quit that job," I said.

"Again?"

"Again, and for good. We have to move. Your new life begins now."

"Oh. Should I pick up the dog?"

The smart answer would have been yes, but I wanted to see the widow one more time if I could. So I said, "No, we'll get him together."

"Right. See you in an hour."

She was so quick and decisive. I hoped she'd make it through the training. For that matter, I hoped *I'd* make it through the training. The Morrigan's vision was very much on my mind, not to mention the consequences Jesus had mentioned.

Before I could make my second phone call, Perun whispered urgently, "Do you have Arizona money? I have none." How sweet of him to be worried about the bill.

"Oh, it's no problem, Perun. The drink's on me," I said. "Especially since it doesn't look like you'll be finishing it."

"Ah. My thanks. I think I go now, Atticus, explore country, find place to hide."

"So soon?" I thanked him for his invaluable aid and hoped that in his exploration of America he would find a town populated by many beefy, hairy women.

"America has such places?" he asked, hope and wonder filling his face.

"I'm sure it does. It's a land of opportunity," I said. He hooked me up with a couple of extra fulgurites for Granuaile and Oberon before he left, and I made sure to dispel the camouflage on his fur cloak outside. "Meeting you was a pleasure," I told him. "It's one of the few things about the trip I can say was one hundred percent positive, in fact. As gods go, you're one of the best I've ever met."

"You are only Druid I ever met," he said, "but I think best also." He tried to leave by pounding me manfully on the back a couple of times, but then decided that was inadequate and crushed me with a companionable hug. It was like getting squeezed between large hairy rocks. As he exited out the back of the Huddle, I tried not to laugh out loud at the collective sigh of relief from the locals. I covered my amusement by taking a long draught of my drink.

The extra alcohol gave me the courage I needed to dial the next number. I punched it in and steeled myself for an unpleasant conversation.

"Hal, it's me. I'm back. And I have bad news."

"Yes, I've been waiting for your call," the new alpha of the Tempe Pack said, his voice tight with tension. "I already know it's bad, but how bad? Are they both gone, or just my alpha?"

"It's uncertain. Better that I show and tell," I replied. "I brought them back, Hal. I did everything I could." I told him where to find me and to bring the new IDs I'd ordered for both Granuaile and myself. "And come in a work van, or maybe borrow Antoine's wheels," I added, referring to the local ghoul who collected and hauled bodies around in a refrigerated truck.

"Tell me this much before I drive out there," Hal said. "Did they at least get their revenge?"

"Yes. They got their revenge. But I never got to ask them if it was worth it."

"I don't think it was," Hal said.

"No. No, it wasn't."

Epilogue

All my old haunts were possible traps now, and the Morrigan's vision of my death had me practically loony with paranoia. Granuaile was already teasing me about my constantly swiveling head, half in jest and half in annoyance; I was making her nervous. Despite her impatient sigh and the rolling of her eyes, I had her park out of sight of the widow's house so that I could call to Oberon through our mental link from up the street.

Oberon, can you hear me?

<Atticus! Stay back! Don't come here!>

He sounded alarmed at my arrival rather than welcoming. That wasn't right. *What? Why not?*

<It's not safe. I'll come to you.>

Is the widow all right?

<No, she is definitely not all right. I'll explain. Do you have a way to get out of town fast?>

Yes. I was sitting with Granuaile in her car, near University Drive.

<Where?>

His question jangled alarm bells in my head. What if I wasn't talking to Oberon? That scene from *Terminator 2* where Schwarzenegger imitated the voice of John Connor and the T-1000 imitated the foster mother replayed in my head. I wasn't sure if such a switch could be accomplished magically, but I didn't want to take the chance. Instead of answering him, I asked a question of my own. *Oberon, can you get out of the house?*

<I'm already out. I'm in the backyard.>

Jump over the fence and come to the front. By yourself. Right now.

<Don't have to tell me twice!>

"Start the car," I told Granuaile. She nodded and turned the key in the ignition. Oberon appeared alone at the edge of the widow's property in a few seconds, looking south down Roosevelt first and then north to where we were parked.

See the blue car? That's us.

<Coming!> He went from dead stop to full speed in about three seconds. <Hope you got a full tank of gas! We need to drive until we run out and hide in a cave somewhere.>

What are you talking about? I got out of the car and opened the back door for him to jump in. He didn't stop to be petted or anything. He leapt in and immediately started barking at Granuaile before I could close the door.

<Go! Step on it! We gotta get out of here before she sees us!>

Oberon, what on earth? Stop that racket. I ducked back into the car and told Granuaile to get us off Roosevelt Street as I closed my door. Oberon's behavior needed an explanation, but if matters were truly as urgent as he suggested, it would be unwise to demand one before leaving. We could always return if it was a misunderstanding. Granuaile made a U-turn and turned east on University, heading toward Rural Road.

"Where to, sensei?" she asked, checking her mirrors.

"Same place we discussed earlier," I said. "Oberon says we have to get out of town." I turned in my seat to collect an overdue explanation from my hound. *Now you will tell me why we're running. What's happened to the widow?*

<Okay, about two days ago—or maybe it was five, you know, a while ago, I'm not sure—I could have sworn the widow died. She was in her bed sleeping, and I heard this hoarse rattle from her throat, but it wasn't like a snore, you know, so I went to investigate. She wasn't breathing, Atticus. I nudged her with my nose, I licked her face, but I got no reaction. I barked right in her ear and she didn't even twitch. But then I heard the front door open and close, and I left her room to go see who it was. There wasn't anybody there, and that was really weird, because I knew I heard that door, and it wasn't like the cats grew opposable thumbs. I sniffed around for a bit; there was something rotten and I thought it felt colder near the door, but it might have been my imagination. Then I heard the bed creak and I went back into the widow's room, and there she was, getting out of the bed.>

Ah, so she is alive after all?

<Well, no, I don't think so. I don't think that's her. She's dead, Atticus. I saw it and smelled it and heard it.>

Then who's been walking around in her house and feeding you and letting you outside since then? You're not making sense.

<I don't know who it is, but it's not the widow. She doesn't talk to herself anymore and she doesn't pet me and tell me what a good hound I am. She just feeds me silently and gives me water and lets me out every so often. It's creepy.>

Well, maybe she's just in a funk, Oberon. She's been depressed lately.

<So depressed she doesn't drink anymore?>

What?

<She hasn't had a single sip of whiskey since she rose from the dead. I haven't seen her eat either. I'm telling you, Atticus, she's gone. Whoever that is, it's not Mrs. MacDonagh.>

I faced forward and slumped in my seat. Shock upon

shock left my mouth slightly open and my eyes unfocused.

"Sensei? Atticus? What's the matter?" Granuaile flicked her eyes from the road to my face, creases of worry between her brows.

"Drive on," I told her. "Oberon's right. We have to get out of here."

Acknowledgments

My editor at Del Rey, Tricia Pasternak, is eternally encouraging and may be a Zen master of Soothing Anxious Authors. She exudes calm even through her emails. Here is one of her koans to boggle your mind: *What is the sound of one subplot resolving?*

Mike Braff, assistant editor, introduced me to Viking Death Metal, specifically a band called Amon Amarth and one of their songs called "Twilight of the Thunder God." I had that playing on loop while I wrote the last battle scene, and now I'm fighting the urge to buy a double-bladed axe and a drinking horn.

My copy editor, Kathy Lord, and my managing editor, Nancy Delia, both deserve a bottle of something Irish because I've probably driven them to drink anyway—it might as well be the good stuff. They've been a spectacular help, and I'm grateful for their assistance.

My agent, Evan Goldfried at JGLM, happened to know a really cool rabbi, Jenny Amswych, who was kind enough to help me out with the Hebrew. I chose the *kh* spelling instead of the *ch* for the guttural sound, and I hope that doesn't ruffle any feathers. If there are any errors, please lay the blame at my door and not the good rabbi's.

Eli Freysson in Iceland assisted with some of the

Icelandic names, but please don't tease him if I messed up, because I tend to Anglicize things a bit.

I'm grateful as always to my early readers, Alan O'Bryan and Tawnya Graham-Schoolitz. Nick Steinkemper also did me yeoman service on short notice.

Kimberly, Maddie, and Gail Hearne are the most supportive family members a writer could wish for, and I count myself blessed to be a part of their lives.

As with my other books, most of the physical locations (on this plane) are real, albeit used in a fictional way. If anyone does that $75 shot of whiskey at Rúla Búla, drop me a line and let me know if it was worth it. I'll tell you right now that the Smithwick's with the fish and chips is always worth it.

Likewise, the teak motorcycle sculpture at the Huddle in Globe is worth a look. It gets even better after you've had a couple Big Boys. I'm indebted to the owner, Tracy Quick, for a tour of downtown that included a rare glimpse of the old secret tunnels beneath the streets.

You can find me at www.kevinhearne.com. I'm also on Twitter (@kevinhearne), and I hope to see you at a spiffy shindig of some kind. Maybe we'll meet at a sci-fi/fantasy or comics convention, catch a glimpse of Neil Gaiman, and squee in ultrasonic stereo.

Read on for a peek at the first two books
in The Iron Druid Chronicles

Hounded
and
Hexed
by
Kevin Hearne

Published by Del Rey

HOUNDED

I had Oberon stationed as sentinel on the edge of the
lawn, close to the street. As the widow regaled me with
tales of her Golden Age debauchery, I was depending
on him to tell me of approaching danger.

<Atticus,> he said, as the widow was winding up her
tale with a sigh over better days in a better land, <some-
one comes on foot from the north.>

Is he a stranger? I had put Fragarach aside while I
talked with the widow, but now I stood and slung the
scabbard back over my head, causing the widow to
frown.

<Yes. He is very strange. I can smell the ocean on him
from here.>

*Uh oh. That's not good. Stay still and try not to make
any noise.*

"Excuse me, Mrs. MacDonagh," I said, "someone's
coming and he might not be friendly."

"What? Who is it? Atticus?"

I couldn't answer yet, so I didn't. I kicked off my sandals and drew power from the widow's lawn even as I
walked toward the street and peered northward. One
of the charms on my necklace has the shape of a bear
on it, and its function is to store a bit of magical power

for me that I can tap when I'm walking on concrete or asphalt. I topped off the magical tank as a possible antagonist approached.

A tall, armored figure clanked noisily on the asphalt a couple of houses away, and it raised a hand to hail me when I came into view. I activated a different charm that I call "faerie specs," a sort of filter for my eyes that lets me see through Fae glamours and detect all sorts of magic juju. It showed me the normal spectrum, but then there was also a green overlay that revealed what was going on magically, and right now the two layers showed me the same thing. So whoever he was, I was looking at his true form. If he had something similar to my faerie specs, he might be able to see through Oberon's camouflage, but then again, he might not.

He was wearing rather gaudy bronze armor that no one would have worn in the old days. The cuirass, faced in hardened leather dyed with woad, covered too much and restricted movement. He had leaf-shaped tassets hanging down over a bronze mail skirt. He also had five-piece pauldrons and matching vambraces and greaves. It would have been hot enough to wear such armor in Ireland, but here the temperature was still in the low nineties, and he must have been broiling in it. His helmet was beyond ridiculous: It was one of those medieval barbutes that didn't become popular until a thousand years after his halcyon days of slaughter, and he must have been wearing it as a joke, though I did not find it especially funny. A sword hung in a scabbard at his side, but thankfully he did not carry a shield.

"I greet you, Siodhachan Ó Suileabháin," he said. "Well met." He flashed a smug grin at me through his helmet, and I wanted to slay him on the spot. I kept my faerie specs on, because I simply didn't trust him. Without some way to pierce his glamour, he could make my eyes think he was standing three feet away with his hands on his head while he was really plunging a dagger into my belly.

"Call me Atticus. I greet you, Bres."

"Not well met?" He tilted his head a bit to the right, as much as the barbute would let him.

"Let's see how the meeting goes. It's been a long time since we have seen each other, and I wouldn't have minded if it were longer. And by the way, the Renaissance Festival doesn't arrive here until next February."

"That's not very hospitable," Bres said, frowning. Oberon was right: He smelled of salt and fish. As a god of agriculture, he should smell of earth and flowers, but instead he retained the stink of the dockside, owing perhaps to his Fomorian ancestors, who lived by the sea. "I could take offense if I wished."

"So take it already and be done. I can't imagine why else you would be here now."

"I am here at the request of an old friend," he said.

"Did he request that you dress like that? Because if he did, he's not your friend."

"Atticus, who is that?" the widow MacDonagh called from her porch. I didn't take my eyes off Bres as I called back to her.

"Someone I know. He won't be staying long." Time to set up my flanking maneuver. Speaking mind to mind, I said to Oberon, *Remain still. But when I say, get behind him, grab a leg, and just yank him off his feet. Once he's down, jump clear.*

<Got it,> Oberon said.

Bres continued as if the widow had never spoken. "Aenghus Óg wants the sword. Give it to me and you'll be left alone. It's that simple."

"Why isn't he here himself?"

"He's nearby," Bres said. That was calculated to ratchet my paranoia up a few levels. It worked, but I was determined it would not work in his favor.

"What's your stake in this, Bres? And what's with the armor?"

"That does not concern you, Druid. Your only concern is whether you will agree to give us the sword and live, or refuse and die." The last fingers of the sun were waving good-bye over the horizon, and twilight was upon us. Faerie time.

"Tell me why he wants it," I said. "It's not like Ireland has a High King who needs the Tuatha Dé Danann to help him out uniting all the various tribes."

"It is not for you to question."

"Sure it is," I said, "but I guess it's not for you to answer. Fragarach is right here." I gestured to the hilt peeking over my shoulder. "So if I give it to you now, you walk away, and I never hear from you or Aenghus again?"

Bres peered intently at the hilt for a few moments, then chuckled. "That is not Fragarach. I have seen it, Druid, and I have felt its magic. You have nothing in that scabbard but an ordinary sword."

Wow. Radomila's magical cloak just rocked.

And then the green overlay in my vision started to differ from the normal spectrum. Bres was pulling his sword out of his scabbard in a leisurely fashion and watching my face to see if I reacted, so I tried to stay relaxed and let him think I was clueless. Either he knew that I really had Fragarach on my back and he wanted to double-cross me, or he simply wanted to kill me to burnish his reputation. He'd make a fine tale of the battle, no doubt, in spite of the fact that he was planning the equivalent of a stab in the back.

"I assure you it's the real thing," I said to him, and to Oberon I said, *Change in plan. Just lie down behind him when I say. I'll push him over your back so he falls down.*

<Okay.>

Bres's glamour form shrugged and said, "You can give your cheap sword to me if you'd like. It will only delay things, and I'll have to come back again with another offer. But I can guarantee that offer won't be as generous as the one I'm giving you now."

And that was when the true Bres on the green overlay grinned wickedly and raised his sword over his head in a two-handed grasp, ready to split me in two.

Now, Oberon, I said, keeping my face pensive as if I were thinking over Bres's words. I started talking out loud to hopefully mask any sounds Oberon made as he moved.

"Bres, I think you're missing something important," I said, even as he brought his sword down with all his strength and I stepped out of the way to the right at the last instant. His glamour persona was still standing there, smirking, but I didn't pay attention to that one anymore. The green one—the real Bres—had just tried to slay me. While he was hunched over awkwardly on his follow-through, I kicked at the nerve cluster in his wrist to make him drop the sword, then put another one in his face to make him stand back up. It didn't get through his helmet, but any blow to the head is going to make you pull away. Then I pivoted on my left foot and spun clockwise, delivering a roundhouse into his solar plexus before he could set himself. He staggered backward and fell over Oberon in a tremendous clatter of bronze and hardened leather, still not hurt but pretty humiliated by this point. He gave up on the glamour, and the smirking Bres merged with the one on the ground, so that my faerie specs and my normal vision showed the same thing again.

I could have left it there. He was disarmed and no danger to me now, and if any of the Fae had been around to see him fall flat on his ass, he would be shamed in a legendary fashion. Except that he had tried to kill me with a glamour. He would never fight me fairly, because he could not win that way—he'd never been much of a terror on the battlefield. If I let him live, then he would send a series of assassins my way, just as Aenghus Óg had been doing for centuries. I didn't need twice the headache I already had.

Plus, in the parlance of our times, he was a douche bag.

So I didn't leave it there. While he was still on the ground, I whipped Fragarach out of its scabbard and plunged it straight through the center of his bronze cuirass, which offered no resistance to the magical blade. Bres's eyes bulged and he stared at me in disbelief: After surviving the epic battles of ancient Ireland (in respectable armor), during which he could have died heroically, he was going to meet his end in a fight that lasted less than ten seconds because of his own overconfidence.

HEXED

"So how many fallen angels you killed afore this, Mr. Druid?"

"This'll be my first, I reckon."

"Shee-it." Coyote shook his head with a rueful grin. "We're gonna die."

I looked sharply at him. "Are you approachin' this like a suicide trip? You figgerin' it's okay to die and leave me there without no one to watch my back, 'cause you can just come back from the dead anyway? I'll tell ya right now, Coyote, I'm plannin' on livin' a long time after this. If you ain't plannin' on survivin', tell me straight and I'll go get someone else to help me."

"Aw, cool your britches, Mr. Druid. I ain't gonna walk on up to 'im and ask 'im to eat me." Coyote threw up his hands. "All I'm sayin' is this ain't gonna be no picnic. A fallen angel's gonna be a far sight smarter than a reg'lar demon, and more'n a little stronger too."

"All right, then. You got any idea where the demon is?"

"Last I saw, he was perched on one o' their buildings overlookin' a courtyard area. It's got some grass and trees in it, so you can draw power there."

"We're gonna have to go through the school building to get there, though?"

"That's what I 'spect."

"We'll have to go camouflaged. School officials tend to get worried about people bringin' weapons onto their campuses."

Skyline High School is a monolithic building of stucco-sprayed cement block trimmed in hunter green. I parked in the no-parking drop-off zone, because I just didn't care about parking etiquette. I cast camouflage on both myself and Coyote, then got out and opened the cargo area, where I camouflaged both our bows, the quiver of arrows, and Fragarach too. It didn't make us completely invisible, especially in the rain, but it sure helped. Once inside, we'd blend into the bland institutional décor without trouble. Coyote pitched in by giving us something he called "Clever Stalking," which really meant we wouldn't make any noise when we moved. (I'm not sure why he didn't call it Silent Stalking; I suppose Coyote thought it was clever of him to think stalking should be a silent exercise.)

We glided by the reception desk without disturbing the matronly woman sitting there; she seemed to be emotionally involved with a game of solitaire on her computer. There were two full-time employees working at the attendance window (because taking attendance and getting money from the state is the most important job at public schools), but they were listening to parents lie on the phone about why their children weren't in school that day, so they weren't even looking up to see what was dripping all across the industrial carpet in the hallway. The doors to the courtyard gave a high-pitched squeak when we opened them, and the sound of pouring rain caused the attendance clerks to look up, but we slipped out without them spotting us.

Class was in session and the courtyard was deserted. We were underneath a roofed area that traveled around the perimeter, providing shelter for rare rainy days like this but usually offering shade the rest of the year. Thick ropes of runoff water slapped noisily on the concrete before coursing in swift rivulets toward drainage grates.

I turned on my faerie specs and had no trouble figuring out where Basasael was lurking. He was directly across from us, perched on the steel roof, in a Doppler-shifted cloud of wrong. The feathered wings he had eons ago were now leathery and batlike. The rest of him was still humanoid in appearance, just blackened and spiky and pulsing with evil, like a subwoofer vibrating a car's windows and blurring the view.

What made him particularly repellent at the moment was his open mouth, out of which dangled another teenage victim's leg—some poor kid who'd been on his way to the nurse's office, perhaps, or called down to see the counselor. As we watched, the fallen angel's teeth crunched down and his lower jaw slid sideways in a grotesque chewing motion.

Coyote saw it at the same time I did. "Too late to help that one, I reckon," he whispered to my right. I couldn't see him in the normal spectrum, but with my faerie specs on, he looked like a colorful collection of light streams, shifting chaotically within his form but not unpleasantly—just unpredictably. I handed him six arrows out of the quiver.

"I'll put my first arrow through his head; you go for the heart," I whispered back. "Then just keep shootin' until he fuckin' dies."

"Wow, you learn all that strategy from the U.S. Army men?"

I grunted in amusement. "No, I learned it from Attila the Hun, who lived an' died without ever knowin' you were here."

The two of us drifted apart naturally, hunters of old. We did not need to discuss strategy. When it's two against one, the two should separate so that if the target counterattacks one, his back is left open to the other. When we'd formed a triangle—Coyote and I at the base and Basasael at the top—we nocked our arrows and nodded at each other. I slid out of my sandals and stepped into the rain so that I could draw power from the earth. First I filled my bear charm back up, in case I needed to cast something on the sidewalk, then I drew enough to pull back the bow, just as Basasael was finishing off his teenage repast. I held up five fingers to Coyote, folded in my thumb, then my index finger to indicate a countdown, then pulled the bowstring to its limit. I took quick aim and let fly in time with the countdown.

I was already grabbing another arrow as our first volley sank home. My arrow pierced the fallen angel's left eye, and Coyote's thudded solidly into the center of its chest. It screeched on several wavelengths and shuddered my bones as it toppled backward onto the roof, surprised and clutching at the shafts.

Normally, if you shoot something in the head with an arrow, it doesn't have enough motor skills left to reach up and pluck the arrow out. And shooting a critter in the heart generally robs it of the strength to stand up and roar defiantly at unsafe decibel levels. Basasael wasn't normal, for he did both of those things.

A white bubbling wound was left behind in each case, but the fallen angel threw both the arrows down into the courtyard, spread his wings, and crouched in preparation to spring at one of us. He saw us both clearly; my camouflage spell kept us hidden from human eyes but not from his.

"How many arrows we gotta use to kill this thing?" Coyote yelled.

"All Mary said was we'd have to pierce it more'n once."

"Yeah? Well maybe you shoulda pinned her down to a specific number there afore we left, dumbass!"

I agreed with Coyote wholeheartedly, as we let fly with another volley. Basasael knocked Coyote's missile aside with a blurred sweep of his left arm, but mine sank directly into his swollen gut. The force of it toppled him backward again, but this time he knew better than to stay still and let us reload. Ignoring the arrow that was turning his black skin into a white froth before bubbling away to gray, he gathered his legs underneath him and launched himself straight up into the air with a single, powerful stroke of his wings and another mighty bellow of rage I could feel in my teeth. At the apex of his ascent, he folded his wings and dove after his chosen target—me.

The eternal whine of self-pity—why me?—flashed through my brain as I aimed one last shot at the fallen angel. The answers came flooding in: I looked like nothing more than a puny human weakling; I'd shot him in the head and the gut; I was standing in the open, where he could get to me easily, while Coyote was shooting from underneath the shelter of the roof; and, because of the binding Aenghus Óg had put on him, he couldn't leave the area until he killed me. I let fly with my shot and it sailed above his right shoulder, much to my chagrin. Dropping my bow because there'd be no time for another shot, I leapt back under the roof and drew Fragarach with my right hand and another blessed arrow from my quiver with my left.

I positioned myself behind one of the roof's supporting steel posts so that Basasael would have to pick a side to attack from and reduce his speed accordingly. It turned out the post was not something he considered to be an actual obstacle. He simply bashed it aside with his right arm as his wings spread to brake his flight, and the post obligingly ripped out of its moorings and buckled a portion of the roof as if it were made of Nerf rather than steel.

"Don't you feel the least bit ill right now?" I asked. I could see the courtyard through the yawning white hole in his head. It was still boiling and hissing, eating away at his substance—as were the other two wounds—but in terms of real damage it only seemed to have pissed him off.

His feet touched down on the concrete rather than the earth, so Cold Fire was out of the question; he answered me by belching a gout of bright orange flame at my face. It looked exactly like the ball of hellfire Aenghus Óg had thrown at me. "*Hey!*" I shouted as the flame passed over me, giving me a brief sensation of heat but otherwise leaving me unharmed, thanks to my amulet's protection. "You're the bastard who made a deal with Aenghus Óg! You're the one who's been behind it all!"

I heard the squeal of the office doors opening to my right: Someone was coming out to investigate what all the ruckus was. They wouldn't be able to see me or the demon, but they'd sure see the mangled post lying in the rain and a dangerously drooping roof. They'd also be in mortal danger. It's the sort of situation that gets duelists killed: a split second of distraction, flicking the eyes away for a shadow of a moment, and suddenly it's all over. Basasael was counting on it; perhaps he saw my eyes move, perhaps he didn't, but he shook off his surprise that I didn't burn and took advantage anyway. He was still a good four feet away from me, but his right arm shot toward my chest and his fingers *extended,* then his claws did likewise, telescope fashion, aiming for my heart. He wanted to pull one of those Mola Ram maneuvers, ripping my still-beating heart out of my chest and then laughing at me as I watched him eat it. I dodged to my right as quickly as I could, raising my left arm to let the claws pass under, but I wasn't quick enough. I felt four rotten black spikes pierce my side, scraping against the outside of my ribs and penetrating clear through to keep me pinned to the wall.

I grunted in pain and retaliated quickly, because part of him was pinned too: I drove the tip of the blessed arrow down through the back of his corrupted hand and on through the palm. He howled and yanked his hand away, withdrawing the evil claws from my side, and in that moment of reprieve I risked a quick glance to my right.

A wide-eyed female administrator in conservative dress was talking rapidly into a handheld radio. "There's some damage to the courtyard roof and some strange animal noises, but I can't tell what's making them."

"Get back inside, lady!" I yelled. "For your own safety!" That was the best I could do for her just then. Basasael looked as if he was going to move in closer and tear my head off, so I raised Fragarach in a defensive stance and winced at the burning in my side. As the fallen angel bent his knees and hissed at me, arms spread in a wrestler's stance, preparing to spring, it occurred to me that maybe Coyote should have managed to shoot an arrow or two during the fracas.

Where was the trickster? Had he taken off and left me to face the fallen angel alone? He'd been known to do that in several stories told about him: Get the white man to agree to a course of action, then take off at the critical moment and make him look like a fool. I didn't know what more I could do to this creature by myself. Four holy arrows had obviously done some physical damage; he'd loudly announced that he felt pain from them, but he still kept coming. A morbid thought wandered into my consciousness and said hello: If Basasael ate my dumb Druid ass, would the Morrigan be able to bring me back fully functional, resurrected from—what? Angel poop? That raised another question, at once metaphysical and profane: Do angels, fallen or otherwise, have assholes?

Coyote provided an answer in singular fashion. I heard a sickening, juicy squelching noise, and Basasael forgot all about charging me. He stood straight up on his clawed toes, feet together like a wooden nutcracker doll, his black eyes bulging and his throat ululating in a *bean sidhe* howl of agony that made me clutch my ears—or, rather, my one good ear and my one mess of pathetic cartilage niblets.

Coyote shouted *"Ha!"* once and then began to yip in amusement, scampering across the courtyard in his animal shape, taunting the fallen angel, and Basasael launched himself skyward to give chase.

While he was thus diverted, I took the opportunity to sheathe Fragarach and grab the school administrator by the collar, dragging her back to the office doors. She yelped in startlement, and I shouted at her as I tossed her inside, "Put the school in lockdown *now!* Just do it before someone else gets killed!" Every school in America had a lockdown procedure they followed to keep students safe in an emergency.

"What? Who got killed?"

"Take attendance and you'll find out. It's what you're best at, because the gods know it's not teaching them English. Damn kids don't know the difference between an adjective and an adverb!" I needed to shut up. Stress was making me take my frustrations out on this poor frumpy lady who probably never got laid.

"Who are . . . ? Why can't I see you?"

"Lockdown! Attendance! Stay inside!" I slammed the door shut for extra emphasis and hoped that would galvanize her to the proper course of action. Turning back to the courtyard, I saw that Basasael was trying to fry Coyote from the air with his great balls o' fire. Coyote was thus far a mite too fast for him, but I wasn't sure how long that would last or if Coyote would be able to withstand a direct hit of hellfire.

I scurried over to where I'd dropped my bow in the courtyard. It was still camouflaged, so I couldn't see it, and it took me a few frantic moments to stumble into it. The act of bending over to pick it up exacerbated the wounds in my side, and, duly reminded of them, I drew power to close them up and begin the tissue-mending process.

Two arrows left. Coyote had presumably dropped the remainder of his somewhere. I nocked one and tried not to laugh at the image of Basasael flying around with a feathery shaft sticking out between his cheeks. I chose my own target carefully, and the bowstring thwocked as the arrow sailed up and through the fallen angel's right wing. It tore a magnificent white hole through it and began to widen, which caused Basasael to screech and tumble ignominiously to the earth—precisely where I wanted him.